Through the Lens

*He thought I was his muse.
Turned out, he was mine too.*

USA TODAY BESTSELLING AUTHOR

K.K. ALLEN

Copyright

This book is a work of fiction. Names, characters, places, and incidents either are products of the author's imagination or are used fictitiously. Any resemblance to actual events or locales or persons, living or dead, is coincidental.

Copyright © 2020 by K.K. Allen
Cover Design: Sarah Hansen, Okay Creations
Photographer: Regina Wamba
Editor: Red Adept Editing

All rights reserved. Except as permitted under the U.S. Copyright Act of 1976, no part of this publication may be reproduced, distributed, or transmitted in any form or by any means, or stored in a database or retrieval system, without the prior written permission of the publisher.

Contact SayHello@KK-Allen.com with questions.

ISBN: 9798639008924

through the LENS

KK [signature] xoxo

Books by K.F.

Sweet & Inspirational Contemporary Romance
Up in the Treehouse
Under the Bleachers
Through the Lens

Sweet and Sexy Contemporary Romance
Center of Gravity
Falling from Gravity
Defying Gravity
The Trouble with Gravity

Super Steamy Contemporary Romance
Dangerous Hearts
Destined Hearts

Romantic Suspense
Waterfall Effect

Young Adult Fantasy
The Summer Solstice Enchanted
The Equinox
The Descendants

Short Stories and Anthologies
Soaring
Echoes of Winter
Begin Again
Spring Fling

To all my babes in Forever Young. Thank you for your patience waiting for Through the Lens. This one is for you. <3

Prologue

Before you, life came in bursts of muted colors.
Everything changed when you somehow slipped under my skin—and then stole my heart.
Layer by layer, you stripped me bare, leaving foreign skin beneath lost feathers. You blinded me with your light. And with streams exposing my every weakness, I became yours. Your words lit a match against my soul, and the flames licked through me like an inferno. Thick. Heated. Wild. Infuriating.
Still, I'm afraid.
I learned at a young age what can be seen through the lens is often a skewed version of reality. A bent perspective. Manufactured, therefore losing all sense of authenticity.
That was me.
The woman through the lens.
The lie.

TAKE ONE

Downfall

"ALWAYS REMEMBER, YOUR FOCUS DETERMINES YOUR REALITY."
— GEORGE LUCAS

Run-a-Way

MAGGIE

Delicate fabric falls against my skin, causing a wave of excitement to roll through my body. I'm a statue for my stylist, Robin, as she pins the thick, crystal-encrusted tulle together in the back, giving the dress just enough pull at my waist. The gold-and-silver-sequined fabric gathers like an accordion on my chest as the long, flowing skirt grazes the scuffed tile at my feet.

We're backstage at the hottest runway event of the season, mere minutes from showtime. Music pumps through the speakers, perfectly synced to the multicolored lights slashing through the stage's backdrop. Not a single stone was left unturned with this event, which showcases a brilliant fall line of the most well-kept fashion secrets. And I'm wearing the biggest secret of them all.

I'm currently being stuffed into the "dress of the season," which will close the show. It's the one everyone came here to see. And designer Gabriele Amante handpicked *me* to wear it.

Chaos is a delicate term to describe the scene behind me. Photographers are stealing last-second pictures. Models are forming lines at all the directed entrance points. Hair and makeup staff give their assigned girls one last touch-up. Soon we'll all be hit with harsh stage lighting that manages to make even us girls with darker complexions look like relatives of Casper.

Robin places her hands on my shoulders and twists me toward the mirror. "Focus, Maggie." Her thick Russian accent comes off just as harsh as she intends it to. Robin is Gabriele's right-hand woman, and while we've never worked together before tonight, she seems to see right through me.

I glance up, catching a full view of my whole ensemble, and gasp as my pulse takes off at a sprint. The outfit is pure magic. The mirror's reflection reveals all, and my fellow models know it.

As hard as I try to ignore my peers' jealous reactions, I can see the side-eyed glances and pinched smiles. I hear the acidic, low-toned mutterings of disdain.

"Why her?"

"You know who her mother is, right? Talk about a free ride to the top."

"She won't last, not with those proportions."

I resist an eye roll and snuffle the anger fighting its way up my chest. Their comments are ones I've gotten used to hearing over the years. Nothing is wrong with my proportions. And while my mother certainly has influence in the industry, I've been modeling my entire life. There isn't a single opportunity I haven't worked my ass off for.

My fellow models are picking me apart because I was chosen to be tonight's lead model for one of New York's fiercest fashion-forward designers on the catwalk to end all catwalks. My eyes float to the mirror again. Damn, I look good in this dress.

"They're going to talk," Robin says as she fidgets with a piece of loose fabric at my spine. "Let them. Gabriele chose you. He needs you." She places her hands on my waist and squeezes. "Take a deep breath, shut out the noise, and show the world how proud you are to wear Amante."

I release a heavy breath and nod to ease her worries. "I'm ready."

She rewards me with a tight smile and pats my hips one last time. "Good. You look exquisite." Her eyes stop on my breasts, and she cringes. "Hold that thought. Don't move."

As Robin steps away, I close my eyes and try again to tune out the noise. A nagging voice seeps into my thoughts.

"This is it, Maggie," my mom-slash-manager said when I first got the offer. "This is the event that will catapult your career. It's only up from here."

I could see the stars in her eyes as she spoke. Witnessing my career transition from professional model to super model had always been her dream for me. It was a goal she had placed on my vision board when I was nearly four years old, and it had become my ultimate goal as a result.

I remember the day she'd added a magazine cutout to my cork board and explained its significance. The image was of her at twenty-two years old. She was a super star in the world of fashion, with a face that decorated lifestyle and fashion magazine covers. She got paid to attend ritzy events and became the face for high-end cosmetic lines. She walked all the famous runways and went on dates with celebrities to appease her publicist.

She had been at the pinnacle of her career, living a life of glitz and glamour, when she met and fell in love with my father, an up-and-coming football star who played for Dallas. They married and had me not long after. That was when she decided to turn in her modeling career for motherhood, something she would never let any of us forget.

"After walking for Amante, you'll be the most photographed, the most sought-after, and the most talked-about model in New York fashion," she'd said, with eyes bright like she was lost in the spotlight of her past. But the pressure I detected in her words was clear.

Don't mess this up.

At twenty-six years old, my career's current stagnant state signifies failure in her eyes. She has set a ticking time bomb over my head, and it grows louder with each passing year. But for me, modeling is simply a stepping-stone I should have leapt from years ago. Tonight, I plan to do just that.

Tonight, everything changes.

After fifteen years of carrying my robotic self down the runway without so much as a hair color change—which I desperately wanted—and letting every photographer think they owned my time and body, I'm ending it all. I'll fulfill my duties on this catwalk tonight, a dream I'd always thought I wanted, but then I'm moving on. My chance for something more is finally coming.

I feel an invasion of my breast and look down. Robin's hands are there, groping me to her satisfaction as she glues on the soft nude cup and smooths it out to form a second skin. "Good," she affirms, patting one breast and reaching for the final piece of my ensemble. She wraps a thin gold belt around my waist twice and secures it in a knot at the small of my back.

"Now," she says with a finger on her mouth and her brows turned down. "I just need to finish fastening you in the back. She tugs the fabric together across my lower back where the dress is supposed to link together.

Embarrassment colors my cheeks. "It won't close?"

She waves a hand to tell me not to worry then holds up a leftover piece of the dress fabric she'd cut to make modifications. "I'll just stitch this right on to cover the gap. No one will even notice."

Relief flows through me as she goes to work. Robin isn't doing anything abnormal. Last-minute fixes are common in the world of runway fashion. Most of my catwalk outfits were stapled, glued, and stitched together at the last minute to ensure a perfect fit. All that matters is how I carry the fabric beneath the lights, how the fabric sways as I make my signature walk down the narrow aisle, and how I will manage to successfully draw every eye in the house to me.

One last time.

Robin presses the final piece of fabric to the top of my bra cup and steps back to assess her handiwork. "Gabriele," she shouts to her right, jerking her head at me to get his attention.

His eyes grow wide, and a smile blooms on his gorgeous, freshly shaven tanned skin. He begins his strut toward us, pausing mere seconds with each interruption to smile with affection at his models. Then he takes my hands, and his eyes sweep over every inch of me.

"Stupenda, mia cara. Molto bella, Maggie. Semplicemente bellissima." His eyes pour over his work, which is now floating majestically over my body, from the shimmering and perfectly placed sequin, to where the skirt of the dress meets the floor with just a slight amount of overhang. My four-inch stilettos almost did the trick.

Gabriele bends and clutches the fabric at my feet then jerks it up. His narrowed gaze snaps up next, meeting Robin's eyes. "Higher," he snaps at her then points to the shoe rack on the other side of the room. "Go. Fast."

She nods in understanding then dashes off just as he takes a final step toward me, eyeing the space between my breasts. "You're too short, yeah? Shorter than promised." His tone is still friendly, but I can sense his irritation. I have to quickly shake such annoyance because I know the constant criticism, the never being good enough, is just part of the job. Too tall, too short, too slim, too curvy, too plain, too tan—I've heard it all. And even after all these years, I never leave an encounter unscathed. I've just gotten better at taking the hits.

"Five-seven," I remind him. My portfolio doesn't lie. "Hardly short." I wink. "But I've never been opposed to strutting taller heels." I continue teasing him with my eyes to melt some of the edge off.

"Mi dispiace," he mutters as his eyes drift downward. *He's sorry.* "Sei ancora molto bella." *He still thinks I look beautiful.*

I fight back my smile. "The dress is beautiful, Gabriele. Magnifico."

He smiles, his ego fed, just as Robin runs over with a new pair of silver heels—a higher strappy pair with a thin spike.

"No, absolutely not," demands a voice on approach.

Our heads whip right to find Matilda Stevens, otherwise known as my mother-slash-manager—and the long-term thorn in my side.

"Nothing taller than five inches, Gabriele. It's in her contract."

His eyes widen at the nerve of my mother. I hold back my impending cringe and eye roll.

"She's short," he spits, and he knows that's all he needs to say.

My mom glances down and can see the half-inch of fabric flattened on the floor. She bites her lip, eyes me like my height is something I have control over, and nods. "I see. My apologies, Gabriele."

Annoyance whips through me, but I bite my tongue, as always.

Gabriele nods, jaw still tight from the confrontation, as he snaps his fingers at Robin, gesturing for her to strap the shoes on my feet. While she does, he steps toward me again, his eyes on my mother. "And these," he says, yanking at the fabric above one of the bra cups. "Big." He turns back to me. "No offense, mio cara."

My cheeks flame. "None taken."

That's a new one. No one has ever complained about my breasts. They're full, but not gaudy. A 32B is proportionate to the narrow curves of my frame. I shouldn't be offended by his opinion.

As my mom begins to sweet-talk Gabriele, I settle into my new heels. Robin secures them and makes me take a walk. They feel fine. I've walked in higher, but the five-inch rule is just a precaution my mother put into place to minimize the risks that come with a high-profile catwalk. In the last fifteen years, I've seen the worst of the worst—careers ending before they've even begun, industry criticism leading to early retirements, or worse. To say a woman needs tough skin in the fashion world is putting it mildly. She needs warrior armor and an impenetrable heart. I'm still working on all the above.

"Final walk. Where are my models?" The backstage director proceeds to call off the names on her sheet, and one by one, the girls line up to take their final walk.

Gabriele leans in to kiss my cheek. "Walk tall, bellissima. You are my star tonight." With a final rub of my back, he walks off toward the line of models ready to go.

"How do you feel?" my mom asks, worry flooding her face as she takes another glance at my shoes.

I nod, batting past her infectious negativity to remember what's next for me. Something my mom doesn't even know. Something she would never approve of. In fact, I am about to do something she would do anything to stop.

"I feel ready." I say it with a smile because I can't help it. Despite the jealous chatter at my back, my mother's unrealistic expectations, and the high pressures of the night, I'm excited.

My mother nods, her angelic exterior no match for her hard insides. I'm not sure how or when it happened, but many years ago, she changed for the worst and took me along for the ride, a ride I never knew to second-guess in the beginning.

At the time, I wanted what she wanted. I wanted to be adored. I wanted the lights, the fanfare, and the fancy clothes. More than anything, I wanted to love it all. But just because I was born into something doesn't mean it was meant for me.

My mother will never understand that.

"Maggie Stevens," the director calls. "We need you on deck."

I let a breath out, a whoosh that stems from excitement and brings another smile to my face. I start to walk to my place, but a cold hand grips me and holds me back with a tug. I don't even look toward my mother again. I'm afraid of whatever she's going to say but even more afraid of what she'll see in my response.

"You're one walk away from having it all, my dear. *Don't screw it up like I did.*" Her tone is like ice slicing through my psyche. If she only knew.

By the end of tonight, she will.

"And... go."

With a gentle push from the producer, I take my first step, teeter slightly, then right myself onto my needle-thin heels. I stopped thinking of my every move on the runway years ago. Now the technique of the walk comes naturally.

The music has just changed for the closing number. It's a heavy dance beat that works perfectly with the crescendo of the night. Forty minutes is a long show, and these people are ready to see what they came for: Gabriele's signature design from his fall wedding collection. It's spring now, but this piece is the one all second-hand designers are going to try to mimic, overproduce, and sell in their shops this fall. And I'm the first one who gets to wear it.

My cheekbones are high and strong. The upward curve of my lips hint at my love for the catwalk, the lights, and the attention. My eyes are focused straight ahead, never straying from the lens of the camera aimed right at me.

The camera loves me. The people gasp for me. And the lights shine for me. But it just doesn't feel right anymore.

Years of training betray me in the next moment as my eyes flick left to where I know my future is sitting. Regis Malone watches me. He's the producer of a new soap opera titled *Pacific Moon*, set to start taping in LA six months from now. He's looking for a fresh face like mine—at least that's what he told me when we met at a bar in LA before I hopped on a plane to New York for this show. It's the opportunity I've been waiting for, and the timing could not be better.

"An amateur to the screen, with the confidence of a trained actor and the passion to want it all," he'd said as he shut the billfold and stood from his chair. He was a stout man with a booming voice, and wide, prideful eyes. And as he looked down at me, it was clear that he was well-aware of his accomplishments and the power he held. He loved my look, my attitude, my walk, and my natural, but subtle, Southern drawl. He was offering me my first true chance to leave the modeling world behind.

So I invited him to my show in New York to seal the deal, to show him what I do best and what I'm willing to give up for a chance at something new. This isn't my first attempt to break away from modeling. I've been hungry to leave—desperate for it—for years. And acting will give me the opportunity to do just that. After countless secret auditions, and just as many rejections, I haven't given up hope.

But tonight, I can taste opportunity fresh on my tongue like sweet victory. My insides feel electrified with everything to come. It's all unfolding just as I planned.

My walk is perfection. I can feel it in my timing as my steps hit the runway on a steady, midtempo beat. My lips are tugged up just slightly at the corners, a trick my mother taught me to give my resting bitch face a much-needed lift.

I hit the end of the runway and release the one smile I'm allowed. All designers have their own rules for their catwalk, and the one-smile rule is Gabriele's. My eyes connect with Regis's, and I grow giddy inside as he nods his approval like it's a secret message to me. I'm one step closer to my endgame.

I'm so caught up in my daydream that I miss the timing of my pivot. When I speed up my next step to recover my pacing, one of my heels catches in a flowy section of my skirt.

Dread locks up my entire body as I teeter forward off my spike heels with more force than I can manage. Suddenly, there's too much air beneath my shoes and zero chances of saving myself.

It's a short one-foot drop off the stage, but it all happens so fast, it's impossible to find my footing. My palms catch my fall as I slam into cold cement. My head whips forward, and pain shoots up my arms. My knees crash to the hard floor, and now I'm on all fours.

My eyes squeeze shut as mortification slips through my veins. One breath... two breaths... three breaths. *Noooooo.* My insides are sobbing. I can't look up, but I peel my eyes open just enough to see a pair of men's shoes under my nose.

The music is still pulsing through the speakers, but all I can hear are the whispers. All I can feel is the shock of the crowd. And all I know is that everything I had planned for my future—my exit from modeling and my entrance into the world of acting—is now completely tarnished.

Five Star Faye

DESMOND

"Sir, would you like something to drink?"

I pull my groggy eyes from the window that overlooks a field of clouds and the bright-blue sky above it. As tired as I am, I can never sleep on planes. There's something about the altitude and not having anyone to talk to that brings every thought to the surface of my mind — the busy kind of thoughts that could benefit from a hit of a joint. Not that I've done that shit in years. Nowadays, the only highs I believe in are the natural sort like reaching the top of a mountain after a long hike, zooming around town in my ride, cooking a badass five-course gourmet meal from scratch, and sex.

Since I can't have any of the above, I'll settle for the next best thing, something that might just settle my mind when it feels impossible. With a quick glance at my watch, I confirm we'll be in the air another four hours. I look up at the flight attendant and clear my throat. "I'll take a Bloody Mary, thanks."

The man in uniform immediately begins gathering the ingredients, and I shift in my seat. My eyes drift to the warm body beside me, which belongs to an attractive woman with a waiting smile. Her gaze is already on me and possibly has been for quite some time. I wouldn't know since I've been lost in my own thoughts since boarding this dreadful flight. I hate plane rides. I hate sitting. I hate waiting around while the fate of my life is in someone else's hands. All I can do is sit here, wishing to sleep through the entire thing.

"Tough morning?" the woman asks.

My eyes snap back to hers, and I cough out a laugh, remembering why I had my eyes glued to the window in the first place. The last thing I wanted when I climbed aboard this plane was to devote a single second to small talk. Then again, I hadn't noticed *her* yet.

My eyes flick down, taking in her stretchy yellow suit pants and tight white tank top that calls attention to certain enhancements, before moving back up her body and landing on her bright-green eyes. If I were to venture a guess, I would say she's an important businesswoman, maybe an executive at her organization, possibly divorced since she's not wearing a ring. And I imagine she has little free time for anything more than a quick fuck now and then.

I smile at that last thought. *My favorite type of relationship.* When it comes to women, I'm definitely the type of guy who prefers a low-maintenance relationship, and I'm not afraid to admit it. No woman could ever label me as a player because my intentions are clear from the get-go. I won't lead a woman on, and the second any sort of feelings get involved, I'm out.

I flash her a smile. "More like a rough night."

Amusement replaces her smile as she faces forward. "Looking like you do, I imagine you have many of those."

My brows lift at what I'm just going to assume was an advance of some kind. Clearly, she's interested. But in what, I'm not so sure yet. Not that I'm complaining. By the way she carries herself, I would venture another guess that she's got twenty years on me putting her in her late forties. *An older woman who's sexy, bold, and beautiful.* Those are my three favorite qualities, and this spitfire has them all.

I angle my body toward her, my anxious thoughts drifting away. "It wasn't *that* kind of rough night, unfortunately."

There's a pause before her curiosity wavers and she turns back to me. "Do tell."

Discomfort snakes through my chest. I'm not in the mood for meaningless prodding from strangers. They don't need to know my business, no matter how good-looking they are. Best to keep my answers short if I have any chance of steering us back toward safe ground. "I was visiting someone in Dallas. I wouldn't want to bore you with the details."

"Ah, handsome and mysterious. I'm sure the ladies love it."

My mouth opens, ready to tell her that's not all the ladies love, but we're interrupted by a male figure leaning toward us.

"Sir, your drink."

"Thank you." I'm grateful for the interruption. While the mile-high club has always been on my bucket list, mindless banter is the last thing that will take my mind off of the situation I just left.

Red and blue swirling lights.

The cold, unforgiving jail cell that smelled of piss and bad decisions.

The small courtroom and the sympathetic eyes of the judge as she passed her sentence.

It's been the longest week of my life, and I can't wait to get back to Seattle.

I take the plastic cup of ice and Bloody Mary mix first, set it down in front of me, then reach for the vodka shots. For the next few minutes, I sit in silence. I mix my drink, tip the cup against my lips, and let the spicy liquid glide down the back of my throat before sinking back into my seat with contentment.

Numbness is my goal. That's the state I want to be in. Anything is better than reliving the past four days in my hometown of Dallas. It was where I grew up, physically and literally. It was where I met my best friend, who would, for some miraculous reason, take me under his wing and give me an opportunity I never deserved. And it was the home that never really felt like home to begin with.

I reach into my bag at my feet and pull out my camera to start flipping through the most recent photos, a habit when I'm lost in my thoughts. I tap through an entire series of pictures I took in the kitchen of a family friend who I stayed with in Dallas where I made an herb-roasted Cornish game hen with rice pilaf and pan jus.

Cooking is the number one love in my life, so much so that I need to photograph every detail of my finished meals in their most vulnerable form, with steam still billowing from the pan, plated, and in the midst of being decorated with fresh herbs and seasonings.

When I capture a photo, I need it to tell a story in a way that captures all the senses, as if the viewer can taste the meal on his tongue with just one look. I click through a few more photos, freezing on the money shot, the one I'll edit, print, frame, and hang with the rest of my favorites in my cooking school's kitchen back in Seattle.

"Did you take those?" the woman beside me asks.

I power off my camera and turn to her with a lift of my lids. My photos, for the most part, are private, like a journal, but I like to capture the food I create. "I did." I respond to her slowly, hesitantly, unsure if I want her to dig deeper.

Her mouth parts like there's something she wants to say about it, but instead she reaches for something safer. "Now I'm even more curious about you." She narrows her eyes. "You obviously don't want to tell me about where you came from. How about you tell me where you're going instead?"

I laugh, a flicker of irritation sparking inside me—at myself, not the stranger sitting beside me. It's gotten to the point that my discomfort about where I came from is so bad that I can't even talk about it anymore. I wave my anxious thoughts away.

"I'm heading home to Seattle." I toss her a look. "And you?"

Her eyes twinkle mischievously. "Business. Maybe a little bit of pleasure too. We'll have to see." She eyes me curiously. "What is it you do?"

"I'm a chef."

She leans back, an impressed look replacing her curious one. "That explains the photos."

I'm not surprised by her reaction. Chicks dig a man who can cook. But I've found I only enjoy it when I'm at work, experimenting and teaching. When I'm at home alone, I stick with takeout and leftovers. In fact, I usually eat propped up in my man cave, watching sports. It's simple. Simplicity dissolves when there are expectations. And women always come with expectations.

"That's it?" she chides. "That's all I get? What kind of chef are you? And for who?"

My eyebrows lift. "Why the interrogation? Maybe I didn't say for a reason. Maybe I don't want to tell you."

She laughs, a full-on belly laugh revealing creases beside her eyes and a full set of pearly whites. "I happen to have an interest in your profession. I might dabble in the culinary field myself."

"Is that so?" Her amusement triggers something in me. "Please don't tell me you're a food critic."

There's nothing that scares and excites me, in equal measure, more than a food critic poking around the cooking school where I teach.

She leans back with a challenge in her eyes. "And what is wrong with food critics? If it weren't for those with exceptional palates and creative write-ups, some of the best mom-and-pop restaurants in the world would have gone out of business. It's a competitive market, with restaurants on every busy corner. You want your food to stand out from the rest? Then you need someone like me on your side, shouting your unique offerings to the world. That is, unless you have none to show."

My eyes go wide, suddenly forgetting everything I was trying to avoid on my long plane ride home. This conversation just got interesting. "You're shitting me. You're an actual food critic?"

She laughs and holds out her hand. Her diamond bracelet catches the weak overhead light. "Faye Montgomery. Pleased to meet you."

Fuck, I think my heart just exploded all over my insides. "Faye Montgomery?" My eyes sweep over her body again, this time with an entirely new perspective. "As in, *Five-Star Faye*? I love that show." I shake my head. "I didn't recognize you."

She shrugs, a satisfied smile playing on her face. "I'm not surprised. I don't get much TV time. It's about the food and who makes it. That's what's important. That's what we showcase." Leaning back, she folds her arms, which conveniently pushes up her chest. "So tell me about your restaurant."

"Sorry to disappoint you, beautiful, but I don't own a restaurant."

Her eyes furrow in curiosity.

"My buddy and I own a cooking school. Well, he's more like a silent partner. I teach, I certify, and I entertain." I give her a wink, letting my pride for my business show. "We're in a hot spot in downtown Seattle. Classes fill up months in advance. We're accredited and growing our services. It's been a huge success."

Faye's narrowed eyes show her skepticism. "Original recipes?"

It's my turn to lean back and feel somewhat defensive. "All original. All food made from scratch. All ingredients picked up daily from the farmers market around the corner. I wouldn't have it any other way."

"Interesting." She reaches into her purse and pulls out a black business card with gold writing. "You should call me."

I raise my eyebrows, feeling a smirk pulling at my lips. "Call you?" I linger on the question, letting our flirtation brew just a little bit longer.

She rolls her eyes to bat me away. "Not that kind of call. Not yet anyway." She doesn't even blink through her forward comment. "I'd love to check out a class while I'm in town. Maybe your kitchen is a fit for the show."

"You're serious? You want to check out my food? I've seen your show. My place isn't exactly the type of joint you review."

She shrugs. "Maybe not. But we're between seasons, and I'm looking for fresh ideas. I'm just interested in checking it out. If I hate it, I walk, and you'll never see me again."

"That's not going to happen."

"Ah, you're a cocky chef. Humor me, will you? Which part isn't going to happen? Me hating it? Or me walking away?"

"Both."

"Now I definitely need to try your food."

I toss my head back and laugh. "Great. And I get to read your scathing review, written just to spite me."

"Clearly you don't watch the show. The worst that can happen is that you don't get any airtime, and I won't give pity attention for food that doesn't deserve it. You think your food is good? Let me be the judge."

She reaches out her perfectly manicured hand, which I stare at far longer than I really should—not because I'm admiring her soft skin or blinging jewels, but because this is a serious opportunity, one I've been wanting ever since I accepted my chef's hat after four years of grueling culinary training. Growing up, I wanted that so much, but I wanted this more than anything else.

My hand slides out to meet hers. As we touch, my eyes meet her ice-cold blue ones. "You're in for a treat, Ms. Montgomery."

She meets my challenge with a knowing smile. "Oh, I'm counting on it, Mr…" She tilts her head. "You forgot to mention your name."

"Blake." I grin at my James Bond impersonation. "Desmond Blake."

Lobsters Have Feelings

MAGGIE, THREE MONTHS LATER

"Remind me why we're here again."

My sister, Monica, responds with a single look to express her annoyance before she takes off around the low-rise Seattle building. She would have never dared to give me that same look when we were younger—one that makes me boil inside as I watch her patent leather heels snap beneath her. I quicken my steps to keep up. For someone who has the short legs in the family, she makes up for it in speed.

"What do you mean *remind* you?" she asks.

"We need this final class to get our cooking certificates."

My face scrunches in confusion. "Certificates for what? You told me we were signing up for one month of classes, and that became three. I don't understand. It's not like you're going to go out and get a cooking job somewhere."

"Well," she sasses back. "Maybe it will come in handy for you, seeing as you need a job so you can stop mooching. Funny how you can afford that fancy ombre, but not even a little bit of rent."

My face grows hot just thinking about the many times she's slung the word "mooch" since I came to live with her. And I ignore the comment about my hair because this ombre is a necessity, not a luxury. After my fall on the runway, I didn't want to take any risks of being recognized after a social media video of it went viral.

The whole experience was so embarrassing, I couldn't even bring myself to tell my sister. I still harbor guilt over that three months later. When I moved here, Monica was going through some pretty heavy stuff herself. The last thing she needed to worry about was me and my drama. But just because I *temporarily* moved to *her* town and live in her tiny-ass apartment in Bellevue, Washington—a city just outside of Seattle—does not mean she gets to boss me around. As the older sister by four years, that has always been my job.

I swallow my bitterness, knowing that, despite our mutual frustration, I do owe her one. But if she calls me a mooch one more time…

"I already told you I'm meeting with that job recruiter you hooked me up with from BelleCurve on Monday. She thinks she has something for me. Maybe there's some sort of radio job out there, or maybe I can jump on the fashion-design bandwagon like you."

Monica laughs. "Really? You've never sewn a damn thing in your life."

I huff out a breath as I continue pounding the pavement beside her. "I can learn. How hard could it be?"

She shrugs. "You *can* learn. You know the industry. You've got an eye for fashion. Open enrollment is coming up at the Art Institute. Maybe you should consider it."

I scrunch my nose at the mention of school. "I don't know. I guess that's an option if I can't figure things out on my own."

With BelleCurve's creative connections, I have high hopes. Moving from one state to another definitely put a kink in my sudden need for a career change. At least in LA, I had connections—so-called friends who knew someone that knew someone. But moving back is not an option, not yet anyway.

"I don't understand why you even need BelleCurve to help you. When you moved here, you had your sights set on acting. You went and got that agent and everything."

Ugh. If there is a subject worse than my exit from modeling, it's this one. "Well, nothing has come of that yet."

"Are you still auditioning? Don't give up if that's still what you want."

I shrug, desperately wanting to move on from this conversation. I haven't minded that Monica has been too caught up in her own situation to realize I've made a shit storm out of my own. When I moved here, I didn't correct Monica when she thought I would focus on pursuing acting in Seattle. It's what she thought I always wanted to do. Hell, even I had made myself believe that lie. There's just never a right time to tell her the truth.

"I'll find something soon. Trust me. I want off your couch just as much as you want me off."

"I just want to see you happy, Mags."

I give her the side-eye, once again realizing that my sister has grown up a hell of a lot since she moved here, away from my mother and me. I feel a twinge of jealousy at what she's been able to accomplish free of our mother's clutches—the same clutches I should have broken free from ages ago.

The tables have definitely turned, and I can't seem to find my way out from underneath them.

We start up the stairs to get to the second floor, where the cooking school is, when Monica halts and swivels around to face me. "Promise me you'll have fun today. This certificate means a lot to me."

I bite back a laugh. "What's the deal anyway? I thought you were just doing all this cooking stuff to impress Zach. You already got the guy."

She releases her hard look, and her eyes soften. "It's not all about Zach. I actually enjoy this *cooking stuff* now. It's fun, and it's nice to not blow my paychecks on takeout all the time." She sighs. "But don't worry. After today, you never have to come back. I only invited you because I thought it would be fun for us to do together."

My shoulders sag with my exhale as guilt tranquilizes my mood. "I know. So did I. But that was before the instructor turned into a major asshole."

Monica chuckles as we stop at the top of the stairs in front of the main entrance. "Desmond is not that bad."

I huff, not budging from my stance. "You're just saying that because he's Zach's best friend."

"No." Monica shakes her head. "I'm saying that because I've gotten to know Desmond, and while he may be a little rough around the edges, he's actually a good guy. Zach wouldn't have chosen him to run the cooking school if he wasn't."

I roll my eyes at the millionth mention of her boyfriend today. I've officially lost my sister to lovesick-puppy status. "Don't you think it's a little strange to be so fond of two guys who Dad has spent more time with than us? *After* Dad abandoned our family when we were kids."

Monica cuts me a glare. "Please, not this again, M." Our dad gave us the nicknames M&M when we were little. For some reason, Monica became M and I became Mags.

"Why not this again? That's the reality of it, isn't it? Dad disappeared and got himself a new family. Then he took Zach and Desmond under his wing."

"Stop talking about Dad like he's a bad guy. He messed up, but Mom wasn't perfect either, which you'd know if you gave Dad a chance to explain. Just talk to him, and—"

I narrow my eyes, cutting her off, then push my way through the entrance. There's no way I'm letting her go on about what a great guy our dad is now. Having an affair is one awful thing, but starting a new family while completely abandoning the one that already exists? There's no forgiving him for what he did to us.

I shake the negative thoughts from my mind as Gretta, Desmond's assistant, beams at me when I approach. "Hey, Maggie. You ready for certification day?"

Already spun out of shape, I'm about to tell her exactly what I think about certification day when Monica pushes against my side and starts gushing about her excitement. I snort my disdain.

"What's the matter, Maggie?" calls a deep voice from the front of the room. "Sad today's your last day with me?"

My eyes snap to find Desmond Blake—full beard and man bun on point—in all his cocky glory, currently leaning over a countertop while chatting with another female student. *Flirting, no doubt.* It's what he does. It's why the class is filled with ninety percent women and a few grumbling husbands.

Last month when I first laid eyes on his hot, tall, Southern bod, I couldn't peel them away. Our flirtation was on another level, but it didn't last long. I came to find out his flirtation wasn't reserved for me alone. The batting eyelashes, undress-me stare, wicked smile, and syrupy sweetness were all part of his schtick.

"It doesn't have to be, you know?" he continues with a grin. "There are still a few open slots for next month."

My laugh is instantaneous, bubbling up my throat before I can stop it. "The only way you'll ever catch me in this kitchen again will be in your dreams, Desmond Blake. I'll take my certificate and be on my way, thank you very much."

"You'll have to earn it first."

The smug challenge in his tone can't be ignored, and neither can the rattling in my chest as our fierce eyes meet. His are a sharp blue. Mine are a shade of light brown that the camera always loved. The mere fact that this guy can get under my skin is starting to bother me more than his bad jokes.

"Ignore him, Mags," Monica says softly. "He just loves to get you all flustered. I think he likes you."

I bark out a laugh and follow my sister to our side-by-side stations. "We're not in kindergarten, M. Twenty-six-year-old men don't tug ponytails and joke about your incompetencies. Real men will let you know they like you. They'll call you on the phone, open your doors, compliment you for all the little things. Real men act like fucking gentlemen."

Monica bites her lip around her laugh. "It's good to see you still have your Southern roots."

I smile at that, feeling warmth in my chest just thinking about back home where we grew up in Texas.

"Couldn't shake these boots from me even if you tried."

She grins, and for a split second, I forget that I'm supposed to be mad at her for dragging me here. At the end of the day, my sister is my best friend. She's the only person who will ever understand the real me and where I came from. She's the only one who could ever understand the hurt we shared together as young girls. And I would do anything for her, including suffering through another dreadful cooking class.

I look at the empty cooking station in front of me and know I need to suck it up. "All right, one last session of torture, and then you're buying me a drink. Deal?"

"Deal."

"Hey, Maggie."

I jump at the deep voice and turn to find Desmond resting against my cooking station with a wolfish grin. My entire body instantly heats. His bulky arms are clearly visible beneath his short-sleeved black shirt. His teeth are white enough to belong in a toothpaste commercial. And the man looks so good in an apron that I won't be able to look away if I try. I don't even attempt to.

"Desmond," I greet with all the syrupy charm I can muster. "I can't imagine what I did to deserve the honor of your close proximity."

He tilts his head in a gesture that tells me he's accepting my challenge. Banter. Insults. Witty comebacks. It's our thing, which somehow makes this class a little bit more bearable.

"Just thought you should know, I looked you up online the other day. Monica mentioned you used to model, and I was curious."

No. My heart rate spikes with fear of what he's getting to. The amusement in his expression nearly confirms it all.

"And I found a very interesting video," he continues, is arrogance starting to smell like a bad cologne.

Shit. I haven't even told Monica about my fall on the runway, not that she would breathe a word about it to anyone. But she's been so consumed in her own love life that I haven't even attempted to broach the subject. In fact, I'd hoped that video would just disappear right along with my past.

But Desmond knows. Desmond looked me up online and found the fucking viral video. He surely had a laugh at my expense.

"Hope you got enough material for your spank bank because those days are behind me."

"Oh, I got enough material all right, but not for my spank bank." He chuckles. "I had no idea you were so *viral*. Why didn't you tell us?"

He doesn't elaborate, he doesn't call me out, but he says enough for me to know that he saw every humiliating moment of that video. Then he winks and backs away from my station like he didn't just poke at one of my deepest, freshest wounds.

He points a finger at my shirt. "Don't forget to put on your apron. Wouldn't want you to ruin those fancy clothes."

10 MINUTES LATER

"What am I supposed to do with that?" I shriek as Desmond walks away after setting a pinchy crawler at my workstation.

With his little beady black eyes and long thick whiskers, the lobster looks more like a character from *The Little Mermaid* than a meal I'm supposed to prepare. I just know he's going to start singing and dancing at any moment.

"Um," I call out, not daring to look away from the moving critter. "It's still moving."

He glances at me from over his shoulder. "That's what your boiling water is for."

My peripheral gaze catches on my pot of boiling water, and I cringe. "You want me to kill Sebastian? Is Scuttle next?"

I hear his deep chuckle, but I can't tear my eyes away from the longest whiskers I've ever seen. "If you're referring to the crab in *The Little Mermaid*, then you've got your sea creatures confused."

"Yeah, well, I'm not killing that thing either way."

I knew we were cooking a seafood dish today from scratch, but I didn't think Desmond was going to make us kill the damn ingredients first. I glance at an amused Gretta who is setting down the recipe on my stainless steel workstation.

"I don't blame you," she whispers with a shake of her head. "I could never do it."

I can feel my insides trembling. "This is inhumane," I hiss back at her.

She just chuckles and walks to the next station.

I straighten my spine and glare at the set of broad shoulders now making their way to the front of the room. "I *won't* do it."

Desmond swivels around, locking eyes with me. "If you can't prepare the meal, you're free to leave, but you won't leave with a certificate."

My jaw drops. I shouldn't even care, seeing as I never wanted to come to class to begin with. But I'm less than two hours from putting closure on the last three months of classes I've endured. I'm not going to just walk away. I've earned that certificate. "Give me something else to make. You can't make me kill a live lobster."

There's chuckling around the room because, apparently, I'm the only one having a hard time with this. Even my sister is biting her lip with amusement, the traitor.

"I'm not handing out individual assignments. I'm sorry, Maggie, but no lobster means no certificate."

My chest puffs as heat wraps around my body like a raging fire.

"C'mon, Mags, you can do it," Monica says with a gentle nudge. That's her, the eternal optimist. I swear there's never been a dare my sister hasn't accepted in her life.

I don't know how long I stand at my station, fuming, but at some point, Monica is by my side, setting her cooked lobster on my station. "Take mine. He'll never have to know," she whispers. "Now start on the shallots, or you'll get too far behind." She grabs my lobster and plops it in her still-boiling pot.

When I raise my eyes to hers, she just winks and goes on about her mission. I do as she says and prepare the pan and shallots to get them cooking. Then I stare at the poor cooked lobster and contemplate becoming a vegan.

It's not like I eat much meat anyway. I'm more of a salad-with-a-dash-of-olive-oil kind of woman. My one indulgence is pasta on the odd occasion. Besides the whole kill-a-lobster part of class, I find my mouth watering for the ravioli part of the meal.

I manage to mix up the shallots with the lobster and some ricotta and Parmesan cheese for the filling. Then I lay them in spoonfuls on a pasta sheet. *Easy peasy.* Once my raviolis are boiling, I start on the lemon-garlic sauce then set it to simmer.

This whole cooking thing isn't entirely bad, but it doesn't mean I would want to come back here again. After today, I'll be set free, and I can go back to spending my Saturdays on the couch, flipping through fashion magazines.

I'm leaning over my workstation, tapping my fingers on the stainless steel, bored out of my mind, when I hear my sister's frustrated growl beside me. I look at her over my shoulder, noting her flushed cheeks and wide eyes.

She swipes her forehead with the back of her hand as she looks my way. "How are you done already?"

I shrug and stand up, glancing quickly at the lobster ravioli I made from scratch. "It was easy after the whole lobster murder."

She winces. "Don't say that. I'm the one who did the murdering."

"Twice," I remind her, only to receive a heartfelt frown. Just because my sister is braver than me doesn't mean she enjoyed boiling the damn thing. Neither of us have had much experience with cooking, and while she's much better now than she was three months ago, I know she wants to prove to herself that her skills extend beyond fashion design.

I attempt to get off the subject of murder. "Anyway, there was nothing to it. Shred the lobster, prepare a garlic-lemon sauce, and let it simmer on the stove."

Monica turns her focus back to me and squints. "Aren't you forgetting something?"

I look at my countertop and shrug. The hardest part of it all is timing everything perfectly so that one thing doesn't cook sooner than the rest. As a matter of fact, I am quite pleased with myself. The only thing there is a wine bottle chilling in a bucket of ice. I pull it out and flash Monica a grin. "Guess I better crack this baby open."

I dare a look at Desmond while I pour myself a glass. He's at the front of the room, observing the class. Then his eyes meet mine with a narrowed challenge, as if he can't believe I accomplished anything, much less prepared an entire gourmet meal from scratch.

Monica clears her throat, turning my attention back to her while I sip from my glass. "I meant the bread. Did you start your loaf?"

Her words are like a bash on the head. "Oh no." I set down the wine and smoosh my face in my hands. "I completely forgot. Crap. No." That should have been the first thing I did. But I was distracted with the thought of killing the lobster.

I swivel in a circle, suddenly drawing a blank. I don't remember what I'm supposed to do. "Shit," I squeak, a little too loud.

"Is there a problem here?"

Hair spikes on my skin, and a wave of heat rolls through my insides. That's pretty much the effect Desmond Blake has on me now. It used to be flutters in my tummy and flushed cheeks just from looking at him. Then he had to go and open his mouth.

Okay, so his mouth is pretty nice. He even has one of those deep voices that could work me like a vibrator if placed in just the right spot. But the words that come out of it tend to make me want to clench my fists and spew a rebuttal.

"Of course not." I try to control my voice, but I can feel my insides quivering. "Everything is *parfaite*." I push my fingers together and kiss the tips of them. "*Trés bien*."

"This isn't a French dish, Maggie."

"Oh." I can feel my cheeks heat in embarrassment, but I quickly turn my fluster into confidence. I push Desmond aside with my elbow in an effort to reach the stove. "Excuse me. You're distracting me."

He catches my elbow before I can completely turn away and narrows his eyes. His look continues to harden as it travels down to my apron.

"What?" I ask, finding it impossible to hide my utter annoyance. His frozen gaze forces me to look down at the apron I found online. I was sick of wearing the blue-and-yellow Edible Desire aprons, so I opted to buy a bundle of my own. This one is black and reads, "Fuck me, I'm the Chef" in gold metallic lettering. "Oh." I quickly realize Desmond doesn't find it the least bit funny.

Then his eyes snap to mine. "There are kids in here."

I toss my head to the right and look at a young girl with her mother a few stations over. They're laughing and mixing something on the stove, totally oblivious to the scolding I'm getting.

"No one even saw it." Frustrated, I reach around Desmond and pick up my wine. I place the cool glass against my lips, my forehead lifting when I realize he's not walking away. He's just standing there. His brows are furrowed, an angry dimple has popped in his cheek, and wisps of curly auburn hair have abandoned his otherwise perfect-looking man bun. I can't remember the last time I got under someone's skin like this, but I recognize the look because he has the same effect on me.

I take a slow sip, my stare leaving his glassy blue one. Dang, he's attractive. It's unfortunate his appeal ends there. What a waste of a great-looking man.

The corner of my mouth lifts in a smile. "Let me get this straight. You're cool with us drinking but not expressing our creative liberties through our fashion? You should really make up your mind."

Desmond shakes his head and blows out a breath. "Well, it doesn't matter because you're disqualified."

I squint to focus a little harder on his sexy mouth, which made absolutely no sense. "Come again."

"If you think I didn't notice you use your sister's lobster, then you've underestimated me. And I don't see any bread, which guarantees you won't have a finished meal in the next twenty minutes. So..." He backs away before turning completely. "No certificate."

My jaw falls in shock. I don't think I can call it disappointment. I have never loved this class. *So why am I pissed the hell off?*

"Come back next month if you want to take this class seriously," he says as he walks away.

Rage fills my body, causing my muscles to launch forward in his direction. "Don't you think that's a little unfair?" I step around him, causing him to stop walking. "Look, I may not be your star pupil, but I deserve that certificate."

"Oh yeah?" He leans in closer, and I'm fully aware that every eye in the room is on us now. "How so?"

I let out an outraged breath. *Is he serious?* "Because, Desmond, I've put in the time. I made the damn dish. I did everything except kill the poor lobster."

"Yet you'd eat one?"

I growl in frustration. "It's not the same thing."

He shrugs. "Well, I hate to break it to you, but I have rules, and I stick to them. If you can't prepare a gourmet meal from scratch, then you can't take home the certificate. Simple as that. What do you care anyway? You don't even want to be here."

"But I have been here. Every damn Saturday for the last three months."

"The good news is you don't need to retake all three months. One month will do."

"What?" I screeched.

He rights his shoulders. "That's the deal."

"You're such a prick."

The corner of his mouth tips up as he backs away. "I've been called worse."

It's official. I may have disliked the guy before, but now I fucking hate Desmond Blake.

When One Door Closes

DESMOND

Maggie was the first one to leave class, and I would be lying to myself if I denied the fact that I hated to see her walk away. She's a feisty one, enjoyably so. Getting a rise out of her has become the highlight of my Saturday classes. When I first laid eyes on the bronze-skinned vixen with sun-kissed hair three months ago, I couldn't stop sneaking glances. She was the definition of gorgeous: tall, slender yet curvy frame, bold stare, full pouty lips. She looked like one of the girls on my pinup calendar from when I was in high school and far too curious for my own good. But it became clear after a few short weeks that whatever charm I'd initially had on her had already waned.

The more I learned about the former LA model was enough to keep my disappointment short-lived. For one, Maggie hates my kitchen with a vibrant passion. Two, she dresses like she's expecting a runway show to pop up at any moment. Three, the permanently poised look about her tiptoes the line between arrogance and class. Nothing would be wrong with any of the above if it didn't come with a flashing neon sign that screams disrespect for me and the cooking school I practically built with my own two hands.

"Hey," Gretta, my assistant, says as she rushes over to me with a flushed face.

"What's up?" I mumble without looking up. I have my camera poised in my hands, and I'm snapping pictures at every angle imaginable of my finished ravioli dish. One day, I'll do something with all these photos, but for now, I like to take the best ones and hang them on the walls of Edible Desire.

"Is it okay if I jet? I've got this school thing that I can't miss."

I look around at the mess left behind by everyone and let out a frustrated sigh. *What can I say? No?* "Again? The materials for the new shelving finally came in, and I was going to work on the storage closet tonight."

"I'm sorry." Her face appears crestfallen, like she's genuinely sorry, which she might be. But she's not sorry enough to avoid repeating the same behavior day after day. "I can come in tomorrow to clean everything." Her eyes float around the room, and I can practically see the dread buried beneath her expression.

I wave her away while pulling the camera and strap over my head and setting them gently on the front counter. "I'm not letting the mess sit for a day. Just go. Good luck. Maybe warn me next time?"

She lets out a relieved breath and nods. "Yes, of course. I'm sorry."

She rushes off, and the front door closes, leaving me alone to finish my photo session before I pick up a rag to start cleaning. Lucky for Gretta, I'm in a good mood. I usually am after I get done with a class. It's just like that feeling I used to get in high school after winning a football game, when the adrenaline was so high, I couldn't sit still even if I tried.

Who would have thought I would trade in my football gear for an apron? Certainly not me. In high school, I was the ultimate jock. I was the guy chicks stood in line to date despite my frequent spikes of anger and bad reputation for getting into fistfights. And usually, it was me who started them.

Looking back, I didn't have a calm bone in my body until my football coach swooped in and taught me how to release my negative energy on the field. Coach Reynolds gave me a fresh start, a home, and a family. I'll forever be grateful for the way he helped me carve a path to my future. Unfortunately, the man who saved me was the same man who abandoned Maggie when she was younger.

The chime on the door dings, and I curse myself for forgetting to lock up after Gretta left. I'm never going to finish cleaning this place if I can't control the interruptions.

"Looks like you need more help around here."

I look up to see Maggie's sister, Monica, approaching me with a smile.

I return her smile with an amused one of my own as I start to wipe down a workstation in the front of the room. "Looks like you're right," I say without looking up again. I'm already dreading what Monica came here to talk to me about. Surely, it has everything to do with her sister. Maybe if she sees that I'm busy, she'll go easy on me. "What's up?"

"It's about Maggie."

I bite down my retort while she continues. I'll need to tread this conversation lightly. Monica is dating my best friend,

Zach, so I have a soft spot for the girl, one that doesn't mix well with her troublesome sister or my anxious mood.

"I know you two have this… tension, but are you sure you can't look past the whole lobster thing? She really wanted that certificate today."

"Well, then she should have done the work." My retort is snappier than I meant it to be, but as much as I love getting under Maggie's skin, she sure gets under mine too.

"Really?" Monica challenges. "Is it really so bad that she didn't want to kill a lobster? I think it's kind of sweet."

The term sweet and Maggie Stevens do not go together, but I refrain from letting that comment slip from my brain and out my throat. I'm not an idiot.

I stand straight, right my shoulders, and stare back at Monica with as much firmness as I can muster without coming off as a complete asshole. This will undoubtedly get back to Zach, and then I'll have to explain myself to him too.

So be it.

"Look, Monica, it's not just about the lobster. It's about the past three months. She's half-listening in every class, distracts the rest of the students with her heckling, and she makes it obvious to everyone that she doesn't want to be here. Not only that, but she criticizes everything—the food, the kitchen, me." My eyes widen, hoping that I've made my point. "I can't give a certificate to someone who doesn't want one."

Monica is biting her lip, and I can tell she's holding back a laugh. Clearly, she doesn't agree with anything I just said. But she eventually sighs and tries again. "It's not like the fate of the free world is resting on Maggie's cooking ability. Come on, Des. She's going through a hard time right now, and you're right—she doesn't want to come to these classes—but she does it for me. The least you can do is give her the stupid certificate." Monica's eyes go wide at her own words. "I shouldn't have said stupid. I'm sorry."

I know Monica didn't mean anything by it, but her words still sting. "It's fine. I get it."

She tilts her head, her smile morphing into a desperate plea. "So you'll hand it over? You probably already printed it."

I raise a hand and let out a sigh. If there's one thing I have a weakness for, it's a well-meaning pouty woman. I just don't have the heart to disappoint Monica too. "Fine," I growl. Then I walk around the island, slide open the top drawer, and pull out the single certificate that was meant for Maggie. I approach Monica and hand it over. "Tell her congratulations for me."

Monica squeals, oblivious to my sarcasm, and hooks her arms around my neck in a hug. "You're the best, Desmond. Thank you. Now why don't you come have a drink with us downstairs at Shooters? Zach's coming too."

I scrunch my face. "Really? To the bar? He's got a game tomorrow." I know it's preseason for the NFL, but Zach doesn't mess around with his football schedule.

"He's just stopping by for a minute. We haven't seen much of each other lately. But you should come. Give the certificate to Maggie yourself. Maybe you two will even hit it off and stop fighting so much."

I chuckle. "That sounds too much like a double date. I think one of us dating the coach's daughter is enough, don't you?"

Monica folds her arms across her chest. "It's not a date at all. Just a hangout."

Backing away, I shake my head. "I can't. I really need to clean up the kitchen, and then I have a torn-up storage closet in the back room that's screaming for my attention."

Monica relents with a smile and backs away. "Okay, fine. But you and Maggie can't avoid each other forever. She and I are kind of a package deal." She raises her hands in a cute shrug. "You two should just kiss and make up already."

"Ha," I burst out. "That's funny. Zach says the same thing."

"With all the tension between you two, I'm surprised that hasn't happened yet." She sticks her tongue between her teeth and reaches for the door handle behind her. "If you change your mind, we'll be downstairs."

I watch her leave, but thoughts of Maggie linger on my mind as I go back to work. I can't get over how Zach found someone so ridiculously perfect for him. And Monica has a point. Maggie will be unavoidable, at least until she moves back to LA once she realizes Seattle isn't made for a woman addicted to the limelight.

Ugh. I don't know why Maggie Stevens has the power to get under my skin the way she does, but I should be damn happy she's not stepping foot in my class again after today. Except I don't think I am happy, and it has nothing to do with the certificate she didn't earn. I've spent my life staying away from women like her, women who are never able to sit still. Maggie is the type that cruises through her damn life without slowing down to experience the natural beauty of the world. Maggie Stevens wears her beauty like it's a mask, and I don't do charades.

Unable to settle my nerves, I reach for my camera to look through the photos I took in my class. The students signed a waiver when they first registered, allowing me to photograph them so that I could use the images for my website or other promotional material. But for some damn reason, the lens found Maggie more often than not.

I had photos of her tying back her hair, chopping herbs with a concentrated look on her face, and stirring the lemon-garlic sauce. At one point, I even aimed the camera at Monica but caught Maggie stealing a taste of her dish. Her eyes are closed, and her lips are parted. Dare I say, she looks to be savoring the moment like she's dreaming of the taste before the pasta hits her mouth.

I shake my head. Who would have known? Maybe Maggie doesn't hate my class as much as she wants me to believe.

Staring back down at the images of Maggie, I can't help but feel a bit turned on by them. I've never considered my food photography erotic before, yet I'm growing hard at the thought of Maggie wrapping those saucy lips around my —

"Shit," I curse under my breath as I power off my camera and set it back on the island. I don't have time to entertain thoughts of the woman who can't tell the difference between a lobster and a crab. No. I need to clean and then start on the closet before my early night turns into an all-nighter.

Just then, the still unlocked door to Edible Desire opens, and I swivel around to face it.

"Well, hi there, stranger," the woman purrs. "Long time, no see."

I grin at the familiar blonde with the ice-blue eyes. "I knew you wouldn't be able to stay away once you tried my food."

Faye steps forward with a grin and lets the door close behind her. "Well, you were right. I can't stop thinking about it."

Coming from Five-Star Faye herself, I couldn't be happier to hear those words. When I last saw her three months ago, I gave her a taste test to end all taste tests. But then I thought maybe I'd ruined my chances after I let her taste-test *me*.

I've never been against mixing business with pleasure, but after three months of silence, I thought maybe that was all she'd come for to begin with.

"Happy to hear I left a memorable taste in your mouth." I grin, and she lets out a throaty laugh, one that surely comes from years of casual encounters just like the one we had. That should probably bother me, but it doesn't.

I've always had a thing for experienced women. Perhaps it's the idea of relationships never moving beyond a fleeting encounter. No strings. No commitments. No broken hearts. It's easy, fun, and safe—just how I like it.

"I'm actually here with a pitch," Faye says. "Should we sit?"

The swift transition from sexual innuendo to business doesn't faze me a bit. I knew that if she did ever come back, I would sacrifice the sex to give whatever opportunity she was handing me a real shot.

I nod toward the dining section of the restaurant that I keep reserved for private events. It's set up like a dining room with two twenty-foot-long solid wood tables made from a vendor around the corner at Pike Place Market. They're decorated with a long white runner down the centers and gray candles of all different sizes scattered across them.

One thing I will miss if it ever comes to firing Gretta will definitely be her decorating skills. She always knows how to sprinkle class around the kitchen and at events, which is probably why she's been spending so much time at design school. The girl is talented, perhaps too talented for what I've been paying her.

Faye takes a seat on the bench opposite me, looking more businesslike than the last time she stopped by. She's dressed in a crisp navy dress suit, and her hair is pulled up in a half ponytail.

"So, just as you guessed, I love your kitchen—the food, the ambiance. Even the location screams something I'd put on *Five-Star Faye*."

For some reason, I feel like rejection is in my future, which makes no sense. Why would she come all the way here to let me down? According to Faye, she didn't do that.

"But?" I ask.

She smiles. "*But* we decided on our lineup for next season, and Edible Desire didn't make the cut."

My heart sinks, and I'm surprised by my own disappointment. It's not like I need Faye's show. The kitchen does well on its own with zero advertisement, but I've started getting excited about all the potential growth a little extra money could give me.

Growth. It's something that has been in the back of my mind since Zach and I opened the place. The initial idea was completely his, but the moment he handed me the reins, I wanted more. I still want more. Edible Desire can be so much beyond just a cooking school. I have more than enough recipes to open a restaurant and a full-scale catering business rather than the one-man-show catering services I offer now. We could even have a bakery department and open up a food truck at the public street market around the corner. But above all things, I want to hire more staff to keep the kitchen running without me working ninety-plus hours a week.

After meeting Faye, I started to believe all of the above could actually come true.

"That's why you're here? To break the bad news?"

Faye chuckles again. "No, Desmond. I'm not that cruel. After discussing some ideas with the network, the conclusion was that *Five-Star Faye* should stick to reviewing restaurants, not cooking schools. It just didn't fit the show."

Great.

"But," Faye starts up again, "my pitch for Edible Desire gave us all a new idea for a different type of show. A spin-off of *Five-Star Faye*, if you will. One that embraces the challenges of running a successful business like yours. Farm-to-table is all the rage nowadays, and you execute that brilliantly here. You teaching your students how to cook from scratch is identifiable, which is exactly what our average viewer wants to tune in to see.

"Not only that, but you're in a prime location, and the charities you support deserve recognition too. After the network and I talked, our ideas were endless, and we couldn't see you slotted into one thirty-minute show, simply put."

"But how?"

Faye shrugs. "Just do what you do, and my crew will shoot it. I'm picturing more of a documentary-style show."

"Like a reality show?"

She nods and shrugs as though she's still considering her options. "Possibly. We wouldn't dig into your personal life as much as we'd be going behind the scenes of running a cooking school, mixed with the art of cooking from scratch. The ladies will love you, Desmond."

"What's the angle? Isn't there always an angle?"

Faye cringes a little. "I'm hoping we don't need one. The concept is original, and that should be enough. You're a pretty face, Desmond Blake. Just so happens, you make a damn good meal too." She swivels her head to face the kitchen. "What was on the menu today?"

"Lobster ravioli from scratch."

She grins. "Sounds delicious. How'd that go?"

I chuckle as an image of a flustered Maggie floats through my mind. "Great for most."

She laughs. "Why do I feel like whatever went on today would have made a great episode?"

I nod. "You'd probably be right. It was comical at best."

"Well, if you like the pitch, I'd like to get some things down on paper and fly my production crew here to scope things out. I'll warn you—I like to move quickly. I want to aim for a fall series premiere, which means we need to have a pilot in the can in just a few months to get the full green light from the network."

"Just like that?"

Faye shrugs. "Just like that. You've got something special here, Desmond. It's time for the world to see it." She stands up and glances around the room. "Now while you're thinking about it, how about some of that lobster ravioli?"

See Through

MAGGIE

A series of clacks from a pool game going on somewhere in the room almost cause me to drop the phone in my hand.

"Are you at a bar?" My mom's accusing tone still makes me cringe, even though we're thousands of miles apart.

I'm at Shooters, a sports bar below Edible Desire that specializes in billiards. The atmosphere is classy and chic with its windowless walls and dim lighting, which goes perfectly with my current mood. Between the distressing phone call with my mom and not getting that damn certificate, I have every intention of drowning my sorrows in gluten-free liquor.

"It doesn't matter where I am. I just wanted to call you back and tell you that I'm still fine. I'm still alive, and I hope you're fine too."

My mom huffs her dissatisfaction. "You can't possibly be fine. It's been three months, Maggie. Where are you living? What are you doing for work?"

"Can you please trust me when I tell you that I'm doing fine? I just needed some time away. Some… space." I push out the words, trying my best to control my tone.

There's a beat of silence before her cold tone blasts through the line. "The agency is asking for you. They're still trying to book you despite your little absence."

I grind my teeth in response to her words. *Little absence.* She talks to me like I'm a toddler in need of some tough love. But really, everyone knows my mother cares more about her manager's cut than she does about being a mother. I need to tell her that I'm not returning to modeling. It's on the tip of my tongue, but I know she'll freak out more than she already is.

"Mom, stop, please. Just tell them I'm taking a break and that we'll contact them when we're looking again. Can you do that?"

A heavy sigh breaks through the phone line. "Oh, sweetie, you don't need a break. You're just embarrassed because of your fall." Her coaxing words can almost be mistaken for caring. "It's been months. All will be forgiven and forgotten. Falls happen to the best of us."

"That's not what this is about. I just need this time. I need to figure out if modeling is still what I want." I cringe the moment the words hit the air. There it is, the setup to ease the blow.

"What?" Her shriek is so loud, I have to pull the phone away from my ear.

Another crack sounds from the pool table behind me, causing me to jump. My mom always gets me so worked up when we talk. I had good intentions by calling, but this is exactly why I've been avoiding it.

"You *are* at a bar," she accuses. "Are you drunk?" Her voice lowers menacingly. "Are you with your sister?"

I'm definitely not ready to open that can of worms. "What? I'm sorry. Shoot. Can't hear you. I'll have to call you later."

"Maggie Grace Stevens, don't you da—"

"I love you. Bye." I let my final word ring for an extra beat before I end the call. But I don't stop there. I power off my phone, giving my mom zero chance to call me back. My next heavy sigh is one of relief.

By the time Monica joins me after her long bathroom break, I'm finishing my vodka soda with a loud slurp before plopping the lime into my mouth and sucking every ounce of alcohol from its flesh. "Here," I say, sliding her drink in front of her.

"Thanks," she says, as perky as ever. "I'll trade you." She slides a piece of paper in my direction.

I eye it with a glare, and my head snaps toward hers. "What is this?"

Her glass is poised at her lips when she raises her brows. "It's your cooking certificate. Congratulations. You earned that, sis."

I laugh sarcastically. "Not according to the cooking lord himself. What'd you do? Pay him off?"

She narrows her eyes, her excitement dwindling rapidly. And for that, guilt swarms through me. *Desmond has some nerve handing my sister a pity certificate.*

"No, I didn't pay him off," she grits out.

I bite down on the straw of my empty drink, cursing internally. Sometimes I hate that I'm such a pain in the ass. I've been a difficult bitch since the moment I arrived at my sister's office at BelleCurve, even after she was gracious enough to offer me her couch, but it's like I can't help it. The world she's built around her seems to be one big trigger for everything I've tried to avoid.

I stare down at the certificate as guilt continues to cycle through me. Perhaps I should be more grateful for her gesture. She obviously went out of her way to take what should have been mine to begin with. She was only trying to make me happy.

With a sigh, I shake my head and force out a laugh. "Well then, what'd you say to convince him?"

"I just told him you deserve it and that it wasn't fair for him to keep it from you. That's all, I swear."

"And he handed it over to you? Just like that?"

A hopeful smile breaks through her expression. "Desmond's not a bad guy."

"Yeah, well, instead of embarrassing me in front of everyone in class, he should have given it to me himself." *Lord knows I've had enough embarrassment to last a lifetime.*

Monica growls. "Can't you accept the dang piece of paper and move on? Or don't take it. I don't care. I just wish y'all would stop bickering so much. You're my sister, and Desmond is Zach's best friend. News flash, sis—there's no escaping each other. One of these days, you and Desmond will have to figure out how to get along."

Annoyance burns in my chest. "I can tell you right now, that will never happen."

She lets out a frustrated growl and shakes her head. "How about we talk about something else?"

My entire body relaxes at the suggestion. "Yes, please. How's school? How's work? How's the relationship?"

Monica perks up instantly at the mention of all the above. "School keeps me busy, and when school doesn't, work does. I guess that's good since Zach and I barely see each other right now."

Not only is Zachary Ryan a football player for the NFL, but he's *the* star quarterback for Seattle. After meeting him and seeing their connection, I totally understand why my sister is head over heels for the man. They complement each other in a way couples only dream of. He's the chocolate to her strawberry as she often says.

"You knew what you were getting yourself into," I say with a weak smile. We both suffered through the NFL's crazy schedule when we were little and our dad played for Dallas.

Monica bites her lip. "Yeah, well, you try having a sexy boyfriend with zero time to *be together*." She leans and lowers her voice to say the last two words, lifting her brows as if insinuating sex is a crime.

I scrunch up my face but am unable to keep the laughter from slipping past my throat. "Are you horny or in love? Because right now, I'm not sure which it is."

"Both," she says easily before sipping happily on her drink. "I just happen to *really* miss the sex right now. Between all the production shoots I've been working at BelleCurve and Zach's football schedule, we've barely seen each other. I miss him."

I look up just in time to see Zach walking through the door to Shooters. I lift up my hand in a wave. "Here's your hottie now."

Everything about my sister lights up when she sees him. She's off her chair and jumping into his giant arms before I can take my next breath. I have to turn away from their makeout session while I wallow in my loneliness and suck down more of my drink.

"Hey, Maggie," Zach says with a squeeze of my shoulder.

I swivel in my stool and flash him a smile. "Hey, Zach. Ready for your game tomorrow?"

He claps and rubs his hands together, emitting an energy that's impossible to ignore. "You know it. How was class today? Desmond still being a pain?"

I lift my eyes and nod. "Did you ever doubt him?"

Zach chuckles. "Not for a second. Want me to talk to him? Straighten him out a bit? You know I'd be happy to."

No matter the relationship Zach has with our father, he is impossible to hate. I find myself smiling my first genuine smile of the day. "Only if I can watch." Then I eye the certificate in front of me again and swipe it from the table, a burst of adrenaline leading me. "On second thought, I think I'll handle the straightening out myself." I stand from the bar. "Keep my spot warm. This should only take a minute."

Monica and Zach's laughter fade as I exit the bar and take the stairs two at a time to the kitchen entrance. I try the door first, but it's locked, so I knock hard on the glass instead.

A few moments later, the door flings open, and I'm ready to give Desmond the tongue lashing I've quickly prepared. My mouth is already opening, my hands are clenched by my sides, and the first syllable leaves my throat when it catches at the sight before me.

It takes me a moment to realize that the man who opens the door is the same one I just saw in class. But this time he's shirtless, sweaty, and breathing as hard as someone who just ran a record-breaking 5K. He lifts an arm above his head and rests it on the top of the door frame, leveling me with his gaze. But my eyes don't stay on his. Instead, I follow a drip of sweat that's running between his pecs then down the center line of his abs until it reaches his navel. He's wearing pants, thank God. But they're hanging low, and now I'm imagining too much.

Damn. If I didn't hate Desmond Blake, I think I might just love him.

"Back so soon?"

My gaze snaps up to find his eyes twinkling with a devilish gleam. His voice is deep, thick, filled with sex, and masked with humor. For a second, a pang of jealousy hits me over whoever has the ability to evoke more from Desmond than sarcastic quips and cruel indifference.

My skin starts to prickle as warmth washes over me. I can feel the flush in my cheeks as my eyes meet his. And just like the moment we met, I feel like he sees far too much. I swallow, attempting to regain control, but it's nearly impossible when he's dressed like that.

"I didn't mean to interrupt your *activities*, but" — I clear my throat then smash the paper to his chest before peeling my eyes away from his hard body again — "despite whatever my sister said to you, I don't want a pity certificate. I want to know I earned it."

He cocks a brow. "You don't believe you earned it?"

"I do." I stumble a little before righting my shoulders. "But I need to hear it from you."

"Are you saying you need my validation?"

My jaw drops while his words tumble around in my mind. Is that what I came here for? If so, I'm giving Desmond far too much credit. *Time to backpedal.*

"I did earn it, but I'm not going to hang something on my wall that someone had to beg you to give me. I want you to hand it to me and tell me I earned it, or I don't want it at all."

He shakes his head, never losing the twinkle. "I'm sorry to disappoint you, Maggie, but I can't do that. You'll have to come back to class and take it seriously if you want me to reciprocate."

My mood instantly falls, and the attraction toward the nearly naked man in front of me is dissolving at a rapid rate. "Are you going to make me kill a lobster again?"

He sighs and shakes his head. "I don't give a damn about the lobster. I care about those who come to my class and work for the reward. There are plenty of other cooking schools you can go to, pay, never show up for class, and then still walk off with a trophy in the end. Not here. That certificate is equivalent to college credit, and I take pride in that. All of my students should too."

"But I did show up for every class. I was here."

He shakes his head. "No, you weren't, Maggie. You've always been somewhere else, two steps from disappearing completely. Before any of us know it, you'll be heading back to LA like you were never here to begin with."

I don't know why, but this conversation suddenly feels incredibly intrusive. I feel my body begin to shake, and my chest heats with emotion. Desmond has no clue where I came from or why I'm here. He can make all the assumptions he wants, but he'll never see me, not the real me.

"You know nothing about me and my decisions. How dare you assume anything other than what I tell you. You don't know me, Desmond Blake."

He shrugs. "You're right. I don't. But you're as transparent as that makeup you wear. You think it conceals what's underneath? Well, you're wrong. I may not know you, but I see you. You may be able to fake your way through life, but you won't get away with that shit in my class."

My throat tightens at his words, and I'm suddenly reminded of all the reasons I hate Desmond. This conversation now tops the list.

I step back before he can see the tears brimming in my eyes. "I can see through you too. And you know what? You don't care about anything or anyone but yourself."

With that, I jog back down the stairs and fly through the door of the bar. "I'll have another one of these," I say to the bartender while sliding my empty glass toward him. I ignore Monica and Zach's intense stares.

"I'm going to head back to my place," Zach whispers to Monica. "I'll see you tomorrow at the game?"

"Okay," she says, and they kiss for a full minute before he finally gets up and squeezes my shoulder. "Bye, Mags. Will I see you at the game too?"

I shake my head, wishing people would stop trying to fold me into their lives like I'll fit in. I never will, not when it comes to football or cooking or Coach Reynolds. "No, but have a great game." I fist-bump him, and he's gone before I can blink again.

Monica leans in and rests her head on my shoulder. "If it makes you feel any better, you look really hot today."

And then I laugh because only my sister can find a way to lighten the mood when I'm wallowing in my own despair.

Production

DESMOND

After Maggie leaves, I'm in no mood to continue messing around in my storage room. Instead, I grab a folded towel from the bathroom and wipe myself down with it.

I'm walking into the main kitchen when the front door opens again. "Dear Lord," I mutter with exasperation. "What now?" I swear I locked the door after Faye left. But then the mystery is solved when, a moment later, I'm faced with Zach. "Shit." Surely he's here because he's caught wind of the war waging between Maggie and me. *This isn't going to be pretty.*

Zach's eyes are dead set on me as the door shuts behind him. Then his hands move to his hips, and he narrows his eyes. "I don't even want to know what you've just been doing."

"Ya sure? Because I'm saving us thousands in handyman fees by remodeling the storage closet myself."

His face twists in confusion. Zach never has to handle the minor details since I'm always here managing the day-to-day operations.

"Whatever. We'll get back to the storage closet. What's the deal with Maggie? Would it kill you to be just a little bit nicer to my girlfriend's sister?"

"Have you met her? Yeah. Yeah, it would."

Zach sighs his frustration. "I swear to God, dude, your issues with the female species are beyond my comprehension."

I shrug and take a seat on the couch near the entrance, gesturing for him to sit with me. I have a feeling this talk won't be a short one. "It doesn't matter anyway. She was all upset that she didn't get a cooking certificate today. I'm not sure why since she never gave a shit to begin with. But even after I gave Monica the certificate to give to Maggie, Maggie didn't want it. She just stopped by to return it."

"Really?" Zach asks, and I can see that he doesn't entirely believe me.

I shrug in response. I suppose my version of the story might be a little one-sided, but I don't really care.

Zach leans back in his chair, looking almost as exhausted as me. "We'll get back to Maggie. Who was the blond woman I saw leaving the kitchen thirty minutes ago? She didn't look like your typical student."

"You saw her? You should have come said hi."

Zach chuckles. "Nah, I'm good."

"You sure? Because she's pitching our new television show to her network executives at Good Eats. She's already talking about filming a pilot."

Zach's jaw falls. "Don't tell me that was—"

"Five-Star Faye. In the flesh."

"She came back?"

I nod with a huge grin for two reasons. One, he sounds impressed. Two, I might have just distracted him from the whole Maggie issue.

"What is she offering you now besides a ticket to the mile-high club?"

"Dude. You mean, what is she offering *us*? You and me. We're in this together. She thinks Edible Desire deserves its own television show, a behind-the-scenes look at how we run our scratch kitchen and school, or something like that. She hasn't sorted out all the details."

"And you're sure that's a good idea? You're already busy enough as it is between classes, catering, and the private parties." His head swings left and right. "Speaking of being busy, where's Gretta?"

I can't hide the annoyance that washes over my face. "Not here, which shouldn't surprise anyone lately. I think I'm going to have to let her go."

"Oh, man. Really?"

"I don't see any other way around it. She has too many conflicts lately. I applaud her passion for school and all, but she left me high and dry again today."

Zach sighs, and I know he understands. We go through part-time employees as fast as I go through laundry detergent. "Maybe it's time we hire someone for you full-time. Take some of the burden off of you, especially since this television thing seems like something you really want to do."

Now my jaw drops. "Wait a second. I was fully prepared for you to argue with me about the whole Faye conversation. You're okay with the show?"

Zach rubs the back of his neck when he gets all bent out of shape, and he's doing it now. "To be honest, I don't think I should get much of a say. You've been responsible for this place for the past four years. I come and go as I please, but none of this would still be running if it weren't for you."

"Thanks, dude." My chest goes all warm over my best friend's confidence. I never deserved Zach's friendship after the way I treated him when we were younger, but I haven't stopped making up for that time.

"As long as you continue to keep twenty percent of the proceeds going to the charities of our choosing, then I'm happy to leave these decisions in your hands."

There's no question that our charity donations continue. That was part of our whole reason for going into business together. "That means a lot, Zach. Thank you."

He throws up his hand. I knew it couldn't have been that easy. "But I won't back down about Maggie. You need to make this right with her."

"How do you propose I do that? You know she has a problem with Coach, therefore she a problem with me."

"Yeah, well, she has every right to be pissed at him. He is her dad, and he did a real shitty thing."

"But Monica got over it."

"Monica will never *get over it*, Des, never. But she's figured out how to start forgiving him, and that has to happen in her own time, just like with Maggie." Zach stands. "Anyway, just consider going easy on her, please. She's family."

My eyes widen as I look at my best friend. "Family, huh? You proposing to Monica any time soon?"

Zach chuckles. "One day, bro. She's it for me—you know that—which makes Maggie family. Besides, she's Coach's daughter, which makes her family already."

I wrinkle my face. "When you put it like that, you're dating your sister."

Zach grabs a decorative pillow from the couch and tosses it at me with his best throwing arm. Only Zach could cause pain with a throw pillow.

I rub my arm. "Shit, dude."

He points at me. "Watch your mouth," he warns.

I just grin.

TAKE TWO

Neighborly Love

"NOT UNTIL WE ARE LOST DO WE BEGIN TO UNDERSTAND OURSELVES.
— HENRY DAVID THOREAU

Do Not Disturb

MAGGIE

Promo Girl. That's the official title on my contract with White Water, a local distillery currently promoting their new brand of four-times-distilled organic vodka. I knew approximately zero about vodka when I started this gig a few weeks ago, and now I know far too much.

Basically, the jobs I've been tasked with over the past couple of weeks require minimal wardrobe, passing out liquor at twenty-one and up events, and a healthy dose of flirting with potential customers.

Tonight, I'm walking around a high-profile club in Seattle, wearing a skirt that is one bend away from revealing my ass. My mission is to persuade clubgoers to try shots of White Water vodka by plastering a smile on my face and shaking my hips in as many directions as they'll go.

What my potential employer failed to tell me during my interview was that they're a huge sponsor of Seattle's NFL team and therefore attend numerous events surrounding the team. *Just my luck.* Tonight is one of those events where the players are my prime customers. I'm supposed to prance around the VIP area with samples and encourage them to choose White Water for their bottle service. So much for exiting modeling to avoid being objectified.

When I stressed my annoyance to Monica earlier today, she only made things worse.

"Desmond will probably be with them tonight. Be nice," she said as she applied her mascara.

She was getting ready to spend the evening with Zach on their first date night in weeks. It was the first night he wasn't beat up from a game or having to wake up early for practice the next morning.

"What?" I shut off my hair dryer, hoping I'd heard her wrong. "Why would Desmond be with the team? He doesn't even play football."

"He's friends with all the players because of Zach. I think he goes out with them every Friday night. I just didn't want you to be surprised."

Disappointed would have been a better word. Things have actually been going well over the past three weeks. I've been keeping busy with my job, which has made my relationship with Monica stronger now that I'm not constantly in her face. I work at night and sleep during the day, while she has the opposite schedule. We go for happy hours a few times a week and binge movies on my nights off. And until my sister broke the news, I hadn't seen or heard about Desmond Blake and his kitchen from hell once in twenty-one blissful days. Now I find myself spending the first two hours of my shift dreading the possibility of his arrival—or eagerly awaiting it. I'm not sure which since I can't stop thinking about seeing him again.

At eleven o'clock on the dot, Desmond strolls into the club like he's one of *them*. He definitely looks the part, with his plain white tee that fails to hide the number of hours spent in the gym and his ass-hugging jeans like those a true Texan would wear. And his long, wavy hair looks like it's been conditioned and prepped for a magazine cover shoot.

No one would ever suspect that the man spends the majority of his time sporting an apron.

I'm walking toward my prime clientele with a sharp eye and flirtatious smile when I see Desmond's gaze follow me in my peripheral. Balko, Seattle's number one tight end, is the first one to walk up to me, but he doesn't go for the liquor. Instead, he comes right up to my ear and whispers, "Just the woman I wanted to see."

I smirk at him because everyone knows Balko is the number one man-whore in all of Seattle. And with his dark skin, honey eyes, and long lashes, it's no wonder he gets away with it. He is one tall, hot piece of gorgeousness that I wouldn't mind taking home to Monica's couch. Well, I wouldn't mind if he'd chosen a different profession.

I would never, could never, date a football player, not after what my father did to our family. I've seen firsthand how football can ruin lives in more ways than one.

"Easy, Balko." I tame him with a gentle push against his chest. "I'm working again."

"Yes, you are, girl." He puckers his lips, and they almost look as drunk as his eyes do as he looks me up and down. Clearly these boys started the party elsewhere. "When's your shift over? Let me take you home."

"How ya gonna do that?" another player chides. "Carry her on your back? You've got a driver tonight."

"Well, she can come too, dumbass. Plenty'a room," Balko slurs.

I smile at the guy who attempted to rip on Balko. I don't know his name, but I already like him. Hoping to change the subject, I raise a shot glass in the air. It's filled to the brim, and Balko's eyes follow it with interest.

"You get one on the house," I say. "Courtesy of White Water, of course. If you like it, just ask your waitress for a bottle."

A few guys crowd my tray and begin to pass shots around until it's empty. Balko still hasn't left my side, but he manages to grab a second shot, which he's currently chasing with a beer. *Gross.*

The moment he's distracted, I slip through the crowd, toward the bar, where I'll refill my tray. A hand grabs my arm, stopping me on my journey, and I know immediately who owns the grip that heats my flesh. I turn, my eyes darting from the hand on my arm to Desmond's face.

He takes the hint and pulls his hand away. "You know Balko's bad news, right?"

"What makes you think I'd listen to anything you have to say?"

I can practically feel the frustration rippling from his body at my question.

A moment later, he settles in his stance, and his eyes relax. "You may not listen to me in the kitchen, but I hope you'll heed my warning now."

"And you care because?"

Desmond stretches his neck to the side and shrugs. "You're Coach's daughter. Just lookin' out."

I swallow, trying to maintain my strong frame. Why does he have to bring my father into this? "What are you, my protector now? Did my dad tell you to watch out for me?"

Desmond lifts his hands with a shake of his head. "No, he didn't. Look, you can take my advice however you want it, okay? At least I can say I tried."

I nod, tightening my forced smile before pushing past him to the bar. "Okay." I draw the word out slowly. "I appreciate the advice."

Desmond can't know what he does to my insides, how they shake and heat like I'm about to explode. He drives me crazy, and I'm starting to have trouble pinpointing the exact reason why. Between his relationship with my father, his nonchalant arrogance, and the fact that he humiliated me in his cooking class last month, it's probably a mixture of everything.

After our awkward exchange, I try to put Desmond out of my mind for the rest of the night. My efforts are futile. I swear every time my eyes accidentally meet his, he's already looking intently in my direction either at me or at whoever I'm handing a shot to. By the end of my shift, I'm more than ready to escape his intense blue-eyed gaze.

I'm cleaning off my tray behind the bar when he takes a seat across from me. "Last call was fifteen minutes ago," I say to him without looking directly at him. "And I don't pour 'em anyway."

He leans forward. "I know that, smart-ass. I'm not drinking tonight."

I don't look up as I think about what he just said. Then I realize that not once tonight have I seen him with a drink. My eyes flicker up to his, and it's like my body can't help but react instantly. Warmth floods through me. "Why's that?"

"I drive the guys when they go out on Fridays." He says it so casually, like it doesn't bother him one bit to not be partying when the rest of them are.

This time, my eyes stay on him while I speak. "And they pay you or something?"

Desmond chuckles. "They're my friends. I wouldn't accept their money. I just do it so they don't get their asses in trouble."

"And so you can swoop in on their sloppy seconds," I say with a wicked grin.

He mirrors my expression. "Every now and then, that might be the case."

"Can't say I'm surprised," I mutter with disdain on my breath.

"Yeah, well, I think you'd actually be surprised about a lot of things if you opened your mind to them."

I bite the inside of my cheek and lock eyes with him again. "Let me guess. We're talking about cooking again, aren't we?"

He shrugs. "Among many other things."

I shake my head, not wanting to argue. "Look, you don't know me. You don't know why I'm in Seattle, or the type of guys I'm into, or what makes me tick. You know the fraction of the me you've seen in your kitchen and on some viral video. You think you've got me all figured out? Let me make myself clear." I lean forward, keeping my tray between us so it dents his chest when I push against him. "You have *no* idea."

With that, I leave my tray on the counter, swoop down to grab my purse beneath the bar, and walk out to the street. I open my phone to text Monica so I can get the hell out of here, except my cell service proves to be shit in this area.

Desmond is beside me before I can try to connect to the club's WiFi. His arm brushes my shoulder without him throwing me a glance. "I'll give you a lift."

I may have an adverse reaction to Desmond, but his offer is a kind one. "Thanks, but Monica should be on her way."

There's a beat of silence before Desmond sticks his hands in his pockets and leans forward on his toes. "Actually...Monica asked if I could bring you home since I'd already be here." His gaze slides to me and then his dimple appears. "I know, I know. Trust me, I warned her it wouldn't go down well, but I'm willing to take one for the team. Are you?"

I cringe and sigh. "Fine. But you realize I'm staying with Monica in Bellevue, right?"

"Yup. Hop in the front. I'll shove these lugs in the back." He nods toward a large black Escalade with fancy rims and trim. Desmond smirks as if reading my mind. "It's Balko's. He let me borrow it so I could drive his ass around tonight."

I accept that, slide into the front seat, and buckle in. Next thing I know, a group of large bodies and boisterous voices climb into the two rows behind me.

Desmond makes three stops, the last one being Balko's house, where he has to practically carry the football player into his home. Then we trade Balko's SUV for a red vintage car.

"What are you doing with a fifty-eight Ford Fairlane convertible?"

Desmond looks over at me while he pulls open the passenger door. I just impressed him. Who knew it would be so easy?

"What do you know about vintage cars?"

I shrug. "A little."

Once upon a time, my dad used to have a car just like this one. It had the same sleek body style, cherry-red exterior, and everything. It brings back every bit of nostalgia from my childhood in a simple glance.

I slide into the red seat and inhale the scent of its aged leather like it's my first time breathing. I slide my fingers along the front dash while the picture-perfect memories compound. *My mom with her hair wrapped in a scarf and a smile on her face. Monica and I holding hands in the back seat with our noses to the wind and giggling into the breeze.* I still remember the feeling of pride that felt heavy in my chest for having the perfect family—a father who could provide, a mother who was the most beautiful woman on earth in my eyes, and a little sister who was attached to my every move.

If anyone had asked me then if we would stay that way forever, my answer would have undoubtedly been yes. We should have never fallen apart.

I'm inhaling the car deeply as Desmond starts to drive. My thoughts are so deeply buried in the past that I almost forget I'm sitting next to a man I despise. But he doesn't let too much time go by before reminding me of his presence. Clearing his throat, he manages to pull my eyes to him.

"Humor me with your car knowledge. Help me get to know the girl who hates to cook."

I smile at that and sink back into the seat, letting my instinctual anger toward the man to my left dissolve momentarily. "My dad was obsessed with vintage cars. He used to take my family out driving every weekend in a car just like this." A cloud pushed into my mind and hovered over my thoughts, darkening them before I could catch myself. "But that was before..."

Desmond's hand curled around the wheel, and his almost-smile darkened at my words. "Ah, I see."

The casual tone of his acceptance stirs something in my chest, something dark and ugly. I should just keep my mouth shut, but of course I don't. "Not that you'd know what it's like not to have a father around. After all, you had mine."

I can feel the tension quickly rising between us, and I hate myself for causing the change in mood. Then again, he was the one that had to offer me a ride. Maybe he's a glutton for punishment.

"Remember earlier, how you told me I had no idea about you? Well, you know nothing about me either, Maggie. I guess it's best for both of us not to make assumptions."

I snort. "I don't have to assume much. Monica told me how you used to bully Zach when you two were kids. How my dad saved you both from killing each other and took you under his wing. He put you on his football team and straightened you up. You consider him some kind of hero according to her. But did you know that while he was putting all his time and effort into you, Zach, and the rest of that team, he was neglecting his family? Did you know there were two young girls sitting on the porch every night just praying *that* was the night their father would finally come home? Spoiler alert—he never did."

"Maggie stop—"

"No. I won't." Desmond has no idea how much pain I have in my heart because of someone he idolizes. "Instead of coming home to his family, he was off starting a new one somewhere else. You want to know how Monica and I found out?"

Desmond is now fuming. "I don't need to know about his past. That doesn't matter to me."

"His past?" I challenge. "At one point, that was his present, and you were right there with him. That might not matter to you, but it sure as hell matters to me."

"So, then how did you and Monica find out?"

"I found his address and I dragged Monica out of bed in the middle of the night to surprise him the next morning. He wasn't the only one surprised. That morning we met his new wife and two new daughters. He'd replaced us, just like that." I suck in a deep breath. "Still want to get to know the girl who hates to cook?"

"It doesn't matter. Tell me whatever you want me to hear, but it's not going to change my mind about Coach. What he was for you and what he was for me are two totally different things."

I chuckle and shake my head. "Never mind. You'd never understand."

He slams his hands on the wheel and pulls off to the side of the road before we reach the highway. There's an empty parking lot looking out over Lake Union, and before I know it, Desmond is stripping off his seat belt and facing me. "You think I don't know what it's like to feel abandoned by one of your parents? Well, here's your reality check. Try growing up with a father who spent most of his life in and out of rehab. And when he was out of rehab, you'd be lucky to spend a single day with him without him falling off the wagon all over again."

My heartbeat quickens. "That doesn't change my situation."

"Yeah, well, at least you weren't abandoned by your mom too."

The air goes cold. Whatever point I was trying to make earlier suddenly feels wrong. "Where was your mom?"

"Dead."

The word comes out with a chill on his breath, and I shiver.

"She died when I was four," he continues. "Couldn't handle life, so she decided to take hers. I don't even remember her."

"I'm sorry."

He blows out a breath. "So what now, Maggie? You still want to compare your daddy issues to mine? Because while your dad wants to make amends, mine is somewhere in Texas, stealing food from trash cans and getting wasted behind the nearest dumpster, just biding his time until he's back in jail or rehab."

My insides are quaking like an active volcano a second before erupting. Maybe I shouldn't make assumptions about Desmond, but he's just as guilty for making assumptions about me.

"I think you should take me home now," I whisper. I never meant for things to get so intense, but every time I'm near Desmond, it's like I get this overwhelming anxiety that brings me back to everything I've spent my life stuffing deep down into a secret box in my chest, one I swore I would never open again. No matter what I do, I can't escape the key that's forcing its way into the lock, opening the damn thing without my permission. One day, it's just going to burst open, and there's no way in hell I'll be ready for it.

Desmond and I are completely silent the entire way to Monica's, and it stays that way when I exit the car and shut the door behind me. Desmond lingers until I enter the security code to get in and walk through the hall to the elevator, but then he's gone, and I'm terrified of the next time I'll see him. Because for the first time since I met Desmond Blake, I'm the one who feels like the bully.

I'm already an emotional mess when I push my way into Monica's apartment. My head hurts from my fight with Desmond. My eyes sting from the tears that I'm forcing back with everything in me. There's no way this night can get any worse. I just need to sleep it off.

As I enter the apartment and slip off my heels, I hear what resembles a cry followed by an intensely erotic sigh. A squeak of the bed comes next, and if that isn't enough to deter me from stepping another inch inside my temporary home, the sound of a body hitting a wall and a guttural moan sure as shit does.

"Oh my God." My voice comes out louder than I intended, and I slam the door behind me out of habit. It definitely gets the attention of the occupants behind Monica's bedroom door because the silence that follows feels almost deadly.

I don't know why I can feel Monica's wrath before she even swings open her bedroom door, but I just dumb it down to sisterly intuition. And damn, I wish I were wrong.

Unfortunately, Monica's face is filled with fury as she stands there, hands on her curvy hips, wearing nothing but pretty black lace panties.

I raise my hands in apology. "Sorry, I had no idea you two would still be awake."

"Are you serious? Did you not see the sign on the door?"

I look sharply at the apartment door and then rub my eyes, exhaustion taking its toll on my body. "No. What sign on the door?"

Monica huffs out a breath. "The Do Not Disturb sign?"

I scrunch my face, trying to make sense of my sister's words. "You knew I was coming home after my shift, yet you decided to put a sign on the door to tell me to what? Sleep in the hall? No, Monica, sorry, I didn't see your stupid sign. I'm tired." I step forward and throw myself on the couch, desperate for this night to be over. "Sorry I interrupted. I'll cover my ears or something."

Monica stomps forward until she's in front of me. "The sign just said to wait and text me when you got here. Jesus, I can't even have one night alone with my boyfriend."

I'm done with this conversation. "Go to his place next time. I don't know."

"This is my apartment!"

"Monica, it's fine," Zach coaxes as he comes up behind her. Then he wraps his giant arms around her petite frame.

"It's not fine," Monica says with an exaggerated pout. "I barely see you. I just wanted one uninterrupted night with you without having to wake up at the ass-crack of dawn to drive back to Bellevue for work."

He cups her chin delicately, like she's the prettiest and daintiest flower. "It's only one night. We have the rest of our lives."

My chest tightens as I witness their swoony love story play out in front of me, and I hate the feeling of jealousy that follows.

"I'm going to go," he says.

"Wait." Monica tugs him back toward her. "I'm going with you. I'll just have to set an alarm for super early." Before she's even finished her thought, she's in her room, packing an overnight bag.

I don't know whether to be annoyed or embarrassed, so I wrap myself in a blanket on the couch and shut my eyes, pretending to be asleep when they leave.

I don't like to cry. It's never gotten me anywhere before, so I avoid it at all costs. But there's no mistaking the emotion that slips between my tightly squeezed lids and drips down my cheek.

I learned what true abandonment felt like when I was just sixteen, but I always thought that feeling would eventually go away. I never thought I would carry it with me forever.

Persuasive

DESMOND

Routines keep me grounded and productive. Daily checklists are my motivation to never miss a step. In the mornings, I like to hit Pike Place Market early, before the tourists wake up and flood the streets. I shop for fresh fish, handpicked fruits and vegetables, perfectly picked cuts of meat, and select dairy. Everything I need can be found in the best of the best lineup of organic goods. I even grab a few dozen bouquets of flowers to add some ambiance to the kitchen.

I wheel my cart past the fish market, where I just grabbed five pounds of fresh jumbo grilling scallops for today's class. Herbs, spices, and vegetables are next. Then I fill up on wine, cheese, and bread, all locally prepared in and around Seattle.

Zach may have initially purchased Edible Desire, but it was me who turned his empty studio into something locals would be talking about soon after. Faye called it farm-to-table. I had never sought a term for my style of cooking. I just do it how I always imagined it being done.

When I was younger and my dad was sober enough to cook, he was great at it. To this day, I've never tasted a single meal that could compare to his. He had a natural ability to pair ingredients together to bring out mouthwatering flavors in unforgettable meals. It was why Zach's parents didn't even hesitate to hire him as a cook in their restaurant years ago.

I'll never forget when he came home from work one night. He walked through the front door of our apartment with the biggest smile on his face. The Ryans were going to use one of his recipes on the menu from that day forward—fried green tomatoes, my dad's specialty.

Unfortunately, the reason they were open to new recipes was because business wasn't great. A few months later, my father stumbled home with a bottle of booze in his hand, signaling the beginning of the end. He'd just been fired. My dad had been on the highest of highs. When it all came crashing down, the fall shook us all.

Everything changed once my dad got laid off. It was the catalyst to many drunken nights where I had to suffer through frequent vomit, police cars, and a father who took care of his addictions instead of taking care of his son. I hated the downward spiral, and I misdirected my anger toward the Ryan family, namely Zach.

Zach was the same age as me, twelve. We shared some classes together, and we got along well when we saw each other. But my life was a walking, talking hell, and I made it my mission to make Zachary Ryan suffer just as much as I was. That carried on for four years. It was a time in my life I'll forever regret and never stop apologizing for.

Thanks to Coach Reynolds, Zach and I are best friends and business partners. My cooking classes started selling out after the first few months, and it has only felt natural to want to grow things from there. We've expanded to include catering, meal-prep deliveries, and private events. The works. Saturdays are my busiest days, and unfortunately Gretta chose today—Saturday—to call in sick again.

I'm pushing the Edible Desire grocery cart I purchased for my daily market runs when I spot Zach jogging across the street to meet me. "Need help?"

"Uh, sure." I move away from the cart to let him push it. Not because I actually need the help, but because it's funny to watch one of the NFL's best pushing groceries around downtown Seattle. Just to be an ass, I hop on the front of the cart as it curves uphill so he can wheel around an extra 230 pounds.

Zach accepts the challenge with a grin and a flex of his arms. Lowering himself to get the leverage he needs to use his legs instead of his back, he starts to push against it like he would a speed sled during football practice. He digs into the sidewalk with his feet and uses his calf muscles to support the weight.

"All right," I say, jumping off the cart and taking it from him. "Now what the hell are you doing here?"

He stretches his back with a twist at his waist. "I was heading to the training facility and stopped by the kitchen to see you. Then I remembered you'd probably be shopping. Doesn't your assistant help you with this stuff?"

I huff out an annoyed breath. "Gretta? Yeah. She used to, but she called out sick today."

Zach shakes his head. "I thought you were going to fire her weeks ago."

I shrug. "I was, but the kitchen's been busy. I don't have time to search for a new employee, fire an old one, and keep up with everything I need to keep up with."

"Well," he starts slowly. "Maybe I can help."

His tone reflects caution, and knots immediately twist my insides. "Can I just say no and move on about my day? I don't know what you're about to propose, but I have a sneaking suspicion I'm not going to like it."

Zach chuckles. "To be honest, you might not, but you'll warm up to it, and it would solve a lot of problems right now."

I quirk an eyebrow, now curious, because it sounds like Zach isn't only trying to help me out, but himself. And if there's anyone in this world I would do anything for, it's him. "All right, what is it?"

"First, did you ever decide what you're going to do with that studio apartment upstairs?"

I shrug. "I have some ideas."

"Like?"

"Well, I haven't given up the idea of Pop moving here. I've been warming him up to the idea." Just saying the wishful words out loud makes my stomach turn.

Zach winces a little. "I didn't realize you were still entertaining that idea. Are you sure that's a good plan? I mean, I know you want to help him, but at some point he's got to start making some changes on his own."

"I know. Which is why he's still in Dallas and I'm still here. When he's ready, I'll be ready."

"Okay." Zach draws the word out slowly, assessing me with his eyes. "So then, what about right now?"

I shrug. "Why? You got a renter?"

Zach lifts his brows like he's prefacing his words with a warning. "In fact, I do."

Shit. I already know where this is going. "Zach—"

"Just hear me out," he says as he raises his hands.

The lift opens to the second floor, and he pushes the cart inside the storage room. Then he meets me in the main entrance of the kitchen and sits on the couch.

I take a seat on the chair across from him. "Spill."

"I'll spare you the gory details, but last night, I asked Monica to move in with me, and she said yes."

I didn't see that one coming. "Dude, you two have been together for only, like, weeks."

Zach makes a face and shook his head. "No, bro, it's been longer than that, and you know it. Try months. But I've known her for years."

"Jeez, I mean, what's the rush? Is the ten-minute distance really hurting your relationship?"

Zach rolls his eyes. "No, but her apartment has gotten a little crowded."

Oh. So Maggie is causing issues at home, too, and not just in my kitchen.

Zach continues. "Anyway, Monica's lease is expiring at the end of the month, and now that she's going to the Art Institute, she's spending the majority of her time in Seattle anyway. She loves her sister more than anything, but she's going crazy right now, especially since I'm gone a lot during the season. So I asked her to move in, and she said yes. It's a done deal, but that's not what I'm here to talk to you about."

"You want me to rent the studio to Maggie."

Zach cringes, telling me I missed the mark. "Not exactly."

"Please don't tell me you're asking me to let her stay there for free. What about utilities and maintenance of the place? There's no way I can cover those expenses, especially not now that I need to hire someone full-time. Most of my profit goes to charity as it is. If I'm ever going to grow this place, I need the extra income, dude."

He holds up his hands. "Just hear me out. Maggie needs a place to stay, and you need an employee. Why not train Maggie to work the kitchen? She'll live right upstairs, so she'll always be available. And then you'll just need to pay her the difference. You have to admit, the plan is brilliant."

"Yeah, if we weren't talking about Maggie Stevens. Have you met the woman? She hasn't worked a day in her life."

"Don't be a chauvinist ass. She's been modeling her whole life."

"Oh yeah? Then why's she suddenly broke and working for White Water?"

Zach shrugs. "None of my business. Look, I know this is asking you for a lot, and who knows if it will work out. It probably won't. But it would help all of us out in the meantime. You, me, Monica, Maggie. Just please, consider it. But don't take too long. Monica is going to talk to Maggie this week."

I chuckle. "She doesn't already know about this little proposition you're making me?"

Zach shakes his head, which makes me laugh harder.

"You know what?" I hold up my hands. "If you can convince Maggie to work *and* live here, then you've got yourself a deal." My laughter comes harder yet again because I know there's no way in hell Maggie Stevens will agree to spend her days anywhere near me. If for some reason she does agree… Well, I'm not sure who would end up regretting it first, her or me.

Moving Out
MAGGIE

When my sister takes me out for drinks the following Thursday night, I instantly detect that our girls' night out is more than our usual sisterly outing. There's something heavy on her mind, and I can't help but feel like it has everything to do with my rude interruption of her and Zach's sexcapades last weekend. Things have definitely been tense this week, but she isn't the only one still fuming about that night. I can't get over the fact that she knew I was coming home after work and tried to keep me out with a sign on the door.

"Let's just get the conversation out of the way," I say after pulling out the lime from in between my teeth. "You're still mad about last weekend, but what did you expect me to do? Where would I have gone?"

Monica sighs. "I want to apologize for that. Zach insisted that I go to his place that night, but I had to be at BelleCurve for a production at five the next morning, so I convinced him to stay. And well... we stayed up a little late." She blushes and then shakes her head. "That's still no excuse. I was a total bitch to you, and I'm sorry."

When I look at Monica and see the red forming in her eyes, my chest tightens. I reach for her hand and squeeze. "It's okay,

M. Honestly, I've been invading your space for months. I kind of deserved it. I'll tell the manager at White Water that I want more hours. Maybe I can work enough to get my own place somewhere cheap, you know? I don't need anything fancy. All I need is a bed and a lock, and I'll be good."

I laugh because the one thing that has always made me weak is seeing my sister sad. It's why I've always been the tough ass for the both of us. But lately, Monica hasn't needed me in that way. Her sadness now has more to do with the fact that she's letting me down gently. She's kicking me out of her place, and I can't even be mad at her about it.

Monica pinches out a smile and squeezes my hand back. "I don't want you to think it's you. You're my sister, and I love that you're here. I don't want you doing anything crazy and moving back to your old life in LA, but if we continue living together—"

"We're going to kill each other," I finished for her.

Now both of us are laughing, and I wrap Monica in a side hug. "I kind of hate that you stopped needing me."

Monica blinks and swipes at a falling tear. "I'll never stop needing you, Mags. Don't ever think that. I've just been thinking a lot about our living situation. Between all the hours I'm spending in school, my lease ending soon, and Zach, I think I should be living closer to Seattle right now. And so should you."

I perk up at the sound of that. Living in Bellevue doesn't make sense for me anyway with the work I'm trying to get, not to mention where White Water has me currently promoting. "What if we get a bigger place where there's room for the both of us? I can help make some of the payments if White Water gives me more hours, and…" I pause in midsentence when I see the look Monica's giving me. She's already made her decision.

"Zach asked me to move in with him." She takes a breath before opening her mouth again. "And I said yes."

My jaw drops as my brain tries to calculate the duration of their relationship. "That seems a little… fast."

Monica cringes and shakes her head. "But it's not. If you think about how long I've known him then include how many years we've been flirting, and then dating. Even if he wasn't technically my boyfriend for that entire time, it doesn't matter. I'm ready to take the leap."

"I've never seen you all-in with a guy like this before. It's beautiful, actually. You two are so in love, it makes me sick."

She giggles, even though my words were not meant to be a compliment.

"I can't believe I pushed him away for so long," she gushes. "Sometimes it scares me to think of what my life would be like without him. If he hadn't been so patient… I can't even imagine it."

I sigh. I've lost my sister to la-la land for good. Well, shit. "So if you move in with him, then what will I do?"

Monica perks up again and turns to face me completely. Her wide caramel eyes are bleeding with excitement. "Zach had the best idea, which you'll probably hate, but honestly, you don't really have any other options unless you go back to LA and move in with Mom, so—"

"Yeah, not doing that. What's Zach's brilliant idea?"

Monica takes another deep breath. "There's a newly renovated apartment in Seattle, right above Edible Desire."

The moment I hear the name of the kitchen, my entire body cringes. "Of course there is," I mutter dryly. It seems I'll never get away from that place.

"Desmond agreed to—"

"Stop. Desmond's involved in this plan? As in cocky chef Desmond?"

Monica sighs at my interruption. "Yes. He owns the place. But he said he'll let you live there for free."

I feel my eyes widen. Shocked doesn't remotely cover my reaction to what I just heard. I'm tempted to look around for the hidden cameras since obviously this is some kind of joke. "You might need to repeat that." I laugh. "I thought you just said that Desmond agreed to let me live in his rental apartment for *free*."

Monica is practically jumping out of her skin with excitement. "That's exactly what I'm telling you. Free rent. Well…"

I laugh at her "well" because of course there's some sort of condition attached to this offer. "Well what?" Then I shake my head. I actually don't hate this plan so far. "Look, as long as I don't have to talk to the guy or step foot back inside that kitchen, I'm on board with this."

Monica cringes, giving me all the answers I need.

I'm shaking my head before she can jump in and explain. "Nope."

"Just hear me out," she pleads. "It's a temporary thing, but you'd get free rent and still get paid. All you have to do is work for Desmond. The hours are so good too. And you could still work at White Water if you want to."

My sister has some nerve with this proposition.

"Did you honestly expect me to say yes to working with Desmond Blake? At the freaking kitchen, no less? It's like the world met in some secret meeting and planned my demise, and you're the pawn leading me to the end. I can't think of a job I would want less than that one."

Monica tilts her head and gives me an annoyed look. "Wow. Dramatic much? I cannot believe you haven't found yourself an acting gig yet. You're such a natural."

I cough out a laugh. "I won't get to explore any career if I'm sweating over a stove all day. What would I even do there? Desmond knows I can't cook. Zach must have paid him off to agree to this. This isn't a one-sided thing. Desmond doesn't like me either, M."

Monica smiles. "Zach didn't have to pay him. Desmond agreed to it. But you're right about it going both ways. Maybe he doesn't think you'll accept the offer. Either way, he needs to find someone to replace Gretta, you need a place to live, and you need a job to afford it. You two are a match made in heaven."

"Try a match made in hell."

"Sure." Monica shrugs. "But either way, you two need each other."

I try to picture Desmond and me working together, laughing in the break room before cooking class, taste-testing all the new recipes, sharing a drink after work... Then our eyes meet in an emotion-filled stare. He kisses me, and I kiss him back. I grip his long hair in my fist to pull him closer while my naked ass smashes against the nearest wall, and he's...

Whoa, that escalated quickly. I shake the vivid imagery from my mind and focus on my sister's waiting face.

"So you moving in with Mr. NFL is already a done deal?" I ask. "There's no talking you into getting a place with me even if I grovel and promise to get a second job to pay more?"

Monica shakes her head. "Sorry, Mags. But c'mon, let's be realistic. It will take a couple of months for you to have the money to help out, and I can't sign another lease. Think about it. Won't it be nice to have your own place? And since I won't need a lot of my old furniture, you can take what you need to the new place."

I won't express it as exuberantly as I feel it, but having my own things and space has a nice ring to it.

"Ugh, fine, but Desmond better play nice. If he doesn't, I just might consider moving back to LA after all."

Monica grins. "He will play nice, I promise. He wouldn't have agreed otherwise. I think he'll appreciate the help so much. It sounds like Gretta has really put him in a bind."

Sighing, I gesture for the bartender to pour me another vodka soda.

If working with Desmond Blake is anything like being his student, then I don't know if I'll be able to ever forgive my sister for pushing me into this situation.

Welcome Home

DESMOND

I'm refilling containers of condiments and spices in the back room of Edible Desire when I hear a knock on the door followed by the sound of the door opening and shutting.

"Hello," calls out an annoyed voice.

I pop my head around the backroom door to see a woman looking just as irritated as her voice sounded. For a second, I don't recognize the gorgeous woman with gray sweatpants and an off-the-shoulder top. First, she's not wearing a stitch of makeup. Second, her long hair is pulled up into a high ponytail. The only bling about her are the diamond studs she always wears on her ears.

When Maggie's eyes find mine, she sighs. "It's two p.m. I thought we were going to meet upstairs."

I glance at the clock on the wall and curse. "Shit, I forgot." Then I flash her a grin. "Sorry." I walk to the sink and wash my hands then grab my set of keys from the wall and start toward the entrance. She follows me out the door and up the flight of stairs to a set of condos on the top floor.

I turn right and unlock the door to Maggie's new place. Before I push it open, I hand her the spare key. "Lose that, and you pay for the replacement."

She rolls her eyes before zooming in on my key ring. "Wait a second. You have a copy?"

"Of course I do. I have the master."

Maggie narrows her eyes. "So you can just walk in whenever you want?"

"Yes, but I won't. Not unless something is wrong."

"And I should trust you?"

I laugh and shake my head. "You mean trust that I won't slip into your condo and replace your shampoo with Nair?" I shrug. "Guess you can never be too sure, can you?"

Her face darkens. "The fact that you even thought of that terrifies me."

I chuckle. "Maggie. Seriously?" I tilt my head at her, hoping she can see my sincerity. "I'm not going to step foot inside your place. But if it helps you sleep at night, you can deadbolt it when you're inside."

"Okay," she finally says and takes the key from my hand. Then she turns the knob and pushes her way inside.

There's not much to the studio floor plan. The living space is one small room encased in white brick, with one large window that overlooks the back alley. The one bathroom is just large enough for a standing shower, toilet, and pedestal sink. And the updated kitchenette barely holds a small refrigerator, a microwave, and a sink. But as I glance around the newly renovated space, I know Maggie would be crazy to dislike it in any way. Who can argue with free rent plus a new job?

"Okay." She sighs again and points behind me to my door. "Do you own that place too?"

I glance over my shoulder and nod. "Yup."

She snorts. "You're a regular landlord, aren't you?"

Before I can tell her the condo behind me is mine, she's off, perusing the apartment like she's taking measurements with her mind.

I lean against the open doorframe. "So," I start, internally cringing at my lame attempt at conversation. I don't know how I'm going to manage working with the woman all day, every day? "When do you move your stuff in?"

Maggie turns from her spot at the window, where she was checking out the view, and pauses like she has to think about it. "I don't have much. Considering the size of this place, that's a good thing."

"You'll need a bed."

Maggie nods, assessing the space again. "Monica's giving me hers. She's going to have the movers bring over some things once she's all moved into Zach's. I might take her couch, too, if there's room."

"There's more room than you think. You just have to be creative."

She shrugs. "I'll be fine. It's temporary, right?" Her eyes meet mine in a mutual agreement, probably our only one since we met. She doesn't want to be here as much as I don't want to be here.

"Right." Of course it's temporary. Everything Maggie does is temporary. There's no reason I should expect any less from her here. "I'll leave you to it. Just make sure you're downstairs in an hour to start your training. I'll go easy on you today, promise."

Her expression twists into confusion. "Um, today? We never discussed a start date."

I raise my brows. "You're moving in today, right?"

"Yes," she answers, caution filling her tone.

"Then today's your start date." I back away from her door with a wink. "See you downstairs."

"No." She charges out the door and slams it behind her before stomping past me.

I whip my body around to follow her movements, shock pulsing through my veins. "No?"

"You heard me," she says, taking the steps quickly. "I have shit to do. I can't start today."

I quicken my walk, following her down the stairs to the street, where she pulls out her phone and goes straight to the ride-share app. I'm officially panicking. "I already fired Gretta. You have to start today."

Her eyes snap to mine. "Well, I can't. I only came here first to see how much shit I would be able to fit in the studio. I have to get to Zach's place and set aside furniture for the movers to deliver here tonight. Then I need to be here to let them in. I'm sorry, Desmond. I'll start on Monday."

I assess her with my eyes, feeling hopeless and ready to let her walk away when an idea strikes. "What if I take you to Zach's and then drive you back here so you can help me?"

"Nope. I'm good." Her retort is quick and dismissive before her focus returns to her phone.

I look down and growl. "Please don't tell me you're scheduling a ride to take you ten minutes from here. I can take you."

Her face twists at my offer. "It's not the middle of the night in a dingy part of town. I'm perfectly capable of getting to and from Zach's place."

Her finger is hovering above the button to confirm her ride when I snatch the phone away. "And I'm perfectly capable of driving you myself."

"Give me back my phone." She reaches for my hand as I yank it away.

I look down at her with a wicked glare and hold the phone above my head. She jumps in a futile effort to grab for it, causing me to chuckle. While she's tall, I've still got at least eight inches on her.

"I'll give it back when you stop being a stubborn little mule."

With a scream, she stomps her foot on the pavement and crosses her arms. "I can't believe this is my life."

"Better start believing it, darlin'. I can even pinch you if that'll help." Then I let out a sigh and lower my hand to give her back the phone. "Look, I'm already here," I say as she snatches it from my palm. "Let me save you a few dollars and give you a ride. Consider it a housewarming gift."

She scoffs and shakes her head. "You're so generous. Don't you have work to get back to?"

I nod. "Yup, and so do you. We better hurry. Wouldn't want to be late on your first day."

Training

MAGGIE

He starts to walk off, and I follow, making quick work of my feet as he leads me around the side of the building to an alley. Tucked away on the bottom floor of the Edible Desire building is a large metal gate leading to a parking garage.

The second Desmond opens the gate, I spot his car and walk toward it faster than he can lead me. I'm still fuming from his demands, even when he comes up behind me to unlock my door, even when he brushes against me so subtly that I have the urge to lean into him. For a moment, I allow myself to stand still and just breathe. It's about time I start taking hold of my emotions when I'm around Desmond. But then I pull in his crisp scent, which sends a euphoric buzz straight to my veins, and I'm quickly reminded why controlling my emotions is a futile effort.

He pulls open the car door for me, and I slip into the familiar leather seat. An uneasy feeling settles over me as I recall the last time I sat in this very spot. The memories rush over me. My confessions about my father. Desmond's confessions about his. The intensity of our goodbye. Yet I'm back here in the last place I ever imagined I would be.

I snap my head toward Desmond. "You're really going to force me to start work today?"

He sighs and throws me a perturbed glance. "No. I won't force you." His words throw me totally off balance, yet again.

"What?"

"I'll leave it up to you. Just know I wouldn't be making such a case of this if I didn't need the help." He pulls out of the parking spot with his eyes everywhere but on me. "I'll help you get to Zach's so you can do what you need to do. I'll bring you back to the kitchen, and then I'll let you decide."

"Why do I feel like this is a trap? Like you're giving me a choice, but there's only one right answer."

He chuckles. "Maybe that's the case. Or maybe your guilty conscience is doing its job."

I huff and fold my arms across my chest. "Well, it should be my choice. Just because I'm going to work for you and live in your stupid apartment doesn't mean you get to run my life."

"No, Maggie. I don't get to run your life. The decision is yours. But you should remember, the only reason I agreed for you to live in my *stupid* apartment was because you needed a job. It just so happens that I really need the help too. Is that not how you understood it?"

My mouth drops while my mind reels because I'm really not sure why I'm being so stubborn about this. Desmond has a point. I guess I just thought there would be some transition time. Everything is happening so fast. "Fine." I shift in the bucket seat. "Help me get my stuff into the apartment, and then I'll work until the movers come."

In my peripheral, I catch his satisfied smirk. "Okay."

It takes everything in my power not to respond to his smug satisfaction. Instead, I face forward and shut my mouth for the rest of the ten-minute drive to Zach's condo.

We park in front of a moving truck at the curb of a beautiful three-story building. My sister explained the location this morning when she brought me here. We're on the south slope of Queen Anne Hill in Seattle. Kerry Park sits across the street and has the most beautiful views of downtown Seattle's skyline. The Space Needle peeks above the trees, and the hillside seems to stretch for miles. The location is as breathtaking as it probably is expensive.

Zach doesn't air his wealth. In fact, sometimes I forget that my sister is dating a celebrity. If I didn't know better, I would think he was just a normal guy with the hots for my sister.

When Desmond and I walk into Zach's place, Monica is already busy making herself at home while the movers lug boxes and totes in around her. She's adding personal touches everywhere we look—throw pillows, brightly colored paintings, accent chairs—to the extent that it almost looks like a whole different place.

"Whoa," Desmond says, his eyes registering the same shock as I'm sure mine do. "It's starting to actually look like someone lives here. It's about time Zach gets some life on these walls."

For once, I agree with Desmond. When I first saw the place this morning, I asked Monica how long Zach had been living here. She shocked the hell out of me when she said it had been his home for a couple of years. The walls were mostly bare, and there were hardly any personal touches. It was like the guy didn't want to commit to it. I guess now, with Monica in the picture, that's no longer a problem.

Monica is beaming from ear to ear as she shows us all that she's accomplished in the last few hours. Her pride and joy is her new craft room, which is currently a complete disaster. "Zach wanted me to have my own space for creating. But don't worry, sis. When you spend the night, you can take the other spare bedroom."

"Hey," Desmond says. "That's my room."

Monica's eyes shine. "Well, then maybe you two can share. Y'all are best friends now, right?"

Desmond chuckles while I feel a look of horror painting my face. I want to strangle my sister.

"Not quite," I say, narrowing my eyes in Desmond's direction. "But it looks like I'm starting work today, so…" I ignore the huge smile Desmond throws me and continue. "We're just here to grab some stuff and then pick out what I want the movers to bring over later."

Monica looks between us and nods. "Okay. Well, your suitcases are in the living room, and the guys will drop the bed and couch off when they're done here. If you want anything else, just let them know. Whatever stays on the truck will go to storage."

With that, Desmond leads me down the stairs, carrying my suitcases. I hop on the moving truck and label a few select items with the Post-its Monica handed me, and then we're back at the car.

"What's the deal with you and your sister anyway?" Desmond asks as he loads my suitcases into his small back seat. He manages to squeeze them in somehow. "You two are nothing alike."

"Let me guess. She's the nice one, and I'm the bitch?" I pull open the passenger door and wait for him to walk around to his side.

He makes a face at me. "I never said that. She just seems more… outgoing and happy, while you're…"

I cringe as he tries to find the right word to describe my contrast to my sister.

"Not," he finally says. Then he pulls open his door and sinks into his seat. I follow suit with a sigh.

It wasn't the first time someone had called us out on our stark differences, especially since being in Seattle. Thankfully, I never take offense to it. "We've always been that way. Every experience we've faced has shaped us differently, I guess. But I think her moving here alone forced her to mature quickly. She's grown stronger and more independent throughout the years, and I've just become more hardened to the world, less forgiving."

Desmond nods, making me wonder if he truly does understand. "Do you have brothers or sisters?"

"Uh, no," he says simply. "Zach's the closest thing I'll ever have to a brother. We're pretty opposite too. He's always been the super successful one, and I…" He shakes his head, telling me he's not going to finish his thought.

"You don't think you're successful?"

"Nah, it's not like that. I just feel like I'll always be paying for some crime or another. If it's not for being a total jackass as a kid, it's being a shitty son now, or being a boss whose employee wants to skip out on him. I'm in a perpetual cycle of trying to do better, give back, but I'll never escape my past."

My heart is beating fast as I listen to him speak. Desmond gives the air of arrogance like no one I've ever met. I never would have thought his thoughts would be filled with such darkness.

"That's a dangerous outlook, Desmond."

"Yeah, well, you asked."

I have so many questions, but there's one that is already rolling off my tongue before I can prioritize them all. "How could you possibly be a shitty son now? The way you made it sound, your dad gets himself into trouble quite a bit."

He shrugs as he speaks. "In lots of ways." He squeezes the steering wheel and blows out a breath. "I could have stayed in Dallas to continue taking care of him. Instead I moved here, built a business, and started a different life. Sure, I visit him every few months, but is that enough?"

"Yes, Desmond. That is enough. Your father isn't your responsibility. His mistakes aren't your burdens."

"No, but then whose responsibility is he? He has no wife, no other children. He has doctors and psychologists, and police officers. My dad isn't just an addict, Maggie. He's an addict with severe ASD."

"ASD?" I'm racking my brain, but for the life of me, I have no idea what that stands for.

"Autism spectrum disorder. He's considered high functioning, but his ASD combined with his alcohol problem is not ideal. Social situations cause him severe anxiety and make his need for drugs stronger. Alcohol fuels his impulses and since he's not interested in treatment of any kind—"

Desmond stops abruptly and shakes his head. "Sorry. I didn't mean to unload all that on you. It's just an ugly cycle that seems to only worsen as time goes on."

My hand wraps around his right one as it squeezes the gear shift. "I don't mind. I still don't think you're being fair to yourself though."

"The guilt is overwhelming sometimes. It's like, I know I should be with him, but..."

Emotion thickens in my throat. "But what?"

Desmond shakes his head, like he's working himself up to respond, but he never does. Silence falls over us, and I squeeze his hand to tell him that's okay. The air feels heavy, and it suddenly dawns on me that he isn't just the cocky chef with a chip on his shoulder. There's a darkness to him that I feel like I can relate to, even though I know nothing about him at all. I don't know how he grew up or why he quit football after high school to attend culinary school. I don't know why he can't see past his guilt or why it's so crippling that he can't seem to escape it. Maybe Desmond Blake isn't as bad as I've been wanting to believe. Maybe he's just... lost. And I can relate to that feeling.

We pull into the parking garage beneath Edible Desire, and he cuts the engine, gets out, and grabs my suitcases from the back seat. Once upstairs, he sets my bags inside my condo door then walks away without a word. I don't see him again until I enter the kitchen an hour later, ready to start my shift.

I can see his shoulders sag with relief when he looks up and spots me at the front of the room. *Did he think I wouldn't show up?* That Gretta chick sure did a number on him by bailing on him all the time.

"There's some paperwork you need to fill out. Handbook stuff. Tax forms. Direct deposit info if that's how you want to get paid. You can tackle all that first, and then I'll show you how to use the registration system. That will be the biggest help for me today."

As soon as I turn in my paperwork to him, he immediately starts training me on how to work the touchscreen computer at the front of the room. It's the one I always saw Gretta tapping on when Monica and I walked in at the beginning of our classes.

I can't help but wonder if he trained Gretta the same way he's training me. He's currently hovering behind me, close enough for me to take in his crisp, woodsy scent again. His right arm is reaching around my body to show me what each button on the touchscreen monitor is for. Every now and then, his arm brushes mine, shooting a current of electricity through my body. *That's* not distracting. *Jeez.* I should be focusing on everything he's showing me, not the way his words are breathing into my hair.

"If we happen to have an opening for a class due to a cancelation, then you can register them here." He points at a button that says Register on the touchscreen monitor and walks me through how to gather a person's information and take payment. "But everything's booked up for the next few months, so make sure you let them know about future availabilities."

He shows me where he keeps his inventory so that I can start creating welcome packets for today's class. I'm quickly starting to understand why he was so desperate to get me to start today. It's the first day of the month, which means everyone gets a new menu, some recipes to use at home, and some cooking swag. Then he walks me through the menu and explains how he begins to gather all the ingredients he'll need for the day. It seems simple enough.

An hour later, while I'm folding aprons to go into the welcome packs, the kitchen door opens, revealing a familiar woman. She has blond hair, sharp blue eyes, and a black-and-white pinstripe, halter-style dress that looks like it was made for the runway. The deep V-neck of her top calls attention to her healthy chest, making me wonder if she knows Desmond and dressed like this for him. A jolt of something rushes through me, a feeling I don't recognize completely. I don't even know this woman, but she's clearly on a mission. And I'm afraid that mission has everything to do with Desmond.

Her heels, I have to admit, are impressive. They're almost as high as the ones I was wearing when I slipped on the catwalk months ago. Only this woman would never fall. She's too poised, too perfect to ever let something like that happen to her.

I don't know why she looks familiar, though. Perhaps I've seen her in one of Desmond's cooking classes. Or maybe she just has one of those recognizable faces. But she struts forward like she owns the place. "Hello," she says with a bright smile and wandering eyes. She seems to look everywhere but at me until her heels halt in front of me.

That's my cue. I stand straighter and plaster a smile on my lips, ready to deliver the words Desmond trained me to speak. "Welcome to Edible Desire. Are you interested in registering for an upcoming class?" It's what I'm supposed to say if I don't recognize them as a student, but I'm not at all surprised when the woman finds this amusing.

She chuckles and glances around the empty kitchen again. Desmond slipped into the back at some point to finish stocking the pantry, but I'm assuming he's who she's looking for. I wait for the woman's eyes to return to me before raising my brows to let her know she still hasn't answered.

"No, that's quite all right. I'm here to observe class today, actually."

"Oh." I don't hide my surprise. Maybe that's a normal thing that happens in Desmond's classes. But I don't remember any observers from the classes I took.

Something in the woman's tone triggers something in my brain, and her features start to morph in front of me. She becomes more and more familiar until I know for certain I've seen her before. *But from where?* It's on the tip of my tongue.

"I'm sorry," I finally say. "Do I know you? I recognize you from somewhere. I swear I do."

Her smile turns syrupy and proud, like she doesn't get the question often enough. "Maybe. Do you watch my show, *Five-Star Faye*?"

My answer would be a definite *hell no* since I hate cooking, but that doesn't mean I don't recognize her from magazines and talk shows. She's the epitome of a food goddess. "Holy shit, you're Faye. I do know you. I mean, I've seen you before. Obviously, we don't know each other, but—" I snap my mouth shut before my word vomit can continue.

She laughs and reaches out a hand to shake mine. "I'm sorry I didn't introduce myself when I walked in. I was expecting Desmond." She tilts her head, examining me closer. "And you are?"

"Maggie Stevens. I'm Desmond's assistant. Today is my first day, actually. I'm just filling in temporarily to help Desmond out since he lost Gretta."

Her eyes narrow as familiarity reflects back on her face. Suddenly, I want to cower in a ball and hide under the nearest cooking station. "Are you sure we haven't met before? You look familiar too."

I guess it's possible Faye recognizes me from my modeling days. I've been in plenty of advertisements that she's been featured in. But since I'm doing everything to move on from that life, I decide not to say anything about it.

I give her my most convincing headshake. "I doubt that. I just moved here." I start to back up while a blush creeps up my cheeks. "Do you want me to grab Desmond, or…"

She waves a hand in the air. "It's okay. Like I said, I just want to observe. Pretend I'm not here."

Somehow, I think that will be impossible.

Impossible Duo

DESMOND

Faye didn't mention that she was stopping by today, so when I step out from the back room and see Maggie welcoming guests while a familiar blonde watches her from the kitchen island in the front of the room, I can't help but panic a little. *Why did Faye have to stop by today?* My stress levels are already so high from having to train someone who has absolutely zero desire to be here.

I step around the island and grin at the woman with poised everything—posture, eyes, smile. She's a walking, talking sex pot, but that's not why my chest feels like it might explode. She would only be back if she had good news to share. Maybe she has a good update on the pitch.

"Well, well." I speak up to let Faye know I'm in the room. "She's back again. You should warn me next time. I'll tip off the paparazzi to start a little buzz."

She laughs breezily and flips her short hair so it swivels around her face. "Oh, trust me. You'll have plenty of buzz the moment promo starts up. Your pretty face is sure to rack in a whole lot of ratings."

I know she's being flirty, but there's something about the way she entirely omitted the mention of my food that irks me. "Just wait until they see what's on the menu."

"Well," Faye says with a perk of her brows, "I was hoping we could start talking logistics after your class today. Maybe over a glass of wine at Shooters?"

My eyes flick over to Maggie, who appears to be stealing glances at us. Discomfort snakes through my chest as I'm forced to answer Faye. *This is business.* "Sure. But you still haven't told me how the conversations are going with your network. You're talking like we have a show. Do we?"

A slow smile spreads across her face. "Yes and no." She must see my smile fall, because she jumps in quickly. "But hear me out. I've only primed them. I told them all about my rough concept for Edible Desire. So far, they're intrigued."

"Intrigued?" The excitement in my chest deflates like a worn-out tire.

She's quick to catch my disappointment and steps forward with a raise of her brows. "Yes. That's a great thing, Desmond. Trust me. I still haven't delivered a solid pitch to them. I'm still brainstorming that one, which is why I'm here. I'm going to sit through class for inspiration, and then we can discuss next steps."

Disappointment is still heavily weighing on me. I'm afraid I started to think this was a done deal. What if she can't find her hook? What if the network nixes my kitchen show before she's able to give a proper pitch? What if the past three months of dreaming about the kitchen's future has just been a big waste of time?

"Okay." I draw the word out slowly, my mind still reeling. "Feel free to take a seat at the island, and just let Maggie know if you need anything." Then I glance at my new assistant, whose eyes are now glued to us. "I assume you already met Maggie?"

Faye nods, and I can sense there's a question on the tip of her tongue in regard to my new assistant. Or maybe it's a feeling I've made up in my mind after seeing the way Maggie is scoping us out from the other side of the room. I would say Maggie looks jealous, but that thought is laughable. Until an hour ago, the two of us couldn't be in the same room without yelling at each other.

"Oh, yes. We've met. She wanted to know if I was interested in booking a class with you." Faye's flirtatious laugh and squeeze of my bicep don't sway from her usual style, but for some reason—*in front of Maggie*—it's making me want to crawl out of my skin. Maggie's expression as she watches the exchange doesn't help either. Her face turns bright red, and she looks away as if she thinks she's intruding.

Shit.

Faye speaks up again. "Actually, I wondered if it would be okay if I brought in a cameraman today to take some footage home with me for inspiration."

That makes me feel really uneasy. "I don't know, Faye. My class isn't prepared for that."

"The camera will be focused on you. We don't have to show any of your students' faces. And this is just for me. It's nothing we would actually air."

I pause, thinking deeply about what Faye is suggesting. It sounds harmless enough, and if I'm serious about this show prospect, it would be smart to give Faye whatever she needs to create a hard-hitting pitch. I cringe in preparation of my response. "Okay, but only one camera. And you need to be discreet. My students are paying for a class, and I can't have disruptions."

Faye flashes me her brightest smile. "Deal." She walks to the door and lets in a guy with a professional video camera. I'm happy to see there's no big crew with them—it's just a guy, his camera, and Faye giving him instructions.

"What's the camera for?" Maggie hisses to me when I approach her again.

"Faye wants to record me teaching class today. It's just for her, for research purposes. Can you let the students know when they walk in? Assure them that the footage won't be used for any commercial content?"

Maggie doesn't look very reassured, but she nods in agreement.

As students begin to enter the kitchen, I chat them up one by one. I like making real connections with my students. Not only does it make them want to come back, but I genuinely love knowing what brings them in.

There's a mother-daughter pair who hasn't missed a Saturday class in the past six months. They started coming in because the daughter was moving into her boyfriend's house and wanted to be able to cook for him without embarrassment.

At the workstation beside them is a newlywed couple who received a voucher for a class as a wedding gift. It's their first day, and they both seem excited to be here. Admittedly, most of their meals are consumed outside of the home, and they want to change things up now that they're on a budget.

There are a couple of singles that I paired together based on the interest questionnaire that came with their registration packets. And then there are older married couples looking for new adventures to help rekindle the romance. Every story is different, and I love hearing them all.

I definitely luck out with the students who walk through my door. Most of them come because they want to try something new or get better at skills they already have. And with every single story, I feel honored they chose my kitchen to get that experience.

I'm halfway through class when I catch Maggie flipping through a magazine, looking utterly bored. I spent all my time training her on registration that I didn't have time to show her what would help me during the actual class.

When Gretta showed up, she was always great about checking on all the students throughout class. If they needed refills on their beverages, then she was right there. If they had questions for me and I was too busy to get to them right away, she would take notes and deliver them to me. And she did her best to cheer on my students as they worked hard through class. I can see why Maggie wouldn't be comfortable with some of the above, seeing that it's her first day, so I quickly conjure up something else to help her at least look busy.

"Hey, Maggie," I call out while everyone's distracted with my latest set of instructions.

Her eyes snap up, her posture straightens, and her eyes widen. "Yeah?"

That's all she says. Not "How can I help you?" or "Hey, Desmond." But "Yeah?" Like I just bothered her by calling out her name.

I stifle a laugh and catch the amused expression on Faye's face at the exchange.

"Can you help me out with something?"

Maggie narrows her eyes as she slowly slides off her stool and walks the perimeter of the room to get to me. It doesn't faze me that she's taking her precious time. But as she's walking, it's easy to latch on to the fact that the woman knows how to strut on a runway. She's a natural, commanding the room with her confidence and her laid-back hip swing. With effortless bouncing hair and a crossover leg technique that I have a newfound appreciation for, I can't help but wonder what brought her here. Why would a woman with such a unique talent come to live with her sister in Bellevue only to end up unhappy and alone in Seattle?

I've already promised myself that I won't dig deeper into Maggie's past while we're at work. She gets so heated when I ask her questions, if not because I'm subconsciously being an insensitive ass, then because something about the wrong subject triggers memories of her father. If Maggie and I have any hope of playing nice together, then I'll need to try to steer clear of certain subjects. Outside of work, I can't make the same promises.

She's nearing my cooking station when she peers down at the pan of gravy I'm stirring and narrows her eyes at it. "I'm here to help." Then she points at the pan. "But not with that."

I chuckle and move to the side so she can take my spot. Then I hand her the spoon. "I just need you to stir it slowly while I make some rounds and check on everyone."

"Nope." She pops her lips and gives me a fake smile. "Not here to cook, remember?"

Annoyance builds quickly in my chest. "I'm not asking you to cook," I say, keeping my voice low. "I'm not even asking you to pluck the feathers off a turkey. Just stir the damn gravy like this." I stick the spoon in my left hand and start to stir while taking her hand in my right one. She doesn't resist my touch, so I bring her hand up and wrap it around mine so she's stirring with me.

When she continues to stir without complaint, I ease myself backward to give her space so she can move closer to the stove. She slides in front of me, causing me to tense up when her ass glides against the front of my jeans. Clearly, I miscalculated the space between where she would stand and the stove.

She doesn't seem to notice, so I pull away slightly to give my entirely too eager cock some distance. It's been months since I last felt the depths of a woman in that way. Surely the mere presence of a woman is making him react, not the fact that the woman is Maggie.

I look down to find the sauce already thickening nicely. "That's it," I say to her. "Slow and steady wins the race."

I'm still trying to forget about my unintentional dry spell when Maggie turns to look at me over her shoulder then bats her lashes down and back up like she's checking me out. Or maybe that's just my imagination because when the slits of her lids lock on mine, her eyes are screaming murder.

"Think you can give me some space there, Chef? It's getting a little *hard* to stir my gravy, if you know what I mean." She winks, and I feel my face catch fire with her words.

Shit. Now I know what she was looking for with her quick glance down. She saw it. The strain against my jeans was clearly all for her.

"Can I trust you to keep it at that pace?"

She nods without turning around again. "Of course, boss. I won't stop until you say the word."

I smirk, unable to help the flirtation that wants to combat her every breath. "I prefer it when you call me Chef."

With a pop of her hip she nudges me away. I chuckle and turn around to see Faye's gaze locked on us both. Then she catches my stare and raises her brows in some secret question I wish I could ignore. Something is on her mind, and I'm sure I'll be hearing about it later. Why do I feel like that something has to do with my hot new assistant?

I just shake my head to tell Faye that whatever she's thinking is wrong, but when Faye looks back at Maggie with a deep look of concentration on her face, I start to worry. Maggie clearly lacks professionalism, which doesn't bode well for landing a huge opportunity like the one Faye wants to pitch to her producers. Maybe Faye is turned off by the fact that I could hire someone so desperately challenged in the kitchen. Feelings of fear, anger, and doubt swirl through me. I swear, if Maggie messes this opportunity up for me…

Pushing away the internal battle in my head, I make my rounds to chat with the students before coming back to check on Maggie at the main stove. She hasn't altered her movements a bit, which earns a sigh of relief. I turn the heat down and point at the stove.

"Have you ever basted a turkey?"

She shakes her head and folds her arms across her chest. "No, and I have no desire to learn how."

"That's too bad because I'm going to teach you."

"What? No. I don't know what you're about to ask me to do, but that sounds like it's crossing the line."

I slip on an oven mitt, open the door, slide out the rack a couple inches. Then I pull out the turkey and set it on the island. After shutting the door, I turn to her with a serious face. I've gone easy on her today, but I don't want her to lose sight of why she's here. "There's no line. The only arrangement we made was that you would get a break on rent in exchange for taking Gretta's place as my assistant. Gretta never argued with anything I asked her to do."

Maggie laughs. "Really? So then where is she now?"

I glare. "Are we going to have this argument every time I ask you to help me? I don't want to bicker with you in the middle of class."

"Fine," she groans. "Just tell me what to do."

If only Maggie knew that training her is just as hard for me as it is for her. Here I am trying to do everyone a favor, yet every time I'm with her, I feel like I'm the bad guy.

"Okay, everyone," I call out as I look up to face the class. "Your turkeys should be at just the right point to slip them out of the oven and baste them. If you haven't done this before, I'm going to let Maggie demonstrate. Fun fact, she's never done this before either." I grin at the students, who find humor in this fact. "This should be fun to watch."

Maggie shoots me an ice-cold stare before taking the baster in her hand like she wants to stab me with it.

"First, you'll want to suck up that liquid at the bottom of the pan with the bulb. Just squeeze the top to close off the air, plunge it into the pan, and let go. Let's see how Maggie does it."

Something pointy hits my nostril, and the next thing I know, it feels like something is sucking air from inside my nose. "What the…" I jump back to find Maggie doubled over. The entire class erupts with laughter along with her. *She did not just try to stick that bulb up my nose.* The bulb is still in her hands as she tries to contain her laughter while tears stream from her eyes.

"Did you just try to stick that in my nose?"

Another burst of laughter comes from the classroom and Maggie, until it's all too infectious to not join in. When my own amusement dies, I rip the bulb from her hand and toss it in the trash. After grabbing a fresh one from the drawer, I stand behind Maggie and place the bulb in her hand.

"Let's try this again, shall we?" Then I look down and lean into Maggie's ear. "Since you're incapable of doing this yourself, I'm forced to help you." I take her right hand with mine and wrap it around the bulb, then I place my hand around hers and look back up at the class. "Now fill up the syringe and release the liquid over your turkey. You'll want to coat it generously and evenly."

When Maggie still doesn't move, I push her hand down until the suction opening dips into the liquid mixture of chicken stock and fresh seasoning.

"Just like that. Don't be shy with how much you use."

As I'm pushing Maggie's hand toward the liquid again, she turns her head toward me and squeezes her eyes closed.

I chuckle at her expression. "What are you doing?"

Maggie peels an eye open to watch me just as she releases her grip on the bulb. "I can't stand that slurping sound."

"I hate to break this to you, but looking away won't help your problem. Maybe you should start bringing earmuffs to work."

She narrows her eyes again. "And maybe you should bring a better personality."

This time, laughter comes from the one person I didn't expect. Faye has her head tossed back, and she's laughing way too hard.

Ugh. Arguing with Maggie is a huge waste of time. I snatch the baster from her hands and shoo her to the side. She doesn't go far as she watches me cover the turkey in hot liquid.

"When you're done," I say loudly to the class, "go ahead and slip it back into the oven for another ten minutes. You just want to keep the moisture in, but we want to be careful so we don't overcook it. No one wants to eat dry turkey."

I continue to talk through the side-dish recipes while ignoring Maggie's persistent glares. I don't ask her to do another thing until it comes time to slice the turkey.

"Slicing turkey is an art. You want the best cuts without shredding your poor meat to smithereens, so pay attention."

I come up behind Maggie, who stiffens a little while I chuckle. I wrap my hand around hers to demonstrate to the class both the good and bad ways to hold their knives.

"Relax," I tell her so only she can hear. "You don't need such a strong grip. Let the knife do the work, not you."

"I can't relax when you're on top of me like that."

"Do you want me to move?" I ask before biting my lip. "Can you do this on your own?"

She looks up at the students, who are waiting for my instructions, and sighs. "Just do what you need to do. I'll disinfect myself later."

I'm chuckling again when my gaze lifts to Faye, whose eyes are still trained on us. At this point, I don't know what thoughts are floating through her mind, but I'm not sure if I want to find out after class.

My arms are completely around Maggie's body now. I grip her hand that is holding the knife and use my other hand to steady the pan. I demonstrate to the class and Maggie how to properly cut through the meat and gently lay it on a serving dish.

While the class starts to taste-test their dishes, I plate a dish using the food I prepared and set it on the island to snap a few pictures.

"What are you doing?" Maggie asks as I adjust the plate and add pieces of garnish to frame the food.

"Taking photos for the website."

Her eyes float around the room like she's just made a connection. "Did you take all of these photos?"

"I did. But some of them are kind of old now. It's probably time to replace them."

In large frames around the room are lifestyle photos of my food and kitchen, but some were taken years ago.

"They're beautiful." Maggie's eyes are locked on the one to the left of the kitchen. It's probably my favorite of the bunch if I had to pick. Everything about the photo is my idea of perfection: depth of focus, lighting, focal point, and ingredients.

I remember taking the photo in one shot. It was just a lucky moment. All the stars aligned—the setting, the aperture, and the balance were perfect. I don't consider baking my specialty, but I'm still good at it, and this photo is of one of my favorite desserts. It's a fresh berry strudel, a puff pastry folded over and filled with a fresh cream-and-berry mix. The dish itself looks mouthwatering, which it is, but the element of the photo that catches everyone's eye is the powdered sugar falling from the handheld sifter above it. Isolating small elements like the sugar and flour is one of the more difficult photography challenges I've ever given myself, but with the perfect shutter speed and aperture combined to control the amount of light reaching the camera, the photo turned out better than I ever could have planned.

"Thank you," I tell her while continuing to snap more photos of the dish from today's class. "Can you start handing out the to-go containers?" I nod behind me toward the back counter where the plastic boxes sit.

I put my camera away and clap my hands. "I hope you learned a thing or two today. Enjoy those dinners tonight. Maggie is walking around with your to-go containers. Feel free to use as many as you need, and I'll see you all back here next Saturday."

"Thank you, Desmond," answer a few of my students.

I smile and start to clean up my main station, knowing Faye will require my attention as soon as class empties out. I'd almost forgotten there was a camera man with her until I see him packing away his video equipment.

I walk over to Faye. "Do you still want to talk logistics?" I nod my head toward the table we chatted at the last time she was here. "We can chat here if you don't have your heart set on going to the bar."

She stands from the island and pulls her purse around her shoulders. "I think I'd rather meet downstairs. Come when you're done." Her eyes dart to Maggie and then back to me. "Bring the little minx too." Then she struts out of class before the first student leaves.

Bring the little minx too. Faye's statement initially confuses me, and then that confusion morphs into worry. I replay the way Faye was staring at Maggie and me while we worked together in the kitchen, and I'm not sure I want to know what she was cooking up in that brain of hers. I intend to find out, but there's no way Maggie is coming with me.

"Hey, Maggie," I call out when the last student leaves. "Finish wiping down the stations, and then you can lock up." I toss her a key to the front door.

She watches as I walk past her. "Where are you going?"

"Business meeting. Don't wait up." I shut the door behind me without another glance or word.

Perfect Pitch

DESMOND

"So what's the deal with your new assistant? Maggie, right?"

I'm barely sitting before Faye asks the cringeworthy question. I'm not sure how to answer her at first, especially since so much is on the line. The last thing I need is for Faye to get the wrong idea about Maggie and then change her mind about me and the show. I'm determined to make this happen.

"There's no deal. Maggie's temporary and completely impossible to train."

"She's a feisty one, that girl. I like her."

Surely she's fucking with me. "You like *Maggie*? Why?"

Faye chuckles. "You two are hilarious together. The energy in that kitchen was so hot today. Tell me you felt that—the chemistry."

I squint to get a better look at the woman who has offered herself to me more times than I can count. When she stopped by the kitchen last month, I managed to see her to the door after dishing her up some leftovers from my lobster ravioli class. She'd wanted to stay. But I made a commitment to my dreams and I wasn't about to sacrifice them by continuing to dabble in the pleasure of it all.

Now it's my turn to chuckle because Faye must already be drunk. "That wasn't chemistry you witnessed. That was Maggie and I expressing our intense dislike for one another."

Faye bites her bottom lip and shakes her head. "Not buying it. And before you lie to me again, I minored in psychology. I know a bullshitter when I see one."

I grab hold of the beer the bartender just slid in front of me and take a swig, slamming my lids together as I do. If I could only drown out the noise that has come into my life ever since Maggie Stevens appeared in it. I can't seem to get rid of her, whether I'm physically near her or not.

I set down my beer and level my gaze at Faye. "Like I said, Maggie is a friend of a friend. She needed a job, and I needed someone to fill in while I find someone more permanent. Trust me when I tell you she's temporary. As soon as she gets back on her feet, she'll be out of there, and I'll have someone more experienced."

Faye doesn't seem to be listening to what I'm saying. She looks to be on another train of thought completely. "Where did she come from? How do you know her?" Faye has a faraway look in her eyes that makes me squint to make sure I'm not losing my mind.

"Why?"

"Something about her just seems familiar."

"Familiar how?"

Faye shrugs. "I swear I've seen her before, but I can't place it."

"She's from Texas. We grew up in the same town, but I didn't know her then. Her dad was my football coach, and now her sister is dating Zach."

Faye's face twists as she tries to connect all the dots. "Sounds a bit—"

"Complicated?" I answer for her. "It is, and it isn't. But why are you so curious about her?"

Faye shakes her head like she's trying to clear her thoughts. "Remember that hook I was looking for? Well, I think I figured it out. It's something we haven't talked about yet, and I can't let go of it. What I saw up there today truly inspired me."

"I'm listening."

"What if we bring on a cohost? Someone who you could exchange conversation with, kind of like how you and Maggie were today? You mentioned how you didn't want to talk directly to a camera. This solves that problem. Plus, it's funny, catchy, sexy—perfect for the demo we're aiming to please."

I cringe. "I don't know, Faye. I might teach classes of twenty at a time, but hosting a show with someone else doesn't seem like something that would work. What if they can't be counted on?"

"You have some trust issues, don't you, Desmond Blake?" The way she's searching me with her eyes sends warning flags to my brain.

"Oh no. You're not digging into my psyche for show content. I want approval over every episode."

"Desmond, I get it. This is your baby, your one true passion in life." The way she dismisses all of the above like she's heard it a million times grates on me hard. "Just look at my track record if you're having any doubts. I would never make you look bad. That simply doesn't benefit me."

She rests a hand on my knee, and I have to stop myself from slipping it off and walking away.

"I hate to break this to you, Desmond, but as hot as you are, it's just not original enough. Hot guy in an apron? Great. But it's been done before. Our audience is smarter than that."

"I didn't agree to this to be some sex symbol. Edible Desire deserves the recognition. It's about the food, the charities we support, the people who rely on our services. It was never about a hot guy in an apron."

"Yes, I know that. But every show needs a hook. Sure, you'll get some great buzz straight off the bat, but the network is looking for something with lasting power, something original. Our audience craves relatability, and having a cohost who resembles one of your students is just the spark we need, especially if we can find someone you have chemistry with. Someone like Maggie."

My double take gives me whiplash as my eyes grow wide. Not only did she just crush my well-inflated ego, but she thinks someone like *Maggie* would be great cohost? Faye is out of her damn mind. "Nope. No way. Maggie is off limits."

"Why?"

"Because she's impossible. How? Let me count the ways. She's stubborn, she lacks motivation, she's unreliable. I'm telling you, she's only working for me right now as a favor to a friend. I don't need a cohost, Faye."

"Why are you being so difficult about this? What's wrong with bringing in someone who can get your kitchen the recognition it deserves? If you don't want that person to be Maggie, fine. But let me put out an emergency casting call to at least try it out before you completely nix the idea."

I sigh, feeling like I've pushed this too far. "And if we don't like anyone who shows up for auditions?"

"Then I start brainstorming another plan. Just give this idea a chance. I'll have a lineup of interested women outside your front door on Monday morning, and we'll go from there."

Jeez, Faye wasn't joking when she said that she likes to move fast.

"Fine. But whoever *we* choose has to be someone I get along with," I point out. "In addition, it has to be someone who can actually cook." That's another reason why Maggie would make an awful cohost.

Faye cringes. "You didn't see what I saw today, Desmond. I think our pitch should be that your cohost is a total novice, someone a little resistant. Just think about it. If we play up the comedy and sexual tension aspect of it all, the network will eat it up. I could not stop laughing today at you trying to keep your professionalism, and Maggie resisting your every effort. Trust me on this. You want a show? I need that special something, that zest, and I think this is it."

I cringe, still not buying the whole concept. "So we're really doing this? We're really finding someone to cohost the show with me?"

Faye's smile spreads. "Give me some space in the kitchen on Monday afternoon, and it's game on. Just think. As soon as we find her, we'll be that much closer to shooting the pilot. Congratulations, Desmond. Your dreams are about to come true, and it looks like you have Maggie Stevens to thank."

Well, shit.

TAKE THREE

Future and Past

"THOSE WHO SEE THE WORLD THROUGH THE LENS
OF LOVE ARE THE TRUE VISIONARIES."
— BRYANT MCGILL

Building Wings

MAGGIE

One day at my new job, and I think I can call it a success. Desmond and I didn't kill each other. I pretty much have the registration system down. And I even assisted him at his cooking station. The guy might even owe me a raise after that one, especially since he left me to clean up the mess in the kitchen all on my own to hang out with that Faye woman.

After I clean the kitchen, I lock up and wait at the curb for the movers to arrive with all the things Monica is donating to me. To my surprise, she joins them on the ride over and helps me get my new place in decent shape for the cubbyhole that it is.

So far, I have a bed, some curtains, dishes, nearly new cookware, a love seat, and a dresser. When Monica starts to hang some decor from her last apartment "to add some personality to the place," I refuse. Minimal decor is quite all right with me. Anything more than that, and I'll be responsible for removing it when I finally get a place of my own.

"It's temporary," I remind her as I hand her a glass of wine.

She pushes out her lips in an exaggerated pout. "You're not planning to move back to LA, are you? I know you're still trying to find your footing here, but I kind of like having you around."

I laugh and wave my arms around, gesturing to my new apartment. "You like having me around so much, you kicked me out and forced me to live here. Thanks, sis."

She shrugs. "Just consider me the momma bird kicking the baby bird out of the nest. You're welcome." She takes a sip of her wine and lets out a heavy sigh. "Speaking of momma bird, is she still hounding you about leaving LA?"

"Yeah. She isn't happy about it, that's for sure. But I can't keep living her dream when it makes me so unhappy."

Monica is silent for a few beats as she swirls her wine. "When did you realize you didn't love modeling anymore? I mean, I knew you were growing apart from it years ago, but you never did tell me why."

I sigh and play with the stem of my wine glass. "I think over time, I just started to realize that I loved it for all the wrong reasons." My face heats with the admission, but I keep going anyway. It feels good to air the truth after the years of lies I've been telling myself and everyone else. "In part, I loved that I made Mom so proud. I loved the clothes, the attention. Men were always asking me out, and the money was good enough to afford an apartment in downtown LA. I didn't really have any worries, but I also never thought about the future, of what my life would be like when I grew tired of the noise, you know?"

Monica glues her sad eyes to mine. "I get it, Mags. But what about acting? You still want to do that, right? I mean, you're still talking to that agent."

I swirl my wine glass around as I heavily debate how much I should tell my little sister. I've spent years protecting her from the harsh world. But then I remember that I don't need to do that anymore. "Um, to be honest, I don't really have an agent."

Monica's mouth falls open, and I cringe as I continue with my admission.

"I don't want to act either, M. I thought I did, but…" I bite down on my lip, hoping that will be enough information.

"What changed?" she presses.

Memories of Regis Malone bombard my thoughts, and I shudder at the last mental image I have of him. "There was this producer in LA. He wanted to meet me to discuss a role, so I met up with him at a bar. He'd seen me in some commercials and sold me on this new soap opera he was producing. Well, he was so interested that he ended up coming to New York for that disastrous runway event. He said he was going to bring his casting director and meet me the very next day."

I shake my head, trying to alleviate the crippling humiliation I still feel over the entire ordeal. Even though Monica is my sister and the most understanding person in the world, I haven't been able to talk to anyone about my experience with the soap opera producer.

"So what happened?"

I take out my phone and find the video app on which my literal fall from grace will live on forever. All I have to do is search for the words "runway fall New York," and it's the first video that pops up. It has over two million views. I sigh and hand the phone to my sister. I watch her reactions instead of the video because I can't bring myself to ever watch it again.

Her free hand flies to her mouth, and her audible gasp can be heard above the gasp of the crowd's, a sound that will never escape my memory. Her eyes shoot to mine, a mixture of emotions flooding them. "Why didn't you tell me about this before?"

I shrug. "You were going through so much when I got to town. I wanted to help you, not add to your stress."

"You've always done that." She says the words accusingly, like I betrayed her in some way. "You've always put my feelings before your own. I wish you would have talked to me about this, Mags. We could have helped each other."

I nod. "I know that, but I was embarrassed too. Embarrassed, and confused, and angry. I think I needed some time to distance myself from it all. Talking about it might not have helped, but it's helping now."

Monica's eyes swell with tears as she hands me back my phone. "So then what about this Regis guy? Don't tell me he didn't want to audition you after that."

I swallow, knowing this will be the hardest confession of all. "I didn't think he would want to, but I woke up the next day to a message from him, wanting me to meet him to talk about the role. He still wanted me to audition, and I was so happy. I went, of course, but…"

Monica's expression turns fierce, like she already fears what I'm about to tell her. "But what?"

"When I got to his room, he… propositioned me."

"You mean with sex? He wanted sex in exchange for giving you the role, didn't he?"

I have to swallow hard to push back the ball of emotion rising in my throat. "He said I would have a hard time getting an acting job after what happened, but he'd be willing to consider me if I..." I can't even say the words, and I don't have to.

"Please tell me you socked the bastard straight in his dick hole."

I stifle a laugh. Only my sister would find the words "dick hole" to be threatening. "No, but I left, and then I got on the first flight to Seattle to figure my shit out. The only thing I've figured out is that I don't want to go back to modeling or acting."

"Are you sure? Don't let one asshole ruin your dreams of acting, Mags. He's not worth it."

"Acting was just as much my dream as modeling was. It's not what I want now."

"But you're so great in front of a camera. I was always so envious with how natural that came for you. So you think you just fell out of love?"

I shrug. "I'm not sure I know what love feels like anymore. And I might have once said I didn't believe in love in that way, but living here and seeing how much you're thriving makes me want the same thing for myself."

"Oh, Maggie." Monica slips off the chair and sits beside me on my bed. She hugs me from the side as a tear slips from her eye. "You'll find your passion too. I promise. And there's nothing wrong with not knowing what you want to do. That's what school is for, and random cooking classes."

We both laugh.

Monica hugs me harder. "People always talk about taking the leap toward your dreams, taking risks, and building your wings along the way—but there's something to say for taking a leap away from the things that do more harm than good. You'll still build your wings, Mags. And when you finally catch the right current, I think you'll be surprised by how high you soar."

Now I'm tearing up and hugging my sister back. "I love you, M."

"I love you, too, Mags."

Free Ticket

MAGGIE

Monica eventually curled up in bed with me last night, and she's still in my apartment when I peel open my eyes in the morning.

"Morning, sunshine," she sings from my bathroom, far too chipper for me.

I squint at her and groan. "You are not all dolled up already for the game, are you?"

She grins as she smears a thick stripe of gold face paint beneath each eye. "I am."

"It doesn't start for hours."

"Early bird catches the booze, they say."

"No one has ever said that in the history of ever."

She shrugs and continues primping. "You should come with me sometime. I already promised the tickets to some friends today, but maybe the next home game?"

The way her voice picks up at the ends, so innocent and hopeful, it actually makes me want to say yes.

"Ugh, that reminds me," I say, "I have to work the game today for White Water. I probably should be getting ready too."

I should have known Monica's eyes would light at the sound of me going anywhere near a game. "Did you say you're coming to the game?"

"It's just some pregame beer-garden thing outside the stadium."

Monica grins. "Which means you'll be free *during* the game? I'm sure we can find you a spare ticket." She perks up. "In fact, I think I know someone who has one."

Her excitement is palpable, but it only makes me want to climb into a dark hole.

My heart squeezes in my chest. I can't believe I'm actually toying with the idea of agreeing to this. "I don't know. What if I get into the game, and I'm a miserable cow for whoever gives me their ticket? One look at Dad, and I'll probably run for the hills."

"Mags, it's been over four months since you moved here. Are you seriously telling me that you don't even want to see him?"

I swallow back the lump that's quickly forming in my throat. "Do we have to talk about this in every conversation we have? There are no excuses for what he did to Mom and us. And to just disappear the way he did…"

"Mom made it impossible for him to come near us. He would explain that to you if you'd just talk to him."

My eyes snap to hers. "Monica, are you forgetting how we found out about his new family?"

She shakes her head adamantly. "I'll never forget that day," she whispers, and I can tell she's still haunted by the past. "Never." Then she sighs. "Look, I was angry with him for a long time too."

"Not long enough. One conversation, and you already forgave the man."

Monica slams her eyes shut as frustration colors her face. "Because he's Dad, and he's here, and he desperately wants to be a part of our lives again. That's worth something."

"Maybe to you."

She leans in and clutches my hands. "Forget Dad for a second. Remember how much fun we used to have watching the games together? Don't you miss it?"

I don't say no, but I don't agree either. I guess there is a part of me that is curious, that does miss the rush of the game and the roar of the crowd. I used to love football, and being in Seattle has made me kind of miss it. And maybe, just maybe, there's still a little girl inside of me that wants a glimpse of the first man who ever broke her heart. Maybe that little girl does want to heal.

And maybe my sister isn't the entire reason I moved to Seattle after all.

Two hours later, I'm dressed in the uniform White Water hooked me up with for today's event and catching a ride share to the stadium.

I try not to think much about the purple-and-gold fabric I'm wearing because it goes against everything I stand for, namely football and being the subject of gawking and groping hands. It's asset-accentuating, midriff-revealing, made of jersey material, and complete with matching shiny leggings. Luckily, White Water makes it all worth it with their compensation, and all I have to do is strut around with drink coupons. *Easy peasy.* The second my shift is over, I can go home and try to make something more of my tiny studio apartment.

I'm supposed to meet the White Water team lead at a fenced-in area of a restaurant parking lot across the street from Century Link Stadium, but no one prepared me for what I would actually be walking into.

When my ride pulls up to a corner and I see the crazy long line of waiting partygoers that dips back behind the beer-garden area, I stop completely in my tracks. "What the—"

It's only ten a.m. Monica wasn't messing around with that early-bird talk. There are still three whole hours to go before the game. But lo and behold, people are already milling around in full game gear, taking shots, chugging beers, and stumbling around like they're already celebrating a win. It's a full-on frat party, and I look like I fit right in.

I shouldn't be here. Other than this fraud of an outfit I'm wearing, I don't fit in. I'm not sure how I'm supposed to mingle with die-hard fans when I can barely stomach the mention of football.

Before I can turn around and run in the other direction, Bentley, the team lead for White Water, spots me from the front entrance of the gate and starts waving. "Looking good, Stevens," he calls out. "You're just in time."

I force my feet to start moving again and greet him with a warm smile. "Hey, Bentley. Crazy morning, huh?"

"Oh, you haven't seen anything yet." He hands me a bunch of rectangular slips of paper with White Water's brand name and a promotional offer. "Here's your first stack. Try your best to keep these to one per person. Each coupon contains a free drink and a discounted drink ticket. Now it's really important that you take your time passing these out. Don't just shove them at everyone you see. Talk about the brand and get them excited to try it out."

His salesman-like excitement makes me want to stab my eyes out.

"We've already got a line started on the end of the food truck there." He points at a line that almost reaches the back of the gate.

"How long have they been here?"

Bentley chuckles. "I forget you're not from Seattle. We take our sports seriously, and that includes starting the pre-party at seven a.m."

My eyes grow huge. Jeez. No wonder Monica was in a rush to get here. "Everyone's been drinking since seven?" I squeal and stare back at the crowd. "Are they going to remember the game once it's over?"

He chuckles and shrugs. "Not our problem. Kara took the first shift, but the crowd is filling out, so we need you. Do you understand your mission?"

I catch myself before I salute the tall slick-haired blond and simply nod, letting him place the stack of tickets in my hands.

"Great. If you need more, come see me."

I walk off. After only a couple weeks of working with the booze-loving team, I know the drill. Have fun, be part of the crowd, flirt, strut, and through my sexual prowess, sell the Tito's-wannabe liquor like it's the new Smartwater. I definitely don't hate the gig, and I'm happy with the payout. A few events a week combined with my new job at Edible Desire should bring in enough to live on until I discover that perfect dream job Monica is so sure I'll find.

For now, I'm okay with the in-between. I'm okay with not knowing where I'm going to end up. But I hope I figure it out soon, before the anxiety hits and before the feelings of failure seep into my bloodstream like poison.

I don't want to believe that modeling was all I'll ever be great at. There has to be more to this life. Deep down, I can feel that there is.

My smile is currently aimed at a hottie wearing the opposing team's jersey—which I find a strange comfort in—when someone sidles up to my right and hooks their arm in mine. I turn to see Monica with a giant grin on her face. I already saw her in full attire this morning, but now that I'm wide awake and staring at her under a perfect sunlit sky, I can't help but smile.

She looks ridiculously cute with her Ryan jersey over a fitted gold hoodie that matches the stripe around her upper arm. Her hair is pulled up in a high ponytail. Her shimmery purple heart earrings match the getup. And even though she's wearing super cute boots that give her some lift, I still dwarf her in height.

"Hey," I say with a laugh. "How's the pregaming?"

"Amazing, of course," Monica says with a pop of her heels. "I heard the hot chick in the Seattle jersey is handing out White Water drink tickets." She nudges me and wiggles her brows. "By the way, I'm talking about you, sis."

I roll my eyes, rip a few tickets from the stack, and hand them to her with a wink. "Knock yourself out. Who are you here with?"

Just then, the familiar auburn-haired girl I'd come to know as Monica's best friend, Chloe, approaches, smiling, along with another girl I don't recognize. "Hey, Maggie. Good to see you again," Chloe says. "Do you know Jazz?"

I shake my head and greet them both fondly. I'm happy to know that my sister has picked some good friends to hang out with. I hand them both a few coupons, ignoring Bentley's request to keep drink tickets to a one-per-person minimum. Obviously, he didn't mean my friends.

"Did you decide if you want to come to the game?" Monica perks up. "I can start asking around for an extra ticket." She wiggles her brows, and I just laugh.

Chloe jumps in. "Oh! I can ask around too. Gavin's friends are always trying to sell a few tickets."

Monica grins then starts to look around like she's searching for something or someone. "Speaking of your fiancé, where did he go?"

Chloe points at the food truck. "He's hungry, like always."

I look at where Chloe is pointing, and I spot Gavin almost immediately. Then I notice the guy next to him. My chest heats, and I squint to make out the figure better. "Is that Desmond?"

"Yup." Monica laughs. "We usually meet up before the game. There's a bunch of us over there." She points at a corner with a group of tall, round tables pulled together. I never realized Monica had so many friends here, but clearly I haven't made any attempts to step out much, especially not to a game on a Sunday.

Not wanting to dive deeper into conversations about Desmond, I turn my focus on Chloe. "You must be excited about your wedding next week. Monica showed me her bridesmaid's dress, and it's stunning."

Chloe beams, and there's a certain glow about her that squeezes my chest a little. "Excited, yes, but I think I'm more nervous than anything. I mean, we're keeping it pretty small, but my nerves grow crazier every day."

"You're going to look stunning. I'm so excited for you."

Chloe smiles with her appreciation. "You should come."

Monica gasps, and her eyes light up. "Oh my gosh, yes. You can be my date!" She squeals.

I laugh. "I thought Zach was going to be your date."

Monica frowns. "He doesn't know if he can come yet since he's got a game the next day. He needs to get clearance from Coach."

Monica doesn't even blink when she calls our dad Coach, and it weirds me out a little. "Jeez, Dad won't even let him go to a wedding?"

My sister immediately jumps to our dad's defense. "Zach's kind of important, Mags. He'd rather not have his player taking red-eyes when they have a game the next day."

I just shake my head, hoping we can drop the subject of Dad. I should have kept my mouth shut.

"Well, you should come anyway, Maggie," Chloe says with a smile. "You don't need to come as anyone's date. We're having a short ceremony and a big, long reception. Open bar. DJ. You'll love it."

"Please come." Monica bats her lashes up at me with pleading puppy-dog eyes. "There will be so many hotties there too. We'll find you a man." She loops her arm through mine. "Who wouldn't want to date a hot model?"

"Ex-model," I correct her while I laugh at her lame attempt at hooking me up.

Chloe laughs. "I promise, there are plenty of good options. In fact, a lot of them are here today. Come meet our friends, Maggie."

I hesitate for a second. "I should get back to work."

Monica looks up at me with a wink. "All you have to do is hand them one of those babies, and they'll want to be your best friend forever."

I laugh at the reference to the White Water drink tickets in my hands. "Noted."

Chloe takes the lead and introduces me to their friends. She tells them who I am and what I'm doing dressed like a Seattle dancer. And just as Monica predicted, they are overexuberant to meet me. I make my way to the center of the group, where I meet a guy named Justin and his friend Blaine.

All of a sudden, a deep voice speaks up from behind me. "What does a guy have to do for one of those?"

A shiver skates up my spine at the familiar raspy voice that is filled with flirtation. When I swivel around to face him, his eyes widen a few too many inches, and his jaw falls in shock. "Maggie?" he practically squeals. "What are you doing here?" He scans the length of me, and his eyes bulge out a little bit farther. "Holy shit, I didn't recognize you. What are you doing here?"

It's impossible to hold back my laughter. He was hitting on me, and he didn't even know it was me. "Workin'. I'd ask you what you're doing here, but I already know." I wink and hold up a drink ticket. "Looking for one of these?"

He is still wearing his shocked expression as his eyes dart everywhere. They're on my breasts when I slip the ticket into his hand and step forward. "Good to know you don't hate everything about me." Then I brush past him, trying to ignore the rush that fills my blood from the simple touch.

I'm halfway across the beer garden when Desmond manages to catch up to me. "Wait a second. You can't just walk off like that."

I tilt my head and lock eyes with him. "Actually, I can. I'm working, and I have about a million more of these things to hand out. See, this is a job I'm actually good at."

Desmond makes a face and shakes his head. "You said something about me hating you back there, and I want you to know I don't. We may not get along, but that doesn't mean I think badly of you. I like to tease you a lot, and maybe I come off like an ass. You and I—we're just different. And you're good at plenty of things, just not at cooking." He grins at his last comment, like he can't help himself.

I growl and start to push him, then I realize that touching him is too intimate. I pull my hand away like it's been burned. Then I think about something. "Wait a second. Isn't Seattle playing Dallas today? You grew up in Dallas and cheered for the Cowboys growing up, and now you're wearing a Seattle jersey? You're almost as bad as my sister."

Desmond chuckles. "You really expect me to cheer for Dallas when my best friend is leading Seattle to a victory?"

I shrug. "I expect you to be true to your roots. Are you even a Seattle fan if you're just going to change your colors the moment Zach gets traded?"

He raises a brow, and I immediately regret my statement. "Guess I've got six years to figure that out, don't I? Besides, he's not my only friend on the team."

"That's right. Balko is a bestie, isn't he?" I grin, knowing that even though I'm barely saying a word, it's pissing him the hell off.

He huffs out a breath. "Why do I even bother?"

I shrug. "I was wondering the same thing myself."

"What about you? You coming to the game?"

"Nope. I wouldn't really fit in if you know what I mean."

He makes a point of scrolling over my outfit again before chewing on his bottom lip. "I think you would fit in just fine." His eyes snap to mine. "What if I told you I have an extra ticket?"

"I'd say you'd better find someone who can stand you enough to *stand with you*." I grin at my joke while Desmond smirks.

"Maybe it's you who hates me, not the other way around."

"Maybe I do."

"Really? As much as you hate cooking?"

"Worse."

He laughs, and as hard as I'm trying not to flirt with him, I'm afraid that's exactly what I'm doing.

He *tsks* while shaking his head. "That's unfortunate because I bet you'd be an instant Seattle fan if you gave it a chance."

I can't deny that there's an insane curiosity bouncing around the back of my mind—to experience the game again and to see my dad. But becoming a fan is a little much. "Oh yeah? How much do you want to wager?"

I can tell that throws him off track by the way his expression changes from playful to serious. "Wait, so you'll actually go?"

"Do you actually have an extra ticket?"

Desmond digs in his back pocket and pulls out two tickets. "I usually bring a date. Or sometimes I meet a girl here and ask her to sit with me," he says with a proud grin. "But I could let you have this today if you're serious about coming."

I narrow my lids at him. *Did he just say what I think he said?* "You seriously do that? Just meet a random girl and then ask her to sit with you at a football game? How desperate are you?"

"First of all, we stand. No one sits at a football game. But going back to your questions—I've found it's a better way to meet women than online or at the bar. This way, at least we have a common interest."

"Oh yeah?" I challenge. "If your interests are so common, why do they need a ticket to the game?"

He throws his head back and chuckles. "Most of them forego their tickets to come with me. They give their tickets to a friend who otherwise wouldn't have been able to go."

Damn it. I really wanted to make a point but failed per usual when it came to Desmond.

"So let's get back on track," he says. "Are you coming with me today, or do I need to find another lucky lady to accompany me?"

I stare back at the ticket and swallow. "I'm not sure. How much is my presence worth to you?"

He's smiling again. "Well, you'd have to stand next to me through the entire game."

"I might sit, but okay. What else?"

He laughs. "You have to have fun."

I roll my eyes and cross my arms. "You can't force a person to have fun."

"You can at least try."

"Okay, fine. If I stand there for the whole game and *try* to have fun, then what do I get?"

"My company isn't enough?"

I shake my head. "Nope."

"Then I don't know. A hundred bucks?"

I cringe. "I'm not your paid escort. I was thinking more like free meals for a month. Breakfast, lunch, and dinner. You're buying."

"Okay, but one week, not a month. You probably won't even still be in Seattle in a month."

"You have a point." I hold out my hand, and we shake, our eyes locking until I pull my hand away with a sharp gasp. "I need to get back to work. I'm off in three hours."

Desmond grins. "Perfect."

I don't know what has him all giddy, but it's hard to think of anything else but his satisfied smile as I walk around and try to make conversation with the crowd. Everyone seems to be well-intoxicated, which only makes me feel like I have a lot of catching up to do when I finally tell Bentley I'm clocking out.

The beer garden has emptied out quite a bit since I got there, and Desmond is waiting for me at one of the tables with a drink. He grins. "On me."

I laugh because I recognize the signature White Water label on the glass. He must have used one of my free drink tickets to get it. "Remind me never to call you a cheap date."

He winks. "Oh, I'll spoil you rotten today, babe. Beer, hot dogs. I don't know what you models eat, but the only salads they serve at the games have more calories than a pepperoni pizza. So if I were you, I'd opt for the pepperoni."

A bouncy body sidles up to me. "I heard the good news." Monica is grinning from ear to ear, and if I didn't know better, I would think that she expects something to happen between Desmond and me.

"He made me an offer I couldn't refuse. Free meals for a week. I'm no dummy. I accepted even though it means hanging out with this thug."

Desmond gasps in mock admonishment. "I'm no thug. I'm actually quite the gentleman."

Monica looks up at him and laughs. "Okay, then. I'll see you two inside." She points at Desmond. "Take care of my sister. Don't let her ruin your fun."

"Oh no, that's part of the deal," he says as he swings an arm over my shoulder. "She has to have fun."

"I have to try," I correct.

Desmond winks at me. "You won't have to try with me."

False Start

DESMOND

Alcohol is definitely not part of my plan for getting Maggie to loosen up today. Sure, the girl is as frigid as a Canadian winter, but I'm optimistic. How could someone who grew up on football *not* have fun at a live game? What I'm not expecting is for Maggie to take it upon herself to down three shots of White Water vodka in just a few minutes.

"Going a little hard there, aren't you, Mags?"

She shrugs as a giggle slips from her sexy throat. "You're driving, not me."

I chuckle. "That's presumptuous of you. Who said I was driving you home?"

This time, she glares and steps right up until she's under my nose. "This is a pretty shitty date if you're not even going to drive me home."

A laugh bursts straight from my chest. "Who said we're on a date?"

She tilts her head and practically purrs. "You did offer me your extra ticket to the game, one you would have otherwise used to bribe one of these poor women to go on a *date* with you—which, by the way, makes me some sort of saint. So yes, this is a date."

"You going to put out afterwards too?"

Her lips curl up at the corners. "Not a chance in hell."

That makes me grin. "Then our definitions of date are very different."

Maggie snorts. "Who are you kidding? We both know you won't let me find a different ride home after the game."

When she bats her eyes up at me playfully and knowingly, something catches in my chest. We both know she's not wrong.

We walk to the stadium with Monica, Chloe, Gavin, and the rest of our friends. Then we detach when we get to the concession stand near where our seats are.

"Want something to eat or drink?" I ask her.

Maggie looks up at the board then tells me she wants a beer but nothing else. I order two hot dogs, two beers, and a pretzel, then we make our way to our row. Monica's seats are an entire section down and to the right of us.

"Here." I shove a hot dog in front of Maggie's nose. "You should eat something."

She makes a face and pushes the hot dog away. "I can't eat that. Do you know how many toxins are in that thing?"

I shrug and stuff half of a dog into my mouth, chew, swallow, and take a sip of beer. "Probably just as much as those three White Water shots you took back in the beer garden."

"Yeah, well, I'm here, aren't I? Now you and my sister can shut up about the Seattle experience. After today, not another word."

I grin. "You ain't seen nothing like it, babe."

"Stop calling me babe."

"Why? I thought you were my date."

She rolls her eyes, causing me to laugh.

"Relax," I say, setting her foil-wrapped hot dog on the cup holder in front of her. "We're going to have a good time, I'm going to take you home without molesting you, and then you can sleep off your hangover while dreaming about me all night long."

"You are such a cocky one, aren't you?"

I grin. "You have no idea."

We have time before the game actually starts, so Maggie and I settle into our seats. Her eyes are fixed on the field, and I wonder if she's searching for Coach. I don't dare ask for fear our almost-good time will turn into something I'm not sure she's ready for.

A few minutes later, Maggie faces me and opens her mouth. "So you played football for my dad, huh?"

I nod, unsure of where this is going. Something tells me she's not really asking. She already knows the answer.

"Were you any good?"

My mind flashes to a smaller version of me with my eyes on my opponent while Zach danced around in the pocket. If anyone came near him, I was all over it, pinning them to the ground just in time for Zach to launch his next rocket.

"Yeah, I was pretty good."

"But you didn't want to go pro? Or you weren't good enough?"

I shrug. "Guess I'll never know if I was good enough. Football was never my number one. I fell into it because of Coach, but my heart has always been with the culinary arts."

Maggie's eyes soften. "When did that start?"

I lean back in my chair, spreading my legs and thinking back to all the memories of my dad while growing up. He was my inspiration. "My dad was always baking or cooking something. I remember coming home from school to the most amazing smells. He never had to ask me twice to join him in the kitchen. He'd plop me on that counter, and I'd watch him work and help as much as I could."

"Did your mom cook, too, before she..." Maggie's face turns red, and I know she wishes she could take the question back. No one ever likes to ask questions about my mom's death, which suits me just fine because I normally hate answering them.

I smile faintly. "My mom didn't cook. She refused, actually. My dad says it inspired him to impress her with every meal. My mom was a photographer. The first camera I ever picked up was hers when I got old enough to fiddle with the thing."

"That's sweet."

The fact that I just blurted all that out to Maggie doesn't seem *sweet* to me. In fact, it might just scare the hell out of me. I take a swig of my beer instead. "Your turn. When did you start modeling?"

"I was a regular pageant girl," she says, batting her lashes at me, "from four years old until my mom decided it was time to start making actual money. That's when she hooked me up with her old agent, and off I went. Commercial one day, fashion-brand shoot another, and runway event the next. I barely had time for school. Eventually, I had to get a tutor to supplement my time out of the classroom."

"Wow, that's pretty intense for a young girl."

She bites down on her bottom lip. "Yeah, but it was all I knew. My mom's career ended faster than she wanted it to, and I became her little puppet. She lived vicariously through me until I finally called it quits."

"How'd you do it? How did you finally break the ties to modeling? Is it because of what happened on that runway?"

Maggie's face grows red and she shakes her head. "No, I was already on my way out. My heart wasn't in it anymore, but the timing ended up being perfect. I saw what was happening in the media with Zach and Monica, and I knew she needed me even without her saying a word."

She's hiding something, but I'm not going to push it. "A sister's intuition?"

She nods. "Something like that."

"Can I ask another question? A personal one?"

She swallows another mouthful of beer and shrugs. "Why the hell not?"

I smile while searching for a safe way to ask the question. "Do you think you'll ever talk to your dad again? Do you want to?"

Maggie's eyes snap to the field, like she's searching for the man. "There's always been this part of me that wants to see him." She speaks quietly, but there's no mistaking her words. "But then I think about the last time I saw him, and I can't let myself forgive him for what he did."

I don't know why I have this yearning deep within me to make things right between Maggie and her father. The last thing either of them probably want is me getting in the middle of their issues. "Monica and him seem to be getting along," I start, but then I shut up before I can finish my thought. That was probably the wrong thing to say.

Maggie's sharp caramel eyes turn from the field to me. "I don't mean to be rude, but can we talk about something else?"

"Sure," I say slowly as she reaches for the hot dog and pulls it out of the wrapper. Her foot taps quickly against the concrete as she rips open the condiment wrappers, one by one, with her teeth, and then decorates the dog. I have the strangest feeling that she doesn't even know she's preparing to eat the damn thing.

I reach for the camera around my neck and focus on her glossy pink lips. Her mouth is marginally parted, her perfectly trimmed nails have a firm grip on her bun, and her cute button nose is currently inhaling her food.

There's something so innocent about the picture through the lens. On the surface, it's just a woman and her hot dog. There's something lonely, yet flawless about how Maggie appears to me now: seemingly unwanted, perfect beneath the mask of artificial condiments, yet toxic because one taste of her will only spell trouble. But damn, I want to spread her, taste her, and swallow her whole.

Jesus. I swallow and try to shake away my dirty thoughts. In my defense, it's been a long time since I've found true pleasure in a woman. Sure, there was that one time with Faye months ago, but a little fucking around in a hotel opposed to a whole night of tantric fucking are on two different scales of orgasm. And I want the good kind, the mind-blowing sex that fills me repeatedly and becomes an all-night fuck-a-thon.

I'm not supposed to have those kinds of thoughts or feelings about Maggie for so many reasons that I'm starting to lose track of them all. But today isn't about sex. It's about learning how I can work and live near Maggie for the foreseeable future. She may not like me, but she doesn't have to hate me. She'll at least have to tolerate me if I'm going to be her boss and her landlord.

I don't know how many photos I snap before Maggie's head snaps toward me. Her eyes fly wide, and she gulps down her next bite then slams a palm an inch from the lens. "What are you doing?"

I lower the camera and laugh. "Sorry, I couldn't help myself. You were really enjoying your meal."

Maggie's face is bright red, and while I know I caught her off guard, her reaction scares me a little.

"Delete those photos." Her tone drips with warning, but I'm too locked up in confusion to take her seriously.

"What?" I shake my head. She's out of her mind. "No."

"Desmond Blake, delete those photos now, or I will leave."

My jaw drops. "Maggie, stop. They're good photos. Look." I hold the camera up, display side facing her, and tap through each photo. Each one is aimed more at the hot dog she's holding than on her. "I was capturing your food. That's all." I fail to mention how nice her lips look in the photo. Apparently, I don't need to because she already appears to be calming down.

She sits back in her seat and narrows her eyes at me. "Next time, ask my permission first."

I can agree to that. "I will. I promise." I lower my camera to my lap and assess her. "Jeez. Aren't models used to having their picture taken?"

"I quit modeling, remember?" With that, she shoves the rest of her hot dog in her mouth and chews before finishing off her drink. Then she shoves her empty cup against my chest. "Beer me."

I take it from her and stand with a light chuckle. The lines will be crazy since there's only twenty minutes to go until game time, but I think I can still make it back before kickoff. "Anything else? Cotton Candy? Red Licorice?" I tease.

She shakes her head and turns her eyes down to her phone, which she starts tapping away on. "Just booze. Thanks."

I refrain from scolding her on her alcohol intake and head toward the aisle just as Monica, Chloe, and Gavin are walking up the stairs.

"Hey!" Monica lights up. *Why can't I have that same effect on Maggie?* "How's she doing?"

I chuckle and toss a look over my shoulder. Maggie's still got her nose buried in her phone. "One guess."

Monica smiles. "I'll go talk to her." She raises her eyes to Chloe. "Can you grab me a drink? And a funnel cake?"

Chloe grins. Being Monica's best friend, Chloe seems well-attuned to Monica's fixation with food, especially desserts. "Of course." Then Chloe looks at me. "Coming with us?"

"Lead the way."

Gavin gives me a fist bump, and we take the stairs two at a time until we reach the top. Like I guessed, the line is a mile long.

Rocking back on my heels, I eye Gavin and Chloe. "You two ready for the big day on Saturday?"

The two exchange big smiles as Gavin wraps an arm around her. "As ready as we can be," he says. "We've only waited our whole lives for this."

As pessimistic as I am about love, I can see that they radiate devotion toward each other. It's a beautiful thing to witness.

Chloe looks at me with a humorous gleam in her eyes. "Mostly, things are going smoothly. We can't thank you enough for catering it for us. We know you usually have classes on Saturdays."

I shrug. "You booked it far enough in advance, so it's fine. I should be thanking you. One of my goals for this year is to grow the catering department."

Chloe beams at me. "That's so exciting."

"Let us know if there's anything we can do to help," Gavin chimes in. "We'll be happy to spread the word, write a review, anything."

"I appreciate that, man."

After we purchase our food and drinks, I make my way back to the seat to find Maggie alone with a sad look on her face as she stares out at the field. The entire team is out there now, including Coach, and I can only guess that's who has put her in a sour mood. I stifle my discomfort and pass her to sit down.

When I hand her the beer, she thanks me and searches my hands, like she was expecting something else. "Where's yours?"

"I've already had four drinks. That's my limit."

Maggie looks shocked and confused, and I don't blame her. That's the reaction I normally get when I tell people my rule. "Like, in an hour?"

I laugh. "No, in a day."

She looks horrified. "Seriously? You must think I'm an alcoholic."

I'm still laughing. "I don't think that at all. I know plenty of people who get belligerent on a daily basis, and I don't judge."

"But why? Your rule doesn't match your whole... persona."

I'm grinning now. I'm not exactly sure why, but I think I like that she has pegged me all wrong.

"I just like to be careful about what I put into my body. Alcohol messes with more than a person's state of mind. I like to know that I'm in control at all times."

She narrows her eyes and nods. "That's right. You're a control freak." She sets her beer down. "Well, now I don't want to drink this. Thanks for being a buzzkill." She settles into her seat.

"I don't mind if you drink, Maggie. I wasn't trying to make you feel bad. It's just a promise I made myself the first time I got really drunk in high school."

"Why?" she challenges, and it's another question that I am unsure if I want to give her the answer to.

This time, I decide *fuck it*. "Because I don't want to wind up like my old man—that's why."

The expression on her face right now—the one filled with a newfound understanding—is one I wish I could capture. It takes all the resistance I have not to reach for my camera. But almost as quickly as the shock and disbelief wash over her, they dissolve like her face just hit the sun.

"I forgot I'm not the only one with daddy issues," she finally says.

"Yeah, well, at least I still talk to my issue."

She swishes her hair over her shoulder and purses her lips. "Okay, in that case" — she picks up her drink and puts it between her lips while darting a glare my way — "I clearly need this more than you do."

I grin, unable to help the way my eyes fall to her glistening lips. "Guess you do."

Standing Room Only
MAGGIE

The game starts, and Desmond hoists me to my feet when everyone else around us is standing. Cymbals are crashing on the other side of the stadium as horn instruments and drums serenade the players after kickoff. I hate that there's an excitement that flits through me at the crowd's noise and at the way every eye in the house is trained on the field below. The large monitors zoom in on my dad. Wearing a headset, he paces the sideline, deep in conversation with someone on the other end.

The last time I went to a football game was in Dallas against Seattle. Oddly enough, my dad was the starting quarterback. I still have vivid memories of that day, cuddled up with my sister and mom in the press box. Eyes were trained on my dad like he was the only man on the team. Even after the game, reporters stood in clusters, waiting to talk to him. And he always gave the best, most inspiring one-liners during the post-game interviews with the media. I was so proud. My dad was my hero in more ways than one. He was also the first man who ever broke my heart.

And the last.

The scene before me all seems so surreal.

I feel a nudge at my side. "You okay?"

Desmond is watching me, waiting for me to respond. I don't know what to say, so I settle on the truth. "I was just thinking about the last game I went to. My dad was playing, and it was in Dallas against Seattle. Ironic, huh?"

Desmond's eyes turn toward the field as he seems to quickly connect the dots. "Oh, Maggie, why didn't you say something earlier? You were making all those Dallas-versus-Seattle jokes, and I didn't even think."

He genuinely looks sorry. I didn't even have to explain to him why this football game over any other is probably the hardest to watch.

"Do you want to leave?"

I watch his mouth for many beats after his last words, blinking and wondering if I just made up his voice in my head. "You would do that for me?"

He glances between me and the field. "Well, yeah. If you're uncomfortable. I brought you here to have fun, but if it's too much—"

"It's fine," I jump in.

He hesitates a moment. "Really?"

"Yes. I'm a big girl. I'll be fine." I right my shoulders. "Besides, I'm really counting on those free meals." Now stop talking and let me watch the game."

The smile that lights up his face sends a charge of electricity through my body. I don't think I've ever seen that version of the Desmond Blake charm before. It's not an overblown cocky smile. It's just natural and kind of sweet. I snap my head toward the field and try to get it out of my mind, but just like with every other thing about him—his long locks that look healthier than mine, his thick lips that could easily swallow me whole—I can't.

For the next hour or so, I shamelessly sip my booze while he screams his lungs out every time Seattle gains a single yard. And he's not the only one. These fans are rabid, definitely more intense than any I've ever seen before. They're on their feet to celebrate every inch of forward movement and quick to scream profanities when the refs get it wrong. They're practically foaming at the mouth in anticipation of a—

"TOUCHDOWN!" Desmond screams. Then he turns to me in what seems like a slo-mo scene in a romantic comedy. He must have forgotten my cup is still full of beer when he comes in for the hug. His arms wrap around me while I'm fighting to make out the words to warn him that things are about to go downhill fast. He pulls me in for a bear hug as my hand holding the cup shoots out and away to save us from a disastrous spillage. But then he lifts me and starts to jump. Not once. Not twice. But three times, in celebration of Zachary Ryan throwing a touchdown pass that puts Seattle in the lead.

He doesn't even notice that beer has just doused us both until a droplet falls from my forehead to my nose. I can feel the amber liquid sliding over my skin like I've just been hosed down. He releases me, and his mouth stretches wide. I can't hear everything he says, but his apologies are clear. But that's before he realizes that he has been doused too. His perfect hair is now wet and stringy, and his lips are now gloriously shimmery.

Maybe I'm drunk because I kind of want to kiss him right now. And well, I just might.

"Shit," Desmond screams before letting me go and effectively shattering my trance. Everyone around us is still cheering, and I can't even hear myself think let alone hear what Desmond is mouthing to me now.

"What?" I scream over the noise.

"I'm so sorry," he says again as he swipes at his wet face. "I got too excited." Then he swivels toward the field, where Coach Reynolds is giving Zach a pat on his back. "Did you see that?" Desmond leans toward me and booms with excitement. "Did you see that pass to Anderson?"

I laugh because no matter what my feelings are toward football or my father or our memories, Desmond's face right now is priceless. His excitement is contagious, and his hugs are far too good to forget.

"Yes, I saw it," I finally say.

For the rest of the game, I actually watch without a resentful bone in my body. For the most part, I keep my eyes off my dad, and I focus them on Zach since he's the one Desmond and Monica are here to see. I can do that. I can focus on something other than my own past and be happy. Maybe I can even start to fall in love with the game again.

Seattle ends up winning thirty-two to fourteen, and Desmond is high on life. I remember that feeling, that joy, that intoxication that flooded my veins with each win. I remember when I would see my dad after a game and he would smile bigger than I thought possible. And somehow, that smile felt like it was aimed at me every single time.

I won't deny that there's something magical about the way the game brings so many people together, win or lose. To an extent, it doesn't matter how much a person understands the sport. All that matters is what color they wear and how loud they scream.

Desmond leads me down the stairs instead of up toward the way we came in, and my steps feel heavier the closer we get to the field. "Where are you going?" I hiss.

He looks at me like he's confused. "It's faster to get through the tunnel this way. Why?" Then he sees my face and sighs. "Shit. I mean, you can stay here if you want, but I have to stop by the locker room before we leave. It's tradition."

He pulls out two field passes, and I want to smack him. Instead, I fold my arms across my chest and sit. "I'll stay here."

Desmond nods. "I'll hurry. Don't move from this spot."

I watch him leave without acknowledging his request. I can't be mad at him for doing what comes naturally, but what comes natural for him feels so wrong to me. How did our lives become so embedded when we weren't even trying?

The stadium seating is clearing out fast as I take in the field, the lights, and the glory. I should have never come to this game. Coming here only made me miss something I've worked so hard to forget. And I was successful until today.

"Mags?"

The familiar voice is an instant blast to my heart, and my body begins to shake as I turn my head in my father's direction. He looks the same, with a few extra grays tossed like tinsel throughout his full set of hair. Just the sight of him tightens my throat.

"It's really you." He's smiling, despite the way I must look—shocked, terrified, and teetering on the edge of a waterfall of tears. "You haven't responded to any of my calls or texts."

I'm still angry at Monica for just giving him my phone number like it belonged to him.

He searches my expression like he's waiting for me to say something, but I'm struggling to find the right words. I don't know how to greet a man who stripped my childhood from me without a second glance.

He takes two steps up the stairs, slowly, like he's testing the waters. I'm still too surprised to move or speak.

"Did you enjoy the game?"

I swallow over the lump in my throat. He asked a direct question. I can manage an answer to that. "It was great. You're quite the coach."

He lets out a chuckle, the tone riddled with nerves rather than actual humor. "Well, I try, but these boys certainly keep me on my toes."

Are we really trying to have a normal conversation now? Are we going to pretend it hasn't been over a decade since we last exchanged a single word.

"Mags—" he starts.

But I stand from my seat as fast as I can. "I can't do this." I turn toward the aisle and take two steps up the stairs when he's behind me.

"Maggie, just give me a minute."

"You don't deserve a minute. I shouldn't even be here right now."

"But you are," he says, his tone still hopeful.

"Not for you." And that's a lie. It's a straight-up, hurtful, blatant lie. But I can't give him the truth. He doesn't deserve to know how many nights I cried for him or how much I missed him when he was busy making a parallel life because the one he already had wasn't good enough for him.

I pivot so fast, I feel the wobble in my brain.

"Maggie, wait." This voice doesn't belong to my father. Desmond is by my side before I can take another step. He slings an arm over my shoulders. "We're heading out, Coach. Great game tonight. Give Balko a reaming about those penalties, though."

"I plan on it," he says, his tone now sullen. "Drive safe, Des."

"Always."

Desmond leads me out of the stadium, and as soon as we hit the concrete sidewalk, I shake him off and walk furiously in the direction of the parking lot. "You told him I was here, didn't you?"

Desmond jogs to catch up. "Wait a second. You're mad at me? I mentioned I had to hurry to get back to you. How was I supposed to know that he would practically start running to you?"

I suck in a deep breath and whip around to face him. "It wasn't your business to mention me. I wasn't ready to see him."

"Well, I'm sorry." Desmond throws his arms in the air. "I'm fucking sorry."

"Are you? Because you continue to be pretty adamant about the fact that I should just forgive the man since he was so great to you."

Desmond lets out a heavy breath and takes my hand in his. I don't have the energy to yank it away. "I'm not telling you how to feel. I have no right to do that. But you don't need to keep everything so damn locked up inside you."

"There's nothing locked up inside me, Desmond. That's the problem. I'm *empty*. The sooner you realize that, the sooner you'll stop trying to see more."

He's still holding my hand when he pulls me toward his chest, and my tears threaten to spill. "You are so wrong." His eyes search mine. "Do you want to know what I see when I look at you, Maggie?"

I slam my lids together and shake my head. "No." I can't see him, but I feel his lips slide against my ear. I suck in a deep breath in response.

"You hide behind your beauty like you need protection from the world, when really, it's the world that needs protection from you. You're fierce and unapologetic about your worth, which is why it's absolutely crazy to me that you find it so hard to believe you're worthy of love, even when there are people out there in the world who beg you to love them back. Your father isn't perfect, and he made some shitty decisions, but he's a good man. And he wants another shot."

I'm shaking so hard, I swear even my breath rattles. "Here's what you don't seem to understand. There are years of my life I can never have back. Why should I forgive a thief?"

With that, I turn and march the rest of the way to Desmond's car. And I don't make another sound until I'm in my new apartment, alone, with nothing but the walls and windows to hear me cry myself to sleep.

Picture Perfect

DESMOND

I'm flipping an omelet on the Edible Desire stove when I hear light steps approach from the back room.

"Hungry?" I ask without looking up. There's only one person it could be, and it looks like she located the back elevator.

Maggie shuffles over, fully dressed for the day in white jeans and a bright-green cotton shirt. Her long hair has been curled, and it falls around her in waves. I could snap a picture of her right this second, and it would belong on the cover of a magazine. Then again, she is always picture-perfect.

Her long lashes bat down to see what I'm cooking, and then she raises her gaze to me, steadying those gorgeous eyes like she's trying to light me on fire. "Don't you have a kitchen in your apartment?"

I smile. "Yes, but I doubt you would have accepted an invite to my place for an apology breakfast. Sit." I nod across the island to a stool and flip the eggs one more time before slipping them onto a plate.

Her nose wrinkles as she eases herself onto the stool. "What's in that?"

"Not much." I focus on dressing up her dish. I drizzle some fresh queso over her eggs, sprinkle some paprika across the top, then drop a couple pieces of fresh parsley to finish it off. "It's just eggs, mozzarella, spinach, and mushroom." Then I look up. "Is that okay?" I really should have asked her about any food allergies on her application.

Her mouth parts slightly when I slide the plate in front of her. "It's fine, but who makes gourmet eggs at seven in the morning?"

I grin and turn back to the stove to finish my omelet. "Me."

After unloading my food onto my plate, I stand across the island from her.

She peers up at me between bites and narrows her eyes. "You always stand when you eat?"

"You always talk with your mouth full?" I give her a close-mouthed grin and stick my fork in my eggs.

Her cheeks lift slightly and I would do anything to see her full-on smile. "So what's the scoop with Mondays around here? What's on the agenda?"

I do her the honor of swallowing my food before responding. "We'll head to the market to grab the ingredients for some delivery orders. Saturday was the start of our month, so the rest of the week pretty much follows suit. You'll run registration, create more welcome packets, and you'll get faster at it all too, except we don't have classes on Mondays. It's kind of an inventory, cleaning, and prep day around here. Then there's all of the usual daily stuff. Check the mail, voice mails, update the booking calendar on the website. And at the end of each day, I like going over everything we need to do the next day so that I'm not waking up surprised."

"Sounds pretty laid back," she says before placing another bite in her mouth.

"Usually, it is, but today will be more chaotic than normal."

"Why's that?"

"You remember that woman who was observing class the other day?"

She squints. "You mean Five-Star Faye? I never did ask you what she was doing here. Seemed like you two knew each other pretty well."

I ignore the way Maggie studies me after her comment.

"Well," I say, easing my way into the conversation. I'm not sure how Maggie is going to take it when she finds out that not only is Edible Desire a candidate for a television show, but that *she* is the prime inspiration for why there are a dozen or so women on their way to the kitchen right now to possibly cohost a show with me. "Faye initially came in a few months ago to check out my food in case it was a fit for her show. It wasn't, but she thinks it could be a different type of cooking show."

"Wow, Desmond, really? You're going to have your own television show? That's incredible."

I bite down on my lip before deciding to polar plunge into the subject. "It would be, but she doesn't think me alone is enough for great television. Ridiculous, I know."

Maggie laughs softly. "I bet that was a blow to your massive ego."

The way she teases me with her tongue between her teeth and amusement on her face revs me up inside.

"So then what?" she continues. "You get a cooking assistant or something?"

"Exactly. Faye already put a call out to casting agents, and she'll be bringing some potentials by today."

"Cool." Maggie swallows her last bite of eggs and gets up from her stool. The plate in front of her is completely clean, causing warmth to spread throughout my chest. *She liked it.*

"Hungry much?"

She looks up, and her eyes widen after she realizes that I noticed. "Yes, actually. I don't have food at my place yet."

I stuff a final bite of food into my mouth and take the dishes to the sink a few steps away. "We're heading to the market now if you want to grab a few things for yourself."

"Sure," she says. "Since you won't be cooking my every meal after this week. Thanks for breakfast, by the way."

I shrug. I decide to bite my tongue when it comes to who actually won the bet. She seemed to have a great time during the game, but not so much at the end. I still feel awful about last night. I pushed the issues with her dad too hard when I should have just stayed the fuck out of it. "No problem. And no, you get one week of meals from me, and then you're on your own. Next bet, you'll be cooking for me." I wink at her, and her face immediately changes color.

She snorts and steps around to join me at the sink. "That definitely won't be happening, but I do know my way around a dishwasher."

I grin and move away. "Look at that. Maybe we're the dream team after all." I don't have to glance at her to know her squinty eyes are currently throwing darts at the side of my head. "I'm going to go grab the grocery lists, and then we can head out." I snap my fingers as I remember something. "That's something you'll start doing too. Every night, you'll pull the next day's recipes and make a grocery list for us to shop in the morning."

"Okay." She slips our breakfast plates into the dishwasher and catches me smile. "What?"

I shrug. "I didn't even have to ask you to rinse those before you stuck them in the dishwasher."

She laughs, and I can tell I've triggered something. "My mom would have murdered me if she caught me sticking dirty dishes in the dishwasher.

"You'd be surprised how many people do it."

When she's done, she grabs her purse, and I grab the cart. We start down the short slope and head around the corner to the market. I can't help but notice the way her eyes grow wide when she sees the main entrance to Pike Place.

"I thought we were going to a grocery store."

"Nope. Why go to the store when you can walk one block to the best farmers market in the Pacific Northwest?"

We start down the main road, walking slowly as she gazes around. "This place is like a street market on crack."

I throw my head back and laugh. "Welcome to the farm-to-table life, Maggie. Everything is fresh and local. As in, I know exactly where everything is coming from. And whatever I can't buy fresh, like the condiments, we make in the kitchen.

For the first time since I've known Maggie, she looks deeply awed by the way I run my kitchen. My chest puffs with pleasure, knowing I just accomplished something monumental.

"Want to pick out some fresh flowers while I start down the produce aisle?"

She nods emphatically, and I feel like I'm two for two. Maybe working with Maggie won't be so bad after all.

"What's on today's menu?" she asks as she returns with a handful of flowers and rests them in the cart.

"Besides a private party I'm delivering food for, I want to try out a new recipe: meatloaf with a side of mac and cheese, fresh salad, and green beans." I peek at her to see if she has any aversions to any of the mentioned foods, but she doesn't give anything away.

"Simple enough."

I chuckle. "You should know by now, nothing in my kitchen is as simple as it sounds."

A smile teeters on her lips. "Guess you're right, but how hard can making meatloaf really be? It's just a slab of meat, some onions, ketchup—what else?"

"Oh, Maggie. You just earned yourself a cooking lesson when we get back to the kitchen."

She moans and throws me a look that tells me I'm trying to do her dirty. "Really? I thought I had all this training to do."

"Consider this part of your training. I still need to test this recipe, so you'll be my sample student."

"I don't suppose a certificate comes with that?"

I snort. "Not a chance."

We finish our first shopping experience together and manage to make it back to the kitchen without sharpening our claws. In fact, this may be the longest we've been around each other without getting into some kind of fight.

She helps me unload the cart, and then we immediately start on today's recipe. I guide Maggie like I would in a normal class. I don't want to tell her that this actually isn't part of the job. Gretta never helped me cook and test my new recipes. The only time she would sample anything I made was when she would steal food from the refrigerator during her lunch hours.

"Sun-dried tomatoes and basil? Really?" she asks when I hand her the jar of tomatoes I dried yesterday. "That's different."

"It's not all that's different. Instead of breadcrumbs or crushed Cheez-Its, we're going to use the oatmeal we grabbed at the market today."

She makes a face but starts slicing the tomatoes into slivers. I watch the way she holds the knife perfectly, with her fingers tucked back toward her hands so she doesn't cut herself. It looks like Maggie picked up more from my classes than she ever let on.

"Now what?" she asks, resting the knife on the cutting board.

"Do you remember how to cut the basil?"

She makes a face. "I don't think so. Show me again?"

I force back my smile, loving the way she just asked me that. Then I step behind her and wrap my arms around hers. It's completely unnecessary, but I tell myself that this will give me a feel for her technique. In fact, this position is becoming all too familiar when Maggie and I are in the kitchen together. When I'm this close to her, I get to smell the mango scent that rises from her skin and the cherry lip balm I've seen her apply too many times.

"Stack," I say while helping her gather enough basil for the recipe. "Then roll, just like this." I move her hands in mine, ignoring the way my heart pounds heavily in my chest. "And then snip."

She takes scissors to the stems as I step away from her, knowing that at any second, she'll feel closer to me than she ever wanted to. But if I could describe my biggest turn-on, it would be this. Cooking with this woman. There's something about it that's so innocent and intimate at the same time. Yet it's something I've never done with a girlfriend. Not that I've had many of those.

"I bet the ladies you bring home love this."

There she goes, reading my mind again.

"Love what exactly?" I want to hear her say it.

She eyes me with amusement. "A man cooking for a woman. The whole reverse-stereotype thing."

"Is that still a thing?"

"According to the men I've gone out with, yes."

"Well, clearly you've been going out with the wrong men. I promise you, that is not the way we all think. And I'm not just talking about guys like me who happen to own a cooking school. I'm talking about every guy I know that does most of the cooking at home."

Maggie blushes and shrugs before turning back to the stove, where she has the freshly chopped ingredients slow cooking. "I guess I didn't know those kinds of guys really existed."

I watch her face intently as she stirs, wondering who Maggie Stevens really is. Who is the woman behind the camera-ready makeup and trendy clothes? There's no question in my mind that there's more to her than first appearances. I may have neglected to see that before, but now that she's here and unavoidable, I have an intense desire to peel back more and more layers.

And that's exactly what I intend to do.

Auditions

MAGGIE

Desmond is walking me through creating a grocery list based on the recipe for tomorrow when the door to Edible Desire opens. In comes Faye with her short blond bob, tan spike heels, and effortless smile. She's a woman on a mission, seemingly always ready to set the world on fire. I can feel it in her presence, the same way I would when a supermodel walked into the room in Los Angeles.

And right now, the world is Faye's oyster, and Desmond is her pearl. I see the way her eyes lock on him like a prowling tiger ready to pounce. Clearly the two have been more than business associates. It's written all over the way she lifts her lips in a sexy smile.

A jolt of jealousy hits me in the chest, but something about Desmond's reaction relieves me some. When he sees Faye, his jaw locks, and his shoulders stiffen. It's almost like he's growing uncomfortable with the woman who is promising him the world. Or maybe that's my wishful hoping.

"You're early," Desmond says, stepping away from me and leaving a draft behind him as he meets Faye halfway.

"Only by fifteen minutes, darling." She places her hands on his broad shoulders and reaches up on her tiptoes to kiss his cheek. "Everything ready for the crew?"

"I suppose. Do you need me to clear out an area?"

"No, but…" She taps her mouth as she looks around the space. Then she points at a cooking station near the front of the room. "There. We'll put them at the cooking station at the front. Is that okay?"

Desmond shrugs and waves his hand for her to check the station out further. "What are you going to ask them to do exactly?"

"Oh, you know. I'll just go over some basic questions and get a feel for how they take to the camera in a more personal setting. If I'm feeling good about someone, I'll ask you to come in and chat with them a little. Just ask them about themselves, about their cooking history, comfortability level, that kind of thing."

"Sounds like a plan."

After that, Faye begins to wander around the kitchen, inspecting the place, while I move back to the station I'm sitting at in the back of the room, trying my best to focus on the task at hand. It seems easy enough. I'm supposed to write down each fresh ingredient needed then categorize it by food department.

"Hey." Desmond comes up behind me with a piece of paper in his hands. "This is a list of everyone confirmed for classes starting tomorrow. Can you just call and leave a friendly reminder for each one? Start with tomorrow's classes, and you don't have to finish the week's worth today, but I like to give them at least twenty-four hours of a heads-up."

I nod and take a seat on the stool while he walks back over to Faye. Soon, a few men are walking through the door with lighting equipment, microphones, and cameras. They begin to listen to Faye's instructions while Desmond keeps himself busy at the front, prepping a meal for today's delivery.

My eyes are trained on the set designer, who manages to turn what was once a normal cooking station into an eye-catching focal point for the lens.

"Um, sweetie?" Faye calls out.

My eyes snap to hers, confused by the endearment. "Huh? Me?"

"Her name is Maggie," Desmond offers, and I'm thankful for the help.

"I'm sorry. *Maggie*. Do you mind stepping out of the shot? Perhaps Desmond can set you up in the back room so you won't be a distraction."

Oh, hell no. Heat flashes through me, but before I can say anything, Desmond is jolting from whatever he was doing and starts making his way to me. "You can use my office."

When I don't budge, he reaches for the paper he handed me earlier and leans in toward me. "It's only for a couple hours, and it's not like you'll be able to make phone calls out here with the auditions going on."

I blow out a frustrated breath and nod. "Whatever. But I won't let her tell me what to do again."

Desmond chuckles. "I believe you."

I follow Desmond closely as he leads me into the back room, which is filled with rows of scoopable bulk items like grains, seeds, flour, and nuts. There's a set of bathrooms for guests, a locker area for students to place their items while they're in class, and an elevator that I recently learned will take me up to my new apartment or down to the parking garage. In the very corner of the room, tucked behind a storage room, is Desmond's office, which I've never even seen.

He pushes open the door to expose a disaster of a space. There are papers and boxes everywhere, covering his desk, the couch, and the file cabinet. "Just ignore the mess. I'm barely in here."

"Yeah, probably because you can't even walk inside it without surfing across the floor. Holy shit, Desmond. How can you find anything in here?"

He shrugs, seeming to not care. "I don't. Everything is electronic now. Most of this can probably be tossed, but I need to go through it first. I guess Gretta never got around to it."

I bite the inside of my lip to keep from laughing. "No wonder why she flaked on you so much. Desmond, this is pretty bad."

He sighs. "I need to get back out there. Are you going to be able to make your calls in here, or do I need to set you up in the storage closet instead?"

I roll my eyes and push past him toward the desk. I pick up a pile of papers sitting on his chair and place it on another teetering stack on his desk. "I'll be good. I'm sure there's a phone here somewhere."

Desmond's jaw ticks with annoyance. "You'll figure it out." Then he closes the door behind him without another word.

Looking around, I sigh and take a seat before searching for the phone, which I find under another pile of papers. By the looks of it, the mess is just a pile of junk that can be digitally stored and then recycled: recipes, invoices, class lists, receipts, and bills. But I ignore it for the sake of my mission at hand — phone calls, mostly voice mails.

Two hours later, I'm done with my calls and drowning in boredom. I didn't even realize that I'd been organizing the piles of papers on Desmond's desk as I was talking. *Now what?* I look around and frown. This room is so boring. It has no windows and no personality. The only touch of anything interesting is another one of Desmond's signature food photos. This one is of a man's hand pressed into a ball of dough. There's flour everywhere — on his hands, all over the wood table, and on the dough itself. But the coolest part of the visual are the bits of flour in midair that appear to be falling onto the table.

I've noticed a trend with Desmond's photography, and I would be lying if I didn't admit that I am deeply impressed. The man knows how to express his emotions well with words, but he damn well knows how to evoke all the feeling imaginable from a photograph. He has a rare gift, and I'm not sure he even knows it.

I shuffle a stack of papers off a hard black object. It's Desmond's camera. *Well, well, speaking of photography...* I recognize it as the one he had in his hands at the game yesterday. Curious, I pick it up and press the power button.

A photo immediately appears in the display on the back of the camera, and I bite my bottom lip over a laugh. I almost forget about the impromptu shoot of me scarfing down my hot dog. Desmond didn't argue about stopping, but it looks like he'd been at it for longer than I realized. I tap through the photos, admiring his eye for live-action food photography. If that's a thing, Desmond is a master at it.

Before the hot dog shoot, there are the photos I saw him taking during Saturday's class. Meal after meal, I find myself mesmerized with the imagery the man is able to conjure up with a simple photo. I must go through hundreds of photos before I spot one of me again. This time, I'm the prime focus of the photo, and I'm standing at my cooking station, agonizing over my lobster ravioli.

Well, agonizing is how I remember it. But that certainly isn't the same word I would use to describe myself in these photos. I look content, focused, and perhaps like I'm enjoying myself while I get lost in it all.

"Huh." I set the camera down and shut it off. That's when I notice a small monitor sitting near Desmond's computer. I push the power button and jump back when a black-and-white view of the main kitchen comes to life in front of me, sound and all.

There's a young woman, probably in her thirties, speaking while Faye asks her questions from off camera. Now this is interesting. I smile as I cozy in to watch the poor girl get flustered when simply asked to act natural. That's all it takes to get her ejected from the shoot to make room for the next girl that walks in.

Three failed auditions later, I'm still glued to the entertainment, but Desmond's desk is also as organized as can be. I managed to straighten the array of papers into piles: receipts, bills, recipes, and old promotional flyers. Everything is still in desperate need of filing or tossing, which I would have started on if it weren't for the door to the office that opens, causing me to jump.

"What are you doing?" Desmond's tone is accusing. His eyes move over his desk and then to the security monitor that I've been watching like it's showing a daytime soap opera. He moves toward me and pushes the power button to shut off the monitor. "You were watching that train wreck?"

I look up and stifle a laugh. "Yup. But don't worry. I finished all my calls and organized your desk while watching mindless entertainment. No harm done."

His eyes narrow. "I'll have you know, that mindless entertainment is going to bring a lot of attention to this cooking school. And what do you mean you organized my desk?"

I ignore his last question and focus on his first statement. "Attention? Is that what you're after? In that case, why not just have Zach announce he owns the place? That'll bring in all the attention you need."

Desmond scrunches his face. "I want genuine interest only. Besides, Zach's barely around. You think I have the patience to handle the hordes of women that will show up just to see him? I don't have that kind of time to waste."

"I don't think you have much patience at all, but if it's the attention you want, then what does it matter? Besides, since when do you complain about being surrounded by hordes of women?" I laugh at the sound of my own question.

Desmond doesn't appear to be amused. "Like I said, I want genuine attention and interest. Can you imagine if all the students who walked through this door were like you?"

"Hey," I say defensively. *Someone's in a bad mood.*

"Oh, don't get all sensitive now. You didn't want to be in my class almost as much as you don't want to be here right now."

I stand up, wondering how I almost started to tolerate this man—that's a mystery in itself. He's just as awful as he was when I first met him. "Well, we're both stuck with each other, aren't we? So do yourself a favor and get over what I want and don't want. Okay?" I slide past him, nudging him with my elbow as I pass. "Oh, and you're welcome for cleaning up your desk. Maybe you can actually sit at it now."

I'm fuming as I walk out into the main kitchen and notice that everyone is gone. I don't know if they just took a lunch break because there's still lighting equipment everywhere and the camera is still focused on the empty cooking station in the front row. "Whatever," I mutter as I walk behind the large island that overlooks the room. I can't believe I actually thought this could work. *Me working with Desmond? Yeah, right.* We'll kill each other before the end of the week.

Desmond walks up behind me and opens the refrigerator. He hands me a bottled water then takes the cap off the one he grabbed for himself. "Thank you for organizing my desk. You didn't have to do that."

I shrug. "I won't touch it again. I didn't even mean to do it. It just kind of happened."

His lips tip up at the corner, and he chugs half a bottle of water before setting it down on the island. "Be careful. I might ask you to organize the rest of my office. Heaven knows I need the help."

"You need lots of that."

He glares at me again, but this time there's a gleam in his eyes. "Maybe so. How about we start here? I've got another meal to prep before everyone returns from lunch. Will you help me?"

"Sure," I mutter dryly. "Whatever you need, boss."

Desmond walks me through the recipes, and we split up, grabbing ingredients and making different parts of the meal. When I don't understand something, Desmond comes over and walks me through it with a gentleness I never witnessed when I was a student in his classes. He always seemed to get so impatient with me. But he can alter his tune all he wants. It doesn't change the animosity I have toward him now.

"What are you doing?" he asks, approaching me with a light laugh.

I look down at the green beans I'm shelling and shrug. "Removing the bean things."

He tosses his head back and laughs harder. "Why?"

My mouth drops. Is he really laughing at me right now? "Because they're in the pod. Isn't that what I'm supposed to do?"

He shakes his head and steps behind me, a lot like how he did the other day. "You've never eaten a green bean whole?"

I look down at my work and suddenly feel heat spread over my cheeks. "I mean, yeah, but…" I feel totally humiliated. But just like that, all the tension that has built up between us starts to fade away like magic.

He wraps his hand around mine. "Just cut off the ends, like this. Not too much." He starts cutting off the ends of the green beans while his mouth is coming dangerously close to my ear. "We don't want to waste any of the good stuff."

My body is hot all over from the rasp of his tone and the heat of his breath. My heart rate takes off at a mile a minute. Not even the force of my steady breaths can stop it. There's this intensity between Desmond and me that is so undeniable, so unshakeable. I don't even question that he feels it too.

My eyes meet his from over my shoulder, and I gasp at the sharpness in his gaze. Never has a man made me feel so whole with just one look. But it's like Desmond sees me, even the parts I never let anyone see, and he won't stop peeling back the layers until he sees all of me.

I might just let him.

His tongue darts out and wets his bottom lip while he moves in closer... closer... until one slight forward movement is all it will take for his lips to touch mine. Suddenly, it's all I want. But just as my eyes close, I'm startled by the sound of the backroom door opening behind us.

I gasp while Desmond curses so quietly, only I can hear. Then Faye walks in with a knowing smile.

What the— Has she been here the whole time?

She holds up her phone as if to answer my question. "I'm done with my call. Desmond, do you want to grab lunch before we reconvene?"

Desmond takes a step to the side of me, but he looks as if he's struggling with his response. "I need to finish a meal for a pickup later today. Sorry, Faye."

"Dinner, then?" she presses, and for some reason, I get the feeling she's testing him.

Desmond shakes his head again. "I really can't tonight either. Another day, yeah?"

She smiles, tight-lipped, her eyes shifting to me while mine turn down, and then she nods. "You two are quite the team these days, aren't you?"

I let out a nervous laugh, and Desmond's eyes snap to me. Instinct tells me to jump in here. "Hardly," I say with a wink in his direction. "But it pays the bills, you know?"

Faye quirks a brow. "Is that so?"

"Faye, stop," Desmond warns.

I look between the two of them, wondering what the hell is going on, because something feels off, and I feel like I'm in the middle of whatever silent exchange is happening between them.

Faye faces me, her entire body centered toward mine, and I feel like I need to brace myself for whatever is to come.

"Maggie," she starts.

"Faye," I return with all the sarcasm I can fathom.

"I have a proposition for you."

My jaw drops, and I turn to Desmond, who's shaking his head and rubbing his neck like he's already tried to stop this exchange from happening. I wasn't expecting that. There's only one thing she could possibly be talking about, and there's no way in hell I'm getting in front of that camera.

I turn back to Faye with an answer already on the tip of my tongue. "I'm sorry, Faye, but I'm not interested."

Five O'Clock Somewhere

DESMOND

Faye left Maggie and me alone after the last audition, taking her camera crew with her. I guess it's a done deal. Maggie isn't interested in the role, no matter how hard Faye tried to persuade her, and we still don't have a cohost.

The entire dynamic in the kitchen feels like it has shifted. Hours ago, I was one cohost away from having a television show that could help me advance the kitchen. And now I have no fucking clue.

I don't know if I should be furious at Faye or Maggie or neither of them. For the past four years, the kitchen has been mine. Suddenly, the fate of my dreams is resting on two women I never sought after, one of whose hands are currently reaching into the refrigerator and pulling out a beer.

"What are you doing?" I grumble.

"Drinking a beer. Want one?"

I step forward and take the bottle from her hand. "You're still on the clock."

She rips the bottle back and lifts it to her lips. "Consider me clocked out for the day."

There's a layer of spite beneath her tone that sends chills down my spine. I pull the bottle back to me and hold it over her head. "Don't be angry with me. That was all Faye's idea."

"Yeah, well, you didn't try to stop her."

"I didn't have a chance, did I?" I glare down at her with a warning. She's not the only one fired up over this. "And it doesn't matter, does it? You said no. But I can't for the life of me figure out why someone who was practically born in the spotlight would turn an opportunity like that down. Isn't the camera kind of your thing?"

"Not anymore," Maggie growls. Then she makes a jump for the bottle, accidentally bumping her chest against mine in the process. I try to ignore the heat that licks through me at the mere touch of our bodies.

"Excuse me," she says with a stomp of her foot. "I earned that."

"Correction. You'll *earn* it at the end of your shift when I release you for the day."

Maggie crosses her arms and leans back against the island. "Fine. But since we're talking about earning things, what are you even getting out of this show anyway? Do you even want to do it?"

I nod.

"Why?"

"Because I have goals for the kitchen that are reliant on the extra income. The show is a quick way to reach those goals."

"What kind of goals?"

I let out a heavy breath, trying to keep my frustration at bay. "I'd like to expand our offerings. I'd like to hire more employees so maybe I can enjoy a few days off now and then without taking a huge hit."

"Okay." She thinks for a moment. "So maybe you need a little bit of cash. Can't Zach just give you what you need? He is your partner. And according to ESPN, the dude is loaded."

I snort. "You seem to think Zach's pocketbook is the solution to everything. That's not how our partnership works. Zach might have purchased this place, but it's me who runs it. It's me who makes the big decisions. And if I decide to expand, it'll be me who will fork over the dough to do it."

"Okay, suit yourself. Guess a cooking show is the way to go, then." She reaches for something on the counter, and I laugh when I see it's the beer I told her not to drink.

Oh, what the hell? It's Monday, which means no one else will be popping into the kitchen. I reach into the refrigerator and pull another beer out so I can join her. I lean against the island she's now sitting on. "So you really won't be my cohost, huh?"

She shakes her head. "I don't think I can." This time, she cuts me an apologetic glance, and I can feel her sincerity. "But I'm sure Faye will find you the perfect girl."

I blow out another breath, feeling the stress of the day slowly decompressing in my system. "I don't know. You saw some of those auditions. Nothing felt even remotely right."

Maggie twists her lips. "The cohost thing was Faye's idea, wasn't it? What is she looking for exactly? Maybe you can just do the show on your own."

I chew the inside of my lip while shaking my head. "The network wasn't into it just being me. Faye actually got the idea of a cohost by watching you and I work together." I laugh at the memory of how bizarrely well we worked together last Saturday. "*You* were her inspiration."

Something in Maggie's expression has a squeezing effect in my chest. "Faye did make it sound like you needed me desperately." She smiles softly. "Just think. If I did accept, I'd probably have the money to get my own place and get out of your hair."

"It's only been a few days, Maggie. Besides, I don't think it's such a bad arrangement. I know you just started, but you're helping me plenty. And who knows if this show is going to take off. Please don't try to find a way out of here because you think I want you gone."

"Good to know you don't."

"Good to know you care what I think for once." I can feel a ridiculous grin on my face and force it into something more professional. "And I'm serious about the beer drinkin'. We'll make the booze an exception today, but from now on, if you want to have a glass of wine during a class with the rest of the students, that's fine. Or if you want to crack one once your shift is over, fine by me. But no other time."

She tilts her head and presses the bottle to her lips, amused. "You realize what time it is, right?"

I look up at the clock and almost choke on my next sip. "Six o'clock."

"Good thing you don't pay me overtime."

I look back at Maggie, who winks, and then I chuckle. "All right, smart ass, you win. So then what are you still doing here if you're off the clock?"

"Having a happy hour with my new boss. What else would I be doing?"

Ignoring her last remark, I decide to push our newfound understanding a bit further. "What do you feel like for dinner? I owe you a meal."

Maggie hops off the counter and downs the rest of her beer. "No time. I've got a gig with White Water tonight."

"Where?"

She shrugs and tosses her bottle into recycling. "At some concert venue."

A new feeling comes over me, something achy, that makes me feel like I might miss her when she's gone. "I can give you a ride when you're ready to leave."

I'm expecting Maggie to decline my offer, but then she turns to me like she's really considering it and then nods. "Yeah, okay. I need to shower first. Will you be ready to go in an hour?"

"How about you come back down here in forty-five so I can feed you before we leave?"

She grins. "Deal."

TAKE FOUR

Reminder

"EVERY DAY IS THE START OF SOMETHING BEAUTIFUL."
— MATT NATHANSON, ALL WE ARE

Show Time

MAGGIE

Desmond is waiting for me at the curb after our quick dinner. The engine is already running and ready for our getaway. Why he's always so insistent to drive me everywhere is not something I'm going to question anymore, but one thing is as troubling as it is certain — I like it more than I should.

In the back of my mind, I know that the niceties are just that — gestures meant to appease his best friend and my sister more than they are favors to me. I understand that and accept it, but that doesn't change who Desmond is to me. *The cocky chef with an ego the size of the state he was born in.* Yes, things are truly bigger in Texas.

It's all too complicated. It's also something I'm not ready to untangle.

I approach the passenger door with a fluttering heart and no clue what to do with it. I'm wearing a faded jean jacket over a White Water tank top, black jeans, and white high-top sneakers. It's going to be a chilly night, so it's the sexiest I can look while I promote the vodka brand.

As soon as I slip into my seat, I feel right at home. I inhale the old leather like it's oxygen before I notice Desmond watching me from his seat. I face his curious gaze with a bashful smile. "What?" I'm immediately on the defensive, knowing he just caught me inhaling his ride. Can he blame me? It's a sexy beast of a machine.

He shakes his head and shifts the car into Drive. "Nothing. You just looked relaxed for a second, that's all."

"You say that like it would be a bad thing."

A smile tilts his lips as he nods. "You're usually on the edge. You know, hyper, ready to jump down my throat."

"Maybe that's because you were an arrogant prick when we first met."

"I beg to disagree."

"You can beg me all you want, but you were still an asshole."

Desmond scoffs. "I recall flirting you under the table the entire first day you came to class. You seemed to like it too. What happened to that girl?"

"Woman," I correct. "And that was before I realized you have a thing for flirting girls under the table."

Desmond chuckles. "And you were disappointed?"

"More like disgusted."

He shrugs. "Well, I've known you for a few months now, and you've never gotten sick in my presence, so I'd say your version of disgusted is all right by me."

"It's not too late. We are stuck together twenty-four, seven these days. Anything could happen."

Desmond bites down on his bottom lip like he's suppressing a smile, and I can't help but do a double take at his long, disheveled hair, bright-blue eyes, and rugged beard. He's not at all the type I would have ever found attractive back in LA. But for some reason, looking at him now, I can't help but wonder what those whiskers would feel like between my thighs, or what that pouty mouth would feel like on my pink flesh. Desmond may not look like any man I would have ever dated in LA, but he sure as hell resembles someone I wouldn't mind getting it on with now.

"I'm counting on that," he says.

For a second, I have to tear my thoughts away from the mental image of him buried between my legs to remember what I said to prompt that response.

Anything could happen.

I choose not to respond and instead reach for the dial of the stereo. I turn it to my favorite radio station. As soon as I hear Matt Nathanson singing through the speakers, I squeal and twist my shoulders to the beat. I'll always be a country girl at heart, no matter what influence the city has had on me, but Matt Nathanson on the piano is something to be marveled. I've loved him since I caught a concert of his at a hole-in-the-wall bar in LA.

"I love this song," Desmond says, surprising me with an approving nod.

I can feel my eyes light up when I turn to him. "Me too."

I still forget that he was born in the same city as me. But at moments like these when I catch the slight twang of country that slips off his tongue and notice his flare of Southern hospitality evidently displayed in his kitchen and recipes, I realize what attracted me to him in the first place. Desmond reminds me of home.

He starts to drive down First Avenue and shoots me a quick glance. "You going to tell me where this show is tonight? Key Arena? Showbox?"

"Paramount. I probably could have walked." The moment the words are out of my mouth, I cringe, bracing for his reaction.

He cuts me a look, and that's the only response I need.

"Okay, okay. I'm sorry I said anything. I appreciate the ride."

"Good." It's silent between us while we listen to the rest of the song. Then Desmond clears his throat. "How do you like working for White Water?"

I shrug. "They pay me well. The jobs are fun and easy enough for something temporary."

Desmond's brows pull together. "You keep using that word."

I squint in confusion. "What word?"

He throws me another glance. "Temporary."

"I guess I do. It's just… weird being here. Clearly, I don't belong. I'm not sure if I ever will."

"Well, what are your goals while you're here?"

His loaded question throws me off balance, and even after I think about it for a few long moments, I'm not sure how to answer. "I'm just… figuring that out, I guess."

Silence passes between us, and a sort of anger brews inside me. "Why does everyone expect me to have all the answers right now? Why can't I just live in the moment and figure it out as I go?"

Desmond scrunches his nose. "No one is saying you can't."

"Well, it feels like that's exactly what you're saying."

"Maybe that's because it's exactly what you're thinking. It's definitely not what I'm saying. Live your temporary life. Live it loud. Live it proud. Doesn't matter to me. I was just trying to make conversation."

For some reason, his nonchalance only stirs me up more. "Haven't you ever been through a transition in your life? When you didn't have all your shit figured out?"

Desmond chuckles. "If you ever meet someone who does have their shit figured out, then I'd love to meet them."

"You're such a smart-ass."

"I am, but I'm not trying to be right now. You're allowed your little transition period, Maggie. I'm not judging you for it, even though I know that's what you want to believe. You're human. You just left a career you've had practically your whole life. But most people don't just live their life in temporary mode. They live in the present. They set goals for themselves to grow and change and adapt to those changes. Maybe you should just stop calling everything in your life temporary."

I settle back into my seat, adjusting my eyes away from the brawny, rugged man from the South, and direct my gaze out the window. I take in the night lights of Seattle as we cruise down First Avenue. Traffic crowds the roads, but we are still moving at a decent pace, only stopping at the red lights while pedestrians cross the street.

Seattle is a truly fascinating place, and that was one of my first thoughts after moving here. It's a city of blended culture, of loud and vibrant artistic types with wild-colored hair and leather platform shoes. It's also a place where, when the sun shines, happiness bursts from the city's pores. Boats crowd the lakes and sounds. Parks are filled with sunbathers and picnic blankets. Music takes over the Seattle Center. Life is celebrated in its most natural form, and I find it completely addicting.

Desmond pulls up to the curb and brakes a little harder than I expect, jerking me forward and back against my seat.

"Thanks for the whiplash." I smile and bat my lashes at him so he can feel my sarcasm. "I mean, for the ride."

His eyes aren't on me, though. I'm not even sure if he heard me. He's fixated on the marquee of the Paramount, with his mouth agape. It's all lit up with white bulb lights around the name of the headliner.

"No shit," he says. "Matt Nathanson's playing tonight? The guy that was just on the radio?"

I let out a little chuckle. "Yup. Wanna come to the show?"

He twists his face, like he's confused, or maybe a little stunned. "Just like that? Are you serious?"

I shrug. "White Water gave me two tickets in case I wanted to bring someone. I was planning to find some loner outside the venue to see if he wanted to come with me, but I guess you can have my extra ticket if you want."

He catches my joke referencing yesterday's game and narrows his eyes at me. "Do I have to promise you I'll have a good time too?"

I bite my lip and hand him the ticket. "You set the rules. Now it's your turn to follow them."

He snatches the ticket from my hand. "Consider it a deal."

Grinning, I make a move to open the door. "Guess you better go find a parking spot. I need to get to work, but I'll see you inside." I hop out of the car and head straight toward the security guard at the front of the building. I show him my

White Water pass, and he shoos me in with a wave of his hand. "Have a good time."

I give him a smile over my shoulder just as I see Desmond's red car turn into the parking lot down the street. My confused heart pounds in my chest. "Thanks. I think I just might."

Limitations

DESMOND

Maggie is already inside and making her way through the growing crowd with a tray of White Water shots by the time I finally get in. In the time it took me to park and walk back to the entrance, the line to get in had wrapped around the building. Apparently, Maggie has some sort of special access, which makes me reconsider my feelings toward her "temporary" life. The perks of her side job don't seem bad at all. She has flexibility, a decent payout, free booze, and concert tickets. And she seems to genuinely enjoy it all. Maybe a temporary life isn't so bad.

The stuck-up model with designer boots and flawless appearance who initially walked into my kitchen with a confidence level so high, not even I could compete with — is transforming before my very eyes. At a turtle's pace for sure, but she's transforming no doubt. Every time I manage to pluck a feather and piss her off more, I get rewarded with a special peek under the armor she's so carefully built. There is more to Maggie Stevens than meets the eye, and now I'm more curious than ever to discover it all.

She's the first woman I see when I walk into the Paramount, and even as I down two drinks while sitting idly at a high-top table in the back of the concert hall, I can't peel my eyes from her. Maggie dazzles.

"One White Water soda and lime," she says cheerfully as she sets my drink in front of me. "Great choice."

I decided to step out of my comfort zone of beer and support the reason I'm here tonight. "Thanks." I flash her a smile and take a sip of the carefully concocted beverage. "When do you get to join me?"

"Um…" Her eyes drift toward the stage and pause on the crew fiddling around with equipment.

The very moment she looks away, my gaze slips to her fitted, sleeveless tank. It's black with White Water's logo on the front, and a deep slit down the middle reveals her chest. At some point between her exiting my car and me entering the venue, her jean jacket vanished, and the bright-red lipstick on her lips appeared. Her light-brown eyes have never popped more than they do in this moment, and I have the strongest yearning to see the same contrast in natural light through my camera's lens.

When she caught me snapping photos of her at the game yesterday, I was not only shocked by her response but disappointed by it. The photos of her going down on that hot dog were completely natural, vulnerable, and raw. Through the lens, she's the woman with no faults, no worries, and no fears. But on the other side of it, there's much, much more, and her reaction confirmed it. There is something she's hiding.

My eyes are planted on her lips when her gaze shoots back to me. My head snaps up, but it's too late. I'm sure she just caught me staring.

"I'm off the clock when the openers are done, but you don't have to wait for me."

My reactions to her all feel so instinctual, protective even. There's an inflation in my chest as I breathe in slowly, controlling the intake of air like my life depends on it. "I'll be here until you're done." I take another sip of my drink and nod with approval. "These are good."

Her eyes light up, and I get the distinct impression that she's proud of what she's promoting. I wonder if there's an insincere bone in her body. When Maggie hates something, she's vocal about it. When she loves something, she doesn't seem to hold back. There are so many qualities to her that I find sexy. Who would have thought? And to think she's been holding back all this time, masking something so vulnerably beautiful. I want more of it. I want more of her.

"I'll keep 'em coming, then."

I tip my head, and she starts to walk away. I watch her sway as she goes, realizing my physical attraction to her is more intense than ever. I'm taking in every detail of her movements, of her body. She's got length made for the runway and enough curves to make a fantastic lingerie model. I'm not ashamed to admit I've given a proper assessment to her ass and tits, and I've determined they are the perfect size. I can almost imagine how they would feel in my palms. But imagining isn't enough for the raging hard-on making an appearance in my jeans. He's restless and hungry. Fuck that.

He's starved and triggered by the sun-kissed brunette beauty looking entirely too hot to be single.

By the time the opening act starts playing, I'm buzzing pretty well off of two drinks. I need to slow down, but Maggie brings me another one without me even requesting it. "Don't worry, Chef, I'm counting your drinks. The first one was pretty weak, so let's just say this is number two."

"Uh, no." I shake my head. "A rule is a rule."

She narrows her lids and twists up the corner of her mouth. *Adorable as fuck.* "Okay, fine. But I'm more than happy to take one for the team and drive you home tonight if you have one too many."

Her words are so innocent, and for the first time since my last shit-faced experience in high school, I'm tempted to test my limits just so I can have an excuse to let her take care of me. That would be something. Besides Coach and Zach, I feel like it's been me taking care of the world for as long as I can remember.

But instead of saying any of that, I give Maggie a wink and lift my new drink to my mouth. "Sorry to burst your bubble, darlin', but you're not driving my car. In fact, I think you just gave me all the more reason to stop at number three tonight."

She pushes away from the table with a huff and a laugh. "I'll be back by before my shift ends, and then we can get closer to watch the show."

I nod and watch her walk off again, but this time, I notice I'm not the only one. A group of guys a few tables away are following her movements with their beady little eyes. One of them reaches his hand out to stop her as she goes by. I sit up straight, ready to swoop in and pull his hand away if necessary, but I'm not needed.

Maggie takes an immediate step back, gives him a tight-lipped smile, says something, and walks away. The man shifts his stance, his cocky smirk dissolving into something resembling annoyance or discomfort. Maybe it's a mixture of both since his friends are throwing jabs his way. *Serves him right.* And I should have known Maggie could take care of herself just fine.

The opener is on and off the stage within the hour, and just as promised, Maggie approaches me with not one, not two, but three drinks in her hands. Well, two of them are shots and the other is a vodka soda. I immediately start to reject them. "Whoa, Nelly."

Maggie laughs. "Have one or none—I don't care—but I'm taking a shot." She reaches for a glass and lifts it to her lips while staring back at me, waiting. Before she can slam it back, I'm picking up the other shot and lifting it to my lips, mirroring her.

"This is number four. Who's that drink for?"

She grins. "Me. I figure I have some catching up to do."

"You figured right."

We toss back our shots and set the glasses on the table. I reach my hand out to hers. She looks at it for a few seconds before finally slipping her small fingers inside of mine. I'm not surprised by how soft they are—most women's hands are small and soft—but I'm surprised by how much I like the feel of hers inside mine, how they fit perfectly when nothing else about us in my life seems to fit.

We head into the crowd where a herd of concertgoers is pushing their way toward the front of the still-growing crowd. I start to move in their direction with the intention of getting us as close to the front as possible when I feel a tug on my hand and turn around.

Maggie is shaking her head and pointing at the side wall. "I'd be perfectly happy standing over there."

I let her lead the way.

"Ah," I say as I lean against the wood panel. There's a clear view of the stage, and we're free of shoving, sweaty bodies. "This is perfect."

She twists and gives me a full-fledged grin. "I agree. And now I have somewhere I can put my drink." She reaches over me and sets her glass on a tall, round table before facing the front, just as Matt Nathanson makes his way to the stage.

All eyes in the building are on him as he sits down at his piano. He doesn't take a beat of a pause before he's playing the opening melody of "Giants." It's an upbeat number with a chill vibe that gets the crowd moving. Arms are in the air, lips are mouthing the lyrics, and hips are swaying.

By the end of the first song, more people have made their way down to the main floor, filling all the empty spaces around us. Maggie doesn't seem to notice at all. She's still twisting her shoulders to the rhythm and singing every word to that song, and the next one, and the next.

My eyes keep flicking between her and the stage. She's kind of adorable when she lets loose like this, oblivious to everything and everyone around her, including the prick from the bar who starts to inch his way closer. She didn't seem to appreciate his advances earlier, so I don't know what the hell he thinks he's doing now.

The dude has the nerve to sidle right up beside Maggie, appearing drunk as fuck. I don't even think Maggie has noticed him yet, but she scoots closer to me anyway. For the second time tonight, the guy doesn't get the hint. He leans in, presses his lips right up to her ear, and starts to say something, causing her to jump.

I do what I should have done earlier tonight and place a hand on the guy's chest to hold him back. Then I wrap my hand around Maggie's arm and tug her closer until she's standing directly in front of me instead of on the side. "Time for you to find another place to stand, dude." My voice is calm, but there's no misplacing my warning.

He gives me a look like I just threatened his life and cocks his head to the side. "Excuse me?"

"You heard me." I give him a little push with my palm, and he stumbles back as if I socked him. *Yup. Definitely drunk off his ass.*

When his friends help steady him, he starts to charge toward me. His friends are smart enough to hold him back. Then they pull him away completely, earning me an unreadable glance from Maggie.

"What?" I ask with an upward tick of my jaw.

She bats those long, pretty lashes at me, feigning innocence, and shrugs before turning back around. I take note that she makes no move to stand beside me again. Instead, she wiggles her ass mere inches from my front. I try my damnedest not to inhale her sweet scent as I watch her move, but it's impossible. *She really needs to stop moving like that.*

In a desperate attempt to distract her from dancing, I reach beside me to the table, grab her drink, and hand it to her over her shoulder. She sips on it, but her ass fails to stop moving, and I swear if it doesn't, I will not survive this night.

The next song, "Faster," is another upbeat one about the singer's heart beating faster, and how his woman tastes like sunlight and strawberry bubble gum. The words might as well have been written by me about Maggie. The words speak directly to the pulsing between my legs, and my problem only seems to worsen.

Suddenly, I'm all kinds of curious about how Maggie would taste on my tongue. Just a sampler would do. But just like I do with my alcohol, I know I would have to limit it to just that one taste. Any more, and the drunk would be too much. I'm good at setting rules and at sticking to them. Maybe I could do that with Maggie too.

Her hips slow their sway slightly in front of me, but this time, she moves her hair over her shoulder, revealing a naked spot of skin at her neck, which my eyes fixate on. The way I imagine sinking my teeth into that tender spot while she gasps her pleasure into the air has me feeling like some kind of fucking vampire. But my thoughts are swinging like a pendulum, threatening. The weight is so heavy, there's no chance of stopping it on my own.

Not a chance in hell.

Run

MAGGIE

I can't remember the last time I went to a concert and felt like this—free, floating, intoxicated from the music and the audience's energy. There's simply something magical about live music. It's like the surrounding sound streams into my pores with a direct line straight into my soul. Six songs in, and I feel like I'm floating on the puffiest cloud.

I don't stop moving. I can't stop. It doesn't matter if it's a fast song or a slow one. My hips move with each beat as I down my drink then turn around to pass it back to Desmond so he can put it back on the round table. When my eyes connect with his, I realize he's just as into the music as I am. He may not be dancing to every beat like me, but his eyes have been glued to the stage like it's the most fascinating sight, and I can't help but smile at him. "Having fun?" I shout.

He gives me an expressionless nod, but I can see a glimmer in his eyes that expresses something more than total indifference. I consider it a win.

"You?" he shouts back with an uptick of his brows.

My smile widens, and I swivel around to answer his question with a shake of my hips while raising my arms above my head. "Can't you tell?"

Something dark yet endearing flashes in his eyes, something that halts my next breath. I should turn around. I know I should turn around. *Focus on the music, Maggie.* But my body doesn't listen to the screaming voice in my head. My arms start to fall, and the sway of my hips slows, just as one fast song transitions into a slower one.

Timing is everything.

If I hadn't turned around at that exact moment, then I wouldn't be standing here now, locked in a dangerous gaze with a man I should find repulsive. This is the same man who refused to give me a cooking certificate that I worked for for three months. And the man who gives zero fucks about the history I share with my father because he idolizes the man.

The first verse of the song "Run" doesn't help either because Matt Nathanson is singing about watching some woman undress. All I can think about is how Desmond is looking at me in that exact same way. His sharp blue eyes are burning so brightly, and I can't seem to tear my eyes from him.

Then a body chooses that moment to slam into me from behind, pushing me into the man I've managed to keep inches of distance from since the night started. My palms find his chest to break my fall. "I'm sorry," I say, feeling my face flush with my words.

What is wrong with me? Desmond is not someone I get hot and bothered over. He's a jerk. A careless flirt. A cocky chef. And my beating heart only quickens because of it.

I tear my eyes away and start to take a step back, but he's pulling me back toward him faster than I have time to think. I gasp and fall against his chest. My gaze slams into his and holy shit if his cold blue eyes don't electrify every fiber of my being. It's like shock therapy, reviving me from a sleeping spell I've been cast in for months.

I swallow and look down at my midsection, where I felt the pull, and find Desmond's pointer finger hooked into the belt loop of my black jeans. His forefinger has a firm grip on it, so I look back up just as he's leaning down and sliding his scruffy beard along my cheek. Chills shoot over my skin, and I inhale sharply. I don't even trust myself to breathe right now.

"You didn't answer my question." He pulls back slightly and tilts his head, waiting for my response.

tilts his head, waiting for my response.

My brain feels foggy. "Huh? What question?"

His lips tip up at the corner, and there's another gentle pull on my waistband. "Are *you* having fun?"

My heart won't stop beating like it's in a freaking track race. How am I supposed to answer that? I *was* having fun, unquestionably. But now... I have no clue how to make sense of my feelings. Why don't I want him to unhook his finger? Why do I want to find a way to get closer?

"I am," I shout back.

His brows crinkle in confusion, and he leans down again until I can feel that familiar scratchy feeling against my cheek. Then his next breath hits me in the ear, sending a wave of chills over me. *Shit.*

"What?" he asks, like he didn't hear my answer the first time.

I swallow and turn my head so I can speak closer to his ear just as he tugs me closer. Our bodies are practically one now, every inch of space gone between us. I know I should hate it, but I don't, not at all.

"I said I am," I say, this time gripping his shoulders to help steady my position against him. "I can't stop dancing." I pull back, catching the smile that slowly spreads across Desmond's face.

"I can tell."

Heat spreads like wildfire through my chest, to my neck, then to my face. "I haven't been to a concert in years." I don't know why I tell him this. It's not like he needs justification for the fact that I can't stop moving my body.

I don't miss the way his gaze slides down my front and then back up. It's so fast, I almost think I imagine it, but the way his eyes flash on mine again tell me this isn't the first time tonight that he's checked me out. *He's been watching me all night?*

My cheeks heat again at my wishful thoughts. The fact that I'm even considering whether Desmond has been checking me out all night is preposterous. Of course he isn't. But even if he was, I shouldn't care.

"Maybe you should go more often. Where'd you learn those dance moves?"

I make a face and laugh. "I wouldn't call those dance moves."

"Well, whatever it is, I like it."

He's definitely flirting, my subconscious screams. *He has been watching you.* Yup, my face is burning. It's probably as red as the Exit sign at the over Desmond's shoulder. But when I feel the tug on my belt loop slack and I look up to see his focus has returned to the band, I'm filled with instant disappointment. It's like a balloon just deflated in my chest, and I'm left with no choice than to turn back around in the middle of the most romantic song.

I swivel to face the stage only to feel Desmond's hand snake around my body and slide over my belly. His palm flattens against me, and I feel another pull, this one less subtle than the one on my belt loop, almost possessive.

He leans into my neck and growls so intensely, I'm almost expecting him to swing me back around. But that's not what he does. Instead, his voice penetrates my insides like a rush of adrenaline. "That asshole keeps staring at you."

I look up and immediately spot the douchebag from the bar who thought he could put his hands on me and call me "sweet thing" as I walked by.

"Stay close to me, and he'll get the hint." Desmond pauses a moment. "Or I can let you go. Just say the word."

His voice blows like a fire through me, and I push myself into him further, my back crushed to his hard front. His palm presses against me in response. This isn't one of those moments in my life where I need to read between the lines to know if a guy is actually flirting with me or not. His touch, his deep gravelly tone, and his burning gaze—it's all perfectly clear. There is absolutely zero question whether Desmond wants me as much as I want him. And if he's not hiding it, then why should I?

"Feel free to move those hips again if you want," he rasps in my ear.

My entire body quivers so violently, there's no way he missed it. I'm not one to disappoint. I do exactly as he suggested. The song is slower, so my hips follow suit in a slow grind against him. I'm fully aware of the hardening of his body and the intense grip he has on my waist. I'm aware of the blur of faces and bodies around us that seem to belong to a totally different world now that I'm in Desmond's arms. I'm aware of the song and how every lyric only seems to bring us closer together, if that is even possible. I don't think it is, but it feels like we're completely in sync, maybe for the very first time, fused together in a moment of passion that I couldn't shake if I tried.

Meanwhile, his mouth is trailing from my ear, down my neck, and into that sensitive place between my throat and my shoulder. His lips part slightly, just enough so that his warm tongue can snake out to taste my skin. Soon enough, his lips, tongue, and teeth are running a line back up my neck, and the moment I feel like he's hardened completely, his teeth sink down into my skin, creating a wave of need and pleasure that pulse deep inside me. And then his hands start to roam. They find the edge of my tank, and his thick fingers slip beneath it.

I realize this is Desmond behind me and that there's nothing between us more than whatever this physical, pulsing chemistry is. But damn, it has been a long time since I've been kissed. It's been so long that I can't even remember what it feels like to have a man's lips on mine. And I would be a liar if I say I haven't imagined the taste of Desmond's lips in particular. In fact, it might have been the initial thought I had of him when my eyes found his for the first time.

When I met him, I remember seeing him as this tall, wild-haired, bearded man wearing an apron at the front of class. My pulse sped, my veins throbbed, and my entire being lit with an excitement I had to taper with a hard bite down on my bottom lip. *"Now there's a man who I'd let ruin my lipstick."* Those were my exact words to my sister, Monica, after spotting the hottie in an apron.

Unfortunately, the fantasy didn't last long. All it took was a little background knowledge to sway my attraction, knowledge I'm forcibly pushing from my brain as he searches my neck with his teeth, lips, and tongue. It's one swipe of gentle and sharp that causes me to inhale quickly as I twist to look at the man who has me completely lifted into a fog of sex and music.

Is it bad to want someone so badly that all sanity gets tossed out the window? Because I know, without pause, that I would give myself to Desmond right this very moment.

His long lashes flip up, and his eyes catch mine over my shoulder. Those serious eyes have a devilish gleam, telling me he's just as ready to break down all the barricades we've built between us. Then he moves in, slowly at first, before quickening for the kill just as his lips approach mine. They're just hovering there, making me wait, making me wonder. I can feel the ache between my legs and the heating of my core that follows.

The slow and sweet lyrics fill the space around us, lifting us above my already foggy state, high above the clouds, until I'm merely floating in dangerous proximity to the rain shower sure to drown us both. But I don't care, not when his breath hits mine in one final warning, like a crack of thunder before the sky lights up the night. The lightning is certain to be pretty, but I'm ready to risk the aftermath just for tonight.

My back is still to him as I close the gap to reach his lips, and I linger there for just a moment. All my questions about the way they feel against mine are answered in a mere instant. They're thick, just like his hands. They're soft and slick too—slick because he just wet them on my skin—skin that still burns from his touch.

But Desmond doesn't allow me another second to memorize his mouth. He's pressing his lips around mine, molding them firmly with his. One hand continues to search my stomach while the other one grips my waist and pulls me around so I'm facing him again. His hand moves to my back, and he bends me slightly while deepening our kiss.

My hands circle his waist just as his tongue dips into the small space he created with his mouth. I've never thought a man's tongue was erotic until this moment, but here Desmond's is, tangling with mine, forcing me to clench my thighs to hold in the incomprehensible ache. When my tongue swipes back at his, his groan is deep and guttural. He grips the back of my thighs and lifts me over his hips. My arms loop around his neck, and my legs wrap firmly around his waist until I'm practically towering over him in height.

The weight of the world lifts, and all I'm aware of is Desmond—his lips on mine, his grip on me, and his throaty groan as my mouth parts wider just for him.

I don't even notice the ending notes of the song ringing out into the crowd until a voice booms through the speakers. "Now that's the effect I want my songs to have."

Something about the singer's words cause me to freeze in midkiss, and Desmond does too. I pull back from him, my wide eyes searching his. "Please tell me he's not talking to us."

Just then, the crowd breaks into cheers and applause, and Desmond leans to the side to see the stage. His face says it all, and I cringe internally before he confirms my worst fears. "I'm afraid he is."

I look over my shoulder, immediately blinded by a spotlight. "Oh shit." I flip my head back. "You should probably put me down now."

Deep disappointment flashes in his eyes, but he nods and helps me unravel my legs from his waist before setting me down. I flip back around just as everyone's attention returns to the singer and his next song. "This one is for the two lovebirds in the back row."

I'm mortified. My face roasts with the singer's words. A piano tune starts, accompanied by Matt's voice. The song has a retro video game vibe, and I immediately recognize it as "Kill the Lights."

I don't stop Desmond from wrapping his arms around my waist again. It almost feels like a small shield for the embarrassment that just fell upon us a moment ago. He's shaking behind me with laughter before leaning into my ear. "Look at that, Mags. Guess we have a song."

My entire body heats at his words because I know he's right. Lord knows I'll never be able to hear this song again without thinking about that kiss.

I look over my shoulder to find his hooded eyes on me. "Wanna get out of here?" His tone drips of sex and hope.

Without thinking about my answer for a single second, I nod.

Backseat Memories

MAGGIE

"Come," a raspy voice says in my ear.

I freeze for a second, my brain and feet having a hard time connecting. Then I feel a tug on my hand, followed by Desmond's body moving away from me. He's leading me toward the exit, and I go along with him, my heart pounding fiercely in my chest. My hand rests firmly in his as he pulls me out the front door and down the street. Then we find his car in the crowded parking lot.

He opens the sleek red door, leans down, folds up the front seat, and stands. "Well," he says with a grin, gesturing to the back seat with a pointed look in its direction. "What are you waiting for?"

When I don't move, he slips into the back seat first and then reaches out for my hand. "I'm not ready for tonight to be over. Are you?"

I shake my head, trying desperately to breathe normally around my speeding pulse. "No." I fit my palm into his and feel a tug when he pulls me into the back seat. I fall into him and laugh. "Are you crazy?"

He winks and reaches over me to close and lock the car door. "Just a little bit." Then he pulls me onto his lap so I'm straddling him. He doesn't make a move to kiss me, but his hands are running up my thighs with a firm grip while his tongue darts out to wet his bottom lip. His hooded eyes burn into mine, and he lets them linger there a few beats without saying anything at all.

"We need ground rules," he finally says.

I narrow my eyes. "For what exactly? I'm not kissing you again, Desmond Blake. That was a one-time thing."

He chuckles and shakes his head. "You're so full of shit." His hands move up to my ass, and he grips it firmly before sliding me closer. I gasp as my hot center lands directly over his hard length.

"That was a mistake in there, and you know it."

His smile morphs into a cocky smirk. "That was the opposite of a mistake." He tilts his head, his gaze filled with curiosity. "But are you telling me you didn't want to kiss me?" He lifts his brows with a challenge.

I blow out a breath. "No." I bite down on my bottom lip, wishing it was enough to shut myself up. But my heart is in charge now. "That's not what I'm saying, not at all. I think that was obvious."

He nods. "Oh, it was." His palms leave my ass and move up until his fingers are crawling beneath my shirt. They move straight up my back to where the clasp of my nonexistent bra should be. Being a small-chested girl has its benefits at times.

I wish I could capture the moment Desmond realizes that I'm not wearing one. I swear, he doubles in size between my thighs. He lets out a quiet groan that I would have probably missed if I weren't so in tune with his every move.

"Just because I let you kiss me back there doesn't mean I'll do it again now. That was dumb, reckless."

"It was just a kiss, Maggie. It wasn't dumb or reckless. And I do want to do it again." He rolls his hips up, pushing himself into me through our clothes, and I react with a groan.

"See?" His eyes drift down my body. "Look what I'm doing to you. I'm not even inside you yet."

"Yet?" I ask in astonishment. "That indicates you will be inside me at some point. Spoiler alert: that won't happen."

"You sure?" His grip loosens on my back, and disappointment fills me. "I'm more on the optimistic side of this scenario."

I swallow and nod, showing him I'm firm on my words. "I'm sure you are, but there are so many reasons this is wrong."

"Name one."

"You're my boss."

He smiles so wide. "I am, aren't I? Well, I assure you, I don't have a fraternization policy, so…"

"Whatever. We're stuck with each other for the foreseeable future. It's just not a good idea."

"One reason. That's all you gave me, and it was shit. You got nothing else?" He lifts his hips again, this time rubbing against me in a way that makes my lower belly swirl with flutters. "Give me one more reason, and I'll back off. But you better make it good."

I suppose all I have to do is lift off him and make it clear that I don't need to give him a reason to not kiss him again. All

I have to do is say no. But I don't say no. I don't lift myself off of him. I stay and conjure up another reason we shouldn't be doing this. And I'm not just doing it for him. I'm trying to convince myself too.

"We hate each other."

That makes his lips curl even more as his head moves up and down slightly. Then he cups my neck with his palm and brings me to his lips. "That could make for some hot sex. I'm not opposed to giving it a try."

A fire burns in my belly as my internal struggle dies a little inside me. Desmond is incredibly sexy and undoubtably amazing in bed. But is that what I want? An extraordinary lay based on nothing more than my burning need to be with a man again despite his numerous faults? I suppose I haven't been opposed to meaningless sex before, but somehow it feels different with Desmond, like I'll be cheating on that little girl inside of me whose heart still breaks over her father's betrayal.

Desmond is still painfully hard beneath me. It takes everything not to grind against him and relieve some of my own buildup. Months without sex hasn't made me feel so wound up and needy until this moment, and I shudder as my imagination starts to go wild.

"Tell me something you hate about me."

"What?" I ask, my eyes opening and landing on his burning blue ones. "Why?"

He shrugs. "If we hate each other, then there's no possibility of falling in love, which is what neither of us wants, right? So we play it safe, embrace the hate, and have lots of sex."

I roll my eyes. "That is the stupidest idea ever."

"Is it?" He quirks a brow, and I realize with a jolt to my chest that he's not joking around. Desmond wants to have sex with me. Well, he wants to have sex with my body. I would be a liar if I didn't want the same with him. But my heart resembles a gorilla's fist as it pounds like crazy against my ribs. I can't even think straight. Casual sex is a thing. People do it all the time. *So why can't I?*

I narrow my gaze and draw in a slow breath of courage before opening my mouth again. "I hate your…" My mind is whirling, trying to conjure up a single thing I hate about this man. Not long ago, I would have sworn that I hated him with a burning passion. My gaze catches on his hair, which appears more disheveled than usual. I start to run a hand through it. "Hair."

He chuckles lightly. "You hate my hair?"

I nod, my eyes glued to his angry locks of dark brown as I run my nails against his scalp. "You're the first man I've met who has hair nicer than mine."

His eyes close as he relaxes under my grip. "Has anyone ever told you that you give good hair sex?"

I bite back my laugh and shake my head. "I think you might be the first."

"Hmm," he moans before his lids fly open, revealing the same hooded gaze. "Now kiss me."

"What?" I start to pull back, but he holds me by the waist.

"You tell me one thing you hate about me, and then you kiss me. When you're done, it's my turn."

I sigh and decide to play along with his stupid game. Besides, I wouldn't mind kissing Desmond again. For someone with such a cocky mouth, it sure knows how to move.

So I press my lips to his, feeling an instant buzz in my chest and head. I playfully pull on his bottom lip with mine. It's a dangerous move, but who the hell cares at this point. It's only a game. It's only sex. And this is only a kiss.

An innocent, slow, intricate, mind-blowing kiss.

My lips part his, but instead of exploring his mouth and tongue, I slide left to right against his lips. I'm testing the terrain like I'm preparing for a hike, giving myself one more chance to back out of whatever adventure lies ahead.

But just as I feel like I'm the one with all the power, he pulls back slightly and grins. "My turn." Desmond's fingers slip back under my shirt, and he draws slow, soft lines over my skin. His eyes darken on mine. "I hate that mask you hide behind to protect yourself, the one that refuses to let anyone inside. You're a beautiful woman, Maggie. You shouldn't cover that up."

I swallow at his words and just start making sense of them when his lips land on my neck, right at my pulse. He darts out his tongue to taste my skin then bites down around it before sucking. My entire body goes into a sort of convulsion as he mimics the move again, this time in a different sensitive spot on my neck. I feel like I'm going to combust right on the spot.

I'm still buzzing when he removes his mouth and looks at me, signaling that it's my turn. I'm not sure how I can form a coherent thought, so I blurt out the first thing that comes to mind. "I hate how you flirt with every attractive female in your presence. No smart woman would fall for that bullshit."

Desmond chuckles again and slides his hands up my back once again, running over bare skin where my bra should be. "Good thing you're a smart woman." His eyes darken on the spot, and his head drops back against the seat. "Well, aren't you going to kiss me?"

This time, I move to his ear, bite gently on his lobe, then take it between my teeth like he did with my neck. When I pull back, I wonder how long this game can continue before we're naked in the back seat of his car.

His eyes flash, and his hands slip to my front, over my breasts, causing me to suck in a breath. "I hate how sexy you are," he says with another lift of his hips. "And I hate how much I want you."

The next thing I know, I'm on my back, and Desmond's on top of me, his mouth moving from my mouth, to my ear, and then to his favorite spot on my neck. I slam my eyes closed and turn my head toward the back of the passenger seat to give him room to venture.

My breaths become ragged as he drags his mouth from my neck to my cleavage, dipping his tongue inside my shirt while his hand slides up beneath my shirt to cover my breast. My entire body shudders as his fingers glide over my nipple. Pleasure shoots straight down to my core from Desmond's dangerously addictive touch, and I'm so ready to give in.

He pushes up my shirt, and his mouth is hot on my nipple, stealing licks, just seconds from devouring me whole. And I desperately want him to do just that. But when my eyes open again, they connect to the back of the passenger seat, specifically on something strangely familiar, causing the fog to clear from my mind and an ache to burn hot in my chest.

No way. No fucking way.

I scramble to move Desmond off of me, to sit and yank my shirt down as I shake the fog of sex from my mind. I blink a few times, trying to make the image now branded in my mind fade from sight. But I can't escape the heart-shaped image that's carved into the old red leather of the passenger seat.

It's not a coincidence.

I'm not seeing things.

I carved that heart into the back of the passenger seat when I was nine, but before I could put the "M&M" inside it for my sister and me, my dad caught me and sent me straight to time-out. I'd never seen my father pissed off before that day.

"You okay?" Desmond's voice breaks through my memories.

Did he really just ask me that? My eyes snap to his as my frown deepens. "Where did you get this car?"

His expression morphs from confusion to understanding so fast, it almost makes me sick. I scoot away from him, my back landing against the side wall of the car. When his mouth opens but he fails to speak, anger engulfs me like gas on a fire.

"Answer me, Desmond."

His shoulders sag, and his face transitions into shame. "It was a gift from Coach after I graduated from high school."

My jaw drops, and my stomach heaves as my heart breaks all over again. "He just... gave it to you?"

His eyes dart between mine before slowly nodding. "I used to fix it up for him until he got so frustrated, he didn't want to mess with it anymore. So he said I could have it since I was able to take care of it." Then he lets out a sigh and shakes his head. "If you're wondering why I didn't tell you, it's because I didn't want you to get all upset about it. It doesn't matter, Maggie. It's just a car."

My eyes bulge wide as I press my body back against the seat. Suddenly, the space is suffocating, and there's nowhere to run. "Just a car?" I can feel my insides shaking as my voice grows in volume. "Just a car?" I glare at Desmond with all the venom I can muster. "Did you know my dad used to take me on secret drives, just me and him, when I'd get in a big fight with my sister or my mom? He'd take me to get ice cream, or to play at the park, and we'd just have fun together and talk for hours." I swipe the first tear that falls with the back of my hand. "Did you know that before he disappeared from our lives, he promised this car to me? It was supposed to be my car, Desmond. Mine. And now it's yours." I blow out another frustrated breath and reach for the door handle.

"Where are you going?" Desmond growls.

"I'm leaving. I'll walk back. Or I'll find another ride. But I'm getting out of this damn car."

Desmond follows me onto the sidewalk and slams the door behind him. "I'm not letting you walk home alone, Maggie. Get in the car. I'll take you back."

I just shake my head and keep walking. I'll be fine. The condo is only ten minutes from here if I can focus on my direction. I'll get home on my own.

When Desmond realizes I'm not going to stop and turn around, he jogs to catch up to me, his angry breathing only a few feet behind me. "I didn't do anything wrong, you know." He growls out his words, revealing his frustration at our situation." I'm not your father."

I whip around to face him, still walking backward. "No. But you're a reminder, and that's bad enough."

TAKE FIVE

Wedding Bells

"IN A SEA OF PEOPLE, MY EYES WILL ALWAYS SEARCH FOR YOU."
— UNKNOWN

Heavy Weights
DESMOND

If I'm thrown off my routine or unable to check a box, irritation sneaks in like a crippling anxiety. Suddenly, it's like I'm struggling for whatever control I can maintain while slipping outside myself. My anger spikes. My mood shifts. And anyone around me becomes a target on my warpath.

Before I met Coach Reynolds, my life was void of the routine that keeps me sane now. Grappling was my normal, and every day felt like a fight just to move through it. The only way I ever felt like I was in control of my own feelings was when I was unleashing my darkest demons, giving into the anger, the insecurities, and the utter disappointment I had for myself and my life.

It didn't help that my father was a raging alcoholic. At the time, he hadn't yet been diagnosed with autism spectrum disorder, not that I would have known what to do with that information when I was a young teen.

When I was a kid, dealing with my father each day was like playing Russian roulette. I would wake up, spin the cylinder, and take my chances. I didn't know what type of mood he would be in or what would set him off to become the version of himself that sent me running. I refused to let my peers get too close to me because I was too embarrassed for anyone to know what was really going on at home.

Things seemed to only get worse the older I got. Instead of running away from the angry drunk my father would become, I was picking him up from bars, tucking him into bed at odd hours of the day, and thanking the Lord he was too messed up to take a swing at me. Not that he would have made contact anymore. I was bigger at sixteen than most of the boys my age. And I'd learned how to fight since it was the only thing keeping the fear in my peers' eyes. That fear I'd instilled in them was the only thing that protected me from hurting more than I already was inside.

"No excuses." That was what Coach would always shout at me the moment I tried to blame one of my teammates for my volatile behavior. "You've got anger inside you, son? Good. So do we all. Use it on the field, but we're not your enemies." He would say those words just inches from my face. "Look around you, Blake." He would point to a row of downturned heads on the benches in front of their lockers. "These men are your brothers. And this right here"—he used his arms to wave around the entire locker room—"we're family. We protect each other however we need to. If that means taking a beating in order for Zach to have time to release that ball, then take the damn beating. Because if he gets sacked, that's on you. Be there, Desmond. No excuses."

Lord knew Zach had taken plenty of beatings from me prior to us joining that team. So of course, my answer was simple. "Yes, sir." I would say those words without fail every single time. And every single time, I meant it, until the reminders were no longer necessary.

In a way, football taught me how the world worked. It taught me right and wrong, forgiveness and how to trust. It taught me how to protect myself without resorting to violent retaliation. But above all, it taught me what a true family bond was like. And Coach Reynolds was the glue.

How he could have ever been something less to his own family is beyond me. I can't picture it and don't want to. Until Maggie Stevens entered my life, I didn't have to. Sure, I know what Zach and Monica went through to be together, but that's none of my business. With Maggie, I can't help but feel a twinge of guilt for her situation.

My workout on Saturday morning is my first opportunity all week to relieve some of the building tension. Maggie hasn't spoken to me at all since that night at the concert. She's shown up to work and done her job without complaint, but not a single word has been muttered in my direction. She's pissed off because I didn't tell her where I got that car, but would she have been any different if I'd told her sooner? I'm pretty sure the answer is "not a chance in hell." So I've rewarded her silence with an air of indifference, speaking only when necessary. *We'll talk when she's ready.*

I'm currently pushing a weight into the air in midgrunt when Coach Reynolds walks up behind me and lowers his hands beneath the barbell. "That's it, son. Give me another one of those. Focus on your breathing."

Focus on your breathing is code for "calm the fuck down" in Coach-speak.

Breathing is one of the first things he ever taught me about how to control the terrible anger inside me. But that isn't all. He taught me the responsibility of being on a team, which in turn helped me direct my impulses in a positive direction. He taught me compassion and empathy by understanding that my anger dwelled from a lonely childhood in which my father had become my child in a way. He gave me a family through football and the occasional dinner at his house, which helped immensely with my self-esteem and feelings of inclusiveness. He taught me respect. Respect for others. Respect for family. Respect for myself. Overall, he gave me the ticket to better myself with the skills he knew I already possessed, and I'll forever be grateful. But I'm still nowhere near perfect.

"Good," Coach says while he helps to lift the bar and secure it.

When I sit up, he takes a seat next to me on the bench. "I haven't seen you work out like that in quite some time. Everything okay with your dad?"

I spin the cap off my water and take a long chug before shrugging my shoulders and looking at the floor. "Is anything ever okay with Pops? He's out of rehab. Got a call from the facility last night."

My father's episodes have become a clockwork thing in the past four years. Hence my frequent travel back to Dallas, the last time being the trip when I met Faye. He'd just gotten out of rehab, and I rushed there, hoping that if I spent time with him when he was freshly sober, my chances of getting through to him would be better. I've found that the only way to speak to him when he's halfway coherent is when he's either in jail or at the rehab clinic. But no such luck. He wasn't at his apartment when I arrived there. And then I saw the flashing lights of the police car a few blocks away.

"I should probably get out there soon to visit him."

Coach nods. "Sounds like a good plan." He tilts his head at me. "Something else bothering you?"

How well this man knows me is almost scary. I shrug again. "Besides your daughter being a royal pain in my ass, life is the same as always."

Coach lets out a light chuckle. "I see. Well, she wouldn't be a Reynolds if she wasn't a pain in the ass, so I'll have to take some credit for that one."

I twist my neck to look at him with confusion. "She's not a Reynolds, sir. She's a Stevens."

The humor leaves Coach's eyes and face, and he nods. "Yes. I know her mom had the girls change their names. She's still a Reynolds."

The firmness in his tone halts me some. "She's also still a pain in my ass."

Coach smiles, but it's not with the same humor as before. "I suppose she's been through a lot. And being surrounded by constant reminders of a man she's grown up hating can't be easy either."

"She doesn't hate you, Coach. She wouldn't still be so upset if she hated you. But she sure hates me."

"Well," Coach jeers with a squeeze of my shoulders, "can you blame her?"

I grin and shake my head. "Not really. Especially since she just figured out I'm driving your old car."

Coach's face falls, and I swear I see his throat bob like he just swallowed a gulp of guilt. "I imagine that didn't go over so well." His eyes glaze over just like Maggie's did the other night. "She loved that car. She would always beg me to take her around the block a half million times." He chuckles at the memory, his eyes turning sad. "She was my first baby girl, you know." His eyes start to water, and my throat closes at the shocking sight. "I had no clue how I would handle being a father to a girl, and then I held her in my arms for the first time. She made it feel so easy. She needed nothing more than love, and I failed her."

My own thoughts are running rampant. I tried to block all feelings for Maggie from my heart and mind this week, but now they're back with a vengeance. "You hurt her pretty badly, Coach."

His eyes shoot to mine, and he sighs with a shake of his head. "Between you and Zach, I can't catch a break. I never would have thought to imagine that you two would find my girls and fall head over heels."

I jump at his suggestion. "No, Coach, not me. Maggie and I aren't…" I shake my head, hoping he'll fill in the blanks.

He creases his brow and locks eyes with me. "Are you sure?"

I bark out a laugh. "Positive. Zach asked for a favor. Maggie needed a job, and Monica needed Maggie out of her hair. It all worked out, for me too. Maggie's filling in at the kitchen until she finds the next best thing."

I say nothing about the possibility that's always been in the back of my mind about Maggie moving back to LA. The truth is, I want that less and less as the days go on.

Coach looks thoroughly confused. "Well, you fooled me. It sure sounds like you care about my girl. Looked like it too at the game last weekend." A few beats of silence pass. "And if along the way, you figure out you do…" His gaze narrows in my direction.

"Yeah, I know, I know. If I hurt her, you'll bury me beneath the bleachers."

Coach chuckles and claps a hand on my back. "Glad we're on the same page."

Through the Trees

DESMOND

After Coach left, I decided to stay at the gym and work out more of my frustration on the treadmill. Five miles later and with Maggie still on my mind, I went home, showered, and now I'm ready to face the big day ahead.

It's a little past ten when I get to the kitchen. Maggie is already there, going over the wedding menu and pulling out the fresh ingredients available while jotting a list down of everything we need to pick up.

"Morning, sunshine," I say while avoiding eye contact. I got a good look at her as soon as I opened the door, and it's definitely a horrible idea to look at her again.

Maggie doesn't have to try hard to look beautiful, and when she puts in the least amount of effort, she seems to look her best to me. Her hair is still wet from a shower, and it's pinned up at the top of her head. She's wearing a simple white tank top that cuts off above her belly, and light-blue baggy jeans that are shredded in so many places, I'm shocked the damn thing doesn't fall apart. She's wearing just enough makeup to mask whatever natural blemishes might be visible beneath, and my urge to know every single freckle and scar is unbearably strong.

After our heated kiss and the way she stormed home with me trailing her in my car the entire damn way, I wish I could give up the fantasies that take over my mind when it comes to her. But I've come to find out that's simply impossible.

Maggie doesn't return my greeting, and I don't expect her to. She's been ignoring me all week, refusing the meals I cook her as part of our bet, but then I'll find that they disappear from the kitchen's refrigerator later on. But communicating is part of the job, and I can't go another entire day without a single exchange. I'm going crazy, and today is important—to the kitchen, to me, to Chloe and Gavin, and to all the wedding guests we're about to feed. Besides all that, Maggie's still my employee and tenant. The silence needs to end.

"I need to run to the market," I say in an attempt to keep things normal and professional. When she doesn't look up or say anything, I continue. "I've got some pasta dough in the refrigerator if you want to start flattening it and cutting up the fettuccine."

Maggie sets her pen down, slides a sheet of paper across the island in my direction, and turns toward the refrigerator. For a second, I just stand there as she takes the ball of dough out of the refrigerator and sets it near the flour and pasta machine I laid out the night before. She seems to know exactly what she's doing, so I take the grocery list she made, turn on my heel, and head for the door.

It's a smaller shopping trip than normal since the only items I really need to grab are some ingredients for the broccoli salad, fresh chicken for the pasta, flank steak to go with the fresh chimichurri sauce, and fresh bread. I'm not going to have time to prepare fresh loaves today, not for 120 guests.

I pay for my groceries and carry them back to the kitchen within thirty minutes of when I walked out. Maggie hasn't left her pasta duties at all from what I can tell. She's completely in the zone, her light brown eyes wide beneath bent, concentrated brows as she focuses on the mission at hand. A mission, might I add, that she's kicking ass at. I set the groceries on the island, unable to take my eyes off the dozens and dozens of long and thick fettuccini, made just the way I taught her in a previous class.

There's a special technique that goes into making scratch pasta. Even with a machine, it's not as simple as it looks. Maggie just made it look like she's been making pasta for years. There's even a hint of a smile on her face as she rolls out the next batch of noodles, catching it easily on a sheet of Saran Wrap.

When she's done, she lets out a heavy sigh and looks up, her chest still inflated as her eyes register something resembling hope. She wants my approval. "Well?" she asks with a shrug as I glance down at her handiwork. "I did it."

I walk around the island to inspect the noodles with an exaggerated effort. I don't need to look any closer to know she made my job look like a walk in the park. I arrive behind her and reach my hand out like I'm going to touch one, but I don't. "All right, should we move on to the chimichurri sauce? I could use help gathering the ingredie—"

She whips around so fast, I swear her hair might fly out of her twisty bun. Her gorgeous eyes narrow on mine, and she steps forward as if she has an inch to spare. She doesn't, causing her to push up against me, her chest heaving with frustration. I don't look, although I want to badly, but it doesn't stop me from picturing my tongue on her tits in the back of my car last week.

"That's all you have to say to me? I did a great job."

I can feel the corner of my mouth tugging up against my will. "I didn't say otherwise."

"You didn't acknowledge how great I did either."

Without taking my eyes off of her, I lean down until my nose is almost touching hers. Then I lick my lips and hear the hitch in her next breath. I like it too much. I like Maggie too much, which is exactly why I need to put forth every effort possible to show her the man she loves to hate. He's the safe version of me, the version I don't have to worry about fucking up every five seconds of the day.

I draw in a slow, steady breath and open my mouth to respond with exaggerated slowness. "I don't give awards for pasta cutting."

With a growl, she places her palms against my chest and starts to push.

I chuckle and grab her hand as she starts to leave, then I swing her back toward me. "Wait a second. Since when do you need affirmations to know your worth? Just doesn't seem like the Maggie way."

She yanks her hand from mine and folds her arms across her chest. "I don't need affirmations. But I sure as hell deserve one after that."

I sigh, unable to piss her off anymore. As much as I love messing with her, she doesn't seem to be in her normally playful mood. "You did great, Maggie, but it hurts to admit it, okay? You nailed it. They're perfect. If you never go back to modeling, you should consider a career as a pasta cook. You happy?"

Although my tone was dryer than dry, Maggie's smile is as bright as the hundred-watt bulb I screwed into the ceiling yesterday.

"Yes, I am, thank you very much." She slips past me and starts to thumb through the recipes.

"Want to make the broccoli salad while I prepare the steak?" I offer, knowing Maggie is in a mood where she has to be the one to call the shots. I figured that out about her last week. If she feels like she's in control, then she's much more pleasant to be around.

She shrugs and plucks a recipe from the pile. "Sure." Then she walks to the grocery bags, grabs the broccoli, and immediately starts to wash the florets.

"If all goes well, I can probably get you out of here by four o'clock. Does that work?"

"That's fine. Monica is swinging by at four thirty, so that gives me enough time to shower. I'll get ready at her hotel."

And that's about how things go for the next four hours as we prepare the food, pack it up, and pile everything in the Edible Desire catering van. As much as I would love to deliver the food hot and fresh, that's just not possible given the fact that I wasn't provided a kitchen on site. The food will be refrigerated until I can get everything on the warmer about thirty minutes before the reception begins.

After the food is secure, we step into the elevator and take it up to our apartments. She walks immediately to hers and only stops to unlock her door.

"Hey, Maggie?"

She shoots me a glance over her shoulder, and I don't miss the fear she carries behind that gaze. What is she afraid I'll say?

"Thanks for your help today. You were a lifesaver."

She shrugs and turns back to her door while pushing it open. "Just doing my job."

I sigh as her door shuts behind her then push through my own. I have time for a quick shower to scrub off the scent of four long hours in the kitchen, and then I'm climbing into the van. I've only been given an address, and that's what I plugged into my GPS before I left the house, so that's where I head, with nothing but thoughts of Maggie Stevens on my mind.

Is this how things are going to be between Maggie and me from now on? Is it just going to be forced conversation, uncomfortable silence, and heated exchanges that stem from a hurt and betrayal I wasn't the cause of? I don't want to live in this uncomfortable space with her. I thought we'd finally gotten over the hump of misunderstandings and hate, but now it seems to have only become more complicated.

I pull up to a parking lot in the park and know instantly I'm at the right place. There's a large gazebo set up in the distance, decorated in bright white lights that match more lights strung from tree to tree, creating a tented appearance throughout the woods. A carpeted aisle is laid out, separating ten rows of seats, six on each side. And to the left is an entirely different setup. Long wooden tables are situated beneath symmetrically lined evergreens and make up enough dinner seating for all the guests. White tablecloths run across their lengths and are tied in knots at each end, giving them the freedom to move with the light breeze. Horizontal black trellises hold up the low-hanging branches, creating a sort of ceiling of trees and lights. And a large, brilliant chandelier hangs from the trellised ceiling.

It's the perfect fall day, ripe with bright-green leaves, a faint spattering of clouds, and a light chill that will feel warm to the wedding party and guests once they're all crowded together for a long night of festivities.

On the other side of the dinner seating is a long row of empty tables currently being clothed in white, and that's where I go. A woman with a headpiece and a clipboard approaches at the same time and reaches her hand out with a curious smile. "Edible Desire, I presume? I saw the van pull up."

I give her my best smile and greet her with a handshake. "That would be me. But you can call me Desmond. And you are?" I assume she's the wedding planner, but I would prefer to have a name.

"Ursula Crestwell, the wedding planner. My sister, Phoebe, is also a bridesmaid. Thanks so much for agreeing to do this at the last minute. I hear you're a family friend?"

"Something like that." I smile. "The bride is my best friend's sister's best friend."

Ursula tosses her head back and laughs. "Sounds confusing."

I grin. "You have no idea." Then I gesture to the long, fully clothed tables. "Is this where I'll be setting up?"

The woman nods. "This is it." She glances at her watch. "It's probably too early now, but we'd like the food to be ready to go by the time the wedding party gets to the reception. They'll walk out, take photos, share a glass of champagne in private, and then we're planning for their arrival about thirty minutes after the ceremony."

I clap my hands together. "Sounds pretty seamless. I'll need to keep all the food refrigerated, but I can set everything else up now."

"Wonderful."

I get to work, setting down the stainless-steel chaffing dishes, filling the water pans, and attaching the biofuel that will later heat the dishes. I set out two end tables with cutlery, porcelain dishes, and napkins. Within an hour of getting there, I've done everything I possibly can prior to the start of the ceremony.

Guests have already started to arrive, and although I'm dressed in all black, I feel the need to step away until it's time to load the dishes into their trays. So I set out into the woods, in the opposite direction than the guests who are arriving, and find a nearby trail that leads me toward the sound of rushing water.

I'm sure I could have heard that same sound, only fainter, back at the wedding spot, but I hadn't even been paying attention. It's amazing what happens when my mind is full of nonsense, yet when I step into the unknown, all my senses come alive.

Snoqualmie Falls is around here somewhere. I've visited them once before on a short hike with Zach when we first moved to Seattle. But even on that day, my mind was full of anger and frustration over my father like it had been for so many years.

When I was younger, fighting to survive despite the rage that always seemed to find me, I knew I was meant for more. I knew that above the shadows was something so much brighter, but back then, the darkness was too much to fight through to find the light. I was practically drowning in the darkness when Coach pulled me out with his stern words and threat to turn both Zach and me in for fighting.

The anger is infrequent now, coming only when thoughts or situations having to do with my father cloud the peace of mind that I've worked so hard to hang on to. I won't turn out like him. I've set up controls, like my limits with drinking, to prevent myself from falling into the same disease that he has. But I worry about the triggers. I worry about the next thing that could set me off and bring me right back to my fourteen-year-old self, who was so damaged and lost he couldn't see straight.

I also worry about my father, and even that can bring on a trigger worth fearing. His ASD is deemed unmanageable by his doctors until he seeks help for his addiction. Other than that, everyone tells me all I can do is wait. *Wait for what?* I'm not sure, and I'm too afraid of the answer to ask the question.

But today, I can hear the heavy waters plunging into the pool beneath the falls. Today, I can breathe in the fresh air and not feel like I'm close to drowning. Today, I can see the beauty in nature and bask in its magic. And if all I have is today, I want to make it worth it.

About a mile in, I can see the top of the waterfall through a gathering of trees, and as I close in on the view, that's not all I see. There's a group of women posing, smiling, and laughing for a photographer. An auburn-haired girl dressed all in white stands in the middle, flanked by a short-haired girl on her left and Monica on her right. Two other girls stand on either side of them. The bridesmaids are wearing seafoam-green silk dresses that bunch naturally at their breasts and fit snugly down their bodies, stopping at their shins.

I'm about to turn away when another woman catches my eye. She's not part of the photo shoot, and she's not wearing green like the other girls. She's wearing a long-sleeved pink dress that ends midthigh and is decorated in long rectangles of shimmering gold fabric. It's formfitting, with a thick band of gold fabric wrapping around her waistline and accentuating her sleek hourglass figure. And damn, her legs are so shimmery and long, I can't stop my eyes from traveling their golden lengths.

Maggie is leaning against a tree, her smile faint as she watches the group of playful women. My chest squeezes as I recognize the sadness and yearning in her eyes. Maggie may not know what she wants yet out of life, but she knows what she's missing out on. She doesn't strike me as a woman who has a ton of friends. With a life built for competition and appearances, I guess that doesn't surprise me. I can't imagine how hard it would be to trust a single soul under those circumstances.

Maggie turns slightly, her brows wrinkling together like she's searching for something in the woods. Before I can turn away, her eyes find mine and widen just as I pull back from the trees that gave me my view. I don't know if she knew it was me, but for the first time ever, I kind of want to be seen.

Something Borrowed
MAGGIE

Leaves flutter in the breeze as I squint to make out the figure that I swear was just peeking out through the trees. Maybe it was my imagination, but I could have sworn I saw a pair of bold blue eyes looking back at me before disappearing completely. Or maybe it was just my wishful hoping that Desmond was on the other side of those bushes.

My feelings for Desmond are becoming more complicated with each passing day. It doesn't help that I'm surrounded by the guy every waking moment. Even now at this beautiful wedding, when my focus should be on the bride and groom who are about to share their first look, I can't stop thinking about him.

Our kiss from earlier in the week still plays on my mind. The memory is so vivid that I can still feel his luscious lips, demanding mouth, and encouraging tongue, not to mention his greedy hands, whispered words, and heated breaths.

I exhale a soft sigh as my body heats all over again. I've never felt more desired than I did that night, and when he pulled me into the back seat of his car, I was more than ready to go all the way. Why not? We are two adults with needs that don't require commitment or love to satisfy. And in that moment with Desmond, I wanted to use him just as badly as I know he wanted to use me. And I was okay with it.

So I thought.

If it was only about sex, then I'm pretty sure the buzz of attraction wouldn't be so strong when we're together. I wouldn't constantly be sneaking glances at him while he's teaching class. And I wouldn't be seeking his approval in the kitchen.

None of the above should matter at all, but clearly, it does

My thoughts are interrupted by a crackling of twigs as the second half of the bridal party moves through the brush. My heartrate picks up speed because this is the moment when the bride and her groom are going to see each other for the first time that day. It's all so romantic, with Chloe staring out at the waterfall, her hands nervously gripping the rail while the bridesmaids slowly trail away to give the couple privacy.

I watch Gavin's face as he spots his bride on his approach. All he can see is her long, flowing, auburn hair set in perfect waves down her bare spine. Her dress is completely open in the back, reaching just below her waist before falling around her legs. She's a stunning sight, but so is he.

Gavin's face is cleanly shaven, and his hair is swept loosely to the side. His black tux makes him look like a version of James Bond, with his tall and muscular build concealed beneath the elegant fabric. And the anticipation on his handsome face as he awaits meeting his bride has my chest swelling with emotion.

My breath catches in my throat when he finally approaches her from behind, and she straightens in his presence. It's no secret that these two are well attuned to one another, but there's such an innocence about them that makes this meeting so raw, so significant. I won't be able to look away if I try.

Gavin reaches for her hand, as if to give her the courage to turn around and face her soon-to-be husband. There's a moment of pause while she pulls in a deep breath, rights her shoulders, and starts to turn. When their eyes catch, it's the most beautiful thing I've ever witnessed.

Chloe's expression immediately fights an onslaught of emotions as her eyes search her fiancé's. Gavin looks equally emotional as he grabs both of her hands and looks her down then back up. At the moment their eyes connect again, their first tears fall. He's wiping hers, and she's wiping his, and then they lean in, whisper something no one around them can hear, and they kiss.

Cheers explode from the bridal party, and when Chloe and Gavin part again, it's with a smile and another swipe of tears. More pictures ensue, and I'm suddenly feeling like an intruder. Monica insisted that I come with them to their photo shoot since none of the wedding guests had arrived yet, but I don't feel right sharing this moment with them.

As the photo shoot continues, I sneak off through the woods and make my way toward the ceremony area. I'm eager to find a spot in the back row, but then a man in all black catches my eye. He has the build of a football player and the hair of a *Sons of Anarchy* cast member. Then he turns around, and a fluttering inhabits my chest. Desmond is devilishly sexy.

He's currently chatting up Phoebe's sister, Ursula, when I spot another figure in my peripheral. "Zach? I thought you couldn't make it."

He greets me with a wink and a hug. "I didn't want to promise Monica in case I wasn't able to, but Coach was kind about it. I just have to jet to the airport at ten o'clock, so no partying for me."

I smile, still emotional from the photo shoot, and feel myself blinking back tears. "You're so good to my sister. She'll be so excited to see you."

He shrugs, like there's no other option. "I love her." Then his grin widens, and he loops an arm around me. "One day, it will be Monica and I saying 'I do.'"

I chuckle and nod over to Desmond, who now appears to be flirting with another woman, this one a beauty around Faye's age. "That's fine and all, but can you leave him at home for your wedding? He'll just try to hit on all the ladies."

Zach bursts into laughter. "True. Well, at least you have nothing to worry about, then."

My stomach squeezes with discomfort. "What do you mean by that?" I ask with a forced laugh. The last thing I want is for Zach to think I care an iota about how Desmond feels about me.

Zach's eyes flick to mine. "You don't have to worry about Desmond hitting on you. I know you're not exactly his biggest fan, which is perfectly fine. Des has a type if you haven't noticed." He gestures over to Desmond, who is still talking with the woman.

I might just feel my heart break a little in my chest. "You mean older women?"

Zach winks and then releases my shoulder, leaving a chill. "Don't say you heard it from me."

I'm still watching Desmond interact with the beautiful middle-aged brunette when he looks over and spots me. His eyes quickly shift to Zach, and then he excuses himself from the woman and starts to jog over.

If I needed additional confirmation that Desmond and I should not be kissing in concert halls or in the back seat of his car, this is it. Desmond has a type, and I'm not it. Clearly, we let the buzz of alcohol and good music cloud our minds. We created a false sense of protection from everything we know we shouldn't want: each other.

"Well, look who decided to show up." Desmond claps Zach on the back while I stay a safe few feet away.

"Couldn't let my girl attend a wedding alone, now could I?" Zach grins, making his true intentions clear.

Desmond rolls his eyes. "Of course not."

"How's the catering gig going? Got everything under control?"

Desmond shrugs. "It's all good. Maggie here helped with all the prep back at the kitchen, and everything's ready to put on the burners when it's time."

I swallow as Desmond's burning blue eyes land on mine when he mentions my name. And even as I look away, I can feel them lingering on me like he's begging me to turn back toward him. Why does he have to look at me like that? We're supposed to hate each other. When did things become so much more complicated?

When you kissed him, you idiot.

But even as I answer my own question, I know complications started much earlier than when Desmond and I kissed. They started from the first day I met him. Our first exchange that was fueled with attraction and something new, only to be shattered by a harsh reality.

"It looks like seats are filling up," Zach says, his gaze traveling to the ceremony area. "I'm going to go find a spot in the back."

I perk up. "I'll go with you."

Zach nods and holds out his arm for me to take.

"Wait, Maggie. Can I borrow you for a second?" Desmond asks.

My heart takes off, beating fast at the sound of my name on Desmond's tongue. I squeeze my lids together and turn to face him. Everything from the past week is suddenly swirling around in my chest and in my head, to the point that I feel like a volcano is about to erupt, and I have no chance of stopping it.

"I'm not a toy," I snap. "No, you can't borrow me." There's so much fury in my tone, even Zach takes notice with a lift of his brows.

"No worries," Zach says, taking a step away. "I'll save you a spot, Mags." Then his eyes float to Desmond in a questioning look before he walks off.

I bite the inside of my lip as my eyes travel back to Desmond's. He's glaring at me intensely. "I was just going to tell you that you look beautiful tonight and that any man who gets to dance with you will be a lucky bastard." He gives a defensive lift of his hands and takes a step back toward the reception area. "But I probably should have saved my breath. Enjoy the ceremony."

I feel like a complete asshole as I watch Desmond walk away. Then I notice an orange leaf, still attached to a thin branch, clinging to Desmond's shoulder blade.

Desmond was definitely in the woods earlier.

And he was watching me.

The Dance

DESMOND

The food is hot and currently ready to be devoured by the 121 guests that arrived, one more than expected since Zach ended up showing. I wonder if Maggie would have come here today if Zach had agreed to be Monica's date from the beginning. And if she hadn't come, would I seriously be contemplating taking Chloe and Gavin up on their offer to partake in the festivities once the majority of my catering duties are complete?

The wedding party starts to trickle in as music plays. The bridesmaids and groomsmen walk in pairs from the small white tents set up behind the reception area to the ceremony, where the guests are waiting. Monica, who is walking down the aisle with Gavin's friend Justin, lights up like a Christmas tree when she spots Zach sitting in the back row.

I've never known Zach to fall so hard for a woman. That always made my desire to remain single forever an easy goal to uphold. Now I'm certain that a proposal to Monica is in the very near future, and then what? I can't be the single bachelor forever, not when my best friend is hitched to the girl of his dreams. Suddenly, staying single forever doesn't sound as appealing as it once did.

I groan at my own thoughts, which are clearly the nature of attending events like this one. Romance is in the air, thanks to the bride and groom, who are making their entrance to the tune of "Stand By You" by Rachel Platten. Bright smiles light up their entire beings as they squeeze the other's hand and wave at the hooting and hollering guests.

Chloe and Gavin's love is one their friends clearly root hard for, and today is sure to be one hell of a celebration. That's exactly what ensues.

Guests start to line up for their food. An adorable little girl with long red hair and freckles on both cheeks starts to bust a move on the dance floor. The bride and groom greet guests who stand in a line to offer their sentiments. And the bar becomes more and more crowded as the night goes on.

When it comes time for the first dance, all the chaos and excitement morph into a beautiful silence that follows the newly married couple out onto the empty dance floor. A spotlight hits them, and the music starts. The song, according to the wedding program, is "Never Stop" by Safety Suit.

Gavin leads Chloe in small steps around the floor, twirling her every now and then before bringing her back into his arms and planting a sweet kiss on her lips. All eyes in the reception space are on them. Tears are falling, hands are clutching, and when I glance over at the long table where Maggie is sitting beside Zach, I have the distinct need to join them. Instead, I keep myself busy, checking on the food and keeping everything hot for the guests.

"Desmond," Chloe says with a laugh as she approaches. I'm currently straightening up, using a butter knife to scrape the fallen breadcrumbs off the tablecloth of the buffet table. "What are you doing?"

I grin and gesture to the empty buffet. "Just trying to keep busy. Congratulations, by the way. This is a beautiful wedding."

Her eyes soften, and she places her hands on her hips. "Thank you, but I'll be forced to leave a horrid review for your services if you don't join in on the fun."

I shake my head, feeling flustered. "No, I couldn't. You're paying me to keep your guests full."

"And you've done that superbly. Now come join us."

Gavin comes up behind her and places his arms around Chloe. "What my *wife* is trying to say is that you weren't just invited here to cater the event. We'd love for you to join us. In fact, I'm heading to the bar now. What's your poison?"

Against my better judgment—and not wanting to be rude—I join Gavin at the bar on the other side of the dance floor. He gets me a beer, and while we're still there, one of the groomsmen buys everyone at the bar a shot of whiskey. Again, I don't want to be rude.

The next thing I know, Zach is joining us at the bar to grab a water, and Gavin is sneaking off to find his bride. "Finally coming to join the party, huh?"

I shrug. "Guess so, dude. Where's your girl? She was pretty excited to see you."

Zach points at a couple of girls in the center of the dance floor. Maggie and Monica are laughing as they dance all-out with some crazy dance moves. Arms are flying, hips are bumping, and I can't help but smile at seeing Maggie have so much fun.

"So what's your deal with Maggie. You like her?"

The question catches me so off guard, I yank my eyes from the girls and narrow them at Zach. Meanwhile, my heart is beating a million miles an hour in my chest. "What? No, dude. We hate each other, remember?"

Zach narrows his eyes. "Yeah, I'm starting to think you two hate each other a little too much. You care about her. I didn't see it before, but I do now."

I scoff and shake my head. "I'm with her all the time, thanks to you and Monica. We drive each other fucking nuts. Don't start this with me, okay?"

I don't know why I'm so insistent on making Zach believe my lies, but he doesn't seem to be buying it at all.

"You're a grown-ass man, dude. Just be careful, okay? Maggie isn't someone you should mess around with if you aren't going to take it seriously."

This time I remain silent, and I know it's as much of an admission as I'll allow. It's not like I'm fooling him anyway. Zach is my best friend. If anyone's going to see through my bullshit, it's him.

Zach reaches around me and squeezes my neck. "Anyway, have fun tonight, dude. I haven't seen you do that since our trip to Hawaii last year."

I sigh, not wanting to point out that I had a great time last week at a concert with Maggie, a night I would love to redo if I could. Except instead of pulling her into the back seat, I would have pulled her into the front. Okay, scratch that. If we're talking about redos, then I would go back to that first night she got into my car when I failed to mention the truth about where I got it.

Zach doesn't stick around. The moment he gets his water, he takes off for Monica, and I'm left peering at the dance floor from the bar.

I try not to glare at Justin, who just asked Maggie to dance and is currently trying to pull her closer to him. She's laughing, leaning into him, and getting a little too comfortable in his arms. They're friends, so I get it. But when one, two, three songs later, they're still dancing together, I start to feel my patience unravel.

I'm two seconds away from throwing a wrench into their little dance-off when Justin whispers something in Maggie's ear then heads toward the bar. And there she is, in the middle of the dance floor, alone. He proceeds to push up to the bar beside me and order two vodka sodas, one of those with three limes. That's Maggie's drink, and hearing him order it is enough of a push for me to leave the bar and move through the dance crowd until Maggie is directly under my nose.

"My turn."

Her eyes snap to mine, and she takes an immediate step back. "Try that again." Her words are fierce and clear. *That's not how you ask a woman to dance.* We may not have known each other very long, but we're both from a place where manners come first between a man and a woman, and my approach was one-hundred-percent wrong.

"Cut me some slack, Maggie. I'd really like to dance with you."

"Why?"

Is she serious? "Because in two minutes, your dance partner will be back with your drink, and I'd like to remind you why you shouldn't dance with him again."

Her eyes freeze on mine before she follows up that cold look with a roll of her eyes. "Oh, really?"

I nod curtly. "Yes, really."

"You are something else."

I step closer and encircle my arms around her waist. She doesn't pull away, causing me to smile. "It's about time you think so."

She places her hands on my chest and tosses her half-ponytail updo over her shoulder, all the while fighting the smile that's already tipping up her cheeks. "It's not a slow song, Desmond. Please tell me you can move those hips of yours like a true gentleman."

I grin at her joke and pull my hands away. "Challenge accepted." I start to move to the beat and wait for her to join in. I might not be the best dancer in the world, but I've got enough rhythm to hold my own. In fact, my love for dancing might just be a close third to my love for food and photography.

Maggie is full-on laughing now, but she's dancing too. "Okay, okay. Does this courage have anything to do with that shot I saw you taking at the bar?"

I grin. "Sounds like someone's been watching me. I'm only on drink number two, so my courage has room to grow."

She groans. "How about you stop counting? Just for one night?"

I ignore her suggestion. That won't happen. "How about you stop running your mouth and dance with me, gorgeous?" I find her hand and use it to tug her toward me. Her body slams into mine, and her smile widens, as if she couldn't hold back her joy even if she tried. And her joy is contagious.

I hold onto the hand I tugged and wrap my other arm around her waist, holding her firmly against me while I move us to the beat. She follows well enough, despite my desperate need to see her smile and laugh again. Then I change direction when she least expects it, causing her to throw her head back and laugh. Everyone around us is bumping and grinding on the dance floor, and sure, we could do that too. But there's something about Maggie that brings me back to my roots. To the days when I would hide away in my garage and secretly teach myself how to dance, all so that I could impress some girl at an upcoming dance.

I'm so lost in the moment, in Maggie, that I don't expect the tap on the shoulder when it comes. Looking up, I register Justin's face. Clearly, he can see that Maggie and I are having fun here, but he's back anyway.

"Hey, Des," he greets with a grin, like we're the best of friends instead of acquaintances who happen to see each other at home football games. Then he grins at Maggie while reaching past me with her drink. "Just how you like it."

Maggie accepts it with a smile, but it falters quickly when she looks between Justin and me. "Um..." she says, like she's about to let us both down gently.

But then Justin holds out his hand, even though one of mine is still around her waist. "How about another dance?" he asks her, completely ignoring me now.

I guess that's one way to steal a girl away without causing a fight—speak directly to her and ignore the guy currently holding her.

The rage inside me is building, but I know better than to take it out on a man with a crush. I've gotten into enough fights to know how this will end if I unleash that beast inside me. *Never again.* It was a promise I made to myself around the same time I made my pledge against drinking too much.

I take a step back, releasing my hold on Maggie. It might be wishful hoping, but I swear her eyes flicker with disappointment as she slides her gaze from me to Justin.

"Sure," she says with ease.

Just like that, I've been replaced. I swallow before turning around and walking back to the bar. I lean my back against it, desperately trying to keep my eyes from Maggie and Justin. I could pick some other girl to dance with, someone who wouldn't move on to someone else so easily, but as my eyes float around the perimeter of the dance floor in a lazy search, a pair of caramel ones catch on mine.

She's dancing with him, but she's looking at me.

My heart is drumming against my rib cage. I should have never let her out of my hold. I should have stayed by her side. I should have fought to keep her in my arms. And that's a lesson I only need to learn once.

My feet start to carry me back to the center of the dance floor where I left her before my mind can think logically about my next step. All I know is that the music is transitioning into a slower one, and Justin is creeping in closer to my girl. *My girl.* Maggie may not belong to anyone, but to me, she's mine, even if just on this dance floor.

I tap Justin's back the way he tapped on mine, and he stalls in midstep just like he forced me to do. When he turns around, his eyes widen in surprise, but just as quickly, they settle into understanding. *Bro code.* And I just delivered it. I ignore him, taking a card from his playing deck, and pin Maggie with my stare. "Would you honor me with another dance, Maggie Stevens?" I'm laying it on a little thick, but her grin is so wide that I know it was worth it.

She turns to Justin with a sympathetic smile. "I'm sorry, Justin. I'm going to dance with Desmond now."

Justin nods, making it no secret that he's disappointed. Then he turns to me with a friendly fist bump before he walks away. And then Maggie is right back where she belongs, in my arms.

This time, I'm not letting her go, not ever.

Without Even Trying

MAGGIE

Everything I've been suppressing in my heart, mind, and soul when it comes to Desmond Blake sparks to life the moment he takes me back in his hold. That's how it feels, and I can't even try to deny it now, not with how swelled my heart grows in my chest as he holds my gaze. A combustible energy sizzles between us that neither of us have a chance at stopping. It's similar to that feeling that swallowed me whole the night of the concert, but something about this feels different.

He's closer now, mentally and physically. Resisting him all week has done nothing to ease the growing sexual tension between us. It might have even made it all worse because I've already experienced the danger of Desmond's touch and the sinful kisses that found their way to my neck, my lips, and my breasts. As much as I know I shouldn't, I want a repeat of that performance but, this time, without interruption. I want to know how we fit together physically, because mentally, in some strange crazy way, like the most complicated puzzle, our pieces absolutely fit.

While my heart is racing, I manage to keep up with Desmond's natural ability to move around a dance floor. Not that there's much room to move, but he carries the beat like it was born in him. His gentle grip on the small of my back palms me in a way that feels gentle yet all-consuming. With his chest pressed to mine, his gaze caressing me without a shred of indecency, and with his feet timed so perfectly to mine, we might as well be tied together. Anyone around us might think we've been dancing this way for years.

Desmond leans forward slowly and presses a kiss to my cheek. Then his lips travel to my ear. "I meant what I said earlier. You look beautiful, Maggie. Tonight, tomorrow, yesterday. I've never thought anything different. And…" He pulls back so he's looking at me. I feel naked beneath his all-consuming gaze. "I'm desperate to ask you not to dance with anyone else tonight, but of course, that's your choice."

If words could light a fire, then his just went straight from his chest to mine. I swallow because I don't know how to make sense of my thoughts when I can't hear myself think over my own heartbeat. "Was that you in the woods earlier today?" I suck in a breath. "Watching me?"

Desmond's smile curves into a faint smirk. "I thought you might have caught me."

I bite down on my bottom lip, suddenly feeling bashful. Just minutes ago, I was in the driver's seat, but now I'm struggling to hold on to the wheel. "I wasn't sure."

"I couldn't take my eyes off you. I haven't been able to all night."

My thoughts are racing a million miles an hour, but one thought pulls into the lead, smoking out the rest and adding to my anxiety. "Are you sure? I'm not exactly your type."

His smile fades, and his lips twist with confusion. "What type would that be?"

I shrug. "That woman you were talking to before the ceremony before you came over to talk to Zach and me." I cringe a little, hating that I feel the need to point this out. "You know. That more *mature* woman."

Desmond lets out a chuckle and shakes his head. "Holy fuck, Zach was warning you away from me, wasn't he?"

When he searches my expression for an answer, I sigh. "Maybe."

He rolls his eyes then brings his gaze back to mine. "I might not have the best track record when it comes to women, but I've always been honest—with them, with you—and I'm not ashamed of my past. And if by my *type*, Zach means that I go for safe women, women who won't expect roses and romance, then yeah. I guess I have a type."

His answer doesn't exactly do much for my nerves. *I should take comfort in knowing that Desmond isn't interested in a relationship since that's the last thing I want with him.* But even as I tell myself that, I'm not quite sure I believe it.

He leans in and places a kiss on my cheek. "I'm not perfect. Never have been. But I'll never lie to you, Maggie. That's one promise I can make you."

We're done talking when Desmond dips me, supporting my arch before bringing me back into his hold. Dancing with Desmond is effortless, just like bantering with him. He's just… Desmond, and like always, the pull I feel toward him is strong, but so is my need to run.

For the next two hours, we dance, drink, and laugh. I almost think he's stopped counting his drinks until he waves away a shot offered to him by Gavin. "I can't man. Thank you, but I need to drive that van home soon."

My jaw drops, and I laugh up at him. "You can't deny a shot from the groom at his own wedding. It's bad luck!" I don't know if I just made that superstition up or if it actually existed, but it sounds good coming out of my mouth. "You've only had one since we started dancing."

"Yeah," Desmond says coolly while glancing down at his phone. "But it's ten o'clock."

"And you're going to turn into a pumpkin?" I tease with a tilt of my head. I don't want this night to be over.

"No, smart-ass, but I do need to pick up the trays and load the van." He hesitates to leave me on the dance floor, and my heart skips a beat. I imagine the reason why he doesn't want to leave me is because he doesn't want me to dance with anyone else.

"I'll come with you and help," I offer.

Desmond blinks like he doesn't understand me. "Really? You don't have to."

"I want to."

"Okay, but don't expect me to pay you overtime."

I roll my eyes and follow him to the catering table. He starts on one side, and I start on the other. We're able to stack most of the trays since they're empty, but the ones we can't, I empty into a few containers that Desmond plans to drop off at a nearby shelter on his way home. After four trips, everything is in the van, and we're standing near the tree, debating whether or not to rejoin the reception.

"Do you need a ride home?" he asks nonchalantly as he plays with his keys.

I open my mouth to tell him no but then have a change of heart. "Monica offered to share her hotel room tonight, but…"

His brows lift in anticipation.

"If you're okay to drive, I think I'd rather go back to my studio."

"I'm okay to drive," he says quickly. "Do you want to stay for a bit, or—"

"Let's go for a walk first. I hear it's pretty out here at night."

"Lead the way."

I swallow and start to walk in the direction of the path that connects to the falls where we took the bridal photos. As soon as we get to the fork in the path, I smile back at Desmond and tug him to the right, toward the sound of the falls.

"Where are you taking me?"

"You'll see." I don't let go of his hand until we arrive at a circular clearing with a balcony that overlooks a brightly lit waterfall. "Now you don't have to spy on me from afar," I tease him with a grin. "You can check out this beauty right here with me."

His eyes are locked over my shoulder at the stunning sight. "Oh, wow. I've never seen it at night."

I grin, enjoying his reaction almost more than my own experience. "It's beautiful, right?"

His palms wrap around the balcony rail beside me, and his eyes are glued to the rushing falls. He releases a breath that relaxes his shoulders. "It's unbelievable."

Everything about the falls appears so much larger than it did earlier. They seem bigger, louder, grander, and alive. I lean onto the rail beside him and shut my eyes. I lift my chin and breathe against the breeze. For how long, I'm not sure, but I know I haven't felt this at peace in a very long time.

"You should do this more often."

Desmond's voice catches me off guard, and I whip my head around to find him with his phone camera aimed at me. My heart sinks as anxiety weaves its way through me. "What are you doing?"

"Admiring the view," he says with a grin until realization strikes. His eyes widen in apology. "I forgot about the permission thing. I should have asked to take your photo first." Then he starts frantically tapping through his phone. "I can delete it."

Before I can think of what I'm doing, my hand is covering his to stop him. "Wait. Can I see it first?"

He glances up at me like he isn't sure he heard me correctly, then he places his phone in my hands. It takes me a second to work up the courage to look down. It's not that I'm afraid of the image I'll see on the other side or that I'm tired of having my photo taken. It's the fact that for the past twenty-plus years, photography has been more about artificial beauty than it has been about art. Through the lens, I was whoever they wanted me to be. Through the lens, I was a lie. But just in the few simple shots I've seen Desmond take of me, I know that, to him, photography is more than creating the perfect moment at the perfect angle with the perfect lighting. Desmond captures moments, he doesn't try to create them. And for that, I don't want him to delete the photo of me. It shows my hair in a disheveled half-ponytail after a fun night of dancing, with natural shadows from the surrounding trees blocking the bright light coming from the falls. I'm everything.

"You're the most beautiful sight when you don't know anyone is watching you. Do you know that?"

My throat closes with emotion before I look up at him. "So this is it, huh? The Desmond charm? And I'm the lucky one who gets to experience it tonight?" I'm trying to keep things playful, because if I don't, I might just start to like what he's saying.

He narrows his eyes. "I mean it, Maggie. You're beautiful all on your own, without even having to try."

I swallow, trying to keep my fluttering nerves at bay. "That was a really sweet thing to say."

As if he knows things are getting a little too serious, his lips tug up at the corner, and his eyes slide down my body then back up. "Well, that dress isn't helping matters."

I shove him playfully as I laugh. "I should have known it was too good to be true."

"What can I say?" he teases. "I'm a really sweet guy."

"No, you're not, but those rare moments when you are just might be my favorite." I pull away from the rail and hold out his phone to him. "Don't delete that photo."

He takes his phone and places it in his pocket, before scooping up my hand in his. "I wouldn't dream of it. It was already on the cloud anyway."

A growl starts in my chest and slips past my throat. "You are something else."

He winks and squeezes my hand. "Ready to go home now?"

"Yes."

The Fifth Drink

DESMOND

It's just past eleven when I walk Maggie upstairs to our adjacent condos. Almost as soon as we got into my van at the wedding site, she fell asleep, giving me far too much time to steal glances at the woman in the pink-and-gold dress. Now she seems awake and as vibrant as ever.

"Thank you for the ride." She's playing with her keys as her eyes shine back on mine, and I don't want her to leave me.

"Always. But you know," I say with a smile and tilt of my head, "one of these days you're going to have to get yourself a ride of your own."

She shrugs. "I don't need one when I have you." She flashes those pearly white teeth at me and turns toward her door to unlock it. "Plus, I'd have to get my license first."

"What?" I cough out the word with my laugh, and she just shrugs before pushing open her door. "Wait." I jump forward until I'm halfway between her door and mine. "I was going to have a drink and maybe light a fire and turn on a movie." I take a breath, realizing how desperate I sound. "Why don't you come over for a minute?"

"Um," she says, looking at her door and then at me.

"I did only have three at the wedding," I remind her with a grin. "Join me?" Then I cringe as I remember how fast asleep she was in the van. "Unless you're too tired and just want to go to bed." I take a step back, trying to lessen the blow of disappointment before it hits.

"I'll come in for one drink." She looks down and then lets out a breathy laugh. "I should probably change first. Give me thirty minutes?"

Jesus, if my heart was dead, her words were enough to jump-start it back to life. "Yeah, okay." I keep my response as nonchalant as possible, not wanting to sway her decision a single bit.

As soon as the door shuts behind her, I'm tearing into my condo, ripping off my shirt, and unbuttoning my pants. With a quick glance around, I breathe out a sigh of relief that I'm not a sloppy son of a bitch. Everything is mostly clean besides a stack of unopened mail on my kitchen island, a few dishes I quickly place into the dishwasher, and my unmade bed, which I fix up in a few minutes. Then I light the fire and turn on the surround-sound speakers to play my custom country playlist. A light soundtrack to the night will be perfect.

When I finish all of the above, I have twenty minutes left to change. Or maybe I should shower.

Before I can decide, there's a faint knock at my door. With a quick glance at the digital clock on my microwave, I start to think I heard her wrong. I swear she said to give her thirty.

I jog from my bedroom to the front door and yank it open. "That was fast—oh." I trip over my words, expecting to see Maggie dressed in sweats and ready for our nightcap. Disappointment settles over me when I notice she's still dressed in her outfit from tonight. I'm expecting her to tell me that coming over will be a bad idea and that she's changed her mind, but then I catch the way she's looking back at me with a bashful smile.

She lets out a light laugh as her eyes bulge at my chest. Then she quickly turns away. "This is embarrassing, but Monica kind of helped me put this dress on, and…" Her voice trails off as she turns around. "I can't reach."

My eyes follow the line of long metal teeth that starts between her shoulder blades and runs down to the middle of her ass. Her gentle curves draw the shape of an hourglass from her ribs to her waist and then to her hips. I don't even realize I've completely gone still from her request until she throws me a glance over her shoulder.

She catches me in my stare, and her brows draw together. "Do you mind unzipping me?"

I clear my throat and step forward, trying to keep my head from spinning before I pass out from the closeness of her. *Jeez.* I haven't even touched her yet, and my hands are shaking just looking at her in that dress. Her half-ponytail is still intact and falling down the middle of her back. With a sweep of my hands, I place the locks over her shoulder before taking hold of the pink fabric between two fingers and gripping the zipper with my other hand. Then I bring the metal down slowly.

Inch by inch, metal teeth unfasten, parting against flawless dark-olive skin and the strapless white clasp of a bra. I lean down and press a kiss to her shoulder, an innocent reaction to the proximity of her. But the way her hair spikes in the area I just kissed tells me she didn't consider it so innocent. I kiss her again between her shoulder blades, then again on her other shoulder, until I've hit the base of her zipper. The fancy fabric she's wearing spreads open wide.

I take in a breath and lean back slightly to peer down her back and confirm what I already know is true. Her plump ass is now uncovered except for her white panties, which are really just a scrap of lace that separates her cheeks. The sight is enough to send my erection jolting to life in mere seconds.

"Shit," I say on an exhale. "I think I went too far. I'm sorry."

She tosses me a look over her shoulder, her eyes shining with amusement. "I'm sure you're used to seeing plenty of asses." She winks. "We're good."

Fuck me.

She starts to take a step back toward her door, but if she thinks I'm going to let her walk away after that comment, she's very wrong. My hand slides beneath the rose-gold fabric of her dress and circles her waist. I lay a palm on her flat stomach and then bring her back to me in one quick move. I'm rock hard against her ass while I press my mouth to her ear and growl, "What is that supposed to mean?"

She shivers in my hold, and her hand covers mine at her stomach from over her dress. "It means you've been around the block, Desmond. I'm nothing special to you."

Anger and excitement fuel me like gasoline on a fire. I'm angry that she feels the need to constantly make assumptions about me and excited because all I want to do is prove her wrong. "Oh, Maggie, you have no fucking idea what you are to me." I press my mouth against the nape of her neck. "You're everything I shouldn't want, but I do. You're the first thing on my mind when I wake up in the morning. And you're the only woman I saw at that wedding tonight. That's what you are to me, Maggie Stevens. What am I to you?"

Her breaths have shallowed, and I can hear her heartbeat speed at the sound of my voice. "You're my boss." She whispers the words so faintly that I almost miss them. "And my landlord."

My hand slips lower until I reach the lace band of her panties. "Is that all?"

I start to lift my hand away from her skin when she starts to shake her head. "No." Her words are still small, but they're firmer now, unquestionable.

I dip back down, this time below her panty line, until I'm slipping between her folds and feeling what I already knew existed. "So wet," I rasp before nipping at her neck. Maggie wants me, and I'm not the type of guy who plans on letting her down. "How long have you been wet for me?" She sucks in a ragged breath, but no words follow, so I punish her by circling her clit with agonizing slowness. "How long, Maggie?" I demand again.

"All night."

Her confession is enough, but that's not all she gives me. I'm still rubbing her clit when her ass rubs against my cock like she's trying to get me off through our clothes. *Wait*, my brain screams. This isn't how tonight is supposed to go. Groaning, I remove my finger and slowly pull my hand out of her dress. Then I grip her small waist and swivel her to face me.

She's breathing heavily, and so am I. It's all the confirmation I need to lean in and slide my tongue across her bottom lip and then her top one, slowly, deliberately, gliding and dipping at the bow. When my lips leave hers, she shudders. I press her to me, my fingers caressing her bare skin at her arch until she's right where I want her, bent beneath me by my direction, but completely at her will. Her mouth is glistening and waiting, her body is hot and shaking, and her breaths are shallow and ragged.

And I'm a fucking done man.

My mouth moves on hers like a hungry lion, more than ready for my meal but willing to wait if it means toying with my prey. I part her mouth the way I parted her dress, slowly exploring and gently tasting. Then I'm delving in with my tongue the way my fingers did her panties.

Maggie doesn't realize this yet, but I like to take my time. I like the agony that comes before an explosive orgasm. And I'm going to love torturing her with slow hands, light touching, and a mouth so dirty, she'll beg for mercy. I should warn her now. The only mercy I'll be giving her is when I finally let her explode on my cock.

When I pull away from her mouth, I feel like she might buckle beneath me if I wasn't holding her up. She clings to my arms, her eyes fluttering open as she does, and then she's pulling in a long, deep breath.

"So how about that drink?" I ask.

She nods, and I chuckle before tugging her inside my condo and shutting the door behind us. I'm not letting her leave to change again.

I lead her to my kitchen and reach into my refrigerator to pull out a bottle of wine and two chilled glasses. "Good?"

Her back is to me, her eyes floating around the room. Then they snap to what I'm holding. "Fine with me."

In that moment, I take in her unzipped dress and my unzipped pants and laugh at the image. She catches my gaze and faces me with a curious smile. "What?"

"I really do love that dress." I step up to the island to uncork the bottle then pour two small glasses. I want a clear head for what I think—hope—might happen tonight.

"Thanks," she says with pinking cheeks. "Monica made it for me."

I knew Monica was a fashion-design student, but I didn't realize her talents extended that far. "Tell her she did a great job, maybe too great of a job."

Maggie grins. "I'll let her know. I'm glad it's still intact." She winks, and I almost choke on my first sip of wine.

"Night's not over."

She turns away so I can't see her expression and continues to walk around my condo. She passes the couch, walks the perimeter of the dining room, pausing at the bench seat under a large window, before making her way to the living room. She runs a finger against the white brick mantle above the fireplace then sits with her back to the flames before narrowing her eyes at me. "Your place is a lot bigger than mine."

I smirk and walk toward her. "I pay a lot more than you do."

She takes a sip of her wine and rolls her eyes. "Well then, maybe I need to find a new job, one that pays me more."

I know she's teasing, but I can't resist a good verbal tennis match. "More than a rent-free condo, free rides, and free meals, plus a paycheck?" Now it's my turn to take a sip while narrowing my eyes in a challenge and keeping my game-winning smile on my face.

"The view isn't so bad either."

Her words surprise me, only because of her casual tone that registers a layer of flirtation as she holds my eyes.

"It's nice to know we're on the same page."

She grins. "For once."

I shrug. "Maybe this is the start of a new story, one where we share many pages."

She lets out a light laugh. "You mean the story where the damsel in distress needs a tall, strong man to fight for her to the death."

I shrug. "Sure. Or the one with the red room, the handcuffs, and the nipple clamps. Your choice."

She almost chokes on her next sip of wine before swallowing it. "I wouldn't put it past you to have a dungeon of sexual pleasure."

"Good point, but I assure you, I don't." I'm studying her expression as she finishes the rest of her wine. All this talk of sex, jokingly or not, is throwing me off track. I hold out a hand, gesturing for her to give me her glass. When she does, I set mine and hers on the mantel. Then I reach out my hand again, my eyes gripping hers. "C'mere."

She takes my hand and stands.

With my hands on her waist and the fireplace burning beside us, I tilt my face down so our lips are inches apart. "I think I'm going to need to kiss you again."

Her lips part on a quick inhale, her light-brown eyes wide and shining. "Maybe you should stop thinkin' so much."

I don't waste a second before closing the distance between us and pressing my mouth to hers in a kiss I can only describe as desperate. I'm desperate to add fuel to the fire that's crackled between us since the very moment we met, a fire that never died even though we both tried to douse it with our resistance. All it took was a little wind for it to burst back to life.

My hands move from her waist to the open back of her dress as her palms slide up my bare chest. With a light touch, I draw my fingers up her skin until I'm holding on to the fabric at her shoulders. With every second that passes, our kiss deepens, our breathing increases, and I'm peeling the fabric from her skin.

Once I've removed the top portion of her dress, the rest falls away—over her sexy hips, around her sleek bronze legs, and down to her pointy heels, which give her already tall stature a few more inches in height. All that's left is a sheer white lingerie set consisting of her panties and a strapless bra that completely exposes her soft breasts and dark-pink nipples. Simple jewelry hangs around her neck and on her ears, and she still has on those killer heels, which I have no plans of taking off.

"Damn." My voice is low and shaky as I take in every ounce of beauty standing before me. "You have got to be kidding." She's a goddess in white. I run a finger along her bra, taking in her swollen nipple in awe. "Is this thing even a bra?"

She looks down and runs the pad of her thumb across one of her nipples. "It's a shelf. You know, to support me without all the coverage. It worked with the dress."

"Fuck yeah, it did." My gaze tracks her finger as it makes a slow circular pattern over her sensitive flesh until I can't take it anymore. I rip her hand away, replacing it with my own while slamming my mouth to hers. Then I kneel onto the faux sheepskin rug, taking her with me until I'm leaning her onto her back and spreading her knees with mine.

"You make me feel drunk," I growl as I tear my mouth from hers and ease my way down her body, stopping only to kiss her breasts, her belly, and then her clit over her panties.

"It's a good thing you stuck with your four-drink limit," she rasps. A moan follows as I swipe away the material between her thighs.

With fabric hooked around my finger and her tender pink skin right there, daring me to take a lick, I chuckle at her words. "I might just have to break my rule." My heavy lids open just enough to meet her confused gaze. "I think I'll let you be my fifth drink tonight." And with a swipe of my tongue, I throw caution to the wind and devour her.

Through the Lens

MAGGIE

Desmond's mouth is something to be marveled. He tastes me like I'm a delicacy too rich to consume quickly, taking his time, running his tongue up and down my center, appreciating every inch, every dip, and every ridge. My fingers move to his head and dig under his hair until I have a good grip on his scalp. Without a word, he understands my needy demand and closes his mouth around that sensitive bundle of nerves. His tongue flattens, spreading wide against me, and then he's sucking my bud between his lips, slowly and gently, before releasing me with a groan.

My head is foggy, and my heart is crashing hard in my chest, but I don't miss the thick digit Desmond slides into my opening or the light growl that climbs up his throat and slips past his lips. I peel my eyes open to catch a glimpse of him as he watches what he's doing to me.

He doesn't try to add another finger like I'm expecting. Instead, he starts to pump me slowly while hooking one of my legs with his free arm and placing his mouth on me again. My insides are quivering, and I swear I'm seconds from erupting when he pulls out his finger and picks up his head from between my thighs.

I gasp, the loss of him washing over me like I've been doused with cold water. "What are you doing? I was so close." I want his mouth back on me so I can unravel on his tongue.

He stares back at me under a hooded gaze, his breathing rapid as he climbs up my body. "Slow and steady." His gaze falls to my exposed breast before leaning down and covering it with his mouth just as two fingers work their way inside me.

I'm abuzz with sensations by the time my insides start to coil all over again. He pushes his fingers deeper, curling them inside me, then flicking and teasing my sweet spot over and over again.

"Don't stop, Desmond," I moan. "Please don't stop." I'm right there, my muscles clenching while a fire builds in my core. Any second now, I'm going to combust. My back arches, and my toes curl, but just as the quickening begins in my belly, Desmond removes his mouth and hands once more. Now he's standing over me, sweat beading on his skin.

"Why?" I cry. This is starting to feel like a dirty game, one I did not sign up for.

He grins and palms himself over his underwear. He's still half-dressed and oh, so sexy. "I told you. Slow and steady, babe. I promise I'll make it worth your while. Do you trust me?" Desmond is hard everywhere, from his tone to his gaze to his hard jaw visible even with his beard. I scroll down, taking in his sexy abs on my way to his long length, which is very apparent inside his unzipped pants.

I sit up then climb onto my knees, flicking my eyes up to his. "Yes." Then I grip the top of his waistband. "Do you trust me?"

He bites down on his bottom lip and nods. I swallow and focus on the man I'm about to undress. I peel away his pants, taking his white boxer briefs with them.

I suck in a breath when his erection springs free. Nothing could have prepared me for the sight of what I would be unleashing. All I know is that I'm suddenly grateful for the fact that Desmond wants to take his time with me tonight. I'm not sure I could have handled anything more.

He steps out of his pants, and I wrap my hand around his length and stroke it in the direction of my mouth. My heart is beating like crazy, and I know it's from fear that once I taste Desmond Blake, there's no going back.

I don't want to go back. I only want to move forward.

I take him in my mouth, swirling my tongue around his length before flattening it against the underside of him. I sheath my teeth and ease down, fitting as much of him as I can down my throat. When I can't go anymore, Desmond groans and takes the top of my ponytail in his fist then glides me up and back down, his greediness growing by the second. I curl the tip of my tongue just slightly, firming it against him to increase the intensity of each thrust while stroking the base of him with my hand.

Desmond responds with a string of curse words and a quickening of his movements. "Holy shit, woman."

I think he's about to let go, and I'm preparing for his hot release at any moment when he shocks me and pulls me all the way off him until I'm staring up at him with wide eyes and heavy breaths. "You didn't like it?"

He rolls his eyes, sinks down onto his knees, and locks eyes with me. Two beats of silence follow in which his lids turn to slits and he releases a long, heavy breath. Then he's gripping the back of my neck and pulling me to his mouth. We blend together, his flavor and mine, and I've never been so turned on in my life.

I'm so into our tangled kiss that I don't notice him grabbing the condom from his wallet until our mouths part and he's rolling it over his length.

His gaze travels the length of me. "I don't think I've stopped being hard since I unzipped your dress."

I'm too worked up to worry about how my next question will sound. "Why did you stop me, then? You were about to come."

Desmond eases me forward so I'm straddling him. "Because I want to watch you come apart when I'm inside you." His eyes are gleaming wickedly. "And it'll be all the more intense when you finally do."

I narrow my eyes. "You're such a control freak." I lower myself until I feel his tip at my entrance.

He chuckles and holds himself steady while I start to ease down around him. "Yeah, but I'm your control freak now." Then he grabs my waist and tilts upward with his hips, guiding me down around him.

My eyes slam closed, and I gasp at the shock of him stretching me to a point that borderlines pleasure and pain.

"Hey," he whispers, placing his forehead on mine. "Breathe, Maggie."

I take in a deep, shuddering breath and nod against him, sinking deeper and deeper, until the initial shock wears off and pleasure is all I'm chasing. I settle at his base and open my eyes before continuing.

His sharp blue stare is pouring into my brown eyes like he's trying to reach the depths of my soul in a silent plea to keep moving. "You okay?"

This time I smile. "Such a gentleman."

A cocky smile lifts his cheeks as his palms find my ass and grip me. He thrusts into me, going deeper than I thought possible. "Are you sure about that?" Then he's moving me, lifting me from him and pulling me back down as my muscles cling to his.

He's biting his bottom lip, watching me move, and I can't help but lean in and take his mouth with mine. I want to—need to—feel every part of him on every part of me.

He groans into my mouth and pulls his knees out from under him and stretching them out. Then he reaches behind him and uses his hands to prop himself up while I take over and start to ride him. As I do, something awakens inside of me, something that reaches beyond pleasure and lightens the weight on my heart. We're face-to-face, heart-to-heart, our slick bodies sliding together. And it's like they were always meant to move this way.

My mind has gone foggy again as I pick up the pace to a stride that will bring me to climax at any moment. I need the release after not just the past hour of buildup, but the past days, weeks, and months. I need this more than I need air, at least that's how it feels as I get closer to bliss.

I'm so close, closer than before, when Desmond growls, sits up, and wraps his arms around my waist. He flips me onto my back, still inside me. He latches onto my bra between the cups, holding it like he would reins, and then starts to rock into me at a pace I know he has no chance of stopping, not this time.

We're too far gone, our hearts and minds tangled too deeply. And I know it's not just me that needs this release.

There's a tightening below my belly, creating a heat that starts to spread to every limb until my head is abuzz once more. I'm reaching the cliff at the speed of a freight train. The moment I hit the edge, there's nothing but sky and sea stretching for miles. A guttural cry slips past my throat, and I'm soaring. Soaring as Desmond's mouth finds mine. Soaring as he pushes inside me for the last time, his warmth filling the condom, filling me, until the two of us are spent.

My body is useless, my muscles a puddle of mush as my mind begins to clear. Our breathing is all I can hear above the crackling fire as he lies beside me. My head rests in the crook of his arm while I curl the rest of my body into him.

He squeezes me closer and kisses the top of my head. "Still think I'm a gentleman?"

I smile and close my eyes. "Verdict's still out on that."

At some point last night, during another round of "Is Desmond a gentleman?" he carried me to his bed, and we fell asleep there. I'm not sure how many times we woke up to go at it again or how many condoms were destroyed in the process, but I'm still in his bed when the sun shines through his large windows. My body is a package of marshmallows, and Desmond's bed is our cloud. It looks like one too, with its soft white sheets, a puffy down comforter, and pillows that hug me in a sweet caress. I never want to leave.

When I look to my right, I have to blink. No Desmond beside me, but then I make out a sound from the kitchen and smile. My senses are coming to life at the smell of breakfast cooking and the sizzle of grease on the stove. I pull myself out of bed and walk to the window, where a white button-down of Desmond's lies. I pick it up and slide my arms through the sleeves, leaving it unbuttoned. I have zero energy to find my own clothes right now.

There's a bench under the window, and I take a seat, pulling my knees up to my chest as I gaze out the window. Desmond's view faces the main street, and just by the activity on the street as people make their way to the public market, I take a guess that it's early afternoon.

"Hungry?"

I snap my head toward Desmond's bedroom door.

He's standing there with a loaded tray of food. "I might have gone a bit overboard."

My mouth starts to water. "Is that French toast? And avocado toast?"

He nods and starts to walk toward me. "And bacon and eggs Benedict and fruit. I didn't know if you liked hollandaise, so I just put it on the side."

The closer he gets, the wider my eyes grow. Strawberries and whipped cream top the French toast, and a cup of syrup sits beside them. There's even a tiny mint leaf sticking from the dollop of whipped cream and a small bowl of berries on the side. "That all looks incredible, and I'm starving."

He chuckles and sets the tray between us as he sits down on the bench. His eyes scroll my attire with a quirk of his lips. "I'm sure you are."

I grin and pick up a fork. "Your girlfriends must feel pretty lucky when they wake up in the morning."

He cocks an eyebrow at me and twists his lips. "Is that your subtle way of asking if I do this for every woman I sleep with?"

I stifle a laugh and hold a forkful of avocado toast to my lips. "Maybe I'm a little curious."

"Well," he says while cutting through layers of egg and ham. "The short answer is no, not to this extent." He still isn't looking at me as he takes a bite, chews, and swallows.

"As in…" I lead, hoping he'll elaborate more.

He sets his fork down and smiles. "Food is my thing, Maggie. I'd be lying if I made you think I haven't used it to my advantage once or twice before. But have I ever given up sleep before to make a buffet of food to make sure a woman was pleased with the options?" He chuckles again. "No. This would be a first. And have I ever wanted a woman to stay after said breakfast was cooked? Not until today."

My lips are parted to eat the blueberry I have pressed to my mouth when heat spreads from my neck to my cheeks. "You want me to stay?"

He slides off the bench, suddenly adopting a serious look as his gaze finds my mouth. "Hold that thought for one minute."

I pop the berry into my mouth as he jogs out of the room, wearing nothing but pair of bright-green boxer briefs. I don't think too much about his exit until he returns with his camera in his hands. "Do that again." He stops at my side and angles the lens down on me.

I pull the shirt over my breasts and look up into the lens, at him, with wide eyes. Panic sets in. "What are you doing?"

He sets the camera to his side and cups my chin with his fingers. "You don't have to be afraid of the lens, Maggie, not with me." His lips tilt up in an almost shy smile. "May I please take your picture?"

My heart takes off, beating wildly in my chest to an unfamiliar rhythm. Something about Desmond's request makes me feel every bit as bare as I was for him last night. Exposed. Vulnerable. But looking back at him with his ice-cold eyes so devilishly innocent, I don't think I can say no.

So I pick up another berry and place it to my lips, and before I know it, there's a click and a flash, followed by another and another. I'm eating my breakfast, bite by bite, while Desmond captures his food and me from every angle. And for the first time since leaving the world of modeling, I don't feel like a puppet. I don't feel like someone's doll to be poked and prodded at until they get their perfect moment. Then I realize the most surprising thing of all.

I trust Desmond Blake.

TAKE SIX

The Cohost

"SOMETIMES YOU WILL NEVER KNOW THE VALUE OF A MOMENT UNTIL IT BECOMES A MEMORY."
—THEODOR SEUSS GEISEL

Moving Fast
DESMOND

I get to the kitchen earlier than normal on Monday morning, and I realize immediately how strange it feels to be off my routine. Between all-day preparations for Saturday's wedding and the time Maggie and I spent locked away in my condo all of Sunday, I knew I would have to start early to tackle the mess I left behind.

I spend the morning changing out the garbage liners, deep cleaning the main kitchen area, and running the dishwasher — all to a Matt Nathanson playlist and with the clearest head I've had in a long time. And I know I owe it all to a certain vixen with a devilish tongue and wicked hip thrusts. But it's more than that with Maggie. She gave more than just her body to me this weekend. She gave me her trust when she let me snap those pictures, and I've never felt prouder of my own art.

Suddenly, I'm inspired to make something more of my art. To take more than live action photos of food to showcase my culinary passion. I love watching Maggie's joy when she tastes my meals. She's like a princess that's been held captive her entire life and has never tasted a single delicious morsel of food in her life. And that's what I want to capture. The innocence of discovery. The first taste of all that's been forbidden.

I'm straightening up the couch cushions in the common area when I hear the door from the back room opening. I look up to see Maggie wearing black skinny jeans and a cream crop sweater with three buttons down the center. Her hair is pulled up into a high ponytail, and not a stitch of makeup can be found on her face. Her look reminds me of the day she was moving in, only on that day, she was a bundle of negative energy. Today, she's a fucking ray of sunshine that I instantly start to move toward.

I scoop her up in my arms with a grin and press my lips to hers like she didn't just climb out of my bed two hours ago. She giggles into my mouth, and I carry her over to the couch before tossing her onto it and pouncing on her. I bury my mouth in her neck, knowing now the effect my beard has on her sensitive skin. I don't even have to look to know that goose bumps just broke out all over her body.

She squeals with laughter. "Stop."

I pull my mouth away and stare down at her. "Sorry, I got a little carried away."

She grins and runs a finger over my matching smile. "I don't mind, but I am on the clock, and I kind of like my job."

I search her caramel eyes and then lean in to kiss her again, this time square on the mouth and with as much passion as I can muster. "It's a good thing, because your boss is a big fan of your work."

She laughs. "Oh, is that right?"

I nod, my gaze now perusing her little sweater, which clearly outlines her breasts. "That's right" I slip my hand up her stomach, over her rib cage, and under her sweater. "He especially likes this outfit. Very appropriate for the workplace." Sweeping a thumb over her nipple, I confirm that she's braless once again and groan. "This is going to make for a very unproductive day."

Maggie places a hand on mine and pulls it out of her shirt with a smile. "I won't let that happen. Should we look at recipes or head to the market?"

"You already pulled the recipes on Saturday and made the grocery lists." Grinning, I pull myself to the side of her so I'm not crushing her with my weight. "And the market opens at nine."

She glances at the clock and frowns. "We have an hour."

My fingers move back to her sweater, to a button between her breasts, and I pop it open. "Looks like we're ahead of schedule, so…"

Maggie turns back to me, and something in her sweet smile effectively melts my insides. I'm putty over this girl, and I don't know what to do about it. My next kiss is tentative and slow. Just because I'm a horny bastard with a permanent hard-on for Maggie doesn't mean she will reciprocate. But when she weaves those long, thin fingers through my hair and pulls me into a deeper kiss, I know I'm not alone.

I've managed to open her sweater and reveal her perfect tits, which appear to be starved for attention. I grip a breast and pull it into my mouth, circling her sensitive peak with my tongue before moving on to the next one as she squirms underneath me. "Maybe we should go back to your place if we're going to do this."

I put her nipple between my teeth and squeeze just hard enough to earn a groan from Maggie, and then I look up into her sedated eyes. "I'd much rather fuck you on this couch if I'm being honest."

"By all means, don't hold back."

My mouth roams her bare skin, exploring every inch with soft nibbles, licks, and kisses, until I'm at her belly. Her back arches beneath me. Her tits are aimed straight for the air, and her body quivers in my hold. I know what she wants, and I have every intention of giving it to her. My hands slide around her waistband before I start to peel it from her skin. I've always loved food, but I've never been addicted to the taste of anything quite like Maggie.

She pushes up her hips to help me slide her pants away when a loud knock comes from the front door. "Shit," I say at her navel, because holy hell, I don't want to stop. Maybe I won't. It's not like whoever is on the other side of the tinted glass will be able to make out that there are two bodies fucking like rabbits on the couch.

"Desmond." Maggie's tone is filled with warning, shattering any fantasy I have of continuing.

"They'll go away," I try.

"I think it's Faye." This time she hisses the words, like someone will be able to hear us.

But it can't possibly be Faye. I haven't heard from her since the dreadful auditions last week. She'd walked out without a word regarding the women she'd just auditioned or what the next plan of action was. I guess I hadn't pushed either.

I wince. "She's either here to let me down gently or to tell me the new plan." I look over my shoulder and see a figure beyond the glass. There's no mistaking who the short-haired woman is. I stand and help Maggie up then sigh when I watch her button her sweater. "Why can't you just be my cohost? You're already my assistant. It actually makes a lot of sense if you think about it."

Maggie bats her bottomless brown eyes up at me, surprised. "I already gave Faye my answer. I can't go back on that now. But I'll still be here with you every step of the way. You still want the show, right?"

"*Want* is a pretty strong word, but I need the funding if I'm going to grow this place. The show just seemed like the perfect opportunity."

Maggie shrugs, and I can feel her trying to play devil's advocate. "A better opportunity could come along."

I shake my head and sigh. "A better opportunity than a television show? I don't know, Maggie."

She smiles and rises onto her toes then presses a kiss to my lips. "Then stop questioning it. Open the door and talk to the woman. If you need me, I'll be right here."

"Okay," I whisper against her lips. "Only because you said so."

Faye's smile is bright and wide when I open the door, but something about it makes me feel uneasy. "Nice to see you again, Faye."

She laughs. "You say that like you're surprised to see me. It's Monday, silly."

I twist up my mouth with my confusion. "You didn't say you'd be back today. In fact, you didn't say anything at all when you left last week."

"Well," she starts slowly and pointedly. "That's because I've been quite busy working on a contingency plan after that disaster of an audition last week. And I've got one." She searches the room until her smile stops on Maggie. "Hi, Maggie."

Maggie waves from the kitchen island. "Hey, Faye."

Faye turns back to me. "Well, aren't you going to invite me in?"

I gesture for her to come in. She breezes by me and heads straight for the couch I was just making out with Maggie on. I stifle my amusement and take a seat on the chair adjacent to her. "So let's hear it." I try to sound chipper to match her mood, but I can't help but feeling like this whole show idea has run into one brick wall after another.

Faye lights up like a Christmas tree. "While I was brainstorming in LA, someone at the network gave me a lead on a young actress looking to break into reality television. She'd make a perfect cohost for you, Desmond."

The word *perfect* triggers me to glance over at Maggie. I half-expect her to jump in and demand the role for herself. *No such luck.* She keeps her head down as she attacks the kitchen island with a scrub brush.

"What are you suggesting?"

Faye straightens her shoulders, her businesswoman negotiation posture. "I'm suggesting that I bring her in today, along with a crew, and we start to shoot some tests for the pilot. Get you two comfortable with each other and get you used to the cameras. If all goes well, then we can aim to shoot the pilot tomorrow, starting with a trip to the market."

"You want to shoot the pilot tomorrow?"

"I warned you, I like to move fast."

"Haven't we already been moving fast? Last week you were determined to cast Maggie, and now you're just going to bring in some random actress?"

She leans over and places a hand on my thigh, her cleavage spilling out of her low-cut black blouse. My eyes betray me, but I tear them away quickly. What was once a fun flirtation with Faye now just feels wrong.

"You'll need to trust me, Desmond. I've only got your best interests at heart. You still want this, don't you?"

She's asking me the same question Maggie just asked, and I can't help but truly think on it now. Sure, the show could do wonders for my kitchen, but do I still want it if we aren't going about it in a way that I'm comfortable with?

I swallow before standing up. My eyes flick to Maggie's for a second, and I almost wish they hadn't. She should be the one standing next to me during production, but the last thing I want to do is put any kind of pressure on her, especially after all the progress we've made. Plus, she's made it clear that she's uncomfortable in front of the camera. Just because she's opened up to me behind closed doors, doesn't mean she's ready to do the same for the public.

Ugh. I feel like there's a rock in my gut, and not even I am strong enough to move it.

"Of course I want this," I finally say to Faye, suddenly feeling completely helpless. "Bring in the crew, then. Let's do this."

Playing the Part

MAGGIE

Desmond is still locked away in his office when Faye's crew arrives and completely takes over the kitchen. The second Desmond walked out, Faye made a quick phone call and opened the door for them all to start piling in: hair and makeup, wardrobe, director of photography, three different cameramen, lighting crew, audio people, and craft services. The entire scene brings me right back to my modeling days.

While my nerves are rattling around inside, I'm also trying to be there for Desmond. So when Faye asks me to run and "fetch" her food and flowers from the market, or when she requests that I run and grab an apron for Desmond's cohost, among various other tasks, I do it with no argument or delay, even though I'm quickly growing more and more worried about Desmond.

When Faye gets into a deep conversation with the director of photography, I slip into the back room and tap lightly on Desmond's office door. "It's me," I say quietly, hoping my voice is loud enough for him to hear. The last thing I want is for Faye to come back here and start barking out more demands, not until I know where Desmond's head is at.

There's a click of the door, and it opens just enough for me to slip inside. Then Desmond shuts it behind me and leans against the door with a heavy sigh. "Is it over yet?"

I tilt my head and hug his waist while staring up into his eyes. "No, but I can make her go away if you really want me to."

He smiles at that and leans down to press a kiss on my nose. Flutters erupt in my chest, and I just don't know how we went from mortal enemies to each other's comfort. I feel like Desmond needs me, and I need him, maybe in ways neither of us have experienced before.

I blush when I think about the way Desmond took his time with me in every sexual encounter we've had so far, always ensuring I came first, always asking me if I was okay after he entered me, and always making sure I was comfortable in any position he wanted to try. I've never experienced a gentle giant like Desmond before, and while neither of us are trying to label things, I know for certain that he is not someone I want to let go of anytime soon.

"Tell me what happened back in LA." He searches my eyes like it's his last-ditch effort to understand me. "I haven't been able to stop thinking about your discomfort around a camera. Did someone hurt you?"

When he asked me to be his cohost earlier, my heart melted, and I almost caved. I wanted to explain everything to him right then and there. About the morning after my fall on the runway, about the creepy producer, about every nagging feeling I've had in my heart since I left LA. Maybe then he would understand why dipping my toes back in that world is so hard for me.

He asked me if I trusted him last night, and I said I did. This is my chance to prove my words and put it all out there.

While I drum up the courage to tell him my story, I pull him over to his desk and push him down into his chair before I climb onto his desk to face him. After a long, deep inhale, I release it then forge ahead. "I already told you how modeling was never my dream. I mean, I thought it was, but at some point along the way, I realized I'd never been given a choice. I grew up in front of the camera. It came so naturally. Obeying direction. Revealing just a little bit more skin. Making love to the camera. And I'd be lying if I said I didn't enjoy the attention or the way looking at those photos made me feel. I felt beautiful and successful, and I worked damn hard at it."

He nods, and I squeeze my lids shut before continuing. "So then you were just upset that it was a career chosen for you and not the other way around?"

"That's a big part of it. I'll never know if I would have chosen it myself. I didn't have any other talents, but then again, I was never given the opportunity to explore."

"So that's why you're here. To explore." He looks down and then back up at me. "Does that mean there's a chance you'll go back to LA if you figure out modeling is, in fact, what you want?"

I search his eyes, my heart tugging with his question. "I'll tell you this much. If I do decide to model again, it won't be through my old agency or with the photographers I used to work for. I'm tired of being an object through the lens, something sexual they can manipulate to sell their products or business offerings."

"Is that how you feel when I take your photo?"

I shake my head, not needing to think a second about it. "When you take my picture, it's different. You see me."

He places his hands on my thighs and squeezes. "I do, Maggie. It's why I'm the way I am with you. It's why I push you and tease you and dig for more. Because I see you, and I want you to see yourself too. You're worth more than they ever made you believe."

"I wish I could believe that. But those photographers weren't the only ones that made me feel that way."

He scrunches his face in question. "Who else?"

I go on to tell Desmond about my lame attempt to exit modeling through acting and about how I was approached by big-shot Hollywood producer, Regis Malone.

I swallow, wondering if it will always be this hard to talk about my experience. And then somehow, I manage to tell Desmond about that awful night in Regis's hotel room when my fantasy turned into a nightmare. My throat is tight as I try to hold back the tears. "On that night, I made a promise to myself to stop looking for my worth through the lens. I came to Seattle to find it." I shake my head and feel Desmond wrap his arms around my waist.

"Jesus, Maggie. I'm so sorry. Why didn't you tell me?"

"I was embarrassed. I went from being at the top of my game on the runway, with a future in acting, to falling flat on my face—literally and figuratively."

Desmond looks up into my eyes, his gaze soft and full of emotion. "That's where you're getting it all wrong. Did you ever stop to think that maybe your previously chosen careers weren't the problem? Maybe it was the people you were surrounding yourself with. When I snap photos of you, you're no puppet to me. You are your most authentic, vulnerable, and beautiful self. I see you through the lens, Maggie Stevens. I see your heart, I see your soul, and there is nothing to be embarrassed about."

Tears drip from my eyes now, and my heart feels incredibly heavy. Desmond and I have come a long way since my first visit to the kitchen. Who would have thought he would manage to mutter the sweetest words anyone has ever said to me?

"What about you?" I ask in an attempt to lighten the mood by turning the focus on him. "Why did you lock yourself away in here?"

He groans and places his head in my lap. "I thought this was going to be my chance to show off all the work I've put into this place. I'm not comfortable doing that with some actress, who I'm sure is amazing, but she can't possibly represent my brand. Not when we've never even met."

I frown, hating that Desmond is feeling this way. This is his moment to shine, and he can't even enjoy it for a single second. "Maybe you should put a stop to it, then. Tell Faye you need to plan the show together, or it doesn't happen. I don't feel comfortable with the fact that she's not giving you a say at all. This is your kitchen, your baby. Don't let her walk all over you."

Desmond growls and snaps his head up. "God, you're sexy when you're bossing me around."

My laughter doubles when he grabs my waist and pulls me off the desk and onto his lap. He cups my neck and pulls me down to his mouth for an explosive kiss, one that has me bursting from the inside and melting into him all at once. "This is probably a bad idea."

"You think?" He runs a line of kisses down my neck and then to the space between my breasts. "Because I can't think of anything better than this."

He pushes his hips up into me, causing a gasp to slip from my throat. He manages to open my sweater, and his mouth is on my nipple when I realize how hard he's become between my thighs. Instinct kicks in, and I start to grind against him slowly because I know that's how Desmond will want to play this. He'll want to take his time with me until I've had more than I can take. Pleasure and pain all blend seamlessly when he's inside me, bringing me to the ultimate state of bliss.

"Desmond." His name is just a breath as I find the perfect friction against him. "You feel so good."

He pulls his mouth from mine and peers up at me.

His eyes are filled with lust, but only for a second. "Damn, you are gorgeous." His palm slides up to my cheek and cups it softly. "So fucking beautiful."

My movements have stilled, so I'm no longer grinding against him, but my breathing only quickens. He has no idea what he's doing to my heart by saying those words.

"Do you trust me, Maggie?"

This time, his question feels heavier than the first time he asked it, and I don't hesitate for a single beat. "Yes."

"Be my cohost. I don't want to do this with anyone but you." He searches my eyes with his. "Only you."

I'm seriously considering his words because I know that, this time, he's serious and not just speaking out of fear or stress. Our connection is natural. It always has been, and there's no way to manufacture something so pure.

My heart feels like it's beating a million miles per hour when I settle on his gaze and bite down on my lip before confirming my response with my heart, mind, and soul.

And then I nod. "Okay, Desmond. I'll be your cohost. I'll do it for you."

DESMOND

Maggie's lips are currently pressed against mine. The news she just delivered has me feeling a million times better than I did before walking into my office.

Then the sound of someone clearing her throat jolts me from my temporary heaven. Maggie tears her mouth from mine and freezes above me. We turn at the same time to see a pissed-off Faye standing in the doorway of my office. Her arms are crossed over her chest and a glare blazes in her eyes.

"Jesus, Faye," I yell. "How long have you been standing there?"

Maggie shuffles off my lap and stands while buttoning up her sweater.

"Long enough." Faye's tone is dripping with disdain, her gaze darting from Maggie to me. "Plan on consulting me first before you replace your cohost?"

A fire burns in my chest. Clearly, she's been standing there quite some time. "Like you consulted me before you brought an entire crew to my kitchen?"

Faye's jaw drops. "I did that for you. As of last week, we didn't have a show. Now we're one step closer, and you want to test your luck bringing in someone new?"

"I'm not testing anything. Maggie's the entire reason we agreed on a cohost to begin with. And one week ago you were ready to offer her the part. Why shouldn't it be her?"

Faye tilts her head. "Are you forgetting how adamant you were that we not cast Maggie?"

"She didn't want it then."

Faye lets out an exasperated sigh looks pointedly at Maggie. "And now?"

Maggie steps forward. "I'm sorry I wasn't ready to agree to this last week, but I am now, Faye. For what it's worth, I believe in this show just as much as you and Desmond."

I wrap an arm around her waist and hold her to me. "Maggie is the best one for the role, as you already know. And she wants it. You have to admit, Faye, this is our best option. No"—I suck in a deep breath—"this is our only option."

"What are you saying?"

"I'm saying that if I'm forced to get a cohost to help sell the show, then that cohost needs to be Maggie."

The air is still as all goes silent. Faye seems to be considering my words carefully while Maggie grabs my hand. The silence stretches, and it's only a matter of time until someone breaks it. What I don't expect is the shrill ring of a phone in the background or the cold chill that runs down my spine.

Maggie reaches my desk first and grabs it while I maintain my staredown with Faye. I'm the first one to break eye contact when Maggie approaches me and places the phone against my chest. "It's for you. The man said it's important, and he wouldn't let me take a message. I guess he tried your cell phone too. It sounds pretty urgent."

My heart is already hammering in my chest when I take the phone from her. There's only one person who would ever call me on my work phone with important news. With my gaze locked on hers in a silent plea for her to stay put, I put the phone to my ear. "This is Desmond."

"Hey, Desmond. It's Mick." The familiar voice of my father's case worker is too somber, too apologetic. It's enough to chill my bones. "Sorry to bother you at work, but it's important."

I squeeze my eyes shut, preparing myself for the worst possible news. It's not the first time I've felt this way when Mick has called, but something in my chest tells me it might be the last. "Hey," I finally say.

There's a slight pause and then a light exhale before he speaks again. "It's your father. He's in the hospital. I don't want to freak you out, but you should probably get here as soon as you can."

No Show

MAGGIE

Desmond left for Dallas on a red-eye last night. He was quiet, stoically so, as he packed a small bag for his trip. I watched as he pulled clothes from his closet and tossed them in his duffel bag, all the while running down a list of things he needed me to take care of at the kitchen. Answer the phones. Call his students to let them know about the emergency cancellations. Donate food in the refrigerator before anything went bad. The list isn't long, but I agreed without hesitation, knowing if there was any little thing I could take off his mind, I would do it.

Even in a state of emergency, Desmond seemed calm and business-minded, but I knew better. The air was thick with unspoken words and questions I didn't know how to ask. I didn't know if he was angry or sad, or how serious the issue with his dad was. But by the way Desmond flew out of here, I could only assume it was very serious.

When I walk into Edible Desire on Tuesday morning, it's with a heavy heart, but it takes me less than two hours to complete Desmond's list. I'm sitting at the reception desk with my cell phone in hand, hoping to hear back from him. While I'm trying to give him his space, it's killing me to not know what's going on or how he's doing. I broke down this morning and texted him to see how he was doing, but I still haven't received a response.

The doorbell of Edible Desire chimes, letting me know that someone is walking in. I left it unlocked in case someone wanted to take a tour of the kitchen or book a class. My intentions were good, but the person who walks in makes me wish I had decided to keep the doors locked.

"Hey, Mags," my dad says, letting the door shut behind him.

This is the second time I've seen him since moving to Washington, and just like the first time, it feels surreal. I spent so many years *knowing* I would never see him again, *adamant* I would never forgive him. So standing in the same room with him is enough to send a jolt straight to my heart. Emotion clogs my throat, and there's even a tiny spot in my chest swelling at his nearness, happy that my daddy's here. Despite that small breakthrough, my guard still stands tall and strong.

"Hey, Dad." I stand and step to the outside of the desk, tilting my head in question. "Desmond isn't here. He had to fly to Dallas." I swallow, the words sticking in my throat.

"I know. Um, actually…" My dad runs his fingers through his hair, the same way he used to when he was uncertain. *His nervous habit.* "I'm here to see you."

His eyes dart to my hands, and that's when I realize I'm wringing them together. *My nervous habit.* I guess some things never change.

"Why?" I don't know what to say, do, or think. So I just stand here and wait. For what, I'm not sure. Maybe I'm waiting for his excuse for tearing our family apart, or for a meaningless apology after years of nothing. I'm waiting for the words I know I'll reject. But what he finally says surprises me.

"I miss you." His response is simple, honest, and sweet.

The small piece of my heart that swelled for him earlier just grew in size. I try to take a normal breath, but it's impossible. My inhale is uneven, catching on air. The corners of my eyes burn with the threat of my tears, and I shake my head, like I have a chance of stopping them.

"I miss you," he repeats. "And I wanted to check on you to see if you're okay." He glances around the kitchen. "Desmond said you've been a big help to him around here and that he left you in charge."

I follow his gaze before looking back at him and pulling my brows together. "Yeah, but I don't see how any of that concerns you."

"I've got a couple hours free if you need some help."

It takes everything in me to refrain from giving him another snotty retort. I don't need to be angry with the man for the rest of my life. If anything, I want to feel free from the haunting memories that arise every time I think of him. Forgiveness worked for Monica. Maybe it could work for me too.

I let out a sigh. "That's really nice of you, but without Desmond, I don't have much to do."

He checks his watch. "Well, how about lunch, then? My treat."

As hard as I want to try, my entire body seizes up at his efforts. "That's really not necessary."

He levels me with his gaze. "It's been a long time. I just want to get to know you. What have you been up to since you've been here? Do you like Seattle? Do you miss LA? I know we can't get those years back, but I don't want to lose any more than we already have."

I swallow past the thickness still building in my throat. "I hear you say you're sorry. I hear you tell me you miss me. But what makes you think I trust any of it?"

He nods and drops his head before picking it back up and looking at me again. "If you need more time, then I'll give it to you. The last thing I want to do is push this, but I'm not going to stop showing up. Whenever you're ready to talk, I'll be here."

"That's just it. I don't want to rehash the past. What's done is done, and I need to find a way to accept that." I can feel my voice already starting to quiver. "I just want to stop hurting."

My dad's entire face crumbles like I've just delivered a blow. "Me too, Mags. I'll live with my mistakes forever. I'll carry them to my grave. But you shouldn't have to. If I could have remained in your life when things blew up between your mother and me, then I would have. And I tried everything in my power to do just that."

"Well, you should have tried harder. Do you realize how mean Mom got when you left? How she poured all of her energy into molding me into something I never wanted to become?"

His face crumbles. "I thought you loved modeling."

I shake my head, my eyes firmly locked on his. "No, Dad. I was told it was the only thing I'd ever be good at, and I believed it. I was told my looks would buy my way through life, and I grasped onto that like it was gospel. I spent nearly my entire life being someone I never chose to be."

His eyes roll up to the ceiling, and I swear they're bloodshot, like he's about to burst into tears. "I thought you were happy." He blows out a breath and looks at me again, this time tilting his head.

"I am happy now, but my happiness has not come easy. I was so young when you disappeared. There were times when I felt like I didn't deserve happiness. If my daddy couldn't love me enough to stay, then who out there ever would? I needed you then, but I'm happy now."

My father's chin is quivering like he's trying to stop his own emotions from shining through. "Are you?"

I don't know why I want to ease his sadness, but it feels important. "I mean, I'm worried about Desmond, and I have a lot of figuring out to do, but I like that I'm figuring it all out here."

His eyes soften. "With Desmond?"

My cheeks heat. "With Monica, and yeah, I guess with Desmond too. He didn't have to give me this opportunity. He had no reason to trust that I would actually be of any use to him."

My dad nods, a smile lifting his cheeks. "Sometimes an opportunity is all a person needs to move forward in life. It's something Desmond has thanked me for numerous times. Zach too. But Desmond is the one who did the work. Just like you're the one putting in the work now. You two don't give yourselves enough credit. Maybe it's a good thing you found each other."

I let out an embarrassed laugh. If anyone had told me that I would be talking to my father about guys, I would have shot them down fast. "You're making it sound like we're something serious, and it's not like that, Dad."

He raises his brows. "Are you sure? It sounds pretty serious to me."

I can feel myself blush even harder. "If things were serious, then I might have some clue as to what is going on in Dallas. He didn't give me many details." Then I realize I might be closer to information than I thought. "Did he tell you much more?"

My dad frowns. "He didn't say much, but he didn't have to. I've known Desmond for a long time. His issues with his father are… complicated."

I think my dad might be trying to protect Desmond's privacy. "I know about the drug abuse and his high-functioning autism. And I know Desmond tries to go see him every few months. Is this normal? For him to get calls like that?"

My dad nods. "Yes, but not because his dad's in the hospital. It's usually because he winds up in jail or has a problem in rehab."

I let out a heavy breath, suddenly feeling anxious. "I just wish I knew what was going on. I hate being here, doing nothing, while he's there." My eyes snap up to my dad's. "I feel like I should go to Dallas. Is that ridiculous?"

My dad shakes his head. "Not at all. He probably needs you, not that he would ever admit that."

"Really?"

"One thing I learned early on about Desmond is that he'll never ask for help. But when he's offered it, he embraces it. He doesn't turn it down."

"But why wouldn't he have just said something to me last night?"

"Desmond's always considered his problems a burden. Deep down, I think maybe he's embarrassed about the situation with his dad. And even deeper than that, he's ashamed of those feelings. Desmond's a good guy, Maggie, but he's shit at asking for help."

I swallow, wrapping my brain around everything my father is saying. Nervous excitement sets in, and in that very instant, I know exactly what I need to do.

Dallas

DESMOND

The beeping of monitors and the stark white walls of the hospital keep me trapped in my own thoughts—for seconds, maybe minutes, maybe hours. I'm not sure, but I can tell morning has come and gone by the rise and fall of the sun through the shaded screen window. My heart feels like it's still stuck in the dark moment of early morning when I first heard the stark news of my father's diagnosis.

"Your father had a heart attack."

The words repeat over and over in my mind along with everything else I'd been told when I arrived. My father got wasted *again*. My father got arrested *again*. But this time, after the cuffs were put on his wrists, he didn't make it into the car. He fell to his knees as he endured a heart attack that landed him in the emergency room.

I stretch my arms and stand from the lounge chair I've been sprawled out on all day. My dad is currently hooked up to a bunch of machines. There's a bag of saline dripping into his veins and a heart monitor keeping a regular beat. I'm told the scary part is over and that once he wakes up, he'll be scheduled for more tests and doctor visits. Eventually, he can move from the ICU and into a regular room, where we can discuss recovery treatments such as rehab, therapy, and medications.

It's all been done before, and no matter how serious my father takes it all in the beginning, he always has a relapse, each one worse than the last. I'm as sick and tired of the broken record as I am terrified and anxious over it all. I don't know when enough is going to be enough. Every time I think he's hit rock-bottom, he proves me wrong.

"Des." My father's throaty whisper freezes me in midstretch. I turn to see his eyes starting to open, revealing the same ice-blue color as mine. "What'd I do this time?" Even in a state of groggy half-consciousness, he manages to attempt a joke.

"Oh, you know." I give him a half-smile. "Same ol' thing. Boozed it up too hard, got yourself arrested, but this time, you added in a little twist and decided to have a mini heart attack while your rights were being read to ya. You always have to make a big production out of things, don't you?"

He coughs and then grunts. "A heart attack, huh? That's a new one."

It's silent for a few beats while my dad seems to take in the space around him again. Then his eyes flit back to me. "Got any new recipes to show me?"

On the flight to Dallas, I prepared for my reunion with my father. It's never long into our conversations before he starts to ask me about cooking, and his questions always start off with "Got any new recipes to show me?"

I smile and pull out my tablet. "I'm going to tell the nurse you're awake. Enjoy these."

My words aren't necessary. The moment my dad lays his eyes on the first photo, he is in another world. He stares at the first one for nearly a minute, taking in every pixel of the photo like he's studying for a final exam. Then he swipes to the next and does the exact same thing with that photo.

I step out of the room, knowing he'll be preoccupied for a while, and walk up to a small desk with a window that oversees my father's room. Kari is the nurse who has been on duty since seven in the morning. She's tapping away at her computer when I approach. "Hey there," she says with a smile.

"He just woke up."

"Oh, wonderful." She checks the time on the wall over her head. "Just in time. I'll check his vitals and see if we can get him a food tray. He's probably hungry."

"I can always run down and get him something if needed."

She smiles and pats my hand. "Aren't you a good son? I've got this. But maybe you should run down to the cafeteria and get yourself something so you can join him."

Now that my father is awake and in good hands, I feel better about leaving. So I nod and take off down the hall, toward the cafeteria. I'm halfway to the main door when the waiting room comes into view. I have to do a double take when I see a woman with a bright-green sweater, dark jeans, and lightened brown hair swooped up in a ponytail. I almost laugh when I think the woman could be Maggie. That just goes to show how much I miss her, especially at a time like this while I'm bored and scared out of my mind.

My steps slow until they halt completely at the same time the woman looks up from her phone. Her eyes lock on mine.

Holy shit. "Maggie?"

She jumps up from her seat and walks over to me. Just the confirmation that she's really here, that she's not just a mirage, gives my heart a hard jolt.

"Hey," she says. "I-I just wanted to be here in case you needed... anything."

The way she's staring back at me, like she fears she's imposing, packs my throat with emotion. I reach for her, pull her close, and engulf her in a giant hug. "I can't believe you're here."

She relaxes into me and tightens her hold. "Of course I'm here. I would have come sooner, but I wasn't sure if you'd want me here." She peers up at me with bloodshot eyes. "Is everything okay with your dad?"

I nod and give her a small smile to let her know everything is going to be okay. For the first time since coming to Dallas, I truly believe it. "He'll be fine. Just a little scare, but he's up and talking about food, just like normal." I drop a kiss on her forehead then bite down on my lip. "Do you want to meet him?"

Her eyes light up. "Yes. Are you sure that's okay?"

I nod. "He's about to eat. Just..." I hesitate, not knowing how much I should explain about my father. "Don't get offended if he doesn't talk much. He's not a talker. And he doesn't really express much emotion, so it's not you. It's just how he is."

She nods, her gaze still locked on mine. "That's okay. I'd love to meet him."

I take her hand and walk her into my father's room, where Kari is pulling away her equipment after checking his vitals.

"How was everything?"

"His blood pressure is a little high, which could be because of the environment. I'll have to check again in an hour, but for now, I gave him something to relax him." She darts a glance at my dad, who is currently engrossed in viewing the photos I left him with. "Although he seems pretty relaxed to me. Keep him that way, okay?" She winks and claps me on the shoulder before walking out.

I pull Maggie around to the other side of my father's bed, where I positioned the lounge chair last night, and step in front of it. "Hey, Dad."

It takes him a second before my voice registers, but then he looks up, his bushy gray brows bunching together. "Huh?"

"I want to introduce you to someone." I nod to my left and smile. "This is Maggie. She helps me at the kitchen."

He slides his gaze to her and stares at her for a full few seconds before saying anything. "You cook?"

She smiles and darts a bashful look at me. "I try. But I'm not as good as your son."

"She's amazing, Dad. Better than when she first stepped foot in the kitchen, that's for sure. She's been a big help."

My dad holds up the tablet and points at the photo he's looking at now. "This you?"

Maggie's eyes bulge when she sees the photo of her eating her breakfast two mornings ago. I still remember how sexy she looked wearing my button-down shirt, and how desperately I wanted to capture all the bits she'd cleverly hidden from the frame. I'd only chosen the photos of her where all her bits were covered, but there's definitely no mistaking that it's her in that picture.

"That's me," she says as she smacks me in the chest with the back of her hand.

My pop doesn't seem phased in the least. "Did you make that?"

Maggie shakes her head. "No. That was all Desmond. But..." She leans down and taps through the tablet a couple slides back to find the broccoli salad she made for the wedding reception. "I did make this."

She's beaming so wide, my chest swells with pride for her. She's come such a long way since we first met last summer.

"You found yourself a sous-chef, I see." My father doesn't smile, but I can feel his approval in his words.

"I guess I have." I nudge Maggie, who smiles up at me playfully. She obviously doesn't believe the term belongs to her, but I think I'm with my dad on this one. She's been more a partner to me than I've ever had in the kitchen.

My dad continues to look through the photos, and Maggie continues to tell him who cooked each meal in them and the event each meal was cooked for. They have their own little conversation going, and I'm happy to stand back and watch my dad engage with someone besides the hospital staff, police, or his aides at the rehab clinic.

We stay through his dinner and fill him in on the television show we're filming with *Five-Star Faye*. And while my dad gives expressionless nods, he's hanging on every word. He even starts to fill Maggie in on stories of his own experience with cooking. We would probably stay longer, but Kari peeks her head in to check his vitals again. His last two blood pressure readings had dropped slightly, but not enough to take him out of the high-risk zone.

"All right, you two. We should give this handsome man some rest. I still don't like where his levels are at, but they should improve with some sleep." She narrows her gaze at my father, and he hands me back my tablet.

"Keep it," I tell him, placing the tablet on the tray next to his dinner. "I'll be back to get it in the morning."

Maggie squeezes my hand. "I'll step outside so you can say goodnight." Then she leans into my father and places a kiss on his cheek. "Good night, Mr. Blake. It was fun talking with you."

He looks at her, eyes big and bright, and then he nods. "You too, Maggie."

When she walks out of the room, my dad pushes his tray away and looks up at me with a knowing gaze. "You're in trouble, son." And then for the first time that I can remember in years, he smiles.

Southern Roots

MAGGIE

The smile on Desmond's face when he steps out of his father's hospital room is contagious. There's something lighter about him than when I arrived. Knowing that his father will be okay surely had a positive effect on his emotions, but there's something else behind those beautiful blue eyes. He has a peacefulness that I've never seen in him before. The Desmond I met months ago was as wound up as a rubber-band ball. It didn't take much to make him snap. I like this version of him. The version that is at peace with his life and his father's condition. Even if it's just for the moment.

He takes my hand and leads me out the front door of the hospital then steers me to a car I assume is his rental. Just one glance at it makes me laugh. It's a tiny red Chevrolet. "How do you fit in this thing?"

He opens my door and chuckles. "I don't, not well."

My amused gaze catches his over my shoulder as I slide into my seat.

"What?" he asks defensively. "I was in a rush, and it was after midnight when I got in. I wasn't going to argue."

I shrug, still pinching back a smile. "I'm just excited to see you try to squeeze in. That's all."

He smirks as he backs away from the door. "That's what she said." Then he slams the door and starts to strut around the car like he's some kind of comeback king. He opens the driver's door, still smirking, and sinks his wide, tall frame between the seat at the steering wheel.

"You did not just pull a 'that's what she said' joke on me."

He starts the car, this time with a full grin. "I did, actually." Then he leans in until his lips are less than an inch from mine, sending my pulse zooming to life. "Thanks for the setup."

He presses mouth to mine, letting his kiss linger. It's like he doesn't want to move too fast, but he doesn't seem to want to pull away either. I breathe him in, finally letting the entire day settle over me until I'm at peace too. I'm here. With Desmond. His dad's okay, and so is he.

I settle back into the seat while he pulls the car out of the parking lot and turns down a city street I vaguely remember. "I can't believe I'm back in this town." As I say the words, I realize how much I once feared returning.

"Is there anywhere you want to go? We've got time to kill until tomorrow."

I think about that for a second, considering all the familiar places that come to mind: my old school, my old neighborhood, the skate park I used to sneak off to just to watch cute boys, the mall, the hair salon my mom would drag Monica and me to every few months. While it's fun to reminisce about those times, I'm not sure I want to revisit any of them now. "Nowhere in particular. Maybe we can just drive around?"

Desmond shrugs. "Sure, we can do that. I'll just cruise around my old stomping grounds. Just let me know if you want to stop anywhere."

It's a ten-minute drive from the city hospital to suburbia. The neighborhoods are all as pristine as I remember, with their perfectly trimmed lawns and brick-accented exteriors. A warm, fuzzy feeling buzzes in my chest when I think of my childhood home, which I know is around here somewhere. I mostly know where we are because of the shared high school football stadium that sits proudly in the center of town. The one that's currently lit up like the Griswald's house at Christmas.

"My dad used to take us to the high school games here when we were little." As I say the words, we get closer to the stadium. The bleachers are packed with kids, the parking lot is crowded, and several school buses line the curb. "Is there a game going on right now?"

"It looks like a pep rally or something. Games are on Fridays." Desmond's forehead scrunches up, and then he nods while turning into a parking spot against the curb. "Want to watch for a little bit?"

One week ago, the thought might have terrified me, but not tonight. Tonight, an excitement sparks in my chest as I feel my face light up. "Yes, let's watch."

I step out of the car in time for Desmond to join me and shut my door. He leans against the car and pulls me to his chest. We can see the field perfectly through the wrought iron fence. The team is currently getting into position on the line of scrimmage when I glance over my shoulder and see Desmond completely glued to the action. Then it hits me. "You played here?"

He looks down at me and nods. "I was born on that field."

The serious tone of his words hits me hard in his chest, and for the first time since I met Desmond Blake, I don't feel that divide between us that once made him my enemy. I feel our connection—in our past, in our present, and in our future. Desmond has never truly been my enemy—I see that now. He's a missing link, a part of me. And I'm a part of him.

My heart is full of emotions at my revelation. I turn to him and cup his face in my hands. Then I lift up on my tiptoes and press my lips to his. When our mouths start to move together, it's not just our lips that connect. Our heartbeats sync too. And when he deepens our kiss, when his tongue finds entrance into my mouth and his arms tighten their hold around me, I can feel every inch of my soul tethering to his.

"Let's get out of here," he whispers, his intentions clear.

"Okay." I'm out of breath but smile as I hear myself speak.

We're back in the car and cruising not too far into a nearby neighborhood when Desmond pulls up to a medium-sized one-story house with the trademark brick exterior and bright, beautiful flowers lining the front. He parks in the driveway, walks me to the front door, and unlocks it with a key.

"Is this your house?" I'm completely baffled, wondering if Desmond comes back to Dallas often enough to have his own home here.

He chuckles and shakes his head. "No, not that I haven't thought of buying one here. This is Zach's old home. His momma still lives here."

My eyes widen. "You're kidding me."

"Nope. She lets me stay when I come to see my dad."

We step through the entrance, and he flips on the lights. We're standing in a living room, and the dining room is straight ahead. A kitchen is to the left, and a hallway to the right.

"Is she home?"

"Nah. She works late most nights, but she'll be home in the morning. Hungry?"

Desmond whips up a fajita dinner with steak and all the veggies he can find in the refrigerator.

I love watching him cook. "You're very comfortable here."

He smiles and loads his plate with food before joining me at the dining table. "I spent a lot of time here in high school, and I lived here full-time while I went to culinary school. It feels more like home than my old place."

I frown at that. "Your dad seems very sweet. It's hard to imagine him any other way."

Desmond nods, his expression showing clear confliction. I suppose he's felt the same way often. "When he's sober, he's amazing. His autism doesn't define him, you know? He would always have these outbursts of anger at the most random times, but it was manageable. Every time he lost a cooking job, he would turn to prescription drugs and alcohol. 'To smooth his rough edges,' his doctor would tell me. But once he goes down the substance-abuse rabbit hole, he can't climb out of it on his own, and he's a completely different person—aggressively impulsive, mean, violent."

"And rehab has never been able to help him?"

Desmond shrugs. "For a short time, sure. But when he's on his own in the real world, he falls back into the same cycle. The truth is, I've been trying to get him to move to Seattle for years. Why do you think that studio was available for you to move into so fast? I've never tried to rent it to anyone because it was always meant for him."

My eyes widen, and my chest squeezes. "And he refuses to move?"

Desmond nods. "He needs predictability. Just the mention of moving sends him into a fit of rage."

I can't imagine what Desmond goes through on a daily basis, missing his father, not being able to be there to steer him down a better path. I can finally understand his feelings of guilt that seem to always live with him.

"You should talk to him again," I suggest. "You say he turns to substance when he isn't being fulfilled with cooking. Maybe instead of asking him to move to Seattle, you ask him to work in the kitchen with you."

Desmond seems to be considering my words, so I take my first bite of fajita. As soon as the food hits my taste buds, I'm moaning, and my eyes roll into the back of my head. "So good." I didn't realize how starved I was, but then I realize I haven't eaten since the small breakfast I had before my father arrived at the kitchen.

"I love that I can make you moan without even touching you," Desmond teases.

I'm so thankful for the lightened mood. I smile and take another bite until we're both enjoying our food.

We clean up the kitchen, and Desmond leads me to one of the bedrooms down the main hallway. It's a small, simple room with white walls and a double bed. There's a tall dresser on one side of the room and a wide closet door on the other side. I'm disappointed to see the lack of personal touch until he opens the closet door to reveal a splash of his culinary school years in the form of clothes, boxes, and stacks of magazines.

"Here." He tosses me an old crimson-and-black shirt with his high school football team's name on it.

I smile and look up at him before biting down on my bottom lip to keep from laughing. "You know, back in high school, this would have meant that we're going steady. You sure you want me to wear this?"

He chuckles and rips the shirt out of my hands before turning back to his clothes. "In that case…" He pulls another shirt from the hanger and walks it over to me then places it on my chest like he's picturing me wearing it. "Maybe you should wear this one."

I look down at the shiny crimson fabric and swallow. It's his old jersey. "Number twenty-four?" I ask with a smile. "That's my lucky number."

His grin widens, and he leans close to my ear, stealing my breath with his words. "That's ironic because you're about to get lucky tonight."

He wiggles his eyebrows, and I push him away with a laugh. "We'll see about that."

Turnovers

DESMOND

Maggie is currently devouring an old *People* magazine she found in my closet, wearing my jersey, which loosely hangs around her body. The bottom of it falls just above her thighs, and she's kicking her legs in the air, making me instantly regret my decision to take a shower. But I need one badly after nearly twenty-four hours in the hospital. So I leave her to her reading material and walk across the hall to the bathroom.

I wait for the water to heat and then step under it, feeling more of the weight from my trip lift away. Today was a heavy day, one I came into alone, not knowing what to expect after my father's heart attack. The fact that I got to have some relatively normal moments with him, and with Maggie too, makes it all somehow worth it. I feel like I got a glimpse of my real father today, the one who loses himself to his disease far too often. And to see his smile again, all because of Maggie, brings to light a new feeling in me, one that has been building ever since the day Maggie Stevens stepped foot in my kitchen.

I'm rinsing the soap from my eyes when I feel small hands roam up my back and around to my chest before sliding down my abs.

"I thought you could use some company in here."

I can feel the upward curve of her lips on my back right before she places a kiss between the blades of my shoulders. "That was a damn good thought." I'm fully aware of the growl in my tone. The fact that Maggie surprised me in the shower only turns me on that much more.

My heart takes off at a gallop as she reaches lower, grips my cock, and strokes me slowly to full mast. She's like a mind reader tonight, giving me everything I need without a selfish bone in her body. She gives and gives until she's sliding to her knees in front of me. She takes me in her mouth and straight down her throat.

I gasp and fall forward, my hand slamming against the wall to fully brace myself. "Maggie," I groan when she's getting close. But my plea only has her gripping my ass harder and pulling me deeper down her throat. "Holy shit." I gasp my words and look down to watch her yank me out of her mouth just in time for my hot juices to hit her neck and slide down her heaving chest while her wide caramel eyes watch my reaction. My entire body explodes in what feels like a second orgasm at the sight of her. She's so fucking hot.

I tug her up to me and devour her lips, sucking them and nibbling them while shutting off the water behind her. Then I'm lifting her so she can wrap her legs around my waist while I carry her out of the shower and into my bedroom. I lay her on the bed while I tower over her, figuring out what I want to do to her first. She's dripping wet, her hair soaking my pillow. Her lips are glistening red and puffy from my kiss. After a few deep breaths, I lower myself above her and stare deeply into her eyes. "I can't believe you're really here."

She smiles softly. "Where else would I be?"

I swallow, her words drifting over me in a warm embrace. "You could be anywhere, Mags. But you chose to be here. Why?"

Her brows bend together, and her smile fades a bit. "Do you really need to hear me say it?"

I bite the inside of my lip, my pulse racing through my body. Then I nod.

"Because I love you, Desmond Blake." Her cheeks push up into a smile again. "Almost as much as I hate you."

I chuckle and bury my smile in her neck before kissing it. My heart is rattling around the walls of my ribs, and I feel like it might just explode. "Well, that's a relief." I pull back to look into her eyes. "Because I love you too. Almost as much as I hate you." I touch her nose with mine, playfully, to tell her I'm joking.

She presses her hips up to where my erection has already come back to life. "You must hate me a lot right now."

I thrust my hips against her and enter in one swift stroke. "You have no idea."

Almost as soon as I'm inside her, my eyes go wide. I'm totally bare, and while we've talked about the fact that she's on birth control and we're both clean, we've never actually had sex without a condom. But damn, she feels good. Now that I'm inside, there's no way in hell I'm pulling out, not unless it's what she wants. I suck in a breath and wait because I think she's making the same conclusion in her own brain.

"Should I get a condom?" I finally ask.

"You can, but"—she bites down on her lip—"I kind of want to feel you tonight."

It's all the permission I need to rock my hips into her once more, slowly, enjoying every ounce of sensation as her walls grip my length. I reach around her and grab a couple pillows to prop her hips higher while never losing my rhythm. With my hands on her hips, and my eyes locked on hers, it's only a matter of time before I feel the early tremble of her pending release.

I hover over her, taking her mouth with mine as she moans out her warning. "Flip me over," she demands.

I don't hesitate to obey. Wrapping my arm beneath her, I slide under her body while she climbs on top of me. Her hands are on my chest, and her hips are already working me at a faster pace than the one I had set. But this time, it doesn't matter. I don't try to control the rhythm. I don't edge her to an orgasm the way I normally like to do. Because this time, it's about more than the art of getting Maggie to her climax. We're making love, and for the first time, I understand exactly what that means.

As our limbs tangle and our kiss grows stronger, I know there's no other woman in the world who could own me so completely. No one but Maggie.

"I should have known I would find you in here, cooking."

Maggie enters the kitchen the next morning, wearing a beautiful smile. My high school football jersey is tucked into a pair of black drawstring shorts she must have found in my closet. She looks refreshed and happy, and I can't help but smile knowing that I am part of the reason for her happiness.

I pull the hot pan out of the oven and set it on the stove before wrapping her in my arms and kissing her square on the mouth. "Actually," I say between kisses, "I'm baking, but don't tell." I wink and smack her ass before turning back to the stove. I slide in a second batch of guava turnovers while Maggie hops onto the counter to watch. "How'd you sleep?"

"Great, except that you're a bed hog."

I chuckle. "Sorry. Now you know why I have a king at home."

She raises her brows as if to challenge my comment. "Is that why? I kinda thought your bed was like your version of a playground. You need all that room to do your tricks."

I smirk and shrug. "I won't disagree with that." I pick up a turnover and step between her legs then hold it to her mouth. "You need to try this. You'll love it. I swear."

Her eyes are wide, and I swear drool is about to start pooling at the corners of her mouth. "How many calories do these things have?"

"Don't worry," I tell her with a smirk. "You worked them all off last night. But if you're really worried, I can put you on another cardio program today."

She narrows her eyes but opens her mouth anyway then leans down and takes a bite from the corner. Her body reacts exactly as I expect. Maggie experiences great food the same way she orgasms. Her entire body freezes, and her eyes roll into the back of her head, then she groans out her pleasure.

She takes hold of the small pastry and finishes it off before eyeing the rest of them on the tray. "What are those called?"

"Guava turnovers," I say proudly. "My dad loves them. I thought we could sneak him in a couple and leave the rest for Rebecca."

"Rebecca?"

Desmond smiles. "Zach's mom." Then I pick up another turnover from the tray and hold it in front of her. "You can have this on one condition."

"What? You're seriously going to hold food hostage from me? That feels wrong."

"Let me photograph you eating it."

"I should have known." Then she laughs and plucks the pastry from my fingers. "Snap away."

I use my camera phone, since I don't have my professional lens, and shoot a series of photos of Maggie devouring her orgasmic breakfast. She's chewing the last of it when Rebecca steps into the kitchen with a full-blown smile on her face.

"There she is," I say before scooping her up in a hug.

She's a petite woman in her late forties with light-brown hair, same as Zach's, and a round, beautiful face. She gives the best hugs and the warmest smiles. If anyone reminds me of home the most, it's her.

"I missed you, Desi," she says, pulling my face between her hands and kissing me on the cheek. "But I think I might have missed your cooking more." She turns and catches sight of the pastry before turning back to me with a grin. "I see you've paid your hotel fee in food."

I smile back. "I have. I hope you'll accept. Although Maggie here might fight you for them."

Maggie has already slid off the counter, and she's extending her hand to Zach's mom with a timid smile. "It's so good to meet you, Mrs. Ryan. I've heard lovely things about you."

Rebecca appears as confused as I would expect as she shakes Maggie's hand.

"Rebecca, this is my girlfriend, Maggie. She's Monica's sister."

Rebecca does a double take, and her eyes widen. "Oh my. Did I hear you right? You and Zachary are dating sisters?" Then she laughs, her eyes crinkling at the corners. "I'm not surprised at all."

Rebecca pulls Maggie in for a hug, and I can feel the warmth from where I'm standing. "Maggie, dear, my apologies for this one over here. I did what I could in the time he spent with me, but I'm afraid he was a lost cause from the beginning."

My jaw drops in mock disbelief. "I take offense."

"You were meant to." She winks and wraps an arm around my waist. "Tell me how your pop is doing. Back to his stubborn old self yet?"

I texted her last night after my dad woke up to let her know. "Yup. We're going back to the hospital now to check in one last time before we head back to Seattle." Then I remember my conversation with Maggie last night. "Actually, I might ask my dad to come with me again."

I see the doubt written all over Rebecca's expression, but she smiles through it, encouraging me like she always does. "I think that would be great if the stubborn old man listens this time. You'd be a great caretaker. But are you sure you have to go back to Seattle so soon? I'd love if you stayed for dinner."

"I wish we could, but we really need to get back to the kitchen."

She understands, and I'm able to chat with her for a bit longer while Maggie changes into the single set of clothes she packed in her handbag.

When Maggie comes back out, she wraps Zach's mom in a hug. "It was so nice to meet you, Rebecca."

"Give my love to your sister."

Maggie smiles. "I will."

Then Rebecca turns to hug me. "Tell that boy of mine that I'll be in Seattle on Thanksgiving, so he better make time for me."

I assure her that I will, and then Maggie and I are hopping into my rental with a full belly and a heavy heart. I hate leaving Rebecca, and I hate that I'm about to see my father for possibly the last time for a few months… unless he chooses to come to Seattle. Maggie was right to mention how much he would love the kitchen life. Maybe it's not too late for him to turn his life around after all.

We pull up to the hospital, and I'm feeling optimistic about things with my dad for the first time in a long time. I'm breathing deeply, my fingers tightly woven with Maggie's. I know that no matter what happens today, I've still got her by my side.

We pass through the main entrance and ride the elevator up to the second floor. We enter the west wing of the hospital, where the ICU is. It always seems to be chaotic here—alarms going off, patients moaning, and beeping hospital equipment echoing in the space. I grip Maggie's hand tighter as we turn the corner and head down the hall.

While everything seems to be business as usual in the hospital, something feels off. The closer we get to my father, the stranger that feeling in my chest gets. A nurse leaves his room. Her eyes are bloodshot, and her cheeks are tearstained. Instead of the normal beeping from yesterday that signaled my dad's heart was beating regularly, now I hear one solid line of noise.

I release Maggie's hand, rush to the room, and push back the curtain. My father's still there with a doctor and three nurses by his side. His gown has been opened, and one of the nurses is holding the two plates of the defibrillator in his hands. I half expect the nurse to apply a shock to my father's chest right then, but judging by the somber faces in the room, I think I may have been too late.

The doctor pushes a button on the machine, stopping the long beeping noise, and places his hands on his hips. Then he looks at me, his sorrowful eyes telling me everything I already know deep in my gut. "I'm so sorry, Desmond."

"What?" I yell. "Why?"

The doctor steps forward, his expression and mannerisms so calm that I want to rage. "Your father had another heart attack, and he went into sudden cardiac arrest. We did everything we could."

"No." My voice cracks, my face crumbles, and my vision is starting to blur. This has got to be a sick joke. This can't be happening. This cannot be real.

"I'm so sorry, Desmond," the doctor says again. "We just couldn't save him." Two solid beats pass followed by two words I'll never forget. "He's gone."

TAKE SEVEN

Hellos & Goodbyes

"EVERY STORY HAS AN END, BUT IN LIFE
EVERY ENDING IS A NEW BEGINNING."
—UNKNOWN

Open Minded

MAGGIE

There's still a heaviness in the air after we return to Seattle on Friday night. I opt to join Desmond inside his place instead of retreating to my own. I can't even imagine leaving him alone right now.

Desmond hasn't spoken much, not that I've attempted to hold a conversation. I've been giving him his space while letting him know I'm still here.

When he crumbled to the floor after hearing the news, I fell with him.

When he was finally ready to say his goodbyes, I stood by his side.

When he started to make the tough calls to family and friends, I held his hand.

And when Desmond had to go to his dad's apartment—which was the hardest day of all—I helped him sort through everything so that he could take away any keepsakes. The only thing he ended up walking away with were some recipe books and his parents' wedding rings. He was shocked him that his dad still had them.

In a way, I would say the past few days were a cathartic experience for him. Each day seems to bring Desmond a little closer to acceptance while he works through the main stages of grief. Shock and denial were probably the shortest stages of them all, with the longest being his anger and bargaining. The guilt he carried from being a helpless bystander in the entire situation was a tough pill for him to swallow. Even if his dad had agreed to move to Seattle, not even Desmond could stop a heart attack.

Desmond excuses himself to take a shower, and I decide to whip him up a small dinner to tide him over for the night. He hasn't been eating much at all, but I'm hoping he'll try now that we're back home. I search through his refrigerator and pantry to see what I can grab without having to run to the market for ingredients, when I get the best idea: a variety of cheeses, a loaf of bread, an onion, mayonnaise, spices, and brown sugar. That's all I need to make Desmond's gourmet grilled cheese.

I've just gathered all the ingredients when there's a knock on the door. I look toward the bathroom, where the water is still running. Desmond probably didn't hear anything beyond the shower water, so I set down the skillet and peep through the hole in the door before opening it.

My heart beats a little faster when I see my dad standing on the other side. He's wearing a Seattle ball cap and a matching sweatshirt with jeans. His head is angled down, and there's a melancholy look on his face, which means Desmond must have reached out at some point. Then I'm struck by a feeling of gratitude for the fact that the two men I love have each other.

I pull open the door, and when our eyes connect, surprise registers on his face. "Maggie—"

Before my dad can get another word out, my arms are around him and squeezing him tight. My throat clogs, and it's impossible to hold back tears. Here I am standing in front of my father when Desmond just lost his. I can't imagine being in Desmond's shoes, especially knowing that I could have had a relationship with my father, but I refused to let him love me.

"I'm so glad you're here."

He squeezes me back. "Are you okay?"

More tears fall even when I try to squeeze them away. "I'm sorry I've been such a pain in the ass."

He rubs my back gently, just like I remember him doing when I was a little girl. "Shhh. It's okay, Mags. You have nothing to apologize for."

"I want to know you too, Dad. I want to be part of your life." I pull back slightly to see his face.

His eyes are bloodshot, and his chin is quivering as he nods. "You always have been, baby girl, whether it felt like it or not. You've always been here." He pats his chest and then cups my chin. "How is he?"

I sniffle. "As good as can be, I guess. He hasn't been eating much, but I'm about to make him something to eat while he showers. Do you want to come in? I can make extra."

He quirks a lip at me. "You're going to cook? You definitely didn't get that trait from your mother."

I roll my eyes. "I've been working in a kitchen, Dad. Besides, it's just grilled cheese. You can't exactly mess that up."

He raises his brows. "Don't be so sure about that." Then he gestures for me to head inside. "I wouldn't say no to that offer. Let's see what you've got."

I smile and shut the door behind us both then head into the kitchen. My dad takes a seat at a stool while I start to heat the skillet.

"When did he let you know?" I ask.

"He didn't."

This throws me off a little, but I focus on dicing the onions, trying not to add to the waterworks.

"Rebecca reached out. I imagine Desmond's been quite preoccupied."

I nod. "He has." I toss the onions and some spices onto the hot skillet. A loud sizzle follows. "I think keeping busy has helped him in some ways. The nights seem to be the hardest for him."

"I can imagine."

Silence passes between us while I start to brown the onions. A few minutes later, I reach into the refrigerator and pull out a beer. I hold it up to my dad in question, and he accepts with a nod. I grab another one and pop the caps off before handing him one.

"So how was it being back in Dallas? You know, before…" My dad's voice trails off, but I understand what he's asking.

"It was nice, actually." I peek at my dad over my shoulder and smile. "Desmond's dad was sweet and adorable. I had a hard time picturing him any other way, you know? And then we drove around our old neighborhood and stopped at Brighton." I take in a deep breath and turn back to the stove to set aside the onions. "I forgot how much I missed those old days when you'd drag us to those high school football games. I never did fall for the game the way Monica did, but I still enjoyed that time with you." I start to smear some mayonnaise on each of the slices of bread. "And then you ended up coaching there. How crazy is that?"

He chuckles. "The world sure does work in mysterious ways. I love that it brought you girls back here to me."

I suck in a deep breath to help steady my emotions, and then I nod again. I'm not sure I trust myself to speak right away, so I focus on adding my butter to the pan and adding the bread. While two slices are heating, I turn to face him while reaching for my beer. "If there's one thing I learned this week, it's that life is truly short. I don't want to live with regrets or what-ifs, or feelings of resentment." I feel heat spreading across my cheeks as I hear myself speak. "Anyway, I love that we're all here too."

"Not really the way I would have ever pictured it," my dad says with a smile. "With my two daughters dating Zach and Desmond. I never even got the chance to threaten them with my shotgun."

I stifle a laugh and roll my eyes. "Miracles do exist."

I turn back to the stove and finish up the sandwiches while my dad and I finish our beers. I don't even notice how quiet Desmond's condo is until the door to the bedroom opens and Desmond comes out in shorts and a T-shirt. "I thought I heard you talking to someone."

My dad meets Desmond halfway and wraps his arms around him in a tight hug. The exchange has me choked up all over again. My dad whispers something I can't hear, and

Desmond just nods, appearing as though he's about to well up with tears too.

"Dinner is ready," I say softly.

Desmond glances in my direction. His eyes landing on the three plates of food I made then flitting up to mine. "Whoa. Did you make those?"

My dad's boastful laugh echoes around the entire condo while he squeezes Desmond's shoulder. "She did. I watched her. I wouldn't have believed it otherwise."

Desmond walks over and starts to inspect his sandwich like I might have poisoned it. Then he takes a bite, and his eyes flutter a little. "Are you serious?" he asks with his mouth still full. "That's damn good. Is this my recipe?"

I shrug while my heart dances. "Well, yeah. It's the only recipe I know."

My dad takes a bite too and has a reaction similar to Desmond's. "This is very good, daughter."

I chuckle. "Thanks, *Father*."

I don't miss the strange look Desmond gives us both. "You two eat," I say while sticking the spices back in the cabinet. "Enjoy. I need to go to my place for a bit. I've been wearing the same two changes of clothes for too long."

Desmond's mouth is still full when he speaks. "At least you've been washing them."

I make a face. "They still feel dirty. I'll be back." I step around the counter and lift myself onto my toes to kiss Desmond's cheek. Then I hug my dad goodbye and smile when he squeezes me a few seconds longer.

"I'll see you soon?" he asks.

I nod and kiss him on the cheek too. "Yes."

My shower lasts as long as the hot water allows. I probably should have opted for a bubble bath instead. My muscles feel tight from the tension I've held over the last week, but the hot water is a gentle reminder that while things might feel different. Everything heals, everything will be okay.

I towel myself off, wrapping myself in the cloth when I'm done. Then I leave the bathroom to find a change of clothes, knowing my father has probably left already.

When I see the figure sitting on my bed I jump so high I think my heart leapt outside of my body. "Holy shit, Desmond, you scared the crap out of me."

He turns from looking out my window and winces. "Sorry. Your dad left, so I thought I'd wait for you here."

"I forgot you had a key," I say gently. Then I walk toward him and sit on my bed to face him. "You okay?"

His eyes search mine for a second before he nods. "I will be. It's just... heavy, you know? I keep thinking about the last time I saw him alive. It had been over a decade since I last saw him smile, and he smiled at me that night."

I scoot forward so my knees are touching his legs. "You never told me that."

Desmond releases a small smile, and I swear a blush is crawling up his cheeks too. "Yeah well. Maybe that's because he was smiling because of you. He told me I was in trouble, and you know what?"

I swallow, my heart pounding like crazy. "What?"

Desmond leans forward and brushes his lips across mine. "My father was right. I am in deep"—he kisses me softly—"deep"—he kisses me again—"trouble." This time, he pulls me back onto the bed with him until I'm snuggled in his arms. "Can we sleep here tonight? I'm too tired to walk back to my place."

As he speaks, his eyes start to flutter closed, and I wonder if there's a different reason he wants to sleep here, a reason he doesn't want to speak out loud. This studio was supposed to be his father's after all. "Of course, Des. I'll get the light."

I leave the bed to flip the switch on the wall, leaving us in darkness except for the glow of the moon filtering in through the large box paned window. Desmond has already stripped himself of his clothes, and he's holding the sheet open for me to slip beneath.

I remove my towel and join him. Our body heat collides as our mouths meet in a slow and tender kiss. It's been days since we last made love, and while I desperately miss him, I know I can't be the first one to make a move.

Our hands roam like we're exploring each other for the first time, and maybe in a way we are. There's no expectation and no agonizing build-up. We're just two souls who had to get lost to finally find their way home. And with Desmond's heart beating in time with mine, we lose ourselves to the rhythm of a new love. A pure love. A love that heals.

Perfect Recipe

DESMOND

Maggie offers to cancel Saturday's class to give me more time to deal with my father's death, but I insist I'm okay. After nearly a week of being away, I'm craving my routine—hitting up the gym, shopping at the farmers market, testing new recipes, greeting and teaching my students, flirting with Maggie.

It was all such clockwork before, but today started out as a struggle. My ass was a lost cause at the gym, mostly due to my low energy level. Shopping at the market seemed like a chore more than ever before. And the thought of faking my smiles through a two-hour class feels damn near painful.

Thank God for Maggie. The moment my students start to arrive, she's at the door, welcoming them with a smile, checking them in, and then chatting up each table just like I usually do. I'm a bit slower to make my rounds like I used to, but I find that with each table I talk to, my mood begins to lift more and more.

The kitchen has always filled me with joy—from the challenge, from the people, and the knowledge that I'm helping my students either at home or in their field of work. The kitchen gives me a purpose, and I'll never take it for granted. Just like an artist who takes a paint brush to canvas, cooking is where I find my escape. In the various tools and ingredients, I get to create something that not only nourishes my body, but it replenishes my soul.

"I know the menu posted online says that we're making zucchini lasagna today, but there's been a change of plans." I wave my recipe in the air while Maggie walks around the room, passing out the new ones. "Today, we're going to make a sausage and broccoli rabe frittata. It was the first dish my father ever taught me how to make." I flash the class my grin. "So this one's for him. Hope you all enjoy it."

We're nearing the end of class when Faye slips in quietly and hangs out in the back of the room until everyone leaves. I'm almost dreading speaking to her again after Monday's dress rehearsal. I left her hanging, and while it was for a good reason, I can't imagine she's back here with good news.

Maggie slides an arm around my waist. "I'm going to head to Shooters to meet Monica. You still up for it?" Her eyes dart from me to Faye, like she doesn't know if she should stay.

"I'll meet you there. This should only take a minute." I lean in and give her a kiss, letting it linger for just a second before I release her. She greets Faye as she passes. Whatever animosity may have existed between the girls last week is no more. Maggie knows Faye isn't a threat, and Faye knows by now what Maggie means to me.

When the door shuts behind Maggie, Faye approaches with a soft smile. "Hey." She hugs me tight and steps back with a tilt of her head. "How are you doing?"

I don't mind the sympathy, but I've started to hate that question. Every minute, every hour, every day is different.

And while the pain feels less like a gaping hole in my chest, I never know how to answer such a simple question.

I take in a slow breath through my nose as we separate. "Just taking it day by day. Working helps. We cooked something in honor of my dad today, so that was nice." I cock my head. Now that the niceties are out of the way, it's time to address the elephant in the room. "I'm sorry the show didn't work out."

Faye's eyes widen slightly and her mouth forms an O in surprise. "Sorry? You don't need to be sorry."

Now it's my turn to be surprised. "I don't? I thought you were here to let me down easy."

Her laugh is light, her eyes still bleeding her sympathy. "No, Desmond. I told you I believe in your kitchen. I'm here to let you know that the studio gave us the green light and a reasonable schedule to work with... if you're still interested."

I can't remember the last time I felt speechless, but there are so many thoughts running through my mind—questions, doubts, excitement—that I'm not sure where to start. "But... how?"

Faye's smile grows. "Do you remember that footage I took of you and Maggie a couple weeks ago?"

I think back to the day Maggie moved in and I put her on the spot to help me cook. "Yes."

"Well, turns out that was all the network needed to see to give the go-ahead. We're approved for one season. My pitch to them was that we will focus on the heart of the kitchen and all it stands for. Farm to table, the charities you support, Seattle life. You'll have final say in the content that gets produced.

Since your brand is involved, we want to make sure you agree on how it's represented."

"Faye, I'm—"

She cringes like she's afraid of my answer. "Ecstatic? Pumped?" she tries.

"I'm impressed, and relieved, and so damn happy." I let out a laugh, feeling a little bit lighter than I did a minute ago. What felt so stressful just five days ago, now feels like a dream.

Faye presses her hands together and pops up onto her toes in the most un-like Faye pose I've ever seen her in. I can practically feel her excitement radiating from her entire body.

"So you're in? Maggie's in? We're doing this?"

I nod, letting the smile push up my cheeks. "If Maggie's still in, then so am I."

MAGGIE

A crack sounds as the cue ball smashes into the top of the pyramid, creating a burst of color as the rest of the balls scatter everywhere. None of them land in a pocket.

"Gah," Monica growls before walking over to her beer. "I'm usually better than this."

I smirk at her and proudly step forward with my pool stick. "That was before you played me. One to zero, sister."

Monica kicks her foot out and taps me on the ass with it. "Less talking. More playing."

Chuckling, I lean over and set up my shot. "Five ball, corner pocket." I lock in my aim and tap the cue ball perfectly.

The five ball sinks and I shoot my sister a cocky wink over my shoulder. "Guess that makes me solids."

Monica just laughs and rolls her eyes. "You're still annoying when you win, you know that?"

After making a couple more balls, I end up missing one. I walk toward the table we're sharing and grab my vodka soda. "I was thinking," I start before Monica walks off toward the pool table. "What if we host a Friendsgiving at the kitchen? Zach's mom and brother will be in town. We can invite some of your friends like Chloe and Gavin." I swallow before attempting my next suggestion. "And ... maybe Dad's family too."

Monica blinks a few times and then nods. "I love that idea, Mags. But are you sure? I know you and Dad are talking now, but I haven't even met his wife and kids. It could make for a super awkward Thanksgiving."

I nod. "I know, which is why we're doing a *Friends*giving. Besides, when is it not going to be awkward, you know? Desmond could use all the family he can get right now. And I'm starting to think ripping the bandage off might just be the best thing."

Monica smiles. "I'm in. I'll buy the chips and dips."

I laugh at her blatant attempt to get out of cooking. While Monica is much more efficient in the kitchen than I, it's still not her favorite thing in the world to do. "Nope. You're preparing with me."

"What? You're dating a freaking chef."

"Yeah, but I don't want him doing all the heavy lifting this year. I'm going to let him enjoy the festivities while you and I cook."

She twists up her face and lets out a groan. "Fine. But only because you let me drag you to all of those classes."

Monica approaches the pool table to take her shot and my eyes wander to the entrance just in time. Desmond's walking through the door with a big smile and more energy I've seen him carry all week. My heart starts to thrum faster in my chest. Faye's news must have been good, but I'll need to hear it to believe it. "Well?"

He stops in front of me and lifts my body so that my feet are off the ground and my face is parallel to his. "We got the show."

Just seeing and hearing his excitement puts a full-blown smile on my face. I squeal and wrap my arms around his neck. "I don't understand how, but I'm so happy for you."

"For us," he corrects.

"No way," Monica says from where she stands on the other side of the pool table. "You guys got the show?"

Desmond nods, not taking his eyes from mine. "Faye showed them some footage from a class her crew taped a couple weeks ago and it was a done deal. You're still doing this with me, right? You're okay with it?"

I don't even hesitate. "Yes." Whatever fear held me back from getting in front of the camera again simply doesn't exist anymore. Not when I'm with Desmond. "Look at that. All your dreams are about to come true."

He smiles and leans in to touch his nose to mine. "No, Mags. All my dreams came true when I met you."

Permanent

MAGGIE

Music plays from the overhead speakers, a mixture of eighties pop, nineties rock, and today's favorites. Desmond and I spent the entire night before putting together a playlist we thought everyone would enjoy, and so far, there aren't any complaints.

Between Desmond, Zach, Monica, and I, we invited over thirty people to join us today. Chloe and Gavin are here with the young girl with the red curls I saw dancing it up at the wedding, along with Jazz and her husband Marco.

Zach's mom, Rebecca, and brother, Ryan, showed up too and are currently seated on the couches talking with my dad, his wife, and two young girls. Ryan is the spitting image of his older brother, though a couple inches taller and thinner. Apparently he's some big-wig baseball player who just turned pro. I don't know how Rebecca did it, but she managed to raise two great men all on her own.

Some of Zach's teammates showed up, too, including Balko, who is currently hitting on a very intrigued Phoebe. That's a bit awkward, considering Phoebe and Justin used to date and Justin is somewhere in the room too.

Sandy, the owner of BelleCurve Creative, is perusing the artwork around the kitchen with her husband. I recently found out she's a good friend of my dad's and Zach's. She's also the reason Monica gets to go to a fancy art school tuition free.

While everyone mingles, Monica and I keep busy in the kitchen. She's on turkey and stuffing duty, while I tackle most of the sides. I've made all the traditional ones, freshly prepared with ingredients from Pike Place Market. We also added the extras that Monica and I thought would be fun to throw in, like our grandma's favorite Southern-baked macaroni and cheese, and a simple turnip au gratin.

All in all, I would say we're kicking ass in the kitchen, but Desmond refused to let us do everything alone, so I put him in charge of setting the tables and playing bartender for the evening.

"Another Maggie special," Desmond says as he carries over a fresh drink. He winks and sets it down in front of me. "On the house."

I laugh. He started calling my vodka sodas Maggie specials because I always ask for three limes. "I think I've earned my keep today."

"Food's not done yet, but... " His eyes roam over the kitchen counters to where we've started gathering and reheating some of the dishes. "Nothing's burning. No one's sliced a finger. No lobsters have died. I'm going to say things are heading in the right direction."

I scoff. "You shouldn't have expected less."

He flashes me a grin. "I'm learning quickly." His eyes flicker down and catch on the text of my apron, which reads "Boss of the Sauce" in glittery rose gold letters.

He tosses his head back and laughs. "At least this one is appropriate for a family gathering."

I grin, remembering that day in class when he refused to give me a cooking certificate. I was wearing a similar apron with much filthier language.

His eyes bulge wide when they catch on something else on the apron. "Wait a second. That's the Edible Desire logo."

I stick my tongue between my teeth and grin. "Monica made it. Actually, she made a bunch of them."

Monica's ears perk up at the sound of her name and she bounces over to stand next to me. Her apron reads "Dessert First," and there's a strawberry beneath it, dripping with chocolate. "Are you talking about my aprons? They're cute, right? I think we should sell them."

Desmond blinks wide. "We?"

"Well, yeah." Monica looks at me and twists her face to tell me Desmond is crazy not to understand. "I can design you an entire line of Edible Desire merch, and you can sell it for profit. I would get a cut, of course."

I grin up at him. "It's actually a great idea. We can make sure they're family appropriate, but I've been thinking of all these ways you can make a little bit extra to support the kitchen's growth in addition to the show, and —" Before I blurt out everything I've been working on over the last couple of weeks, I put a finger up signaling for him to wait. "We can talk about it later. Go mingle. We have things handled here."

He leans down and narrows his lids playfully. "What if I want to mingle with you?"

My cheeks heat, and I have to bite back a laugh. "Later. I've got an important job to do, and I can't have any distractions."

His hands move to my hips, and he tugs me closer. "I'll leave on one condition." He looks between my eyes, and a devilish smile emerges on his face. "Wear that apron for me tonight." Then he slides his lips to my ear. "*Only* the apron."

A chill ripples through my body, and then my lips turn up at the corners. "I think I can manage that."

As Desmond walks away, I catch Monica's mouth drop open. "Sister," she scolds under her breath.

"Hush." I turn back to the sweet potatoes I'm preparing. "You weren't supposed to hear that."

"Well, I did." Then she points at my apron. "I know you want to show him who's in charge of the sauce tonight, but you ruin that and I'm charging you for the next one."

I growl out a laugh as I pick up a rag from the counter and chuck it at Monica. "You're so gross. Don't think I'm unaware of your dessert fetish. I don't even want to know what you and Zach brought for dessert."

"I honestly don't know," Monica says with a shrug. "Zach took care of that one."

"Smile for the camera, girls."

We look toward our dad who has his phone aimed at us with a big grin on his face. We get close together and do exactly as he says. Then Zach comes up behind him and tells him to get in the photo. My dad hands off his phone and comes around to our side of the island. He stands between us and puts his arms around our waists, holding us tightly to him. It's hard not to get choked up when I realize this is the first photo we've taken together since we were kids.

"Dinner smells delicious." He squeezes both of our sides and then turns to face us. "I'm proud of you girls. One of these days, you'll have to come to the house for dinner. Kristin makes some mean pork-and-prawn dumplings."

"Yum." Monica's eyes are so wide, I think she might start drooling.

I laugh at her reaction and push away that initial spark of discomfort at the mention of his wife. The fact that we're all here today is a huge step, and day by day things will continue to get better. I'm ready to push through whatever awkwardness comes to get to a happy place for all.

"We'd love to, Dad," I say. "Just name the date and time. I'm sure the season keeps you busy."

"Sure, but everyone needs to eat, right? Besides, rumor has it we've got a television star in the family now. We might need to work around her schedule." He winks. "When do you start taping?"

A genuine burst of excitement escapes my chest. "Officially January. The goal is to shoot the entire season in January, go to postproduction in February, and start airing sometime in the spring."

"I can't wait." Monica beams. "I'm making all of your clothes. You know this, right?"

"I wouldn't wear anything else."

She squeals and throws her arms around my neck. "I love you, Mags."

"I love you too, M. Now get off of me and finish basting all those turkeys." I smack her ass, causing her to yelp and jump.

We're able to get out of the kitchen for a short time before dinner is served, and I latch on to Desmond while he does his thing and makes his rounds. But unlike in his classes, he's got a beer in his hand, and he's shooting the shit with good friends. The way people respond to Desmond is one of my favorite things about him. I love the fact that he can make practically anybody smile, no matter the circumstance, and the way his quick wit gets him into just as much trouble as it makes people laugh.

I watch him carry on a conversation with my father's two girls, and it's clear they all have a special bond, a bond I hope to one day share with them as well. They know who Monica and I are and seem to be excited to get to know us. The one thing my father did right was telling them about Monica and I when they were younger.

An hour later, the tables are set, and all the food has been laid out, including the four large turkeys, which are a perfect golden brown.

"I can't believe you girls did all of this," Desmond says as his eyes scan the table.

We're the last two still standing as everyone takes their seats, and I have to laugh. "You should have never doubted me."

He wraps an arm around my shoulders and leans down to kiss me. "I never did, babe. Why do you think I was always so hard on you in class? I could tell you were a natural."

"Aww." My insides dance a little in my chest. "And now here we are."

He smiles and then turns to our guests with a clap of his hands. "All right, everyone." He waits for the group to quiet down and focus their attention on him. "Before we dig in, I just wanted to thank everyone for coming to our first annual Friendsgiving." There's a round of loud applause before he continues again. "Today would not have been possible without Monica and Maggie. I think we should all give them some love for all the hard work they put into our meal today."

Desmond looks down at me and winks while everyone expresses their thanks. My face feels hot from all this attention—over cooking, of all things. But Desmond isn't done. There's a sparkle in his eyes as he looks directly at me, making me feel like whatever he's about to say next has something to do with me.

"As you know, Edible Desire is an accredited cooking school. We train amateurs, pros, and everything in between. And when you put in the hours and pass my final cooking exam, you receive a certificate."

I shuffle in my stance and tilt my head at Desmond. What in the world is he bringing this up for? The thought of him humiliating me in front of our friends and family doesn't seem like something he would do, but now I'm starting to wonder.

"Usually I hand out those certificates in class, but I thought I'd make an exception today." He grins and leans over me to pull a manila envelope off the counter. I hadn't even seen it sitting there. He slides out a familiar piece of white paper. A silver seal is on the top, and my name is written clearly on the line.

I gasp while my heart takes off, beating a million times a minute. "You didn't."

He chuckles along with most of the people in the room. By now, everyone knows our story and about that awful day when Desmond refused to hand over a certificate that I felt was so meaningless at the time even though I was stuck on the principal of it all. I'd wanted to prove a point more than I'd wanted to actually earn what I was so desperate to receive. But I get it now.

My throat tightens as tears threaten to spill.

"Maggie Stevens," Desmond says with a grin. "Will you accept this cooking certificate?"

I laugh. "Yes,"

The room bursts into celebration as I take the certificate from Desmond and hug him tightly, not even caring who's watching us as tears slide down my face and his lips find my cheek.

"It's about damn time," I say into his ear.

"I agree," he says back. "But now you know you earned it."

We exchange a smile before retreating to our seats and calling an official start to our feast.

It's probably the longest dinner of my life, but I haven't stopped laughing the entire night. My dad tells stories about Desmond and Zach as teens, Desmond retells the story about the lobster I didn't want to kill, and I recount the story of me tripping at the end of the runway in New York. The fact that I can laugh at all the things that once embarrassed me to the core, makes me happier than I've ever felt. The night is entirely perfect.

"There's only one thing missing," I tell Monica once we're finished eating. I don't need to elaborate for her to know. We've been easing into conversations with our mom over the past few weeks to give her honest updates about our lives. It's the only way for us all to truly move forward together, and while Matilda Stevens was furious on several accounts — that we'd reunited with our father, and that I was officially done with modeling for the agency in LA — she was beginning to accept that we'd made those choices for ourselves.

Monica nods and pulls out her phone then scrolls to Mom's number and dials it.

We step outside together and wish our mom a happy Thanksgiving together, tell her all is well with us, and promise her that we'll visit her in California soon. She's thrilled to hear updates about the television show and about Monica's latest fashion design ventures. And in return, she brags about living the life of luxury with her boyfriend in LA.

When we're done, we walk back into the kitchen to find Zach setting a humongous pastry box on one of the tables. Monica claps her hands together with excitement and happily skips over to her boyfriend. "Oh, I want to see what you brought."

Zach grins and nods at the box. "Do the honors, Cakes."

His nickname for Monica is so adorable and also appropriate considering my sister's obsession with dessert, specifically chocolate-covered anything.

I walk over to stand with Desmond, who has his camera out to snap photos of the reveal.

Monica lifts the cover and sets it aside. Then she gets an eyeful of the cake. It's chocolate with strawberries decorating the top, and underneath them is a message handwritten in icing.

MONICA
WILL YOU MARRY ME?

The look on my sister's face is utterly priceless. Tears well up in my eyes all over again, and I cling to Desmond, needing something to support me while I watch Monica and Zach's proposal play out in front of me.

Monica's mouth opens wide from the shock and she turns to the man who was standing behind her a moment ago. Now he's kneeling, and I swear he's shaking.

"Monica Stevens, I've known you for years, adored you for just as long, and I've been crazy in love with you for the past year. There's no other woman in the world I'd rather spend my life, or share my cake, with." He laughs gently and then pulls out a black velvet box and opens it.

Monica's hands fly to her mouth as she finally figures out that this is really happening.

Then Zach asks the question. "Will you marry me?"

"Yes! A million times yes." She falls to her knees, throws her arms around him, and kisses him so hard that they both fall over laughing. He helps her up and places the gorgeous square-cut diamond on her finger, then they kiss again.

I've never been more moved in my life. Zach had warned Desmond and me about his plans, which is why Desmond was ready with his camera and I dragged Monica outside with me to call Mom when I did. Everything worked out better than we planned.

An hour later, the cake has been devoured, and the kitchen has been cleaned. One by one, our guests leave with their to-go boxes, until it's just Desmond and me alone. He locks up while I run to his office for a quick minute to grab a present I made for him.

We meet back in the front of the room, and he pulls me onto the couch while eyeing the present in my hands. "What's that?"

I bite down on my bottom lip. "Just something I've been working on for the past few weeks." I swallow and search his eyes, finding the courage to say what I need to say. A lot has been going through my mind since we got back from Dallas and accepted the cooking show opportunity. Life has become a whirlwind, and this is my attempt at slowing things down, just for a second. "You inspired me to create something. Something I think you will love."

Desmond stares at the package for a second and then starts to open the wrapping carefully, like he wants to preserve it as much as possible. He pulls out a thick hardback book. It's titled *Fake It Til You Bake It*, and he just gives me an amused smile before he opens it and sees the dedication I wrote.

He starts to turn through the recipe book, page by page. His bloodshot eyes give away the emotion going through his heart and mind. Each recipe is one Desmond created, tested, and put in the approved folder on his computer so he could teach it in class. And each photo is one he took after preparing the dish himself.

"I thought maybe you could have it published. Not that version, exactly. You can exchange the photos, take new ones, but it could be another opportunity to grow."

About halfway through, he gets to the first page of the desserts section and sees the recipe for guava turnovers. He shuts the book and wipes his eyes with the back of his hand then pulls me onto his lap. "I need to stop."

He searches my eyes while I nod. "Of course. Are you okay?"

His chin tips up. "Better than okay." Then he takes my face in his hands and kisses me deeply, holding nothing back. I can feel the weight of the bond that now tethers us in our hearts, and minds, and souls. I can feel his pain that still lingers inside him over his father's passing.

"This is an incredible gift, Maggie. I don't know how you did it, but it means more than you know."

I swallow, feeling his appreciation down to my bones. "I've been thinking a lot about your love for food photography, and it got me thinking about how fearful I was to get back in front of the camera after leaving LA. Photography to me always had such a negative connotation. I was just an object in someone else's eyes, to someone else's perspective, their vision, their direction. Intentions were never clear-cut. Then I met you. And not only are you a brilliant photographer, but you've reminded me how beautiful photography can be as an art when filled with good intentions. Somehow you got me to fall in love with it all over again. But this time, for the right reasons." I laugh at my rambling self. "I just wanted you to see your talent the way I do."

"I've always seen you, Maggie, even when you thought you were hiding yourself from the world and pushing people away. There was something about you that I just couldn't tear my mind from." He smiles. "I'm always looking for something when I look through that viewfinder. Something meaningful. You want to know why I've never done anything with my photos besides hang some of them on the walls?"

I nod, my heart beating so fast in my chest that I can barely breathe.

"Because they're never good enough, so I just keep taking photos, and I just keep searching. But then I started taking photos of you, and I knew I finally found my muse. Maggie, you became my muse without even knowing it, without even trying."

"And you became mine." I touch the recipe book and smile. "You've given me a piece of myself that I never even knew existed. When I met you, I was just a scared and lost woman with no idea where her life was taking her. And then you pushed me and challenged me and never gave up. You helped me find me, Desmond, and I'll never be able to repay you for that."

The corners of his mouth turn up slowly. "Repay me? You're already doing that, babe. You gave me your heart. Nothing about that is temporary."

I curl up against him and rest my cheek on his shoulder. "And it's yours forever."

Epilogue

DESMOND, SIX MONTHS LATER

"That's a wrap on Season One of *Desmond's Kitchen*!" Our director, Franklin, yells the words from the top of his lungs, earning a collective cheer from the production crew. It's a crew of eight packed into the kitchen, along with all of their equipment, and by the chatter erupting in the room, everyone seems to be damn proud of the work we've all put in.

Between the footage being sent to Faye and her cohorts every single day and the major kudos she's gotten from her network in response to the footage they've seen, it feels like everything we once agonized and fought over is finally worth it.

Maggie and I turn to each other after the final shot of our last scene of the season. As she squeals with delight, I'm raising my fist in an air pump to end all air pumps. The joy is practically exploding from me. And when I pick her up and kiss her hard on the mouth with all the production crew to see, I can feel her joy spiraling through me.

We're two halves, Maggie and I, and we fit perfectly together. Her skills complement mine, and vice versa. Same with our love. After my father's death, I didn't have to ask her to step up. I never would have done that. But she did. She stepped up in the best way, picking up my slack in the kitchen, and running the business while I tried to adjust to a new normal.

What's better? She's fallen in love with the kitchen almost as much as she's fallen in love with me which just makes me love her even more.

I growl low in my throat, hating that I have to tear my mouth away from hers, but we have an audience that is probably disgusted with us by now. Maggie and I have managed to get through all our shoots like true professionals, but as soon as Franklin calls "Cut," we don't hold back. Like now.

Maggie is the first to pull away, leaving me with a flirtatious smile and flushed cheeks, before she opens the refrigerator to grab the champagne we purchased this morning. As she's pouring glasses for everyone, I'm making my rounds, thanking each crew member for their time and dedication to the show.

There was a time when I was nervous about what this show could turn into if I let go of the reigns, but Faye came through with her promises intact.

"So what happens next?" I ask Franklin, who is snacking on leftovers from the meal Maggie and I just made.

"You sit back and watch the magic unfold," he says with a brilliant smile.

"That's it?" Maggie asks, looking between us. "Isn't there promotional stuff? And press events?"

Franklin shrugs. "Not my specialty. Faye will be in touch with next steps. But for now, drink champagne, and enjoy your time away from the camera. I'm no psychic, but if I had to wager a guess, the cameras will be back before you know it."

That is the kind of comment I love to hear. Pride swells in my chest and after a single deep breath, I feel thirty pounds lighter.

The crew leaves after a round of drinks and I'm locking up after them while Maggie shuffles off to the back room. She returns a minute later as I'm walking back to the main kitchen. I do a double take when I spot her wearing nothing but a tiny black apron with the words "Fuck me, I'm the chef," on it.

"Do you remember this one?" The innocence on her face is lost when I see the wicked gleam of flirtation in her eyes.

"Um." It's all I can manage as she twirls, revealing her naked body beneath the apron. "It didn't look quite so—bare—the last time you wore it." I grin and start to move faster toward her.

She bites down on her bottom lip and puts her hands on her waist. "That's right. You said this apron wasn't part of the dress code. Should I take it off?"

"Abso-fucking-lutely not." I get to her just as she starts to reach behind her to unknot the fabric, and I pick her up at the waist and set her against the island behind her. "You wouldn't want your boss to complain that you're a walking false advertisement, would you?"

Her eyes widen and she shakes her head. "No, sir. I wouldn't want to get in trouble."

I can't help my grin. "Oh, you've been in trouble since the day you stepped foot in here, Ma'am." My nose brushes against hers as I figure out how I'm going to take my time with her like usual. I'm so wound up already from wrapping the show. The way she's looking in that apron isn't helping matters at all.

She smiles as if she can read my mind and pulls a stool out from under the counter, then slides it out to me. "Have a seat, Sir."

I chuckle and obey, her command sexy as fuck with the added rasp in her tone. Sounds like someone is just as worked up as I am over production completing. Now she's eyeing me like a tiger on the prowl. When she steps in between my thighs, I can't help myself. My hands slide around her body and grab her perfect ass. I rub them gently, savoring the velvety soft skin while my erection fights against my jeans.

I blink up at her while I spread her cheeks and squeeze. *Yeah, I'm not going to last long.* "What are you going to do to me?"

She smiles softly and presses her lips to mine. She kisses me slowly while using the lower rungs of the stool to prop herself up to straddle my lap. "I'm just going to kiss you. That okay?"

"The fuck you are." I growl and thrust my hips against her, then use my grip on her ass to slide her forward and back until I can see in her eyes that she feels the friction. I slip one hand to her front and rub on her clit as I speak. "You're going to turn your ass around so I can get another good look at you."

Maggie steps off the stool and turns until her bare back is facing me. I run a featherlight touch along her spine from her neck down to her luscious ass. The thin string tied together in a bow at her arch is the only fabric covering her back.

"Put your hands on the counter and spread your legs." She does as I say as I pull my pants and underwear down and palm myself. "Now bend over." Then I stand up and nudge my length against her opening. "I'm about to fuck the chef. You ready?"

Before she can even nod, I'm pushing my way inside her, sliding my cock between her legs while she squeezes around me. My little temptress groans out her pleasure, asking for more while I bury myself in her, over and over again.

I'm losing myself in her scent, in her pussy's grip, in her moans and sighs. Fuck me, this will be over quicker than it started if I don't slow the fuck down. But I don't know how to do that. Not when her breasts are spilling out the sides of the apron. Not when she lets out a warning cry to tell me she's about to come. And definitely not when she tightens around me and pulsates her release.

Now I'm chasing my own orgasm. I don't want her riding this one out alone. I want to be right where she is, spiraling into our shared bliss, because we're partners in everything, including this.

Maggie's shaking around me as I push into her one last time. I can feel the hot streams of my fluids filling her while she's still convulsing around me. I swipe her hair from her shoulder and turn her cheek to look at me over her shoulder. And then I slam my mouth to hers to swallow her final moans.

"I might need to change the dress code so you can wear this smock every day." I grin into her mouth while she laughs.

"I don't think your students would appreciate you mauling your assistant."

"True, but—" I twist my face and narrow my eyes at hers at the word *assistant*. "I don't think I like that title for you anymore. How does brand manager sound instead?"

I didn't just come up with that title on a whim. I've been thinking about it for weeks, but I wanted to finish production before we started talking big business decisions.

She pulls back slightly, surprise registering on her face. "Really? Or is that the sex talking?"

I chuckle. "If it was the sex talking, your title would be much different." Then I turn her around so I can face her full on. "Maggie, you practically run this place now while simultaneously cohosting the show. You even scored me a publishing deal for that cookbook idea you had."

"Well," she says slowly. "I kind of used Faye's connections for that one."

"Which was the smart thing to do." I don't know why she always needs to give the credit away for her hard work. "Most people would have been scared shitless approaching Faye about something like that. You've got business smarts, Maggie. And I need that in a manager."

She grins and places her hands on my shoulders. "I don't know, Desmond. This is a big step. Next thing you know you're going to be asking me to move in with you."

I glare at her again. She hasn't spent a single night in her studio since the night after we got back from Dallas. We've been using the studio for food photograph shoots. "Smart ass." Then I touch my nose to hers. "Say yes to the promotion, Maggie."

She tilts her head, her smile softening, and then she rests her forehead on mine. "Yes, Desmond. I accept the promotion. I guess that means you're stuck with me."

I nod before grazing my lips against hers. "Fine with me. There's no one else I'd rather be stuck with."

MAGGIE, SIX MONTHS LATER

Golden Gardens Park is packed like it is on any sunny day — hot or cold. Families are picnicking on the beach, fisherman are trying their luck on the pier, hikers are steadily making their way through the forest trails, dogs are running without restraint of their leashes, and boats are being launched on Puget Sound and gathering near the shore.

I am currently setting up the last of the decorations at our reserved campsite to celebrate the launch of Desmond's new cookbook. Not only is his book filled with never-before-seen live action photos, but it's packed with all the scratch cooking and farm-to-table tips Desmond would normally give in his classes.

Monica, who has been helping me decorate before everyone arrives, just plopped down at one of the picnic benches and is flipping through one of the bridal magazines that practically lives in her purse. She's obsessed with finding the perfect everything for her wedding. A wedding she's only just now started to plan. Between art school and Zach's football schedule, they didn't want to rush anything, so taking the past year to enjoy their engagement before adding in the wedding stress was something they agreed to.

"I'm thinking a spring wedding, what do you think?" Monica flips to another page and studies it like she's done all the others. "I can do all the planning while he's in season, and then we'll have all that time to be together as newlyweds during the off-season." She snaps her head to me and her eyes brighten. "Newlyweds. Can you believe it, Mags?"

I smile and rest my shoulder against hers. "I can, and I'm so excited to help you plan, but today we're focused on Desmond's book launch remember?" I close her magazine and almost feel guilty for the pout-face she makes.

"Fine." She sighs and stuffs her magazine back in her bag. "But you promised to come to the wedding expo with me next Saturday. Will Desmond be cool with that?"

"Yup," I say, standing from the bench. "The new assistant is trained and ready. Thank goodness."

Monica laughs. "You sure gave up your old job fast."

I bite back my own knowing smile. "Hey, I played assistant for an entire year before I finally handed over the reins." Even after my promotion, I wasn't ready to let go of my kitchen duties, but then it all became too much. "I think Raegan will do great. She's young. She's passionate about the culinary arts, and she's into chicks."

My comment earns me pursed lips and narrowed eyes. "Like you have anything to worry about with Desmond. He's crazy about you, and you know it."

"I know, I know. But this way I don't have to worry about *her* heart getting broken, walking out, and leaving me to train someone new. No thank you. I love the work I'm doing now. Between the show getting picked up for a second season, all the work I've done for Desmond's book, and the events we've been scheduling like crazy, I don't have the time to assist during classes. Besides, I think that's a great job for someone who wants to advance their craft, and while I enjoy the whole art of cooking now, it's not what I want to do all day, every day."

"I understand, Mags. You don't have to explain to me. I was just teasing. I'm proud of you."

My chest swells with pride. "Thanks, M. I'm proud of you, too. Three more quarters of school, and then you're done. What are you planning to do after graduation?"

Monica shrugs, her permanent smile brighter than ever. "I'm not making any drastic plans. I'll help out the production department at BelleCurve until I can't anymore. I'm actually enjoying the side jobs I've been getting with personal shopping and custom designing, so I might try to build a brand around that. I'm keeping my options open."

"Well, keep designing clothes for the show and I'm sure word will get out about your talents."

Monica's eyes go wide. "You mean you're hiring me for season two?"

I laugh at her genuine surprise. "Of course I am. You think I'll let Faye choose a stylist for me? Not a chance." I stand and wait for her to join me, just as a few cars pull into the lot. "Oh, they're starting to arrive."

Our dad and his wife pull up at the same time as Zach, Gavin, and a newly pregnant Chloe. Soon enough, more guests start to arrive—students from Desmond's classes, some of the production crew who live locally, Faye, some of the BelleCurve staff, a bunch of Seattle football players. Soon enough there are nearly sixty guests on the beach, playing volleyball, mingling near the fire, and snacking on appetizers. And then Desmond finally arrives.

He pulls up in his red '58 Ford Fairlane convertible that I've started to call "mine," as a joke, and I meet him at the curb. He knew I was throwing him a release party, but I didn't tell him just how much effort I'd put into it. He was probably expecting a dozen people or less, but I couldn't let this opportunity go by without celebrating him properly.

"Um, Mags," he says, stepping out of his car and shutting the door behind him. His eyes are on the beachfront, but he's walking toward me. "What did you do?"

I wrap an arm around him and grin up at his puzzled expression. "I'm throwing you the huge, outlandish party you said you didn't want."

He looks down at me with a playful glare. "Of course, you did. You said it was going to be a small, intimate gathering."

"Everyone is so proud of you, and we want to celebrate." I tug on his shirt a little, batting my eyes up at him, knowing I'll need to do quick damage control in the form of a lot of flirtation. "Humor us. Come join your party." I lift up on my tiptoes and press a kiss to his lips.

He kisses me back with a little growl and a squeeze of my waist. "Fine. You win."

"Like always."

He chuckles. "Is that right? I think I have a game I know I can win tonight if you want to try your luck."

My body heats with his words, and I can feel a blush creeping up my neck and blasting my cheeks. Desmond hasn't changed much when it comes to sex. If anything, he's only become more intense now that he knows exactly what makes me react. "C'mon," I say, tugging on his hand and trying to focus on the task at hand. "If you're nervous, you should try the punch first."

"Why, did you spike it?"

"Yup."

He throws his head back in a laugh, quickly eliminating any tension he drove up with. While Desmond doesn't mind a crowd, he's been somewhat uneasy with all the attention from the show. His classes were already booked before the show started, but now, he's talking about hiring on a couple more full time instructors to add more classes to the daily schedule.

We join the party, and while there are a lot of people here, it's still a chill event. Desmond signs books for everyone, poses for some photos, but all-in-all, it's just an excuse to get together with our friends.

Rebecca and Ryan are back in town too. It's adorable how supportive they are with Desmond. It took me a long time to understand the dynamic of their relationship—with him and Zach's mom, and with him and my dad. But I get it now, and I'm so happy they all have each other.

A couple hours and a lot of laughs later, the sun starts to dip in the sky. The chatter is loud, the music is upbeat, and everyone's had plenty to eat. Well, except for my sister who's sitting with Zach at the fire roasting marshmallows.

I think Desmond senses the party is ending soon, because he gathers everyone near the picnic tables for a quick thank you.

"I really appreciate you all showing up like this and supporting everything we're trying to do with the kitchen. Thanks to the cookbook, we've already been able to do so much this year with our growth through the hiring of new staff and dipping our toes into some new service offerings."

Desmond takes my hand in his and squeezes. "But none of that could have been possible without this woman right here. The cookbook was her idea. She formatted the thing, pitched the book to publishers, and negotiated the deal like she's been doing this kind of thing all her life. Which is why—" he starts with a grin aimed right at me— "I've got a surprise for you."

My jaw drops. "For me?"

He nods and pulls something out of his pocket, then holds it out to me in a fist. My thoughts immediately start to think he's proposing and I can feel my heart crashing around like a pinball in my chest. And then I realize there's no ring box, and I laugh a little at my ridiculous thoughts. There's no question marriage is in our future. We've teased the subject multiple times, but we're both in agreement that we're happy with where we're at for right now.

I hold out my hand to let him drop whatever it is. He releases his grip and a silver key into my hand. A key I recognize before I've even made the entire thing out. I gasp and my head feels light from the shock.

"Now that you have your driver's license, I figure you'll need a car. And well—" Desmond looks up at my dad and winks. "Since this one was always supposed to be yours in the first place, I think it's about time we made that happen."

The crowd cheers loudly and tears start to blur my vision. I don't even have words right away. Then Desmond leans down and places his mouth to my ear. "You already have a key to my condo, to my kitchen, and to my heart but this one belongs to you and you alone. It has always belonged to you,

Mags." He presses a kiss to my cheek and stands up so I can look at him.

What I ever did to deserve such a smart, giving, and talented man, I have no idea, but I'm never letting him go.

"I love you so much. You didn't have to do this."

He grins. "I know. But since I did, why don't you take her out for a spin?"

My dad steps forward and wraps me in a hug. "I'd love to go with you, if that's alright."

I swipe away at the tears that are falling and nod before laughing at how emotional I'm getting over such a generous and thoughtful gesture. "Yes, of course." I look up at Desmond who's smiling down at me. "Are you coming too?"

He shakes his head. "Nah. I'm going to stay here and mingle." He leans down and kisses my cheek then points at my father. "You're in charge old man, bring her back in one piece."

We all laugh as I search the crowd for my sister. "Where's Monica?"

Just then, she bursts through a small group of guests and runs toward us. "I'm coming, I'm coming!"

My dad and I laugh as she catches up to us. Then he loops his arms around both our shoulders as we walk toward my new car.

I start the engine, and my heart flips in my chest at the beautiful sound. When I finally went out to get my license, it was at Desmond's prodding. He told me I'd need it eventually because walking everywhere was going to start becoming impossible if the kitchen continued to pick up steam the way it was.

Now, I know why he was so insistent. Something tells me this has been his plan for a very long time. Maybe even from the moment I told him the car was promised to me first. I don't know. And I stopped caring.

Desmond has done so much for me since I met him, besides giving me a home and a job. He's given me his heart and his encouragement to explore all the things I'm passionate about, whether it's been in the kitchen or not. And while I haven't found one single thing that I am obsessed with like he is, I've been happier than ever before taking the reins on the business side of things.

I drive around the park, taking Monica and my dad through the numerous parking lots, never actually leaving the grounds. But when we hit a straight away, and I can pick up the speed slightly, I can't stop the smile from my face. Monica is hollering in the backseat, and my dad appears to be enjoying the ride as he rests against the door.

"You're a good driver, Mags."

My dad's compliment makes me smile. "Thanks, Dad. Desmond's been teaching me."

He blows out a breath and then chuckles. "I'm not sure if that's a good thing, but it was probably a better idea than having me train you. I don't know how well my nerves would have held up."

I cruise into the next parking lot, relaxing against the wind blowing in my hair and the radio playing softly from the dash. Monica is singing along while my dad flips through Desmond's cookbook. My heart startles when I glance over and realize he's reached the dessert section. He's looking at a playful photo of me in a black bra, a chef's hat, and my tongue between my teeth as I appear to be preparing to eat a donut.

"Um, Dad," I start, but he's snapping the book shut before I can tell him he should probably stop there. There's nothing crude about the photos, but the dessert section does get a little—um—sexual.

"Well," he says stretching out and looking out the window. "I think I've seen enough of that."

Monica howls with laughter and my face heats with embarrassment, but the embarrassment is quickly diminished by Monica uttering her favorite curse word.

"Holy, shiitakes."

"What is it, M?" I glance at her in the rearview mirror and my eyes go wide at where her reaction is directed.

She snaps her head up to meet the reflection of my eyes. "Didn't you carve this heart into the back seat when we were kids?"

A laugh bubbles up my throat. "I sure did. I'll never forgot how mad Dad got at me. If it weren't for that heart then I probably would have never known that this was Dad's old car. Desmond wasn't going to tell me."

I watch as Monica twists her lips with amusement as she connects the dots, then her eyes widen and I forget saying anything at all. "What were you doing in the backseat, Mags?"

"Oh my God." It's all I can say. I'm humiliated. Why can't my sister just shut her mouth for once? I cringe as I sneak a look at my dad, but he looks to be just as embarrassed as me.

"I think it's time to head back."

When I park the car, Desmond is waiting for us there with his arms ready. He wraps me in a hug. "Why does Coach look like that a lobster you refused to boil?"

I look up with a slight laugh. "Let's just say the poor guy will probably never eat dessert again."

Desmond's eyes go wide, making me laugh harder. "Oh, shit."

I nod and make a cringe face. "Yeah. Oh, shit is right. Guess you should have thought twice about dating the coach's daughter."

He narrows his lids and cups my chin in his hands. "Wouldn't have changed a damn thing, Maggie Stevens. You're still the biggest pain in my rear, but you also happen to be the love of my life, so—" he flashes me a grin. "You kind of have to take the bad with the good, if you know what I mean."

I bite down on my lip and stretch onto my tiptoes so I can reach his lips. "Oh, I know what you mean, Desmond Blake. And I wouldn't change a thing either."

Before you, life came in bursts of muted colors.
Everything changed when you somehow slipped under my skin—and then stole my heart.
Layer by layer, you stripped me bare, leaving foreign skin beneath lost feathers. You blinded me with your light. And with streams exposing my every weakness, I became yours. Your words lit a match against my soul, and the flames licked through me like an inferno. Thick. Heated. Wild. Infuriating.
Still, I was afraid.

I learned at a young age what can be seen through the lens is often a skewed version of reality. A bent perspective. Manufactured, therefore losing all sense of authenticity.
But you showed me there was nothing to fear.
I wasn't just the woman through the lens, the lie, like I believed myself to be.
I was your muse.
Turns out, you were mine too.

Let's Connect!

I hope you enjoyed Maggie and Desmond's story! If you'd like to help spread the word about Through the Lens, reviews are the best way to let other readers know how you felt about a story. You can also connect with me on social media and sign up for my mail list. Be sure to never miss a new release, event, or sale!

Subscribe for Updates: www.smarturl.it/KK_MailList
K.K.'s Website & Blog: www.KK-Allen.com
Facebook: www.Facebook.com/AuthorKKAllen
Goodreads: www.goodreads.com/KKAllen
BookBub: www.bookbub.com/profile/k-k-allen
Instagram: www.Instagram.com/KKAllen_Author

Thank You

True story, I used to be so intimidated when it came to writing reviews. Now, I can't wait to publicly thank everyone who had anything to do with me releasing this book. Inspiration comes in many forms, and this story was heavily inspired by so many people that were involved in the creation.

First, I need to express my heartfelt thanks to every one of you who waited for this book. While this book can be read on its own, I teased Maggie and Desmond's romance years ago at the end of *Under the Bleachers*, and they've been on my mind ever since. I can't really explain why so much time went by before I finally committed to writing this one, other than the fact that the Gravity series had a louder presence in my heart at the time. I trusted in that direction, and I trusted my heart again when it was time to finally write *Through the Lens*. Finally! Thank you for your patience. I hope it was worth the wait.

I need to thank my mom AKA @CluttergirlDesigns next. Thank you for your cooking school stories. Maggie's lobster scene was written specifically for you. In general, a lot of Maggie's character was based on your love for cooking and fashion. You are such an inspiration to me, always and forever.

Sammie and Cyndi. I'm so grateful for you two. As always, thank you for putting so much time and heart into reading my stories in their roughest forms. I love you girls so much.

Lindsey, my love. You're not just my boss, but one of my best friends in the world, and I don't know what I'd do without you. Thank you for always being five steps ahead of me. XO.

Renee! You are a dream. Thank you for helping stay on top of my social media game, and for being one of my kick-ass beta readers. I love you!

Brenna and Patricia. You two blow me away. Thank you for everything. You're always coming in with little time to spare to give my books the final reads. I seriously could not do this without you. Mucho love!

To Lynn and Neila, my editing team at Red Adept. I'm always appreciative by how flexible you are with me, amazed by your talents, and so incredibly proud at what comes out of those final edits. Thank you for always pushing me to be a better writer.

To my beeches, Harloe, Heather, and Kate. I know you're not surprised to find your names in here. We only talk every minute of every day. I've never had better, more supportive friends, and I love you all so much. #LoveYouMoreThanMookies

To my cover artist, Sarah Hansen of Okay Creations, and my cover photographer, Regina Wamba. This is a dynamic duo right here and I can't stop staring at the covers you created for this series. Just amazing. Thank you!

To my publicist, Sarah, at Social Butterfly. I adore you so much. Thank you for always being such a positive force and for holding my hand through this one. I am beyond appreciative for your support.

I'm so thankful for all the ladies at Give Me Books. Once again, you stepped up and worked so hard to push this baby in as many hands as possible. You are the absolute best!

To every book blogger and reader who accepted an advance copy and/or promoted *Through the Lens*. I am so grateful for your time and support. You're all amazing at what you do, and this book world would be nothing without you.

To my reader group, Forever Young! This book is for you, babes <3 I hope I gave you all the HEAs you wanted and more.

If you are reading this now, then this last thank you is for you. THANK YOU from the bottom of my heart for taking the time to read Maggie and Desmond's story. It was a rollercoaster. I know. But wasn't it worth the ride?

To everyone. Keep reading. Keep reviewing. Keep spreading the love. Until the next time.

Much Love and HEAs,
K.K. Allen

Books by K.K.

Sweet & Inspirational Contemporary Romance
Up in the Treehouse
Under the Bleachers
Through the Lens

Sweet and Sexy Contemporary Romance
Center of Gravity
Falling from Gravity
Defying Gravity
The Trouble with Gravity

Super Steamy Contemporary Romance
Dangerous Hearts
Destined Hearts

Romantic Suspense
Waterfall Effect

Young Adult Fantasy
The Summer Solstice Enchanted
The Equinox
The Descendants

Short Stories and Anthologies
Soaring
Echoes of Winter
Begin Again
Spring Fling

About the Author

K.K. Allen is a *USA Today* bestselling and award-winning author who writes heartfelt and inspirational contemporary romance stories. K.K. graduated from the University of Washington with an Interdisciplinary Arts and Sciences degree and currently resides in central Florida with her ridiculously handsome little dude who owns her heart.

K.K.'s publishing journey began in June 2014 with the young adult contemporary fantasy trilogy. In 2016, she published her first contemporary romance, *Up in the Treehouse*, which went on to win the Romantic Times 2016 Reviewers' Choice Award for Best New Adult Book of the Year.

With K.K.'s love for inspirational and coming of age stories involving heartfelt narratives and honest emotions, you can be assured to always be surprised by what K.K. releases next.

WWW.KK-ALLEN.COM